LEGENDS OF ZYCONIA
ODYSSEY

Written and illustrated by

Hugh Stephens

First printed in Victoria, Canada

CO-PUBLISHED BY CRYING FLOWER LITERATURE

National Library of Canada Cataloguing in Publication Data

Stephens, Hugh, 1979-
  Legends of Zyconia

ISBN 1-55212-627-7

  I. Title.
PS8587.T46519L44 2001   C813'.6   C2001-910436-7
PR9199.4.S73L44 2001

This book was published *on-demand* **in cooperation with Trafford Publishing.**
On-demand publishing is a unique process and service of making a book available for retail sale to the public taking advantage of on-demand manufacturing and Internet marketing.
On-demand publishing includes promotions, retail sales, manufacturing, order fulfilment, accounting and collecting royalties on behalf of the author.

Suite 6E, 2333 Government St., Victoria, B.C. V8T 4P4, CANADA
Phone   250-383-6864   Toll-free   1-888-232-4444 (Canada & US)
Fax   250-383-6804   E-mail   sales@trafford.com
Web site   www.trafford.com   TRAFFORD PUBLISHING IS A DIVISION OF TRAFFORD HOLDINGS LTD.
Trafford Catalogue #01-0029   www.trafford.com/robots/01-0029.html

10   9   8   7   6   5   4   3   2

This manuscript is dedicated to anyone
who has ever believed in me....
Thank you.

FOREWORD/ACKNOWLEDGEMENTS:

To this date there are more people I am grateful to that have helped me than I can probably remember. So I'll just have to do my best.

First and foremost to one who always seemed there, you know who you are, thank you. Without your love and support over the last couple years I don't know where I'd be. I truly hope you discover what's really important to you. If not, I feel sorry for you, for you have lost what could have been something incredible.

I want to thank Melonie Gilchrist for her overwhelming belief in my talents. You've been there from the beginning giving me the confidence I needed. You've helped me through the good and the bad. I always feel better when we discuss things. No matter where we are or where we go you'll always be my closest friend. Meow-Meow.

Robert Allan is another individual who has helped me over the years. When I first drafted the concept for my novel he began talking about how much money I could make. That I was destined to make millions. Thank you for having faith in my potential. You filled my dreams with grandeur, someday I'll reach the pinnacle Rob.

I have to thank Gina. You've always read my manuscripts whether they were short stories or my book or books in progress. You've always been there to help even though you seem to have such a hectic schedule. And despite being so different we've always had fun together. Remember plastic polly(kill me, kill me) or trust me Rob, he he he. Anyway I've never made friends easily but I've come to think of you as a close friend. Thanks for all the support.

Someone else who has always pushed me to give it my best shot is Amanda Graham. I remember not so long ago how we spent our entire lunch hour discussing the book. You seemed very caught up in it, and that made me feel good. It really gave me the confidence I needed and I really appreciate it. And remember Amanda, 'that's nasty'. Despite our occasional differences I usually get along with my brother Caleb. And I'd like to thank him as well. From what I gather he has some belief in my writing. He once printed up the first part of my book to let his girlfriend Stephanie read it. So he must have some confidence in my abilities.

Steve Cowal is another who climbed on board when I first drafted the novel. He really seemed to like it. As a joke he said I should have added a sex scene. Steve has moved from our area but I'm sure he is succeeding wherever he's gone. If you're reading this Steve, know I'm thankful for your support.

Thanks to Dexter who helped me transfer my manuscript from my father's ancient computer to my new one. That was a great help.

I'd like to thank Maryann for reviewing my book. I haven't seen you much in the last several months, but I hope your doing well.

I suppose I should even thank Tavis Case who seemed to take a slight interest in my writing. You're always good for a laugh Tavis.

Thanks to my parents for actually owning a computer. Without it earlier I don't know if I would have written this book. I appreciate you reading it as well.

I also want to thank Heather Scott for reading my manuscript and for allowing me to read hers. You have a lot of talent Heather.

In my search for someone to review my manuscript I came across Kathryn. When she read some of it she told me it would make an awesome movie. I realized this was very true. Thanks for the help and the comments Kathryn. Maybe in the future the movie idea will come to be. Thanks to my brothers: Nathan, Marcus and Patrick for wanting to read my book as well. They always bothered me for a copy. Thanks to Pastor Kloestra for reading my novel and for your comments. Kade Strong, we've had a lot of strange conversations at the lunch table, but thanks anyway. Brian, how are you man. Stephanie, for reading the part of my book Caleb gave you, I hope you enjoyed it.

To my former guidance counselor, you didn't tell me what I wanted to hear, but that's okay. And to one of my former english teachers, I suppose if you enjoy my book, many others will also. And to anyone, who bought this book and liked it, Thanks.

TABLE OF CONTENTS:

PART 3

PROLOGUE: MINOTAUR MADNESS

Shifting his weight he slowly lifted his head above the boulder's surface. He had a good view from his position. All eight were in sight. The crowd of minotaurs was spread in two small groups in the nearby area. Farther off six of them devoured a downed antelope, while the two closest to Terrek drank, face first, from the muddy river.

He was lucky to be down wind or they would have attacked by now. Terrek sank down behind the rocks and unsheathed his sword. The Council, even though he respected them, was beginning to annoy him. Did they simply decide he was expendable now, is that why they continued to send him on such near suicidal errands? Perhaps the Vicar's hordes were getting out of control and the council was forced to spread its forces much thinner to protect more of Zyconia. If so, he wished they hadn't. The odds would be a lot better if Perrin had been here. Moving slowly to the edge of the boulder he gently slid into the murky water.

Snarling and grunting, the two minotaurs lapped the water up like dogs. Although more intelligent then animals they were a lot less then human. Curiously one of the Minotaurs noticed a slight rustle beneath the ripples on the surface. Suddenly, the minotaur's thoughts were terminated.

Terrek, using the element of suprise, sprang from the depths, his sword swiping cleanly through the minotaur's throat. Not losing sight of the significant other, he leapt back just in time to evade the second minotaur's finely clawed appendage.

The second minotaur now appeared angered by the death of the other and charged Terrek, a foolishly primitive, animalistic tactic. Obviously he wasn't the brightest of his clan. Terrek, rolling sideways on the ground, spun his sword up into the beast's groin. It hit the ground howling in pain as Terrek regained his footing. Sensing an advantage and feeling slight pity for the beast, he quickly relieved it from its agony.

A shrill cry penetrated the momentary solace. Terrek spun, he had let his attention slip too much, the other six minotaurs had forced their way into a small stone home further down river. He broke into a run in the exact direction of the cries.

The inside was dimly lit. As Terrek came through the door he instantly analyzed the grave situation. A beautiful young woman was cornered, with her back to the wall, holding a candlestick and attempting to keep the Minotaurs at bay with a horsewhip. Terrek dove into the crowd and with the element of suprise on his side managed to eliminate three of the six. Finally his sword was knocked clear of his grasp as one of the minotaurs pinned him to the wall with a heavily muscled arm. With agile reflexes the young woman threw hot wax from the candle into the minotaur's eyes.

Suddenly blinded, the animal went berserk releasing Terrek and wildly flailing his head callously around. Terrek hit the floor and rolled over, retrieving his sword yet again. Coming up, Terrek was amazed as the disoriented Minotaur stumbled and fell into one of his counterparts impaling him with both horns. Shocked, the impaled minotaur hit the floor dead. The other rubbed the wax from his eyes just in

3

time to find Terrek's sword entering his chest. He also sank to the floor, and after slight muscular spasms, entered oblivion as well.

In the attempt to retract his sword Terrek was bowled over. Looking back he saw the final Minotaur grab his sword and with a flick of his wrist tossed it through a nearby window. Terrek stood, picking up the horsewhip nearby. The beast eyed him. This one was obviously their leader, he seemed much more intelligent than the others did, even in his posture. The beast lunged but Terrek was too fast and, gathering his momentum, swung himself up over the creature's back looping the whip quickly around its neck.

With sudden loss of breath the minotaur jerked and spun violently, attempting to shake off his smaller captor. Terrek, extremely battle weary, strained his muscles as the minotaur went completely crazy bucking wildly like a horse. Almost completely out of air the minotaur sank to his knees, but at the last second the whip broke and Terrek flew from its back into a nearby table. The table collapsed under the strain, splintering into several distinct shards. Terrek, now panting for breath, raised himself by one arm and slid himself into a standing position against the wall. His vision was slightly blurred and his head ached.

The frightened woman, gathering courage, ran from the wall. Pulling open a cabinet at the opposite wall she frantically rummaged through it's contents retrieving a crossbow.

The minotaur stood, and with a grand effort, charged toward him as the young woman threw the crossbow into Terrek's hands. Totally exhausted Terrek brought the bow to level and fired. The bolt sailed straight through the minotaur's chest. Still effected by it's own momentum, the minotaur flew forward and crushed Terrek against the wall. The last thing Terrek saw before he blacked out was the dead body of the minotaur as it fell to the floor.

The face finally flowed into the existence of reality. Terrek sat up, a rush of adrenaline shot through him immediately.

"Keep calm, the minotaurs are all dead," the young woman said, slight concern on her face.

She put her hands on his shoulders and gently forced him to lie back in the bed in which he now rested. Terrek relaxed and lay back on the pillow. His body ached from battle and his head was so heavy.

The beautiful woman before him smiled slightly as she looked at him out of the corner of her eyes. Her hair flowed down over her shoulders, dimples upon her face.

"Thank you," she said as she placed a warm cloth to his forehead.

"For what?" he said clumsily lost in her beauty.

"For saving my life," she said smiling.

"Oh, yes, sorry, I mean you're welcome," Terrek fumbled.

"My name is Diana, who are you?" she said sweetly.

"My name is Terrek," he replied.

"Well Terrek, you are badly bruised, but other than that you are all right. But you should get some rest," she said firmly. Terrek knew he should get back to Victory City but he was too weary.

"I suppose I can rest if you are taking me prisoner," Terrek joked.

This brought a slight blush to Diana's face as she laughed.

"Well, I wouldn't want you to fall asleep on your horse," she smiled.

"Well, knowing Streak, my horse, I would probably show up dragged along, his teeth clamped tightly on my tunic," Terrek laughed.

This time Diana couldn't contain herself the sheer hilarity of Terrek being dragged into the city by his horse made her erupt with laughter. As she laughed she moved over slightly as her hand rested on his. Just for a moment he looked into her eyes and she looked into his. But her touch had been accidental, she moved her hand away, embarrassed.

"So, Diana tell me about yourself," Terrek began slowly.

At first Diana was shy and a little unresponsive, she seemed to guard herself. But soon they were talking and laughing, sharing things about themselves that they wouldn't tell most. Inside both marveled at how easy it was to talk to the other. Finally Terrek slowly drifted off as Diana watched over him smiling. As he fell asleep he whispered to her.

"Thank you," Terrek said.

"For what?" Diana asked.

"I'm not sure," Terrek answered.

Diana laughed as she changed the cloth on his forehead. Besides the fact that they had shared their lives tonight Terrek felt an unexplained connection with Diana. As though the Maker had drawn him to her. Terrek fell asleep feeling, for once in a long time, totally at ease.

Instantly Terrek was awake. Looking through the nearby window he saw the sun shining.

"How long have I been out?" Terrek asked.
Diana was about to speak when someone entered a nearby door.

"You've been out for nearly a day," the man said.

"Perrin, how did you find me?" Terrek said sitting up, a smile on his face.

"You didn't make it easy, that's for sure, but the Council gave me strict instructions not to return without you," Perrin replied.

"Diana, the minotaurs didn't leave you much here. Do you have any relatives nearby that you can go to live with?" Terrek asked hopefully.

"No I'm afraid my nearest relatives live in Victory City," Diana replied.

Terrek's face brightened.

"You're in luck! That's where we're headed."

CHAPTER 1: THE MAKINGS OF AN ARMY

𝕿errek paused as he reached the large sundial at the entrance to the Council's castle. The glittering lights of Victory City could be seen for miles. He could barely see the city walls, which they had entered not long ago.

The ruling Council's castle sat atop a large hill surrounded by many smaller castles and stone houses as far as the eye could see in every direction. The walls of the city were extremely thick and high and there were fifty guard towers, twenty-five catapults and ten huge crossbows mounted on the top of the wall at intervals all the way around the city. Victory City had great protection from it's enemies.

Terrek was home. He easily dismounted from Streak, his horse, being careful not to cause Diana to fall off. Terrek heavily landed the huge bronze knocker several times and stood back to await a response. Soon one of Terrek's friends from the city, John, allowed them entry. John was shorter than Terrek but he was still very strong and muscular. He wore a suit of chainmail as well as a few sect ions of vital armor.

"Follow me, the Council requested your presence when you arrived," John said smiling.

He led them down the great hall and up numerous flights of stairs before reaching the door to the Ruling

Council chambers.

The guards at the door, familiar with Terrek, stood aside to allow him entry. They all entered as Terrek walked to the center of the room. Terrek stopped, a huge horseshoe shaped table surrounded him as twenty-five men stared directly at him. There was total silence, as if they had been frozen in time, and for a few moments Terrek almost thought they had been.

"So, you are ready for the quest," the comment came from a bearded man named Walker at the apex of the horseshoe, one of the more influential members of the Ruling Council.

"What?" exclaimed Terrek.

"Here's your explanation, Terrek," Walker voiced his concern. "The evil Vicar, ruler of the Forest of Darkness is trying to locate the ancient crystals of Zyconia."

"But I thought his powers only existed within the Forest of Darkness," Terrek interrupted.

"We believe his powers are growing. There have been many sightings of his Sorcerer and Warlock hordes," Walker replied as he continued.

"About a week ago we lost contact with Cantaro castle and soon after Alexium and Cardina Castle. These are our closest outposts to the Forest of darkness, each held about a hundred soldiers. If the Vicar recovers the crystals he would gain immense power and may be able to launch an attack on one of our cities," he finished.

"Or all of them," muttered another council member.

"So, you want me to find the crystals before the Vicar, and you want me to do this alone?" asked Terrek.

"No, not alone. Alone this would be impossible, we have gathered an army of two-hundred of the most skillful warriors in Zyconia. You leave tomorrow...if you accept the quest," finished Walker.

Terrek thought for a moment. "I accept on the condition that I be allowed to have certain people to accompany me as advisors or chief aides."

Walker looked around for objection from the others. "Who?" he asked.

"To begin with, these three," Terrek said pointing toward Diana, Perrin, and John. "The rest I'll collect myself, they all live in Victory City."

"Very well. Be in the Northern Courtyard at dawn, your army will be provisioned and ready to command by then. I would ask that your friends step outside while we give you secret details vital to your success."

Terrek nodded, and Diana, Perrin and John exited. Soon after, Terrek rejoined them outside accompanied by a soldier.

Terrek conversed with his associates, "John, Perrin I'd like you two to stay here at the castle to help organize the army before dawn. Diana and I will descend to the inner city to collect the remainder of my trusted friends."

They both nodded as the soldier with Terrek led them down the hallway. Diana and Terrek descended the staircase.

"Diana," Terrek began, "I never asked you if you wished to join us in this quest, so you shouldn't feel bound. I just have a strange feeling that I can trust you, and you have some healing abilities. But if you still wish me to help you locate your relatives, so that you may go and stay with them I'll do my best."

Diana smiled, "I feel very honored that you want me to go with you. And I do want to remain with you," she said looking into his eyes.

"Thank you Diana, that means a lot to me," he nodded.

Hours later in a deserted part of Victory City an elderly man sat alone praying. He sat in the garden near his home, a large stone building surrounded by a field. The old man was a prophet and his home a temple. The teacher of several followers, he was a great seer and a good man. The man's age was unknown but he had seen many years since his birth. His robes, dark blue, fluttered in the wind. Long white hair and a long white beard dangled from his face. A golden sceptre rested in his unsteady hands.

Suddenly his solitude was interrupted by the call of his name, "Zyron!"

The prophet turned and faced a small group of people; the man in front was the only truly familiar face.

"We need your help," said Terrek as he advanced away from the group towards the old man. The prophet stood and faced them, his eyes on the group behind Terrek.

There was a woman, the most beautiful he had seen in all his years, she had raven black hair, and her figure was very slender and voluptuous. Zyron sensed that she had a beautiful voice. The next person in the group seemed familiar from the past, he was a massive giant and extremely muscular. The other three appeared to be swordsmen Zyron didn't think he knew any of them. Zyron returned his eyes to Terrek.

"So you're back, boy," Zyron breathed.

"Yes Zyron I need you to come wit h me, we must stop the Vicar," replied Terrek.

"The Vicar? I'm too old boy. I've lost all my past vigor; I am not strong like you. Leave me alone to die, I've lived too many years, I can't go with you on your quest it's too much for someone as old as I," Zyron moaned.

"You're never too old to fight for what's right and good, it was you who taught me that. I need your help now more than I ever did in the past, I can't take on this quest alone," Terrek said sternly.

"Why not? You've gone on very dangerous missions before, why do you need me?" asked Zyron.

"I need you because you wield the power of good and you're a great seer. You know the Maker and know how to deal with and resist evil power," he explained.

"I am too old, the power will not be used through me much longer, I can't go, I'm sorry," he whispered.

Terrek stood, perplexed he looked to his nearby group of friends then stared back at Zyron who had turned away from him.

"If you change your mind, be in the northern courtyard of the council's castle by dawn." Terrek turned and walked out of the garden towards his horse, the group he had gathered in the previous hours, looking very puzzled, also turned and left.

Outside the group mounted their horses.

The giant began to speak, "I would have thought that Zyron would always help you, Terrek." Terrek turned to his old friend, who rode a very large horse to support his body.

"Zyron is well past the one hundred mark, I suppose he is right, He is too old, Hemoth," Terrek sighed.

Terrek switched his thoughts to his old friends. Hemoth was the huge giant, Terrek himself only stood slightly past his chest. When Terrek was seventeen Hemoth had saved his life. Hemoth had met Zyron many years back when he came with Terrek a couple of times to visit Zyron.

Although Hemoth was extremely strong and muscular he had no experience with a sword and relied heavily on his club and dagger. Terrek knew that Hemoth's strength would be a great asset on the quest.

The other three were swordsmen and brothers; Zachary the oldest had been one of his best friends for the last few years. Zachary was part of the Council's Elite army just like Terrek and Perrin, and although he could not wield a sword quite as well as Terrek, he was still one of the best in Zyconia.

The other two men were good bowmen, and they also

had some experience with a sword. Their names were Jason and Adam. Although they were in the regular forces they had performed several small missions for the Council's Elite army. Not long ago Terrek helped them fend off a horde of ghouls who had gotten the better of them south of the Ghoul swamp.

Terrek was pulled from his thoughts by Diana's voice.

"Terrek, who was that prophet? How do you know him? You act as though you have known him for a long time."

"I'll tell you later. Right now we have to get back to the castle and help organize the army before dawn," he whispered to her.

Terrek nudged Streak, and Diana held tighter as the horse galloped faster. The others followed suit to keep up.

Terrek stood atop a large hill surveying the plain. Below, the army was fully assembled and nearly ready to leave. Some of the men had decided to bring older members of their families, which Terrek agreed upon. Although he had seen the occasional young boy.

Terrek was an easy commander and had no problem with this. After all, their purpose was more exploration than military. But others would have disagreed since an army that was supposed to number one hundred and eighty men and twenty women healers was now more than double that number.

Diana walked up beside Terrek. "It was very noble of you to let them bring their families."

Terrek looked at Diana and saw that she was now wearing a suit of chain mail and an armored tunic, she also had a dagger strapped to her arm.

"Most of these men are not from the Council's army and are not used to being away from their families, but I

13

fear we may lose some of them on this quest," he reasoned.

Suddenly they were disrupted by a voice behind them.

"Terrek," Terrek turned to see Zyron, the prophet.

"Zyron, you came after all!" Terrek embraced the old man.

"I received a vision last night, I am to go with you, you were right."

Terrek turned happily and introduced Zyron and Diana. A twinkle filled Zyron's eye as he greeted Diana.

They all looked up as footsteps echoed behind him, this time it was Perrin.

"Terrek the Council has provided you with more chief aides," Perrin indicated as he continued.

"This is Ricsis, Jessica and Lynx," Perrin finished. Terrek nodded in acknowledgment as he formed a first impression of them.

Ricsis was a particularly large centaur with a curly black beard. Jessica was a healthy vibrant attractive young woman. But Lynx, he was a wild card. He wore a mysterious long brown robe with a large hood. His hair hid most of his face and a short white beard protruded from the bottom of his hood. Terrek was about to speak to the man but he turned abruptly and left.

"That was rude. Wonder where the Council dug him up?" Ricsis muttered.

Perrin changed the conversation.

"Terrek, Jessica is leader of the healers that are accompanying us," he announced.

"Well, Jessica I want you to have a healer stay with Zyron in one of the wagons. Also I would like you and Ricsis to spread the word to everyone that I will address them shortly," Terrek said.

Jessica held Zyron by the arm as she and Ricsis led him down the slope into the crowds.

Terrek faced Diana.

"Zyron, is my step-father," he explained, "I don't know

14

if he ever forgave me for leaving him those many years ago. He always hated my choice to leave and join the Council's military forces but he agreed that it was my choice to make. But seeing him now I don't know if I should forgive myself."

Diana looked up into Terrek's downcast face.

"You can't blame yourself for his current condition, and all children grow up and leave the nest, it's the law of nature," she rationalized gently.

"Maybe," Terrek said as he slowly spun toward the crowd. He noticed them gathering and gazing towards him. He cleared his throat and raised his voice.

"Comrades, I am Commander Terrek I have been appointed by the Council to be your leader on this quest. You have all been chosen for your specific skills in which you excel, and I know you won't disappoint me. We will head east and camp on the banks of the River of Reflection by night fall. Gather your belongings, it's time to leave." Terrek mounted Streak, his horse, and pulled Diana up behind him.

"We could provide you with your own horse if you'd like Diana," Terrek commented.

"That's all right, I'm fine," she said. Terrek smiled. As they rode through the inner city, crowds of people cheered. It wasn't everyday an army paraded through the streets. Finally they reached the huge eastern gates of the city and proceeded through the wall. Terrek rode Streak down slope until he reached a flat plain. Ahead trees dotted the countryside.

Terrek waved Perrin to come alongside Streak.

"Perrin, I want you to lead the army northeast a little longer then head directly east, Diana and I will be with Zyron."

Terrek rode Streak back around behind the horse riders and approached the wagon where Zyron rested. From the outside the wagon appeared fairly large, its roof and walls were a tent like structure made of some tough animal-skin fabric. Terrek came behind the wagon and allowed Diana to enter the door flaps. Then he tied Streak's reins to the wagon and entered himself. The wagon continued it's journey.

The interior of the tent like structure was dark except for a brazier of coals and a small clay oil lamp. A small number of wheat sacks lay against the front of the wagon. The oil lamp hung from the ceiling near Zyron who was resting on some sacks. Closest to them, Jessica sat crosslegged stirring a small pot on the brazier. An occasional tremor rocked the wagon as it passed through dirt and mud outside.

Terrek stepped over to her and spoke quietly. "You're looking after him yourself?"

"Yes. I know he means a lot to you. I also have a feeling that he is very important to the quest," Jessica replied.

"Thank you Jessica, mix your herbs. Diana and I will stay with Zyron," Terrek smiled.

Jessica smiled and returned to her boiling pot. Terrek and Diana lay back against the sacks close to Zyron. Neither had gotten any sleep the night before while collecting Terrek's allies and Diana soon fell asleep.

Terrek spied the sceptre in Zyron's hands; the gold frame glimmered in the dark. There was a huge blue jewel on the end that seemed to glow, and many smaller gems along the sides. The sceptre was of the finest workmanship he had seen in his life and on the handle the amityus was featured. The Council's symbol?

Many hours later on the bank of the River of Reflection camp was set up and all retired for the night, all but one of evil. A shadow passed the tents as the unknown assailant moved through the camp! Suddenly Terrek felt the sharp pain of a dagger thrust into his shoulder. Terrek leapt to his feet as pain shot down his arm. He swung his arm hard and felt it collide with someone, the assailant fell through the side of his tent creating a large rip in the animal hide. Terrek fumbled with his flint as he lit his torch and, sword drawn, quickly ran out of his tent. Terrek peered around each tent but the assailant had disappeared!

CHAPTER 2: JOURNEY TO THE CAVERNS OF DEATH

℧he morning came swiftly, and Terrek summoned his aides to a meeting in his tent to inform them of the events that had transpired the night before. Jessica stood on one side of Terrek changing the bandage he had put on after the attack. On the opposite side of Terrek stood Diana, worry etched in her features.

"And when you peered out of the tent you saw no one?" asked Zachery.

"No one. I even walked around the camp, but I never caught a glimpse of him," Terrek replied.

"Surely you didn't expect to catch him? It was the dead of night," offered Perrin.

"No, there was a full moon last night. It should have been fairly easy for Terrek to spot him, and the nearest cover would be the small forest to the north and that's at least two-hundred strides from the camp," replied Hemoth.

"Which means that we're dealing with an assassin among us. It is vital to the stability of the quest that we find out who he or she is," Terrek said.

"I suggest a rotation of guards to patrol the camp during the night from now on," chimed in Ricsis.

"Yes, that will be a top priority. Zachary, Perrin, you two will be responsible for setting up the rotation," Terrek replied.

18

"We'll probably need about a dozen guards patrolling at all times," Hemoth suggested.

"I think that is everything for now. You may leave," Terrek finished, his aides vacated his tent and he walked out with Diana.

Outside, the wagons were lined up and hungry people surrounded them arguing. Terrek was about to try and get the situation under control when an angry woman caught a glimpse of him. The woman burst from the crowds and advanced towards Terrek. Quickly Adam and Jason blocked her path.

"I want to speak to Commander Terrek," yelled the woman, "Commander I must speak with you," she pleaded.

Adam and Jason appeared as though they were about to drag the woman away but Terrek intervened.

"Let her through men, I'll hear what she has to say." The woman walked between Adam and Jason.

"Commander we have plenty of food in the wagons but because of the crowds many can't get to it," the woman explained.

"Very well, what is your name?" asked Terrek.

"My name is Juliana, sir," she said cautiously.

"Juliana I appoint you as one of my aides. You will be in charge of food distribution," he said.

Terrek turned toward Adam and Jason, "Round up some soldiers to assist her."

The woman smiled at Terrek, Terrek peered down as a small boy came out from behind her legs. The boy looked up at the tall muscular man before him.

"Are you a real swordsman sir?" asked the boy.

"About as real as they come, son," Terrek replied grinning down at him.

"Well Juliana, you had better tend to your new responsibilities. Don't worry about the boy, Diana and I will look after him," Terrek said.

The young woman walked toward the wagons directing

the people into lines as Terrek took the boy's hand.

"So, what's your name son?" asked Terrek.

"Timothy," the boy replied.

Terrek nodded, "Well Timothy, I suppose we'll have to wait in my tent unt il your mother is finished, come on."

Moments later Terrek, Diana and Timothy were in Terrek's tent, Terrek sat in a large fur covered chair and Diana and Timothy sat at a large oak table nearby. Large hunks of meat and vegetables sat on gold platters on the table, a large barrel of goat's milk sat on the end of the table.

"So Timothy, how old are you?" Terrek questioned the boy.

"I will be nine when the harvest season begins," the boy replied.

Terrek knew this was the youngest child with them.

Timothy stared at Terrek's shoulder, the bandage stained in blood.

"How did you get hurt?" Timothy asked, Terrek looked up at Diana as if looking for some sort of answer in her beautiful face.

"I got hurt in a fight," Terrek replied quietly.

"With who?" Timothy prodded.

"Just someone in the camp," Terrek replied.

"But - but you - you're the Commander of the army," Timothy exclaimed, flabbergasted that anyone would attack Terrek.

This time Terrek didn't have to say anything, Diana began to speak to the boy.

"Timothy you haven't eaten today have you? Well I'm sure Terrek wouldn't mind if you had some of his food, would you Terrek?" Diana asked.

"No I don't mind, go right ahead," Terrek replied as

20

Timothy looked at the food with wide eyes.

Diana gave Timothy a plate and began cutting him some meat. Timothy quickly devoured the food.

Terrek looked up as the sound of footsteps outside his tent came closer, then the door flaps were pushed aside and Juliana stepped through.

"Well what is your report Juliana," Terrek asked in a formal manner.

"Everyone has their rations and are packing up to move on," she reported.

"Very good. Don't forget you're one of my new aides," Terrek said in a commanding tone.

Juliana turned to Timothy. "Come along Timothy, t ime to gather up our belongings."

Timothy slipped from his chair at the table and followed his mother out of the tent as Terrek stood and stretched his legs.

Terrek looked at Diana and began to speak, "I - Diana I've been meaning to ask you, I would be honored if you would join me for dinner this evening."

Diana looked down, away from Terrek, a slight blush crossing her face.

"I'd be happy to join you," Diana said smiling, she looked up at him out of the corner of her eye.

Terrek smiled back at Diana as they began gathering Terrek's belongings into antelope skin sacks.

Meanwhile in a place of great darkness a meeting of evil took place. Where and what this place was didn't matter. The only thing that mattered was the evil that transpired there. The area was dimly illuminated by a brazier of coals, which were situated on the center of a round stone table.

Above the brazier of coals, a strange glowing mist

hovered. Within the mist was the image of a person. Four individuals stood around the table and another stood nearby.

The first had long dark hair and wore a patch over his eye. An enemy had tried to kill him once; he escaped the killing blow and lost his eye. Now the skull of that enemy rested on a large oak pole in a death field on Wicketai (The Island of Evil), his body lay at the bottom of a flooded quarry nearby the field.

The man's features were hard and sadistic, and one would believe his eye could burn a hole into a stone wall. He wore a combination of chainmail and leather armor with a strangely symboled sash over his shoulder. His name was Murack, leader of the Warlocks.

The second was an older man but his age lead no one to believe that he was feeble in any way. This man had very deep evil powers and was not someone to oppose. When he was ten years old his parents sold him as a slave, his master and others pitted him and other young boys in knife fights and bet on who would win. He had never lost. The only visual sign of that past was a scar along his jaw where another boy had come close to slitting his throat.

The man had very rugged features and wore little armor under a large blood red robe with the wicketus symbol on the front. His name was Colar, leader of the Sorcerers.

The third was a Soothsayer. He was an apprentice to the vicar. This man had a huge body and was over seven feet tall, though his back was bowed in a massive hump. His face was twisted into grotesque deformations and his body was so massive that for most of his lifetime he had been forced to live with a group of Minotaurs.

When he lived with the wild Minotaurs he acted as they did and ate what they ate, his nails grew very long until they were like claws and his deformed teeth were long and sharp. Once he fought one of the Minotaurs for dominance. He won, killing it by tearing out its jugular with his teeth.

22

He ate the body over the next few days.

Of these first three he was the most powerful in the dark arts. He wore ragged clothes, which exposed his overdeveloped muscles. His name was Keldar.

The fourth was a mystery. The others had never seen his face but never opposed him or challenged his leadership. Like Keldar, he was very tall and he wore a robe as black as night, a large hood covered his head.

Large, glowing, yellow eyes peered out of the hood. This man was the leader of all evil in Zyconia, nearly everyone knew who he was but almost no one had seen him. He was the Evil Grand Vicar.

The last man close by in the shadows also stared at the glowing mist. Although not as important as the others, he had his own special powers and a band of evil followers. He was leader of the assassin army in Zyconia. His name was Celarus. The Vicar had summoned him.

Everyone gazed up upon the blue mist.

"SO YOUR ATTEMPT FAILED," the Vicar rasped in an inhuman rumbling voice.

"Yes," came a voice from the mist as the person's image lowered its gaze away from the Vicar.

The individual in the mist slowly lifted his gaze.

"My next attempt won't. I assure you," the image replied.

"It had better not. Terrek is the one man in Zyconia who is capable of destroying us," Colar said menacingly.

Murack turned towards Colar, a look of disgust on his face. "It will take a lot more than one good swordsman and a ragtag army of villagers to take down the Dark Circle. You must be growing weak if you actually believe that," Murack sneered.

"I'll show you who is weak Murack," Colar said angrily as his hands began to glow of red light and his eyes glazed over glowing green. Murack took a defensive position.

"ENOUGH!" the Vicar roared. Both Colar and Murack

drew back in fear. The Vicar gazed directly forward not moving his view as he spoke, "IS TERREK THE ONE FROM THE LEGENDS?"

Keldar, who had said nothing until now, stared off into the darkness.

"I have had visions of your overthrow my lord, but the future isn't written in stone. There are as many possibilities as there are stars in the sky. Terrek can be stopped. Terrek can be beaten. Terrek can be killed," Keldar's eyes beamed brightly emphasizing the last phrase as he moved off into the darkness.

"TERREK WON'T LIVE TO FIND ALL THE CRYSTALS, LET ALONE OVERTHROW ME," the Vicar rumbled.

"I WANT THE DEED DONE SOON," the Vicar said addressing the person in the mist, "AS PROOF OF HIS DEATH, I WANT YOU TO BRING ME HIS HEAD."

"His - his head," stuttered the person in the mist.

"YES, HIS HEAD. DO YOU HAVE A PROBLEM WITH THAT?"

"N - no, it will be as you say, my lord," the image replied bowing its head.

"CONTACT US AGAIN WHEN THE DEED IS DONE!" the mist faded out as Murack and Colar moved off into the darkness.

"CELARUS," the Vicar rasped.

"Yes, my lord?" Celarus responded as he stepped forward from the darkness.

"YOU SAW THE PERSON IN THE MISTS. I DON'T COMPLETELY TRUST THE INDIVIDUAL, I WANT YOU TO TAKE SOME MEN AND TRAVEL TO TERREK'S ARMY. ONCE THERE I WANT YOU TO KILL TERREK. WITHOUT A GOOD LEADER THE ARMY WILL COME APART IN DAYS."

Celarus betrayed slight loathing in his face.

"YOU HAVE BEEN NEGLECTING YOUR DUTIES

24

SOMEWHAT IN THE PAST FEW WEEKS CELARUS," the Vicar said.

"I have become tired of this, of the Assassin Army," he answered.

"DO YOU REMEMBER LENK, THE FORMER LEADER OF THE ASSASSIN ARMY? DO YOU REMEMBER HOW HE COMPLETED HIS TIME WITH US WHEN I ALLOWED YOU TO KILL HIM AND TAKE HIS PLACE? SOME OF US MOVE ON, AND OTHERS SIMPLY DIE," the Vicar said with strange emphasis.

Celarus lifted his eyes to the Vicar and thought about what he had just said.

"GO! ASSASSINATE TERREK," the Vicar finished

"It will be done, my lord," the assassin replied in an even tone. Celarus stood there a couple of moments and then turned and disappeared into the darkness.

The army had taken down the tents and now was crossing the shallow River of Reflection. Terrek and Diana rode Terrek's horse, Streak, up and down the river to make sure everyone got across safely. Terrek surveyed the river.

Suddenly Terrek noticed Juliana trying to pull a struggling black stallion across the river. The stallion was acting more like a stubborn mule than a pure bred stallion. Terrek gently slid off Streak's back handed the reins to Diana and went over to help Juliana. Terrek grabbed the stallion by its reins with an iron grip and hauled the horse through the river bucking and kicking.

He returned the reins to Juliana and began to walk back towards Streak. Suddenly he caught a glimpse of something in the water but before he turned his head he tripped on some rocks below the surface and fell over in the water.

Terrek stood up and looked ahead, he had seen the

reflection of one of the crowds of people. One of the men hadn't cast a reflection! Terrek thought he had seen Lynx walking with the crowd. Legend had it that anyone who belonged to the power of evil couldn't cast a reflection on the River. Terrek knew he would have to keep an eye on Lynx from now on, but since he had no proof, he decided to keep this information to himself.

Terrek walked back to Streak slightly paranoid. He had reason to be uneasy, nearby within the dense crowds of the army, one of his aides waited to kill him.

Many hours later, the army drew close to the Caverns of Death. Terrek had invited Diana to join him for dinner that night and so he had set up a small table in the back of one of the larger wagons. Although it was a bumpy ride Terrek was determined to have dinner with her. Platters of delicious food lined the table and delicious aromas emanated from the wagon. Terrek began helping himself to the meat as they talked.

"You really have a way with Timothy, I think he really looks up to you," Diana said smiling.

"Yes, the boy doesn't have a father, which probably makes him very impressionable," Terrek rationalized.

"How can you relate to children so well? I mean, you grew up in a temple with no other children around," she said.

Terrek seemed to think about it for a moment.

"Well, I suppose with Timothy I just did my best in an awkward situation."

"You'd make an excellent father," she said softly. Terrek paused and seemed to slip into another place and time. Terrek's eyes grew sad and he looked toward the floor.

Diana looked at him worriedly.

26

"Did I say something wrong?"

"No, I'm alright," he said quickly recovering.

"Sometimes I don't pay close enough attention to what I'm saying. I'm sorry if I've upset you in some way," she said gently.

"Really, it's all right," he said smiling at her, "I guess I've just been really exhausted attempting to keep everything in the army running smoothly, it's not easy."

Diana seemed relieved but still slightly unsure.

"How about you Diana, where did you grow up?" Terrek asked.

A far away look crossed Diana's eyes as she responded, "I grew up in a small village not far from the cottage where the Minotaurs attacked."

"My mother died giving birth to me, and my father died of a plague that infected our village when I was a little girl. My uncle took me in and eventually we moved to the cottage, but he died a couple of weeks ago."

Terrek began to regret that he had brought this up.

"I was contemplating moving to Victory City to find a place to live only days before the Minotaurs attacked," Diana explained.

Terrek's face was pale as he began. "You have had a great deal of tragedy in your life. I'm sorry."

Diana looked up into his eyes her face full of compassion as she put her hand in his. "You have nothing to be sorry for," she said smiling.

"If anything you've helped me. You came and took me away from all that hurt, gave me something to fill my life with, by letting me come along with you on the quest," Diana said as she leaned toward him.

"Thank you," she whispered as Terrek also leaned toward her.

Their lips met, and in those few moments Terrek felt as though a surge of power flowed through him. They felt that they were the only two beings in existence, that it was just the two of them and this kiss. They forgot that they were on a quest, they forgot the dinner, and they even forgot their very surroundings. It was just the two of them. All too soon the moment passed, both drew back staring into each other's eyes. Neither of them would forget the moment that they had just shared.

"Terrek we've arrived-," Perrin said as he entered the wagon glancing at Terrek and Diana.
Perrin stepped back slipping into a more formal manner; soldier to commander rather than friend to friend,

"Am I disturbing you, sir?"
Terrek looked at Diana.

"No, just give me a moment Perrin," Terrek replied as Perrin moved back out of the tented wagon.

"I have to go, Diana," Terrek smiled at her.

"All right, just promise me you'll be careful," Diana said worriedly.

"I promise Diana," Terrek said, as he leaned over and kissed her one last time on the cheek. Then exited the wagon.

He was in love.

Terrek stopped outside the wagon as memories from his past entered his mind. Looking back to the wagon he became confused. Was he doing what was right?

Outside the wind whistled across the lifeless desolate wasteland known as the Caverns of Death. Chasms and large caverns littered the rocky plain like the rubble of some ancient ruins. The landscape stretched for miles and not far beyond laid the Eastern Sea, a majestic blue strip on the horizon.

Already the army was setting up camp. Nightfall would come soon but Terrek knew his work was not yet finished for the day.

28

Terrek approached his aides who were gathered nearby, close to the mouth of the nearest chasm.

"We'll have to tell everyone not to get close to the chasms. We don't want a tragedy like that on our hands," he began.

"It appears we'll also have to descend into the chasm to recover the crystal," Terrek looked around at his aides.

Then he carefully removed an ancient tablet from one of the pouches on his belt. "Now I can tell you what I couldn't tell you before."

"The Council thought it best that only I should know the most vital information about the location of the crystals."

"This tablet was found not long ago in an old mine outside Victory City. Most of it could not be deciphered, but the part that was led the Council to believe that one of the crystals was within these caverns."

"John, Hemoth, Ricsis, Lynx, Adam, Zachary, Jessica and Perrin you will all come with me into the caverns," Terrek decided.

Then he turned to his remaining aides.

"Juliana make sure the people are allowed a meal before nightfall. Jason you will be in charge of the camp in my absence. And one last important thing, be on your guard in this evil place."

Moments later, a rope fell into the darkness. Down, down, then in an instant it stopped, reaching the cavern floor. And almost right away, one at a time Terrek and his aides descended down the side of the cavern. When everyone had climbed down, Terrek peered around the huge cavern with the light of his newly lit torch.

They headed through a tunnel winding downward in the side of the chasm. Their torches gleamed off the phosphorescent walls. Cracks riddled the walls and other tunnels could be seen through the larger cracks. The walls of the tunnel were very smooth as though it had been formed in some unnatural manner.

Suddenly the group came to a fork in the road. Two separate tunnels curved off in different directions, Terrek took his dagger and marked an X on the wall.

Then he turned around to address his aides.

"We can't afford to be split up in this place, follow me." Terrek spun around and headed into the tunnel spiraling off into the northeast. Tunnel after tunnel, Terrek was forced to choose each time, eventually the group came out into a huge cave.

The cave was immensely wide and its high ceiling was covered with huge spikes hanging down like the malformed mouth of some fang-toothed creature. The walls were covered with phosphorescent dust that glowed, flooding the tunnel with light. It was so bright that Terrek almost didn't need his torch. At least a dozen other tunnels led into the cave from different directions. At the center of the cave was a large pile of bones. They appeared to be human.

Terrek approached the pile; his aides close on his heels. Slowly he knelt down and picked up one of the fragments.

"They appear to be human bones," Terrek said quietly.

"What manner of beast is capable -," Hemoth was cut off by a loud rumbling.

Tremors caused the cave to vibrate.

"What is it ?" Jessica screamed in fear.

Terrek looked around as the tremors escalated.

Then his eyes grew wide with realization as he bellowed. "Deathworms!"

At the same moment the wall on the opposite side of the cave shattered, sending chunks of rock in all directions. Everyone scattered as a gigantic serpentlike beast slid into the cave.

CHAPTER 3: BEWARE THE BEASTS THAT ROAM THESE CAVERNS

The words had barely erupted from Terrek's throat, when the monstrous creature entered the cave through the huge hole it had just made.

The huge worm was the most grotesque beast any of them had ever seen; the very sight of it struck fear into their souls.

It was long and covered in tough scales, the scales appeared greenish grey and were covered with acidic slime. Its face consisted of two main features: a huge, razor sharp, tooth filled mouth and one massive glaring red eye. The worm opened its massive mouth as it spied the group that had invaded its den. Loud high-pitched screeches echoed in their ears.

The worm propelled itself forward as everyone scattered. Terrek quickly moved sideways pushing Jessica out of the worm's path as he leaped high over the worm's back and came down sword first.

Terrek's sword plunged deep into the worm's back as cries of pain and anger rumbled through the cave. Furiously, the worm swung it's huge hind end into Terrek. He flew off the worm's back hitting the wall of the cave. Perrin quickly ran to his aid as the worm turned to renew it's attack.

Meanwhile everyone else, extremely disoriented, struggled to regain their equilibrium, and rushed to attack the worm. Hemoth lifted himself from the cave floor and extended his hand to help Jessica up. Then he turned to help Terrek but was stopped dead in his tracks.

The wall in front of Hemoth shattered as another worm collided into him, knocking him off his feet. A shower of rock shrapnel struck Jessica and Lynx and they were also thrown to the rock floor again. Hemoth once again regained his balance and pulled his club and dagger from his belt.

The caverns quaked again as a third worm shot into the cave through an outer tunnel. Zachary, John, Adam and Ricsis drew their weapons and rushed into battle.

Lynx got to his feet. He had a bruise on his head.

He felt his robe, and found blood. Small cuts covered his left arm. He looked around and saw Jessica, her body huddled on the ground. Apparently she'd been hit by the rocks, harder than he had. Lynx knelt down and listened. Slowly the erratic sound of her breathing reached him, he carefully scooped her up in his arms and moved her away from the conflict.

Perrin's sword streaked across the death worm's eye as it screeched even louder, the beast's agony dominating its vocal cords. Terrek and Perrin staggered back as the second death worm rushed by. Hemoth was clinging to its upper body, his dagger buried deep.

He held his dagger tightly, struggling to remain on its back. He raised his club and brought it down on the creature's face repeatedly. Gaping wounds appeared on the worm's head as it went completely mad shaking it's head back and forth furiously. Hemoth jumped from it's back just before it rolled over, writhing in pain. Amazingly the worm managed to roll back onto it's belly. Hemoth looked around. His club had been thrown half way across the cave. Too far away.

He found himself captured in the glare of the worm's

huge red eye. In just an instant Hemoth saw into the very soul of the beast. Delving into the raw consciousness and purpose of the beast terrified him. He had never felt anything like it in his life; the beast was pure unadulterated evil.

Hemoth's fear nearly paralyzed him but he broke eye contact and quickly searched around for something to use as a weapon. The worm fixed it's gaze on Hemoth, preparing for it's final charge. Hemoth caught sight of a large rock spike connected to the cave floor and threw the whole weight of his body against the spike to knock it over. Hemoth heard the crack as the spike fell to the ground.

The worm, not hesitating any longer, raced toward Hemoth. With one last burst of superhuman strength he hefted the spike up in front of him, directly in the path of the oncoming worm.

With a thud, the noise of the impact resounded through the cave, as the spike sunk deep into the worm's eye, penetrating it's brain. The impact knocked Hemoth against a nearby wall. Exhausted and battle weary, he paused for a moment to catch his breath.

At that same moment Terrek and Perrin moved in for the kill. Now blinded, the worm they faced was considerably easier to attack. Throwing themselves on the worm's back they hacked and sliced at its body with their swords. Soon the worm lay still, and all signs of life faded from its eyes. Terrek and Perrin joined the others against the one remaining worm. It had also been wounded, deep slashes, dripping blood littered it's body. Swiftly they circled attacking as one force, in seconds it also lay dead.

Everyone stood there gazing upon the carnage, their minds soaking in everything that had just happened. Terrek looked around and then turned to examine his aides, cuts and bruises covered his people as they panted for breath.

Lynx brought Jessica over to the group, Terrek eyed him suspiciously as he spoke.

"She's been hurt by the flying rock," Lynx said quietly.

Terrek quickly bent down and checked her breathing looking for signs of any serious injury. She seemed to have been knocked out. Other than that, she had only minor cuts.

"She'll be all right," Terrek replied as he lifted her onto his shoulder and stood up.

"Now let's-," Terrek was stopped in mid-sentence by a loud rumbling.

"Not another worm," groaned Ricsis, but this time it sounded strangely different, a moment later the group felt the cave floor give way. The collapse sent rocks and debris plunging down into the darkness beside them. Terrek felt Jessica slip from his grasp as they hit the water.

Everyone came up gasping for air. Terrek looked up. Far above stood the remainder of the cave floor on which they had just fought. Now Terrek was standing in hip deep water in a tunnel leading off into the southeast.

Nearby Jessica's body floated up and down in the water, carefully he lifted her from the water checking to see if her breathing had been effected by their fall in the water. Her breathing was slow but rhythmic; he lifted her back onto his shoulder.

"Anybody injured?" he questioned as he looked around the group, everyone shook their heads and Terrek squinted, gazing down the long tunnel before them.

"Follow me, this appears to be the only way out," Terrek observed as he started down the long tunnel, the others close behind.

Awhile later, the group was still wading down the tunnel. It hadn't changed, and the water level hadn't changed, but Terrek was beginning to tire. The soft weight of Jessica's body made his shoulder ache. He had to admit that under normal circumstances he wouldn't have minded being this close to a beautiful woman. But this was ridiculous.

Terrek peered ahead straining his eyes. Suddenly he noticed a small point of light. Instantly rejuvenated he pushed his legs forward through the water wading faster than ever toward the faint light. Close behind the others were exhausted, but tried to keep up as best as they could. When Terrek got closer he realized that the light was coming from a small cave entrance on the wall of the tunnel.

He approached the entrance of the cave cautiously and stared into the object that created the light.
In the center of the room stood a pedestal covered in hieroglyphics and ancient writings. The glow emanated from the direct center of the pedestal. Terrek gazed into the object with sheer amazement. A kaleidoscope of colored light radiated from it. The gem on the pedestal bathed Terrek's skin in warmth. This was the crystal of light.

Terrek slowly reached down and plucked the crystal from its nest, the gem was warm in his palm.

He shifted Jessica on his shoulder as he detected a faint noise. Looking up he saw the ceiling caving in. Wasting no time Terrek flung himself and Jessica through the entrance just barely evading the huge rocks. Terrek's Aides rushed over to him and Ricsis helped him up out of the water, Terrek once again retrieved Jessica.

"I have the first crystal," Terrek said as he held it out so everyone could see it.

They all began to talk at once but Terrek cut them off.

"We don't have time to talk here. Let's get out of these caverns before something else happens," Terrek muttered.

Terrek's followers reluctantly pressed on, gradually the water level decreased until they were walking in puddles and mud. The tunnel narrowed slightly and became steep as they began to ascend.

Looking ahead they saw the exit to the surface. Quickly and happily Terrek's team soaked in the fresh air as they climbed through the end of the tunnel into the open air. They were standing in a huge chasm the sky far above, the sides of the chasm jutting up like huge trees that had suddenly grown. The group felt like ants looking at the rock formations that made up the chasm walls.

They all saw the movement at once and turned to see what it was, Terrek's eyes went wide as he saw the gigantic bird not far from where they stood. The bird was chained to the chasm floor with large bronze chains and was watching them with great curiosity. The creature was gargantuan, with a wingspan dozens of strides long. The wings of the bird would undoubtably create wind that would knock any man down. Yet the bird made no threatening moves, it simply stood there observing them like a vigilant statue.

Terrek handed Jessica to Hemoth as he approached the huge bird, then to Terrek's amazement; the bird spoke to him.

"Who are you?" asked the bird in a loud but steady, calm voice.

"I am Terrek," he replied in a guarded, equally steady tone.

"I beg thee kind sir, for my freedom," the bird said to Terrek.

Terrek paused, staring at the gigantic creature, and then stepped forward and hacked at the chains with his sword. The chains, old and rusty, quickly fell apart.

The bird stood and stretched it's wings.

"For centuries I have been chained here kept alive by the power of black magic, to suffer. No one has ever made it this deep into the Caverns of Death. You have broken the power. Why are you here?" the bird asked.

"We have come in search of the ancient crystals of

Zyconia," answered Terrek.

The bird thought for a moment and spoke again.

"Before I was chained here my home was a large sanctuary in which many of my kind dwelt. A large translucent gem sat on a significant altar in the central area. The gem was said to have special powers by the wiser members of my clan. Could this be one of the crystals you seek."

Terrek remembered how the crystal that they had taken from the caverns had been sitting on a pedestal.

"It's possible," Terrek said.

"Then I will take you there. I may be able to convince the head elder to relinquish the crystal to you," the creature explained.

The huge bird carried them all back to their camp. Crowds gathered round as it touched down. Terrek's small group climbed down from the bird's back and Terrek slid Jessica off his shoulder and into the waiting arms of two healers.

"Take good care of her, we need her on this quest," Terrek told them, they both nodded as they carried her away.

Terrek stood in front of the huge bird and addressed the crowd.

"This is Selate. She has decided to join us on the quest. Don't treat her like an animal, because she is as intelligent as you or I. I want her to be given the same respect as you would give anyone else in this camp."

"Tomorrow we shall have a feast, so get some sleep," Terrek said.

At this news everyone cheered. Terrek turned to Selate.

"You can sleep in one of the larger meeting tents. John, show her to her new tent."

Terrek walked toward his tent as the crowd dispersed. Diana, hearing the commotion, appeared in the doorway of her tent.

"Terrek," she breathed as she ran over into his arms.

"You're all right," she said in relief.

"You didn't think I'd stay away too long, with someone as beautiful as you waiting for me, did you?" he grinned. Diana blushed, then she replied.

"You were gone so long I was afraid something had happened to you."

"It would take more than a cave of oversized worms to hurt me," Terrek answered. Both laughed.

"I'm glad you're all right," Diana said smiling.

"Thank you," he said. "I think maybe I should rest now. I'm exhausted."

"Well goodnight, Terrek," she said as she withdrew smiling at him.

"Goodnight, Diana," Terrek replied backing toward his tent.

Terrek entered his tent and sat on his bed, took off his tunic and swiftly lay down and pulled a fur blanket over himself, preparing to go to sleep. Instantly, in his peripheral vision, he noticed a shadow, a dose of adrenaline shot through his body as he spun toward a dark corner of his tent. Terrek relaxed as he saw Zyron sitting crosslegged on the ground.

"Zyron," Terrek breathed. "You should be resting. A healer is supposed to be tending to you. How did you slip by her?"

Zyron behaved as though he had not heard Terrek's statement. "There is evil in the camp. Traitors who were sent by the Vicar."

"Yes, I've already felt their sting," Terrek said, gently patting his bandaged shoulder.

"That won't be the last attempt on your life. Be on your guard," warned Zyron.

Terrek reached down and picked up an oil lamp on the opposite side of his bed and turned back toward Zyron.

"How do-," Terrek stopped and looked around, Zyron was gone.

The young boy tripped and fell to the ground. As he lifted his face from the mud he saw his friend speedily win the small race, shaming his feeble challenge. The other boy reaching the finish, touched the tree in victory.

"I win again Perrin!" he replied as he spun around and came back to help his friend. Perrin reached up, grabbed his hand and stood.

"Maybe I can beat you next time Terrek," Perrin sighed.

"You're a very fast person Perrin, maybe you will," conceded Terrek. Perrin looked to the ground as he and Terrek walked back along the path.

"You just beat me at everything," Perrin complained.

Terrek put his arm on Perrin's shoulder.

"Not everything, you have a lot of great talents I don't have," he said. Both boys continued down the path as the memory blurred and another surfaced.

Both young boys were grown, near adulthood. Standing under a large tree two young couples ate in peace and harmony. Terrek had come with a young woman named Beverly, while a beauty named Lydia had accompanied Perrin. Both young women were beautiful, full of life and ambition.

Lydia had beckoned Perrin away from Terrek and Beverly because she had to speak with him. Out of sight he smiled at her as he kissed her in a playful manner. Lydia was limp in his embrace. Perrin opened his eyes and looked at her a little concerned.

"Is everything all right?" Perrin asked, confused.

40

Lydia turned away from him, taking a few steps. She appeared to be thinking deeply about something.

"You know I am very fond of you Perrin, I'm just not sure we're meant to be together," she said sadly.

Perrin's heart sank.

"What do you mean?" he said slowly, swallowing.

She turned to him and placed a hand on his cheek and looked into his eyes for a moment, then down to the ground.

"My family is leaving Zyconia for the Radrailian Islands in the Northern Sea," she said sadly.

"Then marry me Lydia, I promise you I will make you happy forever," Perrin assured her.

Lydia continued to stare at the ground, slowly she shook her head.

"No, I'm sorry I just don't have that much faith. You will be part of Zyconia's armies soon enough, always off fighting somewhere. I need someone to be with me, a father for my children, I do love you but I just can't –" she choked slightly as she back away, "I'm sorry, it's over Perrin."

Perrin held out his hand as Lydia ran away over the hill leaving him standing alone. The caress of Lydia's hand upon his cheek was replaced with that of the cold wind. A moment later Terrek approached Perrin from behind.

"Perrin there you are. Beverly and I had a wonderful idea to go to Crescent Valley. Do you remember it? It is such a romantic place, I'm sure Lydia would thank you for showing it to her," Terrek said.

Perrin resented the conversation and turned slowly trying to hide his sadness.

"I know you may be a little angry, but I might as well admit to you that I was the one who actually talked to Lydia about you in the first place. I told her what a great person you were and that she would really like you, and things blossomed into a romance. I'm so glad," Terrek said.

Perrin raised his head at the last bit of information, his

blood boiled.

"You – you were responsible for our relationship?" he roared.

"Well not totally. I just thought maybe you could use a little help," Terrek said quietly, surprised at the reaction.

"If I wanted your help I would have asked for it!" Perrin yelled.

Terrek was silent.

"Lydia just ended it!" Perrin cried.

Terrek felt like crawling into a deep hole. He had been so absorbed with Beverly and so happy that he hadn't noticed how quiet Perrin suddenly seemed.

"Maybe – maybe you're better off?" Terrek said, grasping for something to smooth things over. But he knew as soon as he said it that it was wrong.

"How would you know! Leave my life alone! I can handle it myself! Go, take Beverly to Crescent Valley, marry her!" Perrin yelled as he walked away.

"Perrin wait," Terrek called.

Again the scene blurred, flowing forward through time. The tree lined field replaced by a stone castle where Terrek and Perrin awaited the final decision by the officials to allow them entry into the Council's Elite Forces. Finally after the grueling two-month test of physical and mental strength they would earn this just reward.

With a clang the nearby door flew open as several officials entered. Soldiers gathered around in interest. Terrek and Perrin stood wearing the bruises acquired from the last couple of months with honor. The officials looked at them, walking back and forth in unison, and then they stopped.

"Terrek you have more than great potential. We believe you could teach some of the members of our Elite some things. But alas, we find your companion to be less than we expected. He is a great warrior but perhaps not one for the Elite Army," the eldest official said.

42

Terrek stared at them sternly.

"I won't be part of the Elite Army if Perrin isn't accepted. We've been through too much together," Terrek said forcefully.

The officials stared at him, unable to believe he was willing to give up this position for his friend.

"Your heart is in the right place, another quality we admire. Perrin is accepted," the official replied. Terrek nodded as the officials withdrew from the room and the other soldier present congratulated both men on their accomplishment.

Terrek and Perrin sat heavily on a nearby bench. Terrek noticed Perrin's sour expression.

"We were accepted! Why do you look so unhappy?" Terrek asked.

"You were accepted, they only took me because you forced them. They didn't want me, it wasn't on my own merit," he said slowly, as he stood.

Suddenly Terrek stood as well his body becoming massive as it filled the room. Perrin felt himself pulled to the floor by an invisible force. He couldn't move: totally subdued. Terrek's shadow covered him as his face changed and his voice became low.

"What's wrong Perrin, you should be grateful! After all I've done for you!" Terrek said.

Perrin cowered against the floor.

"No!" he screamed.

Suddenly Perrin erupted from the makeshift bed in his tent. Breathing heavily he wiped the sweat from his face. Perrin lay back down, pulled his blanket over his head, and tried to get back to sleep.

The next morning the army and their families gathered together to have a feast to celebrate the discovery of the first crystal. Everyone sat on large logs, or on the slope of a nearby hill. Several boars were being roasted over open fires. Terrek sat at the top of the small hill where he could be seen and heard by all. Diana sat beside him. Terrek's aides were nearby. Terrek stood as the crowd hushed. He began his speech, showing the crystal to the people. The crowd cheered and applauded their leader.

Unnoticed nearby, men of evil slithered into the camp crowds. Several of them sat on the hill whispering amongst themselves.

"Be prepared, we're going to make our move tonight," said a large hooded man.

"Then Terrek will have to give us the crystal," said another.

The men faded into the crowds as Terrek finished his speech and the crowd feasted happily on the wild boar provided.

The wagons were reloaded with the excess food and the horsemen remounted. Again the army followed their path. Diana sat with Zyron in one of the wagons as Terrek led the army, riding on Streak, gazing skyward for guidance from Selate. The huge bird would take them to the next crystal.

Jessica rode up beside Terrek a small bandage draped over her forehead.

"I understand I have you to thank for hauling me out of the caverns."

"I suppose I played a minor part in your survival," Terrek smiled. "I'm just glad you're all right. We can't afford to lose such a gifted healer."

"Thank you Commander, I'm grateful," Jessica said in appreciation.

"You're quite welcome," Terrek finished.

Soon everyone had recrossed the northern part of the River of Reflection without incident. Terrek saw nothing unusual this time, and Lynx was nowhere to be seen. After many hours they reached an astoundingly dense jungle known as the Jungle of Confusion. Selate landed and again everyone set up camp. In the morning they would have to travel through the jungle.

Terrek was hoping to have dinner with Diana. Unfortunately he couldn't find her. After searching for her for awhile he became very worried. He checked with Zyron and found that she had left the wagon just after they had set up camp. Grasping at straws, Terrek went to his tent to see if she was there. Terrek entered his tent to see an unexpected visitor.

CHAPTER 4: ASSASSINS

The man standing before Terrek was at least his height. He wore a suit of chainmail with a sword at his side. His features were rugged and his hair was long and tangled. His face was twisted into an evil grin.

"Who are you? What do you want?" demanded Terrek as he entered the tent. The man sat in a chair at Terrek's table as Terrek moved toward a chair on the opposite side.

"Commander, it has come to my master's attention that you have found something that belongs to him. He wishes it returned," he rasped.

Terrek stood apprehensively, knowing what the stranger wanted, "I have nothing that belongs to your master."

"Then perhaps you'd like to make a trade. For the woman's sake," the stranger said, allowing the last few words to linger on his vile tongue.

Terrek looked into the man's eyes; they had Diana. Terrek grabbed him by the collar nearly pulling him off the ground.

"Where is she? Where is Diana!" Terrek said fiercely. The man's eyes became clouded with fear, for a moment he was almost afraid that Terrek would kill him then and there.

"Harm me, and you'll never see her alive again," the

man mouthed in Terrek's iron grip. Terrek loosened his grip as the man spoke again. "Come wit h me if you value her life."

It seemed he had no choice.

Diana slowly regained consciousness. Her wrists ached; her back was against a tree. She was in a large clearing in the forest, her arms and legs bound tightly. A small fire burned nearby and three large men sat around it talking amongst themselves.

The events that had led up to this came flooding back as she groaned, feeling the pain in her head. She had retired to her tent for the night. When she entered the tent someone had grabbed her. She had tried to scream but a hand covered her mouth, the last thing she remembered was a blow to the back of the head. After that she could recall nothing until now. Where was she?

Suddenly she heard footsteps, the men around the fire turned toward two figures coming towards them.

Terrek and one of their men came into the clearing. Terrek saw Diana, but knew that attacking immediately could risk her life. There were too many men present; he needed to wait for the right moment.

One of the three approached Terrek. "We've been waiting for you Terrek," the man said, withdrawing a large club that hung from his belt.

"I am Celarus, leader of the Assassin army."

Instantly two of the men grabbed Terrek by the arms and before he had time to react Celarus swung his club heavily into Terrek's abdomen. The men released his arms and Terrek fell to his knees. His vision blurred as unbelievable pain flowed through his body.

Quickly the other men relieved him of his sword. Celarus pulled the crystal from his belt, gazing on its illuminated surface with awe.

"We have the crystal, kill him," Celarus said, as he walked from the clearing.

Terrek swiftly stood, gripping the collars of the men on either side of him. Lifting both men off the ground he smashed their heads together.

A loud crack resounded through the clearing. Terrek released one of the men, pulling the other in front of him just in time to protect himself from an axe. The axe crashed into the man's back as Terrek leapt over him kicking the axeman in the head. Terrek grabbed the handle pulling the axe from the man's body. Now he was armed.

Two more men came running into the clearing, the other two, still alive, regained their bearings. Suddenly an arrow struck Terrek in the leg. A moment later, Terrek swung his axe into the chest of the man with the crossbow. Blood gushed across Terrek's tunic like waves of water upon the shore. One of the men grabbed Terrek from behind as another rushed him. Terrek swung his axe back, bringing the broad side of the axe down into the man's head behind him.

Pulling the axe forward he brought it directly into the charging man's head, nearly splitting it completely in half. Terrek ran forward and hit yet another man in the abdomen. As the man crumpled to the ground the last man tried to run from the clearing. But with one final excruciating effort, Terrek threw the axe at the escaping man. The axe caught him in the back and he fell over into a pile of broken twigs. He couldn't let him escape and warn Celarus.

Terrek paused, taking in the carnage around him. He only hoped he wouldn't someday die like these men had.

Terrek rushed to Diana's side. Diana was close to tears as Terrek untied her.

"I'm sorry you had to see that Diana, but there was no other way," Terrek said softly.

Terrek looked off in the direction Celarus had gone.

"Stay here I've got to get the crystal back," he whispered in desperation.

Diana grabbed Terrek's arm. "Be careful, please" she said.

Terrek leaned over, pressing his lips against hers. He gently helped her to her feet as he backed away. She had enjoyed the kiss as much as he had. Terrek picked up a nearby crossbow and handed it to her.

"If anyone tries to attack you, protect yourself with this. Just wait until you see who they are before you shoot," Terrek warned her.

Terrek picked up his sword near the fire and turned back toward Diana one last time to reassure her.

"I'll be all right," he said, then he was gone.

Celarus had left no tracks. He must have some evil powers of his own, Terrek thought. But he could sense Celarus's evil stench on the wind. Terrek knew the Maker was giving him guidance tracking the assassin leader. Terrek was very battle weary, and walking halfway through the forest had further tired him.

Unexpectedly he was hit from behind with an armored boot to his wounded leg. Terrek rolled over and came up ready for a fight. Terrek looked around, no one could be seen. He listened for any unusual sounds; all was normal except for the sound of a waterfall in the distance.

Again another blow hit him in the back, knocking him off balance. Again he turned seeing no attacker. Terrek shut his eyes and concentrated. If he had enough faith he knew he could overcome Celarus. Slowly it came to him; he had the power to beat Celarus. He could sense him now, he was very close. Celarus jumped out toward Terrek and in one fluid motion Terrek grabbed a hold of his foot throwing him into a nearby tree.

Celarus got to his feet scowling.

"You're a better warrior than I thought. The Vicar could use someone with your skills."

"I would never abandon Zyconia to the clutches of the Vicar! He will never be Zyconia's ruler," said Terrek with great passion.

"You're fighting a losing battle; the Vicar's power is growing, and the number of raiders is increasing, soon all of Zyconia will be over run."

Terrek lifted his sword and addressed Celarus.

"Give me the crystal."

Celarus withdrew his dagger, and in a mocking tone replied, "come and get it."

Terrek jumped forward swinging his sword, but Celarus was too quick and the sword buried itself in the tree. Celarus struck Terrek across the jaw with an armored glove, which sent him sprawling. Celarus, seeing an advantage, rushed at Terrek as he staggered to his feet. Suddenly Terrek swung a large tree branch into Celarus's mid-section. Terrek quickly kicked the dagger out of Celarus's hand as he jumped to his feet.

Both men took defensive positions waiting for the other to strike. Finally they both moved towards each other. Swiftly they began trading punches, over and over until both were panting for breath. Eventually Terrek managed to down Celarus with a series of lefts, rights and a final blow to the jaw. Celarus looked at Terrek like a man possessed as he got to his feet. Grabbing his dagger from the ground, he leapt at Terrek. The dagger swished by Terrek scraping his forearm. He yelled in agony as he grabbed Celarus by the wrist.

The noise of the waterfall loomed closer and closer as the fight continued. The only witnesses were the trees and bushes that surrounded them. The dagger fell, sliding across a patch of grass close to the edge of the waterfall. The waterfall was enormous and dropped down so far

51

below them that they could barely see the bottom. At any other time Terrek would have enjoyed the beauty of the mist shrouded falls, but not now.

Both men struggled for the knife.

"Our way is the only way. I'm where I am now because I murdered the former leader of the Assassin army. I've never lost and I never will," exclaimed Celarus in anger.

"Don't you understand, the Vicar doesn't care about any of you he simply uses you, as you assassinated your superior so will you be assassinated when you become of no use to the Vicar," Terrek said.

Celarus relaxed his grip for a moment. What Terrek said sounded so much like what the Vicar had said not long ago. Terrek looked into Celarus's eyes but at the same moment spied a glimmer from Celarus's belt. Terrek might have been able to convince him, but he couldn't afford to wait and find out.

Terrek acted quickly throwing the knife beyond both their grips he grabbed at Celarus's belt. Again they struggled and fell to the ground. Just when Terrek had a firm grasp on the belt, both men lost their patch of ground, which crumbled beneath them. The men plunged down into the pits of oblivion. Terrek felt the belt tear away from Celarus's waist as the assassin leader hit the shallow end of the falls. Terrek tightened his grip on the belt as he hit the dark rushing water.

Terrek lay on a pile of rocks having just pulled himself from the river; rushing water rolled by. He was completely exhausted. His clothes and armor were torn. His hair fell over his face as his chest heaved.

Terrek turned over on his stomach and pulled the belt to him, opening the pouch. Instantly a flood of light blinded him, Terrek rubbed his eyes as he sighed in relief. He slowly got to his feet putting the crystal back inside his own belt. He threw Celarus's belt into the water. Then Terrek remembered Diana, he had to hurry and get back to her.

Early the next morning Terrek gathered his aides for a meeting in his tent.

"It seems we must watch ourselves more closely than we thought," Terrek said facing them. All were present, even Selate's large bird head protruded into the tent from the doorway.

"I never caught sight of Celarus after the fall. I don't think he could have survived it," Terrek said, a twinge of remorse in his voice. He didn't have the chance to see if he had gotten through to Celarus, if he had he would never know.

"I'll tell the guards to be extra cautious. We can't have this happening again," Perrin asserted.

Timothy, tired of the meeting, stirred next to his mother as Terrek spoke again, "that's all, you may leave."

Everyone vacated the tent and Selate pulled her head back from the doorway.

"I said I would kill him, you didn't have to send others," said the image of the person in the mist.

"YOU FAILED THE FIRST TIME, MAYBE THIS WILL ENCOURAGE YOU," the Vicar rasped.

The Vicar stood in darkness. Once again Colar, Murack and Keldar accompanied him around the circular dark table. The coals in the brazier were slowly going out and would soon have to be replenished, the blue mist hung above it waving like a flag in the wind. Colar nudged the coals in the brazier with a metal rod.

"I told you I'd do it but I must wait for the right time," the image explained.

Murack smashed his fist down on the table, "Terrek must be vanquished now. He overcame Celarus the powerful leader of the assassin army."

"We need Terrek killed immediately he is too much of a threat to us. We don't have time," Colar cut in.

"SILENCE! BECAUSE HE HAS KILLED CELARUS YOU WHINE LIKE INFANTS FOR TERREK'S DEATH. YOU WILL HAVE YOUR TIME, BUT TERREK WILL BE DEAD SOON, OR YOU WILL," the Vicar finished.

The mist faded and the image disappeared. The person sat back in a chair, in a tent in Terrek's camp, thinking about what had to be done.

The density of the Jungle of Confusion made it hard to navigate. Terrek had hoped to be at the other side by now. The humidity of the jungle was slowly making him wilt and he felt as though they were traveling in circles.

The army had been trudging through the jungle for hours now with no end in sight. Terrek had planned to reach the other side by mid-day, it was now well past mid-day. The wagons were having a hard time coming through the dense jungle and were constantly getting stuck in the undergrowth.

Adam rode up behind Terrek and Diana, who were riding Streak. "We should be through the brush by now."

"There's vegetation everywhere, and the scouts report that this is all that's ahead, I think we should stop and make camp. We can get our bearings and find the right direction tomorrow."

Terrek thought about this for a moment, "I'm going to speak with Zyron," he said as he dismounted Streak.

54

Zyron stepped from the wagon and surveyed the wilderness before them.

"Your faith is not as strong as it should be, you can't see the illusions created by the Vicar," said Zyron.

Terrek looked at Zyron, puzzled. "Perhaps this will clear things up," Zyron explained as he lifted his sceptre high over his head. The sceptre began to glow as the scene around everyone dissolved from that of jungle to grassland.

Terrek looked back the way they had come, jungle could be seen on the horizon. The Vicar was trying to confuse them to make them turn back. They had already traveled through the jungle! Terrek, exhausted, helped Diana dismount Streak as he announced. "Pitch your tents we're going to make camp."

CHAPTER 5: SANCTUARY OR CENATAPH

$\mathfrak{N}$ightfall. The camp was completely set up. At the center of the camp lay numerous cook fires, surrounding the fires were the wagons, and beyond the wagons the various tents of the army were positioned. Guards marched about the camp performing the nightwatch.

Around the cook fires sat many groups of individuals sampling small cooked animals they had captured in snares and traps during the day. Around one fire sat Hemoth, Zachary, Adam, and Jason. Nearby, Perrin leaned on a wagon wheel carving a small figurine.

"So Zachary, how long have you known Terrek," asked Hemoth.

"About three years. The first time I saw him was in a small Inn at Batera. Terrek and Perrin were on a small errand for the counsel's elite army while I was on a separate errand. We were all at the Inn eating, when an old man burst into the Inn screaming and yelling."

"Apparently four boys had been playing in an old subterranean dungeon close to his home and had locked themselves in one of the old cells. When the thunderstorm had started the dungeon began to flood. When the old man heard their cries he hurried and tried to free them but he couldn't budge the lock."

"Quickly Terrek, Perrin and I were on our feet and out

the door followed by a handful of other men. As we descended the dungeon steps we could see the water rising as it swallowed each step. When we found the cell the water was hip deep. All the men heaved and pushed at the door but to no avail."

"Finally one man brought an axe into the dungeon and all stood back. The axe struck the huge bronze lock several times but did no damage. Suddenly a huge rush of water came through one of the barred windows knocking the axe from the man's grasp. After a futile search in the muddy waters all the men returned to their physical struggle with the door."

"Soon the water was above our heads and most of the men retreated to the dungeon entrance. The young boys climbed the bars to try to keep their faces out of the water but it had practically reached the ceiling. Perrin and I couldn't hold our breath any longer."

"Perrin tried to pry Terrek from the metal door but he couldn't. Terrek held the door with an iron grip. Perrin and I reluctantly returned to the entrance and came out beside the other men. A huge crowd had gathered around the dungeon."

"The moments dragged on and we didn't think he would survive. Suddenly and unexpectedly he emerged. He had one boy over each shoulder and one in each arm. Terrek fell to the ground sputtering and coughing," Zachary paused.

"A few days later, when the water went down I returned to the dungeon. The cell door that the boys had been trapped behind was completely torn off the hinges. I've never really confronted him about it but Terrek had to have ripped that door off with his bare hands."

Hemoth smiled. "When I met Terrek it was during very dire circumstances as well. Only at that time he was the one who needed help. Had I not found him he might not be alive today."

"At the time Terrek was still part of the regular army at Victory City. He had been hunting and ran into some bad weather. By the time I found him he was pinned beneath the trunk of a huge oak. As I first spotted him I thought he was dead. But when he suddenly cried out deliriously for help I knew I was mistaken."

"I tried to wake him from this state of delirium, as best I could. Then straining my muscles I attempted to lift the trunk. It barely moved. I knew that if I didn't get him out soon he would surely die. The nearest village was one day's walk away. So I redoubled my efforts on the trunk. Pain conquered my body as Terrek pulled himself from beneath the tree. For a long time after that I had pains in my arms."

Hemoth concluded the story as he rubbed his right bicep. Everyone around Hemoth looked on. Although he may have had his strength disabled once, he was the strongest man they had ever seen.

Perrin moved closer and tossed a handful of wood shavings into the fire.

"What are you carving, Perrin," asked Jason.

Perrin smiled as he held out the figurine. "A Minotaur, I have nearly thirty different carvings of them now," Perrin smoothed his hand over the delicately featured face.

"I wonder what philosophers would say about creating ones own enemies."

Perrin returned his attention to his work.

Jason eyes were fixed on the carving. He raised his voice. "How did you come to know Terrek, Perrin?"

"You're just determined to interrupt my work aren't you?" Perrin said a grin on his face.

"All right," Perrin sighed.

Perrin returned his carving knife to his belt as he began. "Terrek and I have known each other since our youth. We often played together as children and eventually trained together to join the Victory City army. There was some jealousy between us in our childhood and youth. We always competed, but those feelings subsided as we matured. When we became integrated into the Victory City army we quickly made a name for ourselves as we climbed the ranks," Perrin smiled as he remembered.

"Terrek was the one who became accepted by the Council's Elite army, he told them that he would join only under the condition that they accept me as well. We've been working together ever since."

Jason looked to the fire, "I suppose you've known him the longest."

"Now if story time is over I believe I will return to my work," Perrin smiled.

High over head Selate guided the army ever forward to their next destination. Just ahead the ruins of a huge pillared building lay before them. Could this possibly be the palace Selate had referred to? Terrek pulled back on Streak's reins and dismounted while Selate swooped down from the skies above. Terrek surveyed the area.

The huge structure was completely lined by decaying moss-ridden pillars supporting an overhanging stone roof around the perimeter, which stretched in a complete circle. The building was massive and without feature, solid stone walls all the way around. Directly in front of him was a single huge bronze door, barely connected to its hinges. Vines and overgrowth covered most of the building. Another living creature hadn't visited this structure in a long time.

Terrek faced Selate. A strange expression was ingrained in her features. Terrek's best guess at the emotion would be confusion. This was obviously not the sight she expected to confront her. The grinding of wagon wheels ceased as Terrek's aides rode up behind him, he handed his reins to

Diana.

Terrek faced his aides. "Zachary, Jason, Adam, Lynx and Hemoth follow me! Perrin keep things under control until I get back."

A loud clang echoed through the halls of the great structure as the huge bronze door collided with the miry stone floor. The small group entered a large room and scanned the immediate area. The sight that greeted them was gruesome.

Giant stone slab tables littered the room and sprawled across them and on the floor were the remains of at least a dozen huge bird skeletons. Selate drew back in terror as a low guttural moaning escaped from her throat, a rippling of distortion fluttered across her facial features.

In pity Terrek attempted to ease Selate's pain. "You were gone from this place for centuries Selate. I guess the magic put upon you prevented you from aging, but they did. They've been gone a long time. I'm sorry."

The others, their faces solemn, quickly moved past Terrek and Selate to scout the room.

Selate turned her face from the painful sight and buried her sadness in her wing. Tears streamed down her ruffled feathers. Terrek looked on, full of sorrow for the strange being. Obviously this had been the only family she had ever known, and now with all her kind vanquished she was alone in the world.

Selate began to recover herself and through sobs she managed. "I'll lead you to the central meeting area, follow me."

It took several minutes to transverse a huge hallway that led them to a circular room even larger than the last. Flowing from the ceiling to the floor rays of light shone through the opening of collapsed sections of roofing.

60

Terrek seeing a hieroglyphic covered pedestal at the center of the room cautiously approached, looking for the glimmer of another crystal.

The pedestal was vacant.

Nearby something else caught his eye. On one of the stone tables scrolled in large letters over the surface read:

> "To any avian or other winged kin,
> we have been attacked by unknown creatures.
> Even now they are attempting to invade our
> Sanctuary by destroying the bronze door of the
> east passage. I only hope they don't discover
> the crystals hiding place, I -"

The message stopped abruptly. Obviously, judging the dire distress of the words, the writer had been disrupted by something or someone.

Selate was distressed once more as she spoke. "How could something like this have happened? Our entire avian society was pacifists! Why would anything attack us?"

Terrek examined the table. Then something off to the side caught their eyes. Another skeleton. Only this one was human.

Terrek instantly faced Selate, but this time rage filled her eyes. "It was your kind, your kind are the murderers!" Her body seemed to vibrate under some unseen strain. "You - you're all murderers."

Selate's wings erupted, a torrential explosion of bluish-green, and with one flourish Terrek was knocked to the ground.

"Murderer!" Selate cried, as anger twisted her face. She sprang from the floor and flew away through one of the larger breakages in the ceiling.

"Selate wait!" his words fell on deaf ears as Selate immersed herself in the clouds above. Terrek lowered his head. Why now?

Getting to his feet he stared down at the human corpse in disgust. He appeared to have been pushed back onto his own weapon. It was true it was his kind that had caused this. They had come all this way for nothing. There was no crystal and now they had lost Selate.

In frustration he pulled back his foot and kicked the ancient decaying corpse into piles of splintered bone. He was about to leave the same way he came, but the human skull rebounding off the pedestal shattered a hidden compartment. A second later a large green gem rolled out onto the floor followed by three small tablets.

Sorrow ruled her mind and body. She exerted every muscle as if the strain would release her mind from torment. Spiraling down from the sky she came to rest on a small hill. How could Terrek's kind be responsible for such atrocities? True, he was a fierce warrior but he was so kind and gentle. How?

No, she realized she could not lay blame on him. In her society it had been different. Everyone in the Sanctuary had been so innocent. They operated almost as a collective mind, one individual would be responsible for the entire group.

The first realization she had of how innocent they were came from the harsh experience she had just escaped from in the caverns. She and a few members of her clan had been scouting the area for a place to set up a new colony. A great wizard had captured them and she'd been chained.

But the others had resisted. Eventually angered the wizard so much that in a fit of rage he recklessly destroyed both the avians and himself. The magic had held her there inanimate for what seemed forever. If it had not been for Terrek she would still be there.

Dragging herself back to her original thoughts she made

her decision. No, Terrek's society is much different. He should not hold any blame for this.

Selate felt a presence at her back and knew who it was. She looked out over the grassland away from him.

"I will rejoin you now, but I can't say that I can ever really completely respect you or your kind in the same frame of mind as I did. Some of you don't have the same souls. They are corrupt and sadistic. It's going to be more difficult for me to trust now."

Terrek spoke gently, "I'm sorry about all of this, I wish I could change it. But this quest is to prevent evil individuals from dominating Zyconia. Perhaps, as we strike out against them, you will gain some measure of peace in the knowledge that we are stopping men like the ones that killed your family."

Selate faced Terrek his face soft but unyielding. Selate felt her grudge against him melt away.

"Thank you."

CHAPTER 6: MOOR APPARITION

The tablets were old and primitive but John was well aquainted with all ancient Zyconian dialects and had little trouble deciphering most of them. The army was now heading out across the eastern part of the central grasslands. Outside a thunderstorm raged. The rain hammered down like a million furious teardrops. John sat in the back of one of the tented wagons. Around him sat Terrek, Zachary, Diana and Hemoth. The strong wind tore at the roof of the wagon.

"These two tablets are a legend which tell about a great city which sits atop the Utopian Mountains?" Terrek said, holding them up.

"Yes, as near as I can tell. It speaks of the people of this city and that they are very hospitable. It says that there is another of the crystals in a vault deep beneath the city. But the legend also says something about hand to hand combat between a human and some great beast known as the Father Minotaur," John described.

"Well, I don't know anything about the father Minotaur, but I know we have to get that crystal. We're already headed toward the Utopian Mountains, we should reach the base soon. Chances are that if we travel well into the mountains we can escape most of the storm," Terrek said.

"We'll all be better off once we're away from the storm.

It's the rainy season, and the horses are getting pretty spooked by the thunder and lightning," reasoned Zachary.

"I'm going to relieve Perrin and lead the army ahead myself. I'll take Diana to sit with Zyron and keep him company," explained Terrek.

"You will sit with him, won't you Diana?" Terrek asked

"Of course I will," Diana said putting her hand on his shoulder, "be careful."

"I will," he whispered as he kissed her.

He slowly waded through the swamp. If seen, he wouldn't have been recognized as human. Much of his armor and wardrobe had been damaged or torn. Seriously wounded he struggled on. Blood, dried and some still oozing, covered his face and body. His eyes were partially glazed and bloodshot, ashen against the destruction of the storm. The wind hammered upon his staggering frame as exhaustion racked his body.

Violent moans escaped his throat and his eyes rolled back in his skull, blood dripping from the sockets. He stumbled yet recovered and continued, intensely focused on his goal.

The storm still raged although they had reached the base of the Utopian Mountains and were now slowly beginning their ascent. It wasn't as difficult as many thought it would be. The mountain, although very rocky, rose gradually and wasn't steep. The storm was the worst obstacle.

Selate, feeling much better now after leaving her home, was tucked away in one of the tented wagons to escape the rain. The night before, Terrek had sat up with her while she remembered everything good about how the Sanctuary used to be. She told him many interesting stories about her clan. Some were even entertaining tales. She was at peace with her past now; it was time to look to the future.

Terrek pressed on up the mountain. Close behind, Zachary, Hemoth and Jason rode their horses. Although Terrek had trained Streak extensively to ignore the thunder and lightning, even the weather was spooking him. Terrek put on a lambskin cloak to protect himself as much as possible. Large moors loomed ahead.

Suddenly out of the corner of his eye Terrek caught sight of an erie picture.

"What is that!" one of the soldiers cried from behind Terrek. Terrek slowed his horse and raised his gaze.

"A demon from the depths of hell!" cried another.

"Calm yourselves!" Terrek yelled over the storm.

Not far ahead a humanlike creature stood atop a large moor waving its blood streaked arms in the air.

"Eeeeeeeecccchhhhh," a shrill scream echoed from its throat as its tattered rags and battered limbs blew in the wind like a cryptic ragdoll.

It lowered its arms.

Suddenly a flash of lightning illuminated its face. Terrek became slightly disturbed.

"Celarus!" he whispered, deeply perplexed.

Slowly he moved toward the moor. Finally one last moan escaped Celarus's throat and he collapsed sideways and tumbled off the moor. His body hit the ground with a thud and rolled unto its back. The soldiers gathered around staring down at the broken form. Terrek knelt down beside the form and shone some torch light on the blood-streaked face.

"Celarus. He's obviously delirious," Terrek said to Zachary, Jason and Hemoth.

"All right get him into one of the wagons, bring some healers to him," Terrek bellowed.

CHAPTER 7: UTOPIA CITY

Celarus shivered, a man possessed. Terrek assumed the shiver was in response to an internal chill. Celarus had been this way for most of the night. Two healers sat on either side of him. One attempted to feed him while the other tended to his wounds and attempted to bring feeling back into his chilled body. The storm was over and a feeling of calm had descended on the army. Many silently wondered why Terrek would help such an archenemy.

Terrek sat near the entrance of the tented wagon observing Celarus closely. Diana sat beside him, her arms around him, half asleep on his shoulder. Terrek felt sorry for Celarus. He obviously had taken the worst of the fall they'd shared. He must have been wandering deliriously for days and then encountered the storm. Terrek mentally winced with pity, but he was glad it wasn't him lying there in agony.

The problem was what to do with Celarus if he managed to survive. They couldn't just set him free. In no time he'd be back as leader of the assassin army, terrorizing and killing innocents. But he was another human being and he was in pain. They couldn't just let him die, and Terrek couldn't bring himself to kill an injured, unarmed man. Even if it would be a mercy killing in his present state. Miraculously Celarus's shaking slowed and his eyes opened wide.

"Terrek - Terrek," Celarus rasped.
Terrek gently woke Diana and moved beside Celarus so that he could see him.

"What is it ?" Terrek said, a hint of hostility in his voice.

"I - I realize now you were right. I just spent so long obeying the Vicar that I forgot what was really out there, how decent so much of Zyconia is. If I could go back to my youth now I would change so much. But I guess since I'm going to die now it doesn't matter anymore," Celarus swallowed as tears filled his eyes.

Terrek suddenly felt severe anguish, like his soul was bleeding inside.

"It does matter, it matters to me and it matters to the Maker," Terrek said emotionally, squeezing Celarus's arm.

"I'll do my best to make sure you live," Terrek continued, "so you'll have a chance to change all that."

"We're in sight of Utopia City. Terrek, I think you should come out," Perrin interrupted.

Celarus's face became distorted again as his shivers returned in full strength.

Celarus grabbed Terrek by the shoulder. "Te - Terrek wait I must warn you - I - I - warn must – he, you," Celarus once again became delirious.

Terrek held Celarus as still as possible. "What is it you must warn me about," he asked levelly.

"Celarus can you understand me?" Celarus gave no sign of acknowledgment.

"He can't hear you," replied one of the healers.
Terrek slammed his fist into the wooden floor in frustration, then stood and left the wagon.

Terrek stepped out of the wagon and ran into someone listening at the door. Terrek apologized as he lifted the man by his arm to his feet. Instantly he realized it was Lynx.

Lynx backed away quickly. "Sorry Commander, I didn't mean to block your path," he said quietly. Lynx turned and disappeared into the crowds. Terrek starred after him, paranoid and suspicious.

Terrek gazed into the distance. A small stone city could be seen on the slope opposite them. Diana stood beside him.

"Alright, we can't assume that the tablets were right and that these people are really hospitable, so a small group of us is going to have to go over to make first contact," Terrek said addressing his aides and the army behind them.

"Hemoth, Perrin, John, and Jason you will come with me. Zachary you are in command in my absence, make camp for now," he ordered.

The army dispersed.

Diana put her hand to Terrek's cheek and stroked his dark hair back.

"I know I say this a lot, but be careful out there, alright," she said worriedly.

"I will," he promised as he held her close. Gently he pressed his lips against hers. He could feel the rising and falling of her chest. She was so delicate, so fragile, yet seemed stronger than he did sometimes, in so many ways. He drew back and looked into her eyes trying to ignore the rising thoughts in the back of his mind.

"I'll be back soon, I promise," he whispered as he stepped back to join the others.

They stood in what appeared to be a central street yet there was no sign of life. The entire city, although not decaying, seemed lifeless. Terrek, Hemoth, Perrin, John, and Jason stared in all directions.

Finally Terrek broke the silence.

"Where are all the people?" he exclaimed.

The group shook their heads; they were as puzzled as he was. Terrek examined the streets and walked over to look into the dark windows of the buildings.

"Commander, I think I hear low music coming from this building," yelled Hemoth who had wandered down the street.

They all walked to Hemoth's position and listened. Terrek heard a low drumbeat as well as some strange whistling pipes. Terrek entered the huge structure's doorway and looked down a short hallway. He could barely make out the start of a staircase spiraling downwards.

"Did anyone bring a torch?" Terrek asked.

They shook their heads.

"Draw your weapons. Follow close together. Stay alert!" Terrek ordered.

Terrek strode to the stairway and walked down the steps. The room below was even darker but Terrek made out a small door on the opposite side. The music was getting louder the farther they went. Wherever it was coming from couldn't be far off.

One by one they went through the doorway. Terrek had great difficulty seeing now. He heard a slam and the room instantly became pitch black.

"What happened?" asked Terrek.

"Door shut behind us," Jason said apprehensively.

Hemoth felt his way to the door and thrust his fist against it.

A loud clang echoed as Hemoth drew his hand back in pain.

"Not only that, the door's made of iron," he said.

Terrek walked toward where he thought the opposite wall would be.

"There's got to be another way out."

"Wait, did you hear that?" asked Perrin.

"What?" asked John.

"I thought I heard something move," Perrin whispered nervously.

Instantly an eruption of several forceful movements and the sounds of impact caused Terrek to spin around in the dark to where the others were.

"Perrin, what's happening?" yelled Terrek fearfully.

Silence.

"Hemoth, Jas-" Terrek was cut off in mid-sentence by a violent blow to the back of the head. Falling on his chest he attempted to lift himself from the floor and received another crack to the back of the skull.

Pain filled his head as he lifted himself from the sand. Lifting his head his mind was assaulted by the details of his surroundings. Cheering filled his ears.

He was in the center of a large coliseum. He was in a circular pit with wall several times his height. There were two doors in the walls one the size of a man and one fit for a giant. Both were made of unadorned, smooth iron. High above the walls, all the way around the pit sat many cheering men, women and children. They appeared thinner than most Zyconians, their skin slightly darker.

In one area, blocked off from the rest of the crowd, sat twelve very old but identical looking elderly men. They wore jewel adorned robes and their white hair was pulled back, not a strand out of place. They didn't cheer. They examined him with a cold collective stare. Terrek knew that they were important. One of the elders sat in a chair more prominent than the others.

Terrek assumed that this was their king. He wore a large amulet around his neck. Terrek looked up and saw that the coliseum had a ceiling. He assumed that he was still inside the structure he'd entered.

Terrek looked around and realized that his comrades were lying on the sandy floor as well. He quickly woke them. They stood and waited to see what would happen next.

From above the prominent elder lifted his arm and a large net and a spear were thrown into the pit. Suddenly a great cheer arose from the crowd.

Terrek and the others saw the huge metal door rising, to reveal what was behind it. The door rose completely but there was nothing but darkness. The crowd sat in suspenseful silence.

Terrek's stomach churned.

Then all at once a sight emerged that horrified them. Before them was a minotaur unlike any of them had ever seen. It was at least double the height of a normal minotaur and had huge twisted horns. This creature held all the familiar characteristics of it's smaller kin except for one difference, it had only one gigantic glowing eye. This strange, cycloptic minotaur ambled forward and caught sight of them.

Terrek looked at the net and the spear, then at a pile of stones nearby.

"Perrin, Jason, John quickly, you have to distract it, grab a handful of rocks and throw them at it. Aim for the eye! Hemoth follow me!" Terrek ordered.

Terrek and Hemoth ran across the pit floor and grabbed the net. Each took one side and ran toward the minotaur. The others began shooting stones at the beast which, after being struck in the eye, blinked and raised his arms to ward off the stones. Terrek and Hemoth quickly wrapped the net around the Minotaur's legs, and Terrek called to the others to come swiftly.

"We have to do this fast, heave!" Terrek bellowed.

All five of them pulled on the net and the giant toppled

to the sandy floor. Terrek ran speedily across the beast's back and grabbed its horns. He turned to ask Hemoth for the spear, but the beast lurched up and stood erect smashing one of its horns into the wall of the pit. Terrek, clinging to the other horn, was just high enough to jump to safety in the crowds, but he wasn't about to leave his comrades. The Minotaur spun its head back and forth trying to throw Terrek off, then it brought its arms up and began swinging at him.

"Quickly, throw me the spear!" Terrek yelled in anticipation.

Hemoth lifted the spear and tossed it up into Terrek's grip. Terrek stood on top of the Minotaur's head and lifted the spear in both hands for an instant. Then all at once he brought it down with an echoing crack through the creature's cranium. The Cycloptic Minotaur released one great, deep-throated yell of agony before falling straight down.

Terrek jumped clear as it fell to the ground. Hemoth and the others helped him to his feet. Everyone in the coliseum was dumbfounded. Amazed looks plastered the crowd. Even the elders, who had shown no emotion until now, seemed surprised by what had just happened.

The elder in the prominent chair stood.

"Guards," he called.

Terrek's group tensed up. Would they now have to fight hand to hand too? Surprisingly, the guards entered above the pit wall and herded the crowds out. Finally only the twelve elders remained.

The standing elder moved from their view and moments later appeared in the smaller doorway in the pit wall. The elder slowly approached Terrek, and held out his palm. Sitting in his hand was a purplish translucent crystal.

"Take it, indeed you have earned it," the man said. Terrek, puzzled, looked at the man and took the crystal from his hand depositing it in the pouch on his belt with the other two crystals. Terrek was about to speak, but the man stopped him.

"Many years ago we left lower Zyconia to escape the evil and create a utopian society, but when men like the Vicar learned what we had accomplished, they tried to destroy us. This is why we have moved underground and have left the once great city lifeless. At one time we possessed three of the crystals. All but one was stolen.

That was before we were given the beast. You are not the first to come looking for that crystal. We were told that whoever vanquishes the beast is the crystal's rightful owner. You are the one. You have also entertained us, so we wish you to take these," the old man said.

The old man held out a map and fastened his amulet around Terrek's neck.

"The amulet will help you, trust me, and the map will lead you to two of the other crystals," said the old man as he headed toward the small door.

"If you go through the larger door you should find a staircase that will lead you up to a door to the street," the elder explained.

"You said you were told that whoever kills the beast is entitled to the crystal, told by whom?" asked Terrek.

"Ask not now," replied the elder.

"If you wish your army may take food and water, and whatever else we may provide, I will have my men help you reprovision," he offered. Then he turned and left.

When Terrek and his group returned to the rest of the army the entire city was bustling with people waiting to meet the conquerors of the great father Minotaur. The Utopians were all gracious and ready to lend a hand in reloading their wagons with supplies for their continuing journey.

74

While their wagons were reloaded, Terrek asked the head elder if he could help him decipher the hieroglyphics on the third tablet that they'd recovered from the avian Sanctuary. Fortunately the elder was able to translate. The tablet told them the location of another crystal, in the Swamp of Ghouls, which was close to their present location. After they had all said their farewells, they headed off down the mountain.

Terrek had been on the outskirts of the Swamp of Ghouls before, fending off several of the little evil monsters with Jason and Adam. That had been enough of an experience for him. For some reason he couldn't shake the ominous feeling that something sinister was going to occur in the swamps.

CHAPTER 8: THE SWAMP OF GHOULS

The wind blew across the slime-laden plain. The sky above was dark. All that became visible ahead was swamp. Here and there small, horrid, dead looking, leafless trees dotted the landscape, perhaps as remembrances of the flailing arms of the many victims that had disappeared beneath this grimy sea of mucous. The foggy mist was acidic and nauseating. Gutteral, unnatural, gurgling noises echoed across the bubbling surface. All that was evil was not visible for, not far beneath the surface, dangerous predators waited to strike.

Terrek surveyed the swamp and stood atop a large rock so that the entire army could see him.

"The wagons are obviously not going to be able to travel through the swamp. However, after deciphering one of the stone tablets from the avian Sanctuary we believe that there is a crystal somewhere in the swamp. Perrin will take all non-military individuals and the wagons and travel around the swamp to meet the soldiers, who will be led by me, on the other side."

He paused for a moment then continued. "The soldiers will be separated into teams in order for us to cover as much of the swamp as possible. Be on your guard. There are small troll-like beings inhabiting the swamp and, although alone they are not particularly strong, they often travel in packs of a dozen or more. Before you realize it, you may be pulled beneath the swamp to be devoured, so remain alert."

"Perrin, keep Celarus alive, I want him to survive. Do you understand?" Terrek said strongly.

Perrin nodded.

Terrek led the soldiers toward the swamp as Perrin headed away in search of a route around.

One person didn't feel that he should be grouped with the non-military, and that was Timothy. Just as the soldiers were out of sight he peered out of the back of one of the wagons in the rear, and seeing that no one was watching, he jumped out and ran in the direction Terrek had taken.

Terrek's team was made up of Diana, Hemoth, Zachary, John, Juliana as well as a half dozen other soldiers. High above, Selate surveyed them all, ready to swoop down at the first sign of trouble. They all had weapons drawn and rode closely together. Terrek led Streak while Diana sat atop the horse nervously holding her dagger. They all knew danger was imminent.

Instantly a splashing noise startled them all as about four dozen ghouls aggressively surfaced, surrounding them.

The ghouls had grey, human-like, lizard heads, dwarf-like bodies and small clawed hands.

They hissed and growled as they closed in on the group. All at once they sprang forth, blanketing the team. Several clung to the horses while others attacked the soldiers. They hurriedly hit and hacked at the ghouls desperately trying to fend them off. The ghouls themselves bit and clawed everyone they clung onto.

Terrek killed the couple that had jumped upon him and began killing the ones clinging to Streak with Diana's help. He also helped those nearby that were struggling. Everyone was fighting hard; the fear of being pulled into the murky depths of the swamp made everyone frantic. The ghouls seemed to be overwhelming them at first, but Terrek saw that if everyone banned together they would overcome them.

Hemoth was a great warrior in this situation. Because of his size, the ghouls had a very hard time keeping him occupied, so he was free to knock the ghouls away from the others.

A dark shadow flashed across the swamp. Terrek looked skyward to see Selate swooping in low.

"Scccrrreeeeee!" Selate's scream, although it hurt their ears, sent the ghouls scrambling back beneath the muddy water. Terrek felt like cheering but he quickly made the group press on before they could be attacked again. Selate flew across the swamp away from them and they again heard her scream but this time from a distance.

Suddenly everyone heard the splashing of footsteps from behind.

"Commander Terrek, Mother I've found you!" it was Timothy addressing Terrek and Juliana. Terrek was about to chastise him when he noticed several ghouls gathering on a small tree behind the boy.

"Timothy watch out!" Terrek ran towards the boy. Just as the ghouls were about to pounce on Timothy, Terrek plowed into them. Timothy quickly ran to his mother as Terrek fell into the pile of ghouls. Horrified, Hemoth and Zachary, the closest soldiers, rushed toward Terrek as his head sunk beneath the water. The others followed. Hemoth grabbed for Terrek's hand as it slipped beneath the surface. And just for a moment their fingers locked. Then, in an instant, he was jerked away.

"No!" cried Hemoth as he frantically moved his arms

around below the surface grabbing at anything solid. Zachary, John and the others followed suit and Diana dismounted Streak and quickly began to help.

Some began diving below the surface but the water was too dirty to see anything. Here and there large pits of mud were discovered on the bottom. Perhaps he'd been pulled into one of them.

They continued combing the waters until their arms were numb.

Their search slowed.

"I don't see him," one of the soldiers called.

"We have to keep looking!" Diana screamed through her tears.

"Please," she begged.

Hemoth nodded and bent down to search, everyone else followed suit but with grim expressions. The wind howled through the swamp rattling the few trees and chilling them to the bone.

Juliana held bawling Timothy tightly in her arms, a grave look on her face. She was near tears as she thought:

Were the ghouls already devouring Terrek?

Where was their leader now?

END OF PART ONE

CHAPTER 9: ESCAPE FROM THE SWAMP OF GHOULS

The soldiers looked out across the swamp. Their leader was gone; slowly, gradually they stood, waiting for orders from one of Terrek's aides. Hemoth stood nearby, Zachary and John also stood. Diana still frantically searched the muddy water. Not far off they heard splashing noises, obviously more ghouls were moving toward their position. Juliana looked at Hemoth, surprised that they had stopped searching.

Hemoth spoke in low tones with Zachary and John, he turned to the other soldiers.

"It's time to move on," he ordered.

Diana looked up in disbelief, her emotions raw and unhindered.

"No! Please we have to keep looking, please," she begged as she ran toward Hemoth.

Hemoth looked sympathetically at her as he picked her up, put her over his shoulder, and stepped toward his horse.

"Put me down, we can't leave now, please, don't! Terrek!" Diana screamed as she went hysterical, clubbing Hemoth in the back with her fists. This had little effect.

"What about Terrek? We can't just leave him here!" Juliana asked Hemoth.

Hemoth pushed Diana up onto his horse and

momentarily faced Juliana.

"He's gone, we can't just stay here. More ghouls are bound to attack," he said in a low tone trying not to let Diana hear him.

Juliana turned, frustrated, and reluctantly mounted her horse with Timothy.

They all took one last look as they headed away.

 Suddenly a violent splash was heard nearby.

Zachary jumped from his horse.

"It's Terrek," he yelled.

He swiftly sprinted through the swamp. Terrek struggled desperately to stay above water; both his hands were locked onto a nearby tree branch. Terrek was pulled under as the branch snapped, but this time Zachary grabbed firmly onto the sleeves of his tunic. Zachary turned and lifted with all his might, but instead he felt himself being pulled into the watery pit. His head also went below the surface, but Hemoth reached him, and clamped his other hand.

Hemoth, not about to lose a second chance to save his friend, heaved skyward. With a sickening, gurgling noise Zachary was pulled above the water. Sputtering, Zachary was barely conscious. Amazingly he still held Terrek's arm. Hemoth swiftly grabbed Terrek's arm as one of the other soldiers carried Zachary to safety. Hemoth strained his muscles as Terrek slid up out of the mudhole.

Terrek looked dead. His eyes were partially open but glazed. His pupils had rolled up into his head. A lot of his clothing had been torn away, his upper body was revealed and one leg of his pants had been torn away revealing his well-muscled leg. Large cuts and bruises covered his entire body. His face was dark and pale. His body was cold. He wasn't breathing.

No reflex.

No breath.

No hope.

No life.

But somewhere a will existed that wouldn't let him die.

Suddenly Terrek began coughing up water. A loud series of choking and shivered sputtering escaped Terrek's throat as he began breathing. His eyes opened slightly as though he were half asleep.

Diana ran to him tears streaming down her face.

"Terrek – Terrek!" Diana sobbed as she held Terrek's head in her hands. She sat him up in the muddy water and put her arms around him.

"Diana," Terrek said slowly.

Diana trembled as she held him, crying.

"I thought I'd lost you, I thought I'd lost you," she cried as she held him tighter, as though she'd never let him go. Hemoth, Zachary, John and the others looked on. Relief flowed through the team.

Much later all the teams made it through the mudpit and rejoined their families, who Perrin had guided safely around the swamp. Terrek's tent was pitched and a healer was brought to him. Although exhausted, Terrek strongly insisted on hearing the reports from all his chief aides.

They all gathered around the makeshift bed in his tent. He lay exhausted with several animal furs covering him. Diana sat beside him staring down at him strangely. She appeared deep in thought. Terrek attempted to ignore her peculiar behavior.

"We managed to recover the crystal in the swamp Commander," proclaimed Ricsis retrieving a bluish purple gem from his belt.

Terrek looked pleased, though his face remained pale. Ricsis handed the gem to Terrek who deposited it in his belt. Ricsis smiled as he told the tale of its capture to him and the others.

"The team I led, as well as two of the other teams, converged at the center of the swamp. There, a large pedestal rose from the depths. On the top surface sat the crystal. Almost as soon as we arrived more than a hundred ghouls came up out of the water and attacked. After a great battle Adam climbed the large pedestal and retrieved the crystal. We then fled to escape ghoul reinforcements that we saw moving toward us on the horizon."

Ricsis looked at Adam. "Adam deserves most of the credit. He climbed the pedestal, risking being pulled off by the ghouls to take a fatal fall. If they'd succeeded in pulling him off they would have had no problem dragging him below the swamp. It took great courage to do what he did." Everyone acknowledged Adam in respect and congratulated him, shaking his hands and patting him on the back.

"You are a great warrior."

"You all are," Terrek said proudly.

Terrek smiled as he looked at them, even Lynx.

"You all may leave now," Terrek said. Diana stood, but thought again and decided to stay.

Terrek looked up at her.

"I didn't think I was going to escape that pit, but somehow this helped," Terrek said holding up his amulet. Diana looked at it but said nothing.

"As I was being dragged under I tried to hold my breath and break free of the ghouls' grips but there were too many of them. Even through the muddy water I noticed the amulet glowing and when I clasped it in my hand I felt extreme strength flow through me. I was instantly revitalized. It seemed as though I had a new breath in my lungs and my strength had magnified tenfold. Still frantic, I struggled away from the ghouls and headed toward the swamp surface. The ghouls followed. I guess my newfound strength wasn't to last forever," he said referring to his near death experience.

Terrek finished his story and again looked at Diana. She seemed unresponsive. Terrek lowered his eyebrows in worry.

"Is something wrong Diana?" asked Terrek.

Diana stood up and slowly paced his tent. She appeared to be deep in thought. Gradually she turned and faced him.

"Diana?" Terrek spoke her name quietly, this time deeply concerned.

"I've always lived my life under great strain. I've never really asked for anything from anyone and I've never let myself get too close to anyone. Perhaps I always knew they'd go away and I'd just end up alone again. Maybe I just have never met anyone who I felt able to share my deepest emotions with. I know I've never met anyone like you. You're so strong, yet you're so caring, so kind, and so gentle," she confided.

Diana stared directly into his eyes all her emotions emptied her soul with one accurately attributed phrase: "Terrek I love you."

Silence.

Terrek's eyes became clouded and he coldly turned over in his bed and buried his face in his furs. Diana looked toward him puzzled.

"I think maybe you should leave," Terrek said in confusion and sorrow.

Diana lowered her head and lifted her hands to her face as she began to cry.

"I - I don't understand -" Diana sobbed.

"Leave, I said! Get out!" screamed Terrek emotionally. Diana turned and ran from his tent, tears streaming down her face. Terrek turned over, his own face streaked with tears. His mind wandered to a place deep within his past.

She just didn't understand.

If she only knew.

CHAPTER 10: THE CALM BEFORE THE STORM

The army had camped for two days. Terrek was virtually back to normal, at least physically. Celarus too had shown drastic improvement. Celarus still remained unconscious, but the healers that tended him thought he had a much better chance for survival now that his shivers had stopped. They all were glad for the rest that they had now, but they knew it would soon be time to move on. Terrek and Diana hadn't talked since the night after he had escaped the Swamp of Ghouls.

Terrek sat on the edge of a nearby wagon watching John demonstrate his skill with the design of a new crossbow he had built. The crossbow had a small wooden compartment on the underside of the bow, which encased five extra arrows. As one arrow was released the soldier would simply pull back on a small lever and the bowstring would be drawn back and the next arrow in the case would be sprung into place. It was a great accomplishment. John was a man of many talents. Besides being able to translate ancient texts, he was also an expert in state of the art weapons design.

"It's excellent, John," Terrek said quietly.

John smiled and pulled the trigger releasing one of the arrows; it hit the bullseye of his target.

"You should probably have a hand full of soldiers help

you create duplicates. Your new crossbow could be of great use to us," Terrek finished as he started walking toward his tent. John looked in Terrek's direction; his face lost its glee.

"Terrek?" John asked.

"Not now John," Terrek replied.

Terrek sat in his tent in a small chair. Emptiness cascaded from all points of his surroundings. His brain was an amalgamation of confusion. So many emotions spiraled through his mind, but the feeling at the forefront: pain. He thought about the future. He thought about the past. He thought about the living. He thought about the dead. His insides ached and he wondered. Yet he shut himself off from his hopes. They were not to be. He couldn't have what he once did.

Perrin entered and approached Terrek.

"Terrek I -" Perrin began.

"Get out Perrin, not now," Terrek said coldly. Perrin moved back out of the tent, "as you wish, Commander," Perrin muttered.

Terrek sat back and stared at the ceiling. Moments later another face entered his view. He frowned but said nothing. What was the use, no one would leave him alone anyway. Hemoth sat down on an adjacent chair and looked at the floor.

"You're worried that it might happen again, aren't you?" Hemoth asked bringing his hands up to support his temple and peering directly at Terrek. Terrek neither moved nor adjusted his gaze in any way and when he answered it was in a low tone.

"Yes," he managed.

Hemoth looked down again.

"Zyconia is a volatile land, prone to death and destruction. What if I wasn't there? What if it happened again? How could I ever live with myself?" Terrek said.

"But you can't just shut yourself off, how can you ever remain sane if you do?" Hemoth asked.

"I can't, don't you get it?" Terrek yelled jumping to his feet and knocking his chair aside.

"Didn't you see how much pain it was when it first happened? I just can't live that life again! Didn't you see how much I wanted to die?" Terrek cried, horrendous misery and horror etched on his face.

Hemoth, disturbed by his emotional eruption, became edgy and also stood. Terrek turned away from him and lifted his hand to his face in torment.

"Just go!" Terrek said.

Hemoth approached Terrek one last time and put his hand on his shoulder.

"Terrek," Terrek struck his arm away. Hemoth rubbed his arm as he turned around and left.

The Vicar stood alone. His essence shared between two places. This time the traitor from Terrek's army met the Vicar on a non-corporeal plain. Reality was alien to this existence. Everything here was a blur except them. Their surroundings appeared as mist. The Vicars eyes glowed as he spoke.

"I'VE DECIDED TO LET TERREK CONTINUE ON HIS JOURNEY," the Vicar said.

"What?" asked Terrek's traitor dumbfounded.

"I HAVE OTHER PLANS NOW, THE CRYSTALS WILL BE MINE, TERREK WILL DIE WHEN I CONQUER ZYCONIA," he explained.

The individual looked around puzzled.

"I WILL NOT EXPLAIN MYSELF FURTHER," the Vicar roared.

"I understand, my lord," stated the individual.

"SOON ALL OF ZYCONIA WILL BE AFLAME WITH MY POWER, AND ONCE THAT HAPPENS, NO ONE WILL BE ABLE TO STOP ME," rasped the Vicar.

The individual again was perplexed, but not wanting to anger the Vicar, kept it hidden.

Both dissolved with their surroundings resuming their corporeal states of consciousness.

Diana sat with Zyron her eyes red and raw. She said nothing. Zyron watched her. His soul cried for her. He wanted to tell her, so many things, but he knew he couldn't. It wasn't his place. It wasn't the right time. All he could do was try to keep her from her own desperation. He brushed his hand across the sceptre's blue gem. In time, he thought. He moved toward her to try to speak with her.

Terrek headed out, the army followed close behind. He rode Streak, alone. Desert stretched out before them forever. Terrek was still tired. Even Streak seemed tired. However, the army was energized and full of life. Terrek was both resentful and envious of this.

Jessica rode up beside Terrek and spoke gently, "I wanted you to know, I think Celarus is going to survive."

"That's good. He may yield a lot of vital informat ion the Council can use against the Vicar and his minions," Terrek muttered.

"Yes," Jessica said as she ventured to broach another subject.

"Terrek, I know you are having problems with Diana and I want you to know that if there's anything I can do, all you have to do is ask," she said quietly.

Terrek glared at her.

"There is no problem, Jessica," he said flatly.

"Oh," she said quietly backing off from the subject.

"Return to your duties, Jessica," Terrek said coldly.

"Of course, Commander," Jessica lowered her gaze and guided her horse back into the crowds behind. No one could seem to stay out of it could they, he thought. They were traveling to a part of Zyconia that he'd never seen before. Deserts were not his favorite place to be. The council hadn't even explored this region.

Terrek looked up. The wind began to pick up. Sand blinded him. Swirling clouds of granules peppered everyone.

"It's a sand storm!" someone yelled from behind Terrek.

He pulled a small animal skin from his horse's armor and wrapped it around his head as a hood.

"Just keep moving!" Terrek yelled to those behind him.

The army pressed on as layer upon layer of angry sand attacked. The sun became clouded and the world became dark. They were forced to protect themselves placing garments to their faces to protect their lungs. Yet they moved on, and soon the wind subsided.

Terrek, aggravated, looked at the map they'd received at Utopia City spread before him. He lifted his eyes and stared out at the Silent Sea less than a hundred paces away.

"According to this map the crystal should be on that sea," Terrek said.

Terrek looked toward the shore and saw the remains of a small wooden boat.

"I'm going down to the shore to determine if that craft is sea worthy, Zachary make camp," he commanded.

Terrek looked at his aides, "Perrin, Hemoth, Jason, and

Jessica you will come with me."

"I'm coming too," Diana said aggressively. The rest of Terrek's aides parted to let Diana through. Terrek's face was pained.

"If you wish," he said.

The shoreline was rich with vegetation, and it appeared that the old fishing boat floated well enough. Terrek ordered everyone into the boat and Hemoth grabbed two oars and began rowing.

"The map says the crystal should be here," Terrek said, straining, his eyes combing the lake's surface.

"Maybe it's on some sort of small reef or floating craft," offered Perrin.

Hemoth slowed, his arms tired.

"It feels like something is grabbing at the oars," Hemoth said eerily.

Suddenly a huge tentacle swung up across the middle of the boat. Expressions of horror swept across their faces. With a downward thrust the boat was torn to splinters, and its crew was sent flying into the water. Tentacles wrapped around all of them as they were pulled down, down, down into the dark depths of the Silent Sea.

CHAPTER 11: KALDORIAN OBJECTIVE

Terrek looked around. He was completely soaked.

Surprisingly, he hadn't blacked out from their ride with the huge squid, but his compatriots lay groggily on the stone floor. They were in a large stone room, it's only features a large metallic door at the top of a dozen steps, and a clear pool that entered a spacious aquatic cave below. The pool is where the squid had brought them into the room. The aquatic cave led outside to the bottom of the lake. Somehow they had been brought to some sort of undersea room. It was amazing.

Terrek helped Diana to her feet. He winced when he saw the bruise on her arm, she merely pulled down her sleeve and moved away from him.

"Where are we?" asked Hemoth stupidly, as though one of them had the answer. Terrek looked toward the iron door. Footsteps could be heard beyond.

Suddenly the door swung aside and three strange creatures came down the steps.

The creatures seemed to have human bodies. Yet their skin was blue and scaly. Their eyes were smaller than those of men, and they had fins on their backs. Their hands were thin and bony. They looked like some kind of fish beings. Their appearance was disturbing but their faces were inviting.

"Greetings," they chimed in unison, "welcome to Kaldoria."

Terrek stepped forward a bit nervously.

"Greetings."

The creature in the front appeared to be female; she had long brown hair and a shapely figure. She was attractive even though she had blue skin and a fin on her back. She was their leader.

"I am Velerion and these are my servants, Malican and Berathus," she said indicating the fishmen to her left and right. At the top of the stairs stood six fishmen. Velerion didn't introduce them. Terrek assumed they were guards.

"Come with me," Velerion said ascending the stairs, "we will give you a tour of the city."

"City?" Terrek asked.

"City." Velerion replied.

They all followed.

Velerion led them through a temple like structure. Many fishmen appeared to be praying toward a large curtain of darkness. For some reason one end of this temple wasn't lit. Terrek had never seen the Maker worshipped in this manner before.

As they exited the temple they stared in awe at the huge dome high above. They were standing on a road in front of the temple, many buildings could be seen in all directions. They were at the bottom of the sea and Kaldoria was an undersea city encased in a transparent dome. Terrek stared at Velerion.

"Your amazement is understandable," Velerion said walking down the street as they followed.

Velerion continued. "Long, long ago our kind lived on the ocean floor but over time we gained extreme knowledge. We want to take our place in the world above, this is why we have harnessed a mystic power of our own. It helped us to change ourselves, we can now live in your world. It may be possible to raise our city from the sea floor with this power."

Velerion led them to a large tower that connected to the top of the glass dome.

"This is our fastest way to the surface," she said indicating the tower. The base of the tower had a large bronze door.

"Inside is a metallic compartment. When anyone enters, the pressure in the volcano beneath increases, and the compartment is shot up through the dome to the surface."

Terrek took note of the tower's location.

'So why have you come, Terrek?" asked Berathus.

"We have been sent by the Council to seek the ancient crystals of Zyconia," replied Terrek.

"The - the Council," Velerion seemed perturbed.

"Follow me, I think I might know what you're looking for," Velerion spun around.

The group entered one of the larger buildings of the city and headed for a nearby staircase. Jessica saw a beggar in a large chair nearby, his arm was badly bandaged so she went to the man while the others descended the staircase.

At the end of the staircase stretched a large subterranean chamber. Here, oil lamps and torches lit the walls. Terrek and his aides stood at the center of the chamber. Velerion and her servants approached a dark corner of the room and put their hands on a huge shadowed bulk.

"What are you doing?" asked Terrek.

"Watch!" exclaimed Velerion.

The bulk suddenly aflame with light revealed a wide pedestal that glowed by the reflection from a crystal.

Terrek's group exchanged glances.

"Is that what you've come for?" asked Malican.

"Yes, is there any way you'd part with it," Terrek asked.

"I'm afraid not," Velerion said. Suddenly moving sideways, she slapped her arm against the wall. A huge cage fell from the ceiling, trapping Terrek and his aides. Terrek grabbed the bars. "What are you doing?"

Three figures moved into the room from a nearby tunnel. He recognized the person in the lead.

"Terrek, at last we meet again, the mighty Commander of an Elite army designated by the Council. I see you've done well for yourself," Murack said stepping into the cave.

"Murack!" Terrek bellowed in disgust and loathing. Terrek's eyes filled with hate as they transfixed on Murack. The other two figures moved from the shadows. Terrek didn't recognize them. It was Colar the leader of the Sorcerers and Keldar the soothsayer apprentice to the Vicar. Keldar stood back as Colar pressed forward.

"You know Terrek?" Colar questioned Murack. He looked at Terrek through the bars. Terrek's hands tightened on the bars and flowed blue with the strain.

"We share a past don't we Terrek?" Murack said smiling. Terrek wanted to kill him.

Colar looked at Murack, puzzled, but decided not to question him then. Velerion moved beside them and looked at Terrek.

"The citizens of Kaldoria are Necromancers, Commander Terrek. We put our faith in the dark arts and worship our own demon goddess called Phremona. We wish to live on the surface but the Council's rule is not to our liking. What the Vicar proposes is. When you first arrived we had no idea who you were, but the Dark Circle promised us great power in the Vicar's empire for our cooperation in your capture," Velerion explained coldly.

Velerion pointed at the crystal on the pedestal.

96

"This is the mystic power that will help us raise the city," she said.

"But first the Vicar has need of it," she said lifting the crystal from the pedestal and handing it to Colar.

"The Vicar humbly thanks you, it will be returned to you soon, I assure you," Colar stated.

Murack approached the cage.

"We require these as well," he said tearing a pouch from Terrek's belt. Terrek threw his arms through the cage grasping at it but Murack moved back and opened the pouch.

"Velerion, I believe our time has come to leave," said Keldar in a deep voice from behind them.

"Keldar is right," Colar said walking into the shadows with Keldar.

"Maybe we'll meet again Terrek, but I doubt it. Velerion, sacrifice them to your goddess," Murack smiled.

"Malican, Berathus show the Vicar's men to the surface tunnel, I've duties to perform," Velerion looked at them with fire in her eyes.

Unseen, a dark figure moved behind her in the shadows.

The Vicar's men stood at the mouth of the tunnel.

"This tunnel has been dug under the sea floor and up to the surface. It will lead you to the shore," Berathus said.

Nearby, five of Velerion's servants saddled their horses. One of them, hooded approached Murack.

"Tie this to my horse," Murack said to the servant handing him a sack with all five of the crystals, "tightly," he growled.

The servant moved toward the horses, Murack and Colar faced Berathus and Malican.

"Just so you realize, the Vicar has no intention of

returning the crystal," Keldar said.

A look of extreme surprise crossed Berathus and Malican's faces as swords slid into their stomachs. The men quivered for a moment as their lives drained from them. They had received the reward for their loyalty to the Vicar. Murack tore his sword from Berathus's belly as Colar removed his from Malican's, both bodies fell to the tunnel floor. Their faces abstract and prostrate against the flat surface. The servants looked at them in terror.

"Move off or you'll receive the same," threatened Keldar.

They mounted their horses and proceeded down the tunnel untouched.

Terrek, Perrin, Hemoth, Jason and Diana had been herded into the temple now filled to the brim with fish beings. The temple was larger than they'd remembered. Velerion stood on a raised platform at one end of the temple, while Terrek and the others stood in a small cage on another platform at the center of the temple. Covering the floor around the platforms, hundreds of fish beings roared with bloodlust.

Terrek suddenly realized someone was missing.

"Where is Jessica?" He looked at the others. They exchanged glances.

The opposite end of the temple was still dark. Velerion raised her arms and the crowd quieted.

"This day we are privileged to see five of our visitors humble themselves before Phremona. As an act of the surface world's submission to us they have decided to lay down their lives before her. This will be the beginning of such sacrifices," she announced, savage passion filling her eyes. At this the crowd roared once again.

Terrek looked at Velerion's face. It seemed transformed

to him. He saw her for the wicked Necromancer she was, instead of a beautiful female he thought her to be. Her face furrowed and sweat dotted her brow as she continued to stir up the crowd, their cries for death growing more and more intense. She seemed to draw strength from this madness. Soon her voice reached a pinnacle, every word a sadistic hyperbole of evil.

"Now, let them feel the heat of Phremona! Let them feel her power!" she screamed.

Velerion raised her arms. Terrek and the others felt the cage move. Terrek stretched out his arms to balance himself as a look of terror crossed his face. Suddenly the cage lifted from the platform. Slowly it levitated in the air. Everyone inside was mortified.

"Velerion, wait!" Terrek's calls were lost in the roar of the crowd.

Velerion's face tightened and her eyes closed. Suddenly, some unknown power lit the darkened end of the temple.

Terrek and his group gasped.

A snakelike eel statue sat against the wall. The eyes glowed as blue sapphires in its golden head. Fins covered the sides of its body and it's mouth dripped of glowing liquid. Directly in front of the idol was a large lava pit. Panic stricken Terrek and his aides looked around for some way out of this.

"Call on Phremona, let her know we are sending her new servants for her demonic army of the dead," Velerion cried swaying in a trance.

Terrek looked at the lock on the cage. No way out. He looked at Diana painfully. Were they to die?
Slowly the cage started to move, levitating toward the lava pit. Terrek and the others seemed like mice trapped in a cage. All in the temple transfixed their eyes on the lava pit. The fish beings began chanting. It started out in a low rumble, but quickly got louder.

"Phremona, Phremona, PHremona, PHRemona, PHREmona, PHREMona, PHREMOna, PHREMONa, PHREMONA, PHREMONNAA, PHRREEMMOOONNNAAAA," it filled the temple.

Unexpectantly, someone ran up behind Velerion on the platform. Velerion had no sense of her surroundings; her mind had completely separated from reality.

With violent action the iron rod the person held collided with the back of Velerion's head. She hit the floor.

"Jessica," Terrek smiled.

Suddenly a rush of fear hit all in the cage as the cage fell straight down from midair. With the sickening crunch of breaking bones the cage landed on the crowd below.

Terrek's group was unharmed, however most of the fish beings underneath the cage were dead. The fall had broken the cage.

Terrek and his group jumped from the cage and quickly fought their way through the entranced crowd and scrambled up onto the platform where Jessica stood. The crowd, shocked and in disbelief, unconscious of their surroundings and unsure what to do gave them little offense.

Jessica handed Terrek and the others their weapons as they ran from the temple. They came out onto the street.

"Stop them!" cried a fish being soldier from one of the nearby buildings.

Farther down the city streets, a number of fish being guards ran toward them.

"Follow me, there is a tunnel to the surface," exclaimed Jessica.

They all turned, but Terrek spied the tower nearby.

"I've got a better way, come on!" he yelled.

They all ran to the metal door and entered the compartment inside. Once inside Jessica applied the latch on the inside.

"Wait, we can't leave without the crystals," Terrek said.

"We don't have to worry Commander," Jessica said holding up a sack.

"I disguised myself as one of Velerion's servants, and Murack handed them to me himself, but I think he'll be disappointed when he discovers he's carrying a sack of stones tied to his horse," she smiled.

A series of clanging reached their ears, the fish guards beat on the outside of the door.

"There's got to be a way to make this thing go to the surface of the sea," Terrek said, they all searched frantically.

Instantly Hemoth stepped on a large panel in the floor. The panel sunk and everyone felt a rumbling.

"I think I found it," Hemoth said.

In a flash Terrek and the others hit the floor as the compartment was blasted by the release of lava up out of the dome and through the seawater.

The metal compartment hit the shore. After a few moments, they all staggered out a little nauseous but otherwise unharmed.

"I feel like I've attempted to ride a wild stallion," Perrin groaned.

Terrek looked down the shore, his lungs seemed refreshed. Something about Kaldoria's air didn't seem right. Maybe it was just too stale.

"Come, we'd better leave the Silent Sea in case Velerion wakes up and wants revenge. We got what we came for," Terrek said gripping the sack tightly.

Terrek and the group walked slowly down the shore toward the camp.

CHAPTER 12: FOG VALLEY AND THE CRYSTAL OF DARKNESS

Terrek now had five of the crystals and the Vicar's plans for their possession had thus far been avoided. Fortunately, they hadn't been followed by any of Velerion's fish being guards, and were much too far away to be tracked down. He felt rejuvenated. He'd faced all of the experiences so far with all the courage he possessed, and he was a stronger soldier because of the experiences. A stronger warrior. A stronger person. But as he thought about his triumphs he also thought about his sadness, Diana.

"We humbly beg your forgiveness my lord, and ask that you spare us, and give us another chance," Murack asked pleadingly.

The Vicar looked down on his men with contempt. Yet had he wanted too, he could have killed them by now.

"YOU ATTEMPTED TO RETRIEVE THE CRYSTALS WITHOUT MY KNOWLEDGE IN ORDER TO IMPRESS ME, YET YOU ARE SO INCOMPETANT THAT ONE OF TERREK'S AIDES MANAGED TO FOOL YOU, AND YOU END UP GIVING ME THESE!" he rasped holding out the sack of rocks.

He threw the rocks at them but they dared not move.

"YOU ARE A DISGRACE TO THE DARK CIRCLE. YOU SHOULD BE DESTROYED, NOW! BUT I AM NOT AS ANGERED BY YOUR RIDICULOUS STUPIDITY AS I WOULD HAVE BEEN HAD I NOT ALREADY A PLAN IN MOTION TO STEAL THE CRYSTALS MYSELF. I SOLELY WILL RETRIEVE THEM. THE SPY I HAVE IN TERREK'S CAMP TOLD ME THAT CELARUS IS ALIVE," the Vicar paused.

At this they all raised their eyes in shock, but their faces dropped again quickly, not wanting to anger the Vicar any further.

"THE SPY TOLD ME THAT CELARUS HAS DECIDED NOT TO FOLLOW THE PHILOSOPHIES OF THE DARK CIRCLE ANY LONGER AND WILL PROBABLY ATTEMPT TO AID TERREK. BUT THIS POSES LITTLE DANGER. BY THE TIME CELARUS REGAINS CONSCIOUSNESS I WILL POSSESS THE CRYSTALS AND ZYCONIA WILL BE IN EXTREME JEOPARODY," he explained.

"I always suspected Celarus was a traitor," Murack hissed under his breath.

"SILENCE!" rumbled the Vicar.

All three jumped. Keldar, Colar and Murack raised their gaze slightly like whimpering dogs. When it came to the Vicar they were cowards.

"BUT YOU ALL WILL HAVE A VITAL PART IN ANOTHER PLOT I HAVE IN MIND. A PLOT TO CONQUER ALL OF ZYCONIA, END THE COUNCIL'S RULE AND CAPTURE VICTORY CITY," the Vicar finished.

As the army moved further into the valley the fog got thicker. Terrek led them, once again atop Streak. Behind

104

him most of his aides rode their horses, although a few were farther away. Jessica once again sat with Zyron, as did Diana. Deciding that Selate was as much an Aide as anyone Terrek gazed skyward to see her large bowed frame cross what little sunlight could be seen through the haze.

Terrek had never visited this part of Zyconia and was slightly on edge exploring the new area. He knew that somewhere beyond the fog lay the Central grasslands. According to the map in the northern part of the grassland there was a gigantic structure. The structure was a sleek metallic tower surrounded by a vast maze.

From all the Zyconian legends he had ever heard, Terrek knew that there were only six crystals. They only had to capture one more of the ancient gems and everyone could resume their normal lives. Walker and the rest of the Council would be very pleased, and although he didn't care one way or the other, perhaps he would be promoted to a higher position, perhaps High Commander of a grand army or Subcouncil of one of the Council's larger outposts.

Jessica had reported to him not long ago that Celarus was regaining his strength rapidly and might be conscious any day now. Terrek took this as good news, he knew the Council would have many questions for him. The strategic information he revealed to them would be invaluable in the battle against the Vicar. More than that, he knew Celarus would be a free man, no more would he be blinded and suffer the oppression of the Vicar.

Keldar stood. He forced his essence to bleed out allowing the Vicar's will to enter. Placing his hands on the object before him he concentrated. His eyes transformed and affixed on the gem he held, staring straight ahead.

They glowed.

They beamed.

His powers were deep but he was about to go beyond anything he had ever done.

Fierce evil passion encapsulated him.

His mind exploded into splinters of fragmentation.

His emotions raged with the purest form of horror.

His spirit merged with the gem and the process began. His entire being spun and careened through the whispers of time.

Spiral.

Stationary.

Away.

Apart.

Optimum.   Red.   Eibbor.

Power.

Wish;

Have.

}Espylacopa{

Nothing.

Talk.

Lem.   How.

Soon.

Decision…

Adnama.   Anig.

Ethic... .. .

Leave IV

Arm.   Naive.

Languish.

Tsirhclig.

Defuse.

…Survival…

Nivag.

Coallesce.***

Einolem.

Senile.

Rest.   Fire.   Purity.

106

Ha-Lo-te-ve...

                          Devastation.

  Flow.

                   Creation.

           (Life)

       Ignorance.

  Mistakes.

           -Unhappiness-

                     Hurt.

                Pain.

           (Death)

Deconsecretional... contrapactional... Kaitronctatution... ..
… .. … ..

~Barathic Satricant~   Inauguration

               Everything.

                   -dissolution-

              Nothing.

           -absolution-

              Something

                  -desecration-

                     ..Anything..

  ....Lost...

Thoughts protruded and hid. All was jumbled and exhilarating. His mind sped across air, fire, earth and water. He realized the thoughts of thousands over whole lifetimes in a mere moment. He knew the power as he had never known it before, and he couldn't handle it.

Keldar's body twitched, his eyes flickered. Slowly his movements escalated into convulsions. He had to break free but with the sheer sadistic passion in his soul he forced himself onward. Pain exploded throughout his body his hands scorched by the invisible power unleashed within the object he held. The burning continued.

It was unbearable. Keldar released the object. He fell to the ground, unconsciousness.

The Vicar stood opposite Keldar. He held the dark gem a few moments more, energy flowing through his arms, and then he pulled it to him.

He looked down at Keldar's massive, immobile body. He was strong in the forces of darkness, but he was not the Vicar. He had to learn. The Vicar didn't need Keldar to encapsulate the pure evil into the object he handled, but this way it was less strenuous.

The Vicar held up the object they had fused. It emitted a dim light. The surface was cracked yet smooth and sickeningly triangular. It wasn't a genuine article, but it would serve its purpose when the time came.

It was a seventh crystal: the crystal of darkness.

The fog was so thick ahead that some of the soldiers started wandering, not being able to tell the position of those in front of them. Terrek ordered his army to quicken their pace. He'd feel much better when they reached the Central grasslands.

Terrek heard shrill screams off to his left and behind him.

"Perrin, Zachary follow me," Terrek called, though he could barely see them through the floating vapor.

Terrek shifted Streak and moved off to the east. He could hear two horses close behind. Perrin and Zachary. Suddenly Terrek stopped.

"Perrin! Zachary! Stay back!" Terrek yelled.

He heard their horses rear up. They dismounted, as did he. Before them, a large pit sat, and not far below lay two of Terrek's soldiers and their horses. Large iron spikes that covered the floor of the pit had heavily impaled both horses and riders. With torch light Terrek examined the pit.

Obviously they had been riding too fast and hadn't seen it in time through the fog, or perhaps the pit had been covered over. Terrek grimaced and lowered his head. He knew they had no time to retrieve and bury these men. Terrek returned to the front of the army and halted them.

"It appears that there are hidden traps in the valley. We don't want to risk lives needlessly. Therefore, I have decided that Perrin, Zachary and I will slowly move forward through the fog with torches and long staffs to test the ground for traps. All horses will follow single file behind us. And all wagons single file behind them," Terrek finished giving everyone the signal to move forward.

Terrek moved his staff out in front of him and gently nudged Streak. They traveled on without incident.

Camp was once again pitched and Terrek stood outside his tent surveying the cookfires nearby. On their way out of Fog Valley they had uncovered and evaded seven more traps similar to the one that had pierced two of his soldiers. Terrek felt grieved for the men. He knew he would always remember their faces not for ambition or enthusiasm, but for tragedy and death.

Terrek's thoughts were interrupted by two of his men nearby who were pointing skyward. Terrek looked up. It was Selate. Something was wrong with her. Suddenly she fell out of the sky and collided with a nearby tent.

Terrek, horrified, ran to her aid. He looked at her as she lay in the smashed tent. Others gathered around. Her eyes were bloodshot and her breath was labored. Terrek looked toward another group of tents nearby.

He looked up and saw Jason.

"Quickly go get Jessica tell her to bring a couple of

healers and come quickly."

Terrek sat outside the tent Jessica had Selate in. All of his aides also waited, even Diana who paced, and occasionally looked at him very concerned. During the long amount of time they'd been sitting there loud screeches echoed from the tent. Terrek was disturbed to say the least, but was afraid to enter.

Finally Jessica exited the tent everyone surrounded her. The first thing that caught their eyes was the blood that covered her hands. Terrek stared at her with wide eyes.

"What's going on?" yelled Terrek, very worried.

Jessica looked at him slightly alarmed, but a smile came to her lips.

"It seems you have some new additions to your army, Commander. Selate just gave birth."

CHAPTER 13: MAZE OF MINOTAURS

Terrek sat in his tent deep in contemplation. Selate gave birth to twenty-five avian infants. Apparently all the avian females that left the sanctuary with her to find a suitable location to start a new colony had also been impregnated. Selate had assumed when she didn't give birth after being bound for centuries by the evil power of the wizard in the caverns that her pregnancy had somehow been aborted. Now they all saw that her pregnancy had only been stalled by the Wizard's power.

Terrek couldn't let the army continue their journey after Selate's birthing, which was why they'd been stranded here for the last three days. But Terrek was lucky, because the avian life cycle was nothing like any other species in Zyconia. When avians are born their growth accelerates into overdrive and they become fully-grown within a week. Selate had already informed him an hour ago that it would be okay if they moved on, as her offspring had just learned to fly.

Terrek went over the events that had happened since he'd left Victory City, they were incredible. In the last couple of weeks he had seen more adventure than most men do in their entire life, but something wasn't right, and he knew what it was.

It was quite a sight for Terrek. He looked to the skies.
Twenty-six shadows flashed past the sun. The army moved
with him from behind. Streak, refreshed, galloped with
renewed vigor. Terrek was beginning to really believe they
would accomplish their quest more than he ever had before.

Diana sat with Zyron. Jessica sat nearby, her attention
on her mixing pot of herbs. Zyron reviewed Diana's face;
her hurt would not leave her, not without gaining some
form of an explanation.

"You're allowing your bitterness to rule you, my
child," Zyron warned.

Diana seemed to snap from her self induced trance, "I -I
don't understand."

"No, you don't," Zyron replied.

Diana looked at him. "Why doesn't he just tell me," she
said sadly, frustrated.

Zyron put his hand on hers. "Give it time."

She relaxed against the sacks.

The large cathedral was dimly lit. A long walkway led
down the center of the floor. Rows of torches burned on
both sides of the walkway down to the end. At one end of
the walkway was a door. On the other end, elevated, was
the Vicar's throne.

The throne was vacant, but standing in front of it was
Keldar. On one side of the walkway stood Colar and on the
other side stood Murack. A long line of Warlocks and
Sorcerers moved slowly down the walkway. Each new
warrior would briefly stop and stand before Keldar then

move toward an alternate door to their left.

Keldar's eyes smoldered as the next warrior moved in front of him.

"Kneel down," he said without emotion.

The warrior stared vacantly and kneeled.

"You are the spawn of Evil. I purge you of all the Maker has influenced upon you and fill you with demonic power. You have pledged your allegiance to the Vicar, and will destroy all who oppose him, until your death," Keldar said passionately.

"Until death," the warrior said crossing his arms tightly across his chest and placing his palms on his shoulders.

"Until death," replied Murack and Colar in Unison.

Both men's eyes glared. Murack being on the warrior's left placed his palm on the left side of the warrior's head. And Colar on his right placed his palm on the right side of the warrior's head. Keldar pulled an iron pole from a nearby brazier. On the end of the pole an iron symbol was connected it was red hot because of the brazier. The symbol was the symbol of evil, the Wicketus.

The warrior closed his eyes.

He released an excruciated cry as Keldar pressed the burning symbol to the center of his forehead. He exhaled violently as Keldar pulled back. The burnt symbol remained forever scorched deeply into the warrior's skin. Smoke drifted from his head as he slowly got to his feet, turned and exited through the nearby door.

The next warrior stepped into place.

It was early evening. The sun hadn't set yet which allowed Terrek and the others to see what lay before them. Not far away a huge maze with high walls surrounded a smooth black metal-stone tower that reached toward the clouds. No one had seen anything like it anywhere in all

Zyconia.

The maze of walls was made of stone and many types of vines and thorny fauna. It stretched over a vast area. The tower, at the exact middle of the maze, jutted skyward. It seemed to glisten in the near sunset rays. The very top of the tower was a bulb with a large spiked steeple. It had been carefully and perfectly constructed. Every little curve, every little angle seemed omnipotently crafted.

Terrek slid off Streak's back.

"Make camp, it's time to finish what we started," Terrek ordered.

He knew the last crystal had to be within the tower.

They found the maze entrance, it was fairly prominent. The entrance was a single molded hole in the stone, but on either side of the molded door was a torch. Both burned endlessly, one with a bright white flame the other with a flame of darkness.

They entered their leader at the head. Terrek had chosen Hemoth, Perrin, Zachary, Adam, Jason, and Lynx to accompany him, he'd left Ricsis in command. Terrek chose a long alley between the walls of the maze and beckoned for the others to follow.

Selate nurtured her young. Most avians had been fairly fertile. It wasn't uncommon for her kind to have so many. She was very proud that she bore the winglings. Even now they were starting to understand her speech.

When Selate realized at the Sanctuary that she was the last of her kind, she felt as though she had nothing left in the world, but with the birth of her newborns, she knew that the avian race would continue. They would not cease to exist when she died, and to the rest of Zyconia and her children, she would be remembered as the mother to a new race. She was very proud.

Diana had moved with Zyron and Jessica to the wagon where Celarus rested. Terrek wanted a few trusted people to keep watch over him. His health had drastically increased and he was bound to be conscious very soon.

Juliana appeared at the door flap of the wagon and entered. Timothy lingered at the door and seemed to be playing with the stones on the ground outside.

Juliana sat down beside Diana. Zyron slept, and Jessica tended to Celarus who lay nearby.

"How are you doing, Diana?" Juliana asked compassionately, a caring look on her face.

"I'm feeling unwell. I'm just not sure where I stand with Terrek right now. Maybe I shouldn't have officially stated how I felt," Diana replied sadly.

Juliana put her hand on Diana's shoulder, "I know he really cares about you as well. I don't know what's going on in his mind, but there must be something more. Something hidden," she seemed to be pondering the unknown.

Suddenly inhaling violently Celarus systematically sat up in his makeshift bed. His eyes were wide. Jessica steadied him by holding his arm. He was weak, but he seemed all right. He even had most of the control over his bodily movement back.

Celarus stared at them and stated seriously. "Where is Terrek, I must speak with him right now!"

The walls of the maze in many areas appeared as though they had been created from the top down. They were made of layer upon layer of silt and limestone. Here and there fossilized animal remains covered the walls. It was as though some unseen force had dropped from the skies and scooped out this maze.

The maze had obviously been here for a long period of time, as the overgrowth in numerous areas was thick and stringent. The only thing that seemed unusual to Terrek were the small patches of brown fur or hair that had been left when something got caught in the thorns along the walls.

Terrek drew his sword. The others copied his movement. Slowly he moved down the alley. He heard scratching nearby.

"Where is that coming from?" Hemoth whispered.

"It sounds close," Terrek stated.

They heard a growl from above. Looking up they saw a horde of minotaurs climbing down from the walls. Swiftly they began jumping from the walls toward the group. Terrek and his men positioned themselves back to back ready for the battle to begin.

CHAPTER 14: TOWER OF DESCEIT

Minotaurs surrounded the seven of them from all sides. Terrek looked at the others, and decided on action.

"Follow my lead," Terrek said cautiously.

Terrek suddenly threw himself from his spot into the crowd of minotaurs swinging his sword. The first thing his blade caught was the throat of one of the beasts. The minotaurs appeared ready to mob Terrek but his men waded into them, attacking.

Hemoth was right in the middle. Compared to the others his height and strength gave him an extreme advantage over the foe. He stood almost a head taller than most of the monsters, and was able to kill many with a single blow of his club to their heads. He spun like a juggernaut, dispatching minotaur after minotaur. The beasts began backing off slightly.

Terrek and his men broke through the mob of minotaurs and ran down one of the nearby alleys. The minotaurs took up the pursuit. At the end of the alley there was a small courtyard. Terrek moved to the center.

"Time to use our new weapons," Terrek said.

Everyone pulled a crossbow from their backs and pointed it at the opening to the alley. With a violent spray of arrows the minotaurs dropped like dead flies as they crashed to the muddy ground in front of them.

John's new multiple shot crossbows came in handy when there were too many enemies. The few remaining beasts unhurt or wounded, fled.

The warriors lowered their weapons.

Darkness descended and the group was forced to travel by torchlight. They made their way through much of the maze, the tower was very close now. In fact, the base couldn't be more then a couple hundred strides from them, even though they were forced to follow the long alleys of the wretched maze.

Terrek thought about what they might find within the tower. It would be amazing if they managed to enter a door and the crystal simply sat there on a pedestal in the center of a room. This was unlikely.

"How long?" rasped the Vicar.

"They will be here, my lord, give them time," said the dwarf at his feet.

The tiny man had sold his soul by allowing the Vicar to enter such a sacred place. He'd given up all he had to serve him. The tower was now a hot bed of deceit. Had the Vicar not been given entrance to this place his power wouldn't have had a chance to manifest itself, but already the Vicar was forcing it throughout the structure. Soon it would be too late.

Right now he knew, in other parts of Zyconia his men were preparing. Soon, he thought. Very soon. The Vicar glowered across the large room. A musty odor filled the air. Directly in front of him sat a large pedestal.
On it sat a crystal.

The base of the tower was free of imperfections and crevices. The only distinguishing feature was the astonishing porthole ingrained in the base. Terrek stared at it. It didn't seem real. It was there, but it wasn't. It wasn't a solid iron or wooden door; it was a celestial gateway.

The entrance itself appeared to be some sort of flowing blue mist, insanely thick. They couldn't see beyond the surface. A faint echo emanated from beyond like the far away sound of rushing water. Images appeared to start to form until they thought there was something there but they faded, like illusions.

Terrek moved to the group.

"I don't like stepping into the unknown like this but it appears we have no choice. We'll have to enter. Follow close," he ordered.

Terrek exhaled. Slowly he moved toward the doorway followed by the others in single file. He paused for a moment, then entered, each man followed: except for one. The traitor.

The moon was full.

Guards slumbered in the small towers on the walls of Victory City. The night was welcomed. All the soldiers were exhausted. For a reason unknown to them, their superiors had been forcing them to perform more drills then they ever had before.

A few guards slowly paced the wide walkways atop the city walls. They couldn't help but occasionally lean on their spears for rest.

One of the guards, seeing that no one was close by, sat on the ledge. His shift was almost over anyway. None-the-less he would keep a lookout.

He lifted his gaze toward the rolling hills away from the city. Even at night the lights of the city illuminated much of the surrounding countryside beyond the walls.

Suddenly, a far off flicker on the horizon caught his eye. Slowly a distant thundering grew. More and more flickers appeared. The guard stood and squinted. He exhaled deeply, his features white.

An army was moving toward the city.

Terrek stepped through and as he did he lost sight of the door. Horrified, he moved toward where it had been. There was merely empty space. Where were his aides now? Had they been trapped outside?

He scanned the area around him. Nothing seemed as it should have been. He felt as though he was in a dream, but it was very real.

All around him darkness prevailed. He felt the darkness as though it was a substance. He stood solidly but couldn't make out a floor or anything solid for that matter. He didn't feel that the darkness was restricting his vision because, surprisingly, he could see his feet, arms and body with perfect clarity. True darkness would have made it more shadowy and difficult to make such things out. He felt as though the darkness merely enclosed around the space where he stood.

He moved forward. His legs were rubber. His equilibrium was a little unsettled. Terrek was unsure which direction to take, as there were no objects of any kind from which to determine direction. Sensing that the darkness was an oppressor, he wanted to conquer it.

"Hello?" he bellowed.

The word vibrated across what seemed a great expanse, and someone answered.

"Hello, my love," a sweet tone replied.

120

Terrek spun in the darkness to face a beautiful woman a few strides away. His mind went crazy.

Jessica stared in disbelief at Celarus.

"Impossible, I - I don't know whether to believe you or not," she said, astonished.

Celarus had told them who the traitor was, but Terrek didn't know. It was hard to believe one of his aides would betray him, and it was even more difficult to believe it when it came from the mouth of one of their former enemies.

"I'm telling the truth," he said, aggravated.

Jessica looked at the others. They were also unsure.

"I know you still think of me as the enemy. But if this was all a ruse I could have escaped by now. I have mentally renounced the Dark Circle's philosophies, this is why I nearly died. If I'd retained my powers I could have healed myself. And why would I lie about this? What would it accomplish? While you stall here, Terrek and the others could be in great danger."

Silence.

"He speaks the truth," everyone faced Zyron.

"We're going to have to send some soldiers in to try and find them," said Ricsis.

"No," Zyron stated, "I must go alone."

"Beverly!" Terrek breathed.

It was a single, longing and reawakening release echoing from the depths of his heart and soul.

He conquered the space between them and embraced her. She was solid. This wasn't some sort of sick twisted dream. Their lips met, and he caressed her cheek. He drew

121

back, barely able to believe it was her.

"How, here - I -" he became silent as she put her finger to his lips.

"Shhhh," she smiled.

He looked into her eyes. "I never thought I'd see you again. For months afterward, I prayed in agony to the Maker for death. Wanting to rejoin you so much, I suppose I never let you go."

She looked at him, saddened. Tears of endless joy streaked his cheeks.

"Maybe it doesn't matter how you got here just that we're together now," he said incredibly happy.

"That's right," she said, as they kneeled down beside eachother, "we're together now."

Terrek laid his head against her lap. She gently stroked his hair from his eyes. Terrek relaxed to her touch.

A small boy came out of the darkness.

"Jonathan!" he cried.

The small boy kneeled down in front of him and hugged his large arm.

"Father!" he said happily.

"I've told Jonathan that we'd be reunited again," Beverly said.

He looked at the little boy with love in his eyes; his face was just as he'd remembered it.

"So much has happened that I must tell you, both of you," Terrek said.

"We don't need to think about that ever again," she said softly.

Terrek's mind jarred for an instant.

"What do you mean?" he asked weakly.

She rubbed his neck. "We can all be together as a family again. You never have to worry about anything ever again. You can stay here with Jonathan and I and never have to think about any problems, the Vicar or Zyconia ever again."

Terrek's soul felt poisoned. He jerked away from her and stood. She looked at him as though hurt.

"The Vicar will destroy Zyconia, and my friends will forever wonder what became of me. Why can't you come with me, help me finish what I started?" he asked.

"Trust me my love, we can be happy here. This place is whatever we desire it to be. We can have anything, be anything, be anywhere and be with whomever we want. All we have to do is will it. We can be together forever," she soothed.

He looked into her eyes, his heart cried for him to give in, to allow himself the happiness.

"All you have to do is forget everything out there. The first step is to be rid of your responsibilities to the outside. Please, hand me the crystals," she said gently.

Terrek looked at her and loosened the sack on his belt. He held the sack in his hand.

"Yes," she said softly.

Terrek tightened his grip on the sack and fought back emotions.

"No!" he screamed.

She looked at him sadly.

"You're not really Beverly. You've been conjured up by the Vicar to trap me here. No, I won't abandon Zyconia. If you were really Beverly you would want me to fight for what I believed in no matter what," he said fighting his emotions, which had been reduced to shreds.

Terrek turned away from her. The small boy ran to his father and grabbed him by the leg.

"Please father, I want to be with you. Please don't abandon us."

Terrek looked into the child's eyes. In essence it was his son. The child's eyes were glazed and crying. He begged his father not to leave him. Tears erupted from Terrek's face, emotions bled him, and his breath became labored. He stroked his hand along the child's face, such an innocent face.

He looked at Beverly. "He lost his father once through death. Would you allow us to die again, Terrek?"

Terrek's face vibrated with pain. His chin shook.

"No, I -" he cried, a sad, emotionally confused look on his face. His soul cried to the Maker for peace.

Terrek knelt down and looked at the boy, carefully he ran his fingers across the smooth face and through his hair. Then he shut his eyes tightly to shut out the sensation.

"Go to your mother!" Terrek cried.

The child, crying, ran to Beverly who now also cried.

"Go back to that, from which you came," he said sadness breaking him.

"Terrek please -" screamed Beverly.

Terrek began breathing hard.

"Go away!" he screamed, emotions catching in his throat. All his feeling welled up inside. He tightened his eyes. Streams of tears covered his face.

He turned and took one last look as Beverly and Jonathan faded away into the abyss. Terrek fell to his knees. Eternal sadness flowed. He felt sick and his vision blurred. Part of him wished he had died with them but a larger part knew he couldn't.

Terrek brought his hands to his face and cried.

After a long time Terrek rose. He had to continue. For the first time Terrek noticed a bar of light nearby. As he moved toward it, he saw that it led into a dimly illuminated hallway. Terrek felt his equilibrium change and he looked around. Behind him the hallway stretched as well. The darkness that had surrounded him was gone. He knew he must be in the head of the tower.

He continued along the hallway, the light beyond getting brighter. He entered a large stone room. At the center stood a pedestal and atop, a large glimmering crystal.

"SO YOU CONQUERED THE WOMAN!" asked the Vicar.

Terrek, terrified, spun toward him and drew his sword. Suddenly, a dwarf that had been hiding in the darkness nearby pulled the sack of crystals from Terrek's belt. Terrek swung at the tiny man and caught him in the neck. The Vicar raised his arm and an invisible barrier surrounded Terrek. The dwarf hit the floor. Terrek looked at the fallen dwarf.

"PITY, IT'S SUCH AN UGLY EMOTION," the Vicar sneered.

The Vicar picked up the sack and kicked the near dead carcass of the dwarf into a dark corner. Terrek heard the dwarf's death hiss as it's life and soul emptied.

Someone else stepped from the darkness. Terrek stared at the traitor.

"THIS IS HOW I KNEW YOU WERE COMING HERE COMMANDER. I GUESS YOU NEVER SUSPECTED THE TRAITOR IN YOUR MIDST TO BE YOUR CLOSEST FRIEND!" the Vicar roared.

Perrin stood there looking at Terrek. His face betrayed little sign of guilt. He glowered with pure satisfaction.

Terrek looked at him, saddened.

"Why Perrin? How could you do this? Do you realize what you've done?" Terrek asked quietly.

Perrin's face became clouded, but only for a moment.

"Ever since we were children we've always been together. I've tried to remain with you, but you've always done everything so much better than I ever could. I want something of my own Terrek. Something where I am in command, and am not always second to my friend. No more," he said turning away.

The Vicar took the gem from the pedestal. He looked at Terrek one last time then led Perrin away. Terrek hit the

125

barrier with his fist. Once again he was pained.

Terrek lifted his head to the footsteps. Zyron entered the room, the others who had been with him outside the tower followed, they all looked saddened.

Terrek saw long rows of soldiers behind them.

"The Vicar was planning to use the tower as a massive dungeon. These are his prisoners; their number exceeds five hundred. They have given their oath to fight the Vicar and join us," explained Zachary.

Terrek nodded to the few dozen he could see outside the door, obviously there were gigantic crowds beyond.

Hemoth looked at Terrek. "Sorry Commander, we were imprisoned by the Vicar on some sort of evil plain of darkness. We each faced something impossible, I guess we just didn't have the strength to resist. If not for Zyron pulling us away, we might have forgotten everything, and you might never have seen us again."

"I faced the plain myself," Terrek said emotionally.

"I know," Zyron said sadly, "I felt your spirit."
He raised his hand and the barrier around Terrek ceased to exist.

"Come, let us leave this place," Zyron said.

END OF PART TWO

CHAPTER 15: CLOSURE

Terrek returned to the camp. It was all over, he thought.

He and Zyron went to his tent as Zyron had asked to speak to him. He sat in his fur-covered chair while Zyron stood. Terrek lowered his head and rubbed his face, massaging his temple.

"You saw her within the mystic plain didn't you," it was a statement.

Terrek looked up slightly, but otherwise was unnerved. Zyron spoke again. "Inside you there has never been any measure of peace since it happened. You could never let what you blamed yourself for go. You just couldn't let it rest. Even though she was gone, they were both gone."

"But when you were in the mystic plain," he continued, "I felt you let the blame and hurt go. I know it was harder than anything you've ever faced and you even feel like you've betrayed Beverly, Jonathan, and their memory. But you deserve the peace. Simply because you've forgiven yourself and let yourself live again doesn't mean you will ever forget them. But don't pollute their memory. Remember them for everything special you had together and not for the tragedy, or what you think you could have prevented. No one can change the past. Remember the love not the pain."

Terrek focused directly on Zyron. He had already come

to many of the same realizations and conclusions himself, but he needed to hear this. After all this time, all of his emotional and mental wounds had been torn open, but this had somehow healed him. He still felt pain, but he knew Zyron was correct.

If Zyron had said these things when he attended the sacred double burial those few years ago Terrek wouldn't have let himself listen or understand. After all this time he felt, closure.

"I know you're right," Terrek said somewhat reluctantly.

Zyron paused a moment then pressed a bit further.

"I know you also realize that she would want you to continue your life and allow yourself happiness. Even the happiness you once felt with her. You have another chance, don't let it slip away."

He approached her. She sat on a dead stump attempting to string a crossbow. It was slightly entertaining watching her, she didn't have the physical strength. It was a difficult task. Many strong soldiers had difficulty with this.

When she saw him she placed the bow next to the stump and moved toward her tent. He felt a pang of hurt but he had to talk to her.

"Diana, may I please speak to you?" he called.

She looked at him hopefully. He actually wanted to talk to her.

"Step into my tent," she said softly.

Terrek paced back and forth. The words were all composed in his mind it was just difficult to speak. Diana looked at him. She knew whatever he wanted to say to her was hard for him.

She took him by the hands and sat him in a chair opposite her.

"It's all right," she reassured him, an understanding look of affection on her face.

Diana reached out and put her hand on his leg.

"Whatever it is please just tell me. I can deal with it, I promise. I know whatever it is must be hard for you, but you've got to tell me. Leaving me in the dark isn't going to help you, but maybe telling me will."

Terrek sighed and leaned forward taking her hands.

"Nearly five years ago I had a wife and a child," he began, reliving the past.

"Her name was Beverly. We were so young but we were so in love, and, for a time, we were so happy. Soon after our marriage we had a child, Jonathan. He was supposed to be the first of many. We made our home in a small village called Derta just south of Victory City, and for a long time we were such a blissful family. Everything was so perfect, so real," he stuttered slightly, feelings welling up in his throat.

Diana squeezed his hand; she was on the verge of tears as well. She'd never seen him like this before.

Terrek swallowed, "Beverly and I spent every moment we could with eachother, and I taught Jonathan all I could. He was always so innocent, so full of curiosity and wonderment," he said smiling through tears.

"One day the Council sent me with a large army to a nearby mine because the Vicar's hordes were attacking it for the gold within. While we were gone the village was attacked by a large band of assassins sent by the Vicar. When word came to the army that Derta had been attacked, with about two dozen soldiers I raced back to the village. By the time we arrived, the village had been razed to the ground," Terrek faltered.

Diana began crying and lowered her face.

"The entire village was burned to cinders. I - I was frantic when I arrived. I moved through the rubble like a madman. Many of the others with me did the same. When I approached where our home used to sit I saw their bodies," he said now trembling.

Diana raised her head horrified. Terrek's words came in choking gasps.

"I approached slowly, and looked down at them. They were so close to one another. Beverly's hand seemed to be reaching for Jonathan. She was partially buried under fallen rubble, and her body was so burnt it - it was so hard to tell it was her. Jonathan lay there, covered in blood. Jonathan, face so innocent, now never to feel wonderment again," Terrek's composure was gone.

His insides collapsed. His body shook violently. Terrek couldn't stop the tears. Diana moved forward from her chair and tightened her arms around Terrek, hugging him.

Terrek, hurt beyond belief, pressed on.

"And I fell to the ground and screamed. Had others not been present I would have killed myself, then and there, but the soldiers restrained me, and took me away from the village."

"I later discovered that Murack was the one who led the raiders against my village. After that, I made a blood oath to kill him, and have pursued him many times. He has always evaded me. For so long I died inside every time I thought of them, and I hated myself so much for not being there. I thought I could have saved them," Terrek explained.

He pressed his face to her shoulder.

"How I wish I'd been there, just to have had a chance to help them, or die with them."

They both trembled. A single convulsion of emotion.

"I'm so sorry, Terrek. I had no idea. But you can't blame yourself, you couldn't have known," Diana reasoned

"I know," he nodded slowly.

"This is why I turned away from you. I'm so afraid that it might happen again. If I got close enough to anyone and something happened again I wouldn't be able to handle it," he continued.

"I'm afraid," he said drawing back, looking into her eyes, "but I will try."

"I love you, Diana. I'm not quite sure when it started. I guess it built up little by little as we spent so much time with one another. I know you love me as you've told me. I just need you to know I feel the same way, and that there's no one I'd rather spend the rest of my life with," he revealed.

He redirected his emotions, "Diana, will you be my bride? Will you marry me?"

Dumbfounded Diana soaked in the information. Suddenly she leaned forward and began kissing Terrek. Passionately.

Terrek stood in his tent. Although emotionally drained, he felt much better than before. All his aides were present except one, Perrin.

"No one could have known, Terrek," Zachary said, "but I know you must feel betrayal like no one else. I myself knew him for a few years, but you grew up with him. You knew him better than anyone."

Terrek felt remorse. He wondered deep down if maybe he had never acknowledged Perrin as an equal. But he had never expected this of him. Perrin had led them all into this trap. Didn't he realize what the Vicar stood for?

"I fear we have failed in our quest. The Vicar has the crystals. I don't know how dangerous that makes him, but I feel as though Zyconia will be lost. I have no wish for that to happen but we are so far from Victory City, let alone the Forest of Darkness, I don't see how we can strike at the

Vicar," Terrek explained.

Terrek's aides thought.

Selate moved her head in closer from the outside of the tent.

"There might be a chance. My winglings can now fly almost as swiftly as I can, and I can fly many times the speed your horses travel. If you let some of your soldiers mount my winglings we can fly to The Forest of Darkness and attack the Vicar."

Terrek faced Selate with a smile on his face.

Nearby, Celarus entered the room. "You'd better send the rest of your men toward Victory City. The Vicar once said, when he decided to conquer Zyconia, that the first city he would take would be Victory City."

The avian winglings were lined up single file. Terrek had chosen fifty of his best warriors to come with him. Celarus, Hemoth, Zachary, Lynx and Zyron would ride with him on Selate's back. Ricsis was left in command. He had strict orders to race for Victory City as quickly as possible and help ward off the Vicar's murderous hordes.

"You're sure your new children can handle this Selate," he said as he climbed onto her back.

"Trust me, they may be newborns but they'll follow their mother," she said.

Diana ran to Selate.

"Terrek wait!" Terrek slid from the bird's back and focused on her.

"I'm coming with you. No more 'be careful'. This time, I'm not letting you out of my sight," she said aggressively.

Terrek was a bit edgy about it but he knew she wouldn't take no for an answer. He nodded and pulled her up behind him.

The Vicar entered his temple cathedral and faced the front wall. Magically it rippled and disappeared. Beyond was an area nearly as large as the cathedral itself. A huge circular platform levitated high above the floor and a spiraling staircase led to its surface. High above the platform a grand opening in the ceiling allowed one to observe the dark, ominous clouds gathering overhead in the sky.

Perrin remained on the cathedral ground floor watching with shuddering fascination as the Vicar ascended the spiral. On the surface of the circular platform a large hexagonal stone table sat. The table was covered with hieroglyphics. They were the cryptic writings of the demons themselves. The most distinguishing characteristics of the table were the seven carefully crafted grooves on the surface. Six spanned the table on the outer edge, while the largest lay at the center of the table.

The Vicar removed the crystals from the sack he had obtained from Terrek. Carefully he placed the first six octagonal shaped crystals in the outer slots. Then he removed the seventh pyramidal crystal of darkness from his robe and placed it in the central dwelling.

The outer crystals glowed with atrociously blinding light. A high pitched tone erupted from the six crystals, but slowed as tiny beams shot from them directly into the crystal of darkness. It began to glow with a dim grey light from wit hin.

The Vicar raised his arms toward the skies. The dark clouds far above the temple swirled and spun like a torrential hurricane.

He lifted his voice, "DARK LORD, FROM WENCE ALL EVIL HAS COME, HEAR ME NOW AND ANSWER MY CRIES. ALLOW YOUR SERVANT HIS GREATEST TRIUMPH THAT IT WILL BE GREATER

133

TO YOUR GLORY. FILL ME WITH YOUR POWER SO
THAT I MAY FEED UPON THE ROTTING
CARCASSES OF ALL WHO WOULD OPPOSE AND
DENOUNCE YOU. EMPOWER MY SOLDIERS AND I
TO STRIKE AGAINST YOUR ENEMIES. ALLOW THE
SEALS OF HELL TO BE BROKEN AND RELEASE
ALL MANNER OF DEMONIC POWER TO ME."

The Vicar released a sadistic, animal cry from the shaft
of his throat. Spontaneously, psychedelically colored
flowing mists appeared around the Vicar. Slowly they were
drawn into his body. Strange cries that didn't seem to be
coming from him, echoed around his form as the mists
disappeared.

Perrin looked on unnerved. The scene disturbed him
deep within. Had he made the right choice?

CHAPTER 16: DARKNESS DESCENSION

𝕿he avians tore up the skies with their enormous wings.

Terrek held tight to Diana. If any of them were to fall from this height, they would surely die. It would be nightfall by the time they reached the Forest of Darkness. Not that it mattered; it was the Forest of Darkness after all.

Celarus would lead them to the Vicar's temple; hopefully it wouldn't be too heavily guarded. The Vicar's hordes would all be attacking across Zyconia, and they would never have thought anyone, let alone Terrek, could infiltrate their lines so quickly, especially from the air. But Terrek knew enough not to underestimate the Vicar's abilities. He was extremely intelligent, and probably prepared for every contingency.

The Vicar allowed his mouth to utter things that were impossible to understand. His words instilled disturbing passion as well as paranoia in Perrin who looked on, totally disturbed.

Slowly the central crystal of darkness beamed. Then, all at once, a beam of tremendous brightness and intensity erupted from the crystal, shooting straight up through the open ceiling, into the dark clouds above.

Instantly, the power was released on the land of Zyconia tenfold. Evil was suddenly unleashed like it had never been before.

Throughout Zyconia all of the Vicar's men became impassioned with uncontrollable bloodlust and power. Their abilities multiplied and they fought like men possessed.

Far away the Swamp of Ghouls boiled and sizzled. Suddenly the subsurface ejected its yield. Hundreds of ghouls emerged on the surface and charged beyond the swamp's edge in search of their next victims.

An inextricable amount of Deathworm larvae hatched in the bowels of the Caverns of Death. Their growth ultimately accelerated.

The sandstorms of the Northern Desert were raised with such ferocity that no one could travel through. The fog in Fog Valley became acidic causing all animals within to die or be severely scorched before escape.

Minotaurs everywhere in Zyconia went on a berserk rampage through many villages and inhabited areas.

Feelings of evil spread like wild fire all through the population of Zyconia.

But one of the most important things was the power increment infused into Velerion's body. The Vicar probably hadn't completely realized how far reaching the flow of evil would be. But at that moment Velerion woke from a deep sleep, diabolically hyperactive.

She felt her powers of levitation increase and tested them. She stared through a nearby porthole, which allowed her to observe the sea floor. Outside the porthole, there was a huge rock. She concentrated and saw it shoot from the floor of the sea upward.

She now had more power than she ever thought possible. She closed all channels to her mind and laid her hands on the floor. The entire dome, which held her city, groaned. The structure was under immense pressure. Ever so slightly it began to detach and rise to the surface. Yet it settled back to the bottom. She had to harness the power more completely.

Ricsis strode forward. He was the only one who traveled like the others but without a horse. His body had been a great convenience on numerous occasions. They had to move quickly, there would be no telling what was happening in Victory City right now.

Ricsis heard two horsemen approaching. They were traveling fast.

"Halt!" Ricsis yelled.

The men eyed them with hope as they blurted out their

message.

"We have been sent by the Council. They require mercenaries to battle the Vicar who has attacked Victory City. Many villages near the city have already been occupied, and although the Council has lost contact with it's other cities, they believe the twin cities Batera and Geritus have been attacked, as well as Vatiria in the southern grasslands," the soldier managed through quickened breath.

"The entire countryside is being heavily raided, and although the Victory City army has managed to keep the Vicar's hordes out off the city, that is only because of the huge walls. We won't be able to hold out much longer," the man finished.

Ricsis looked at them and turned to John who was on a horse beside them.

"Continue on your way and spread your plea, we will go to Victory City," Ricsis told the men.

From their position Terrek could barely make out the huge courtyard in front of the Vicar's palace, the temple of evil. They were deep enough in the forest not to be detected.

Celarus came up behind Terrek. "We'll wait unt il the palace guards go on forest patrols before we attempt entrance. That way there will be much less opposition."

"It feels fairly strange to me," Terrek said smiling, "being comrades with a former enemy I nearly fought to the death."

Celarus thought seriously for a moment, "I guess it would. But I'm attempting to make up for all the evil I've done in the past. If we stop the Vicar's invasion, we prevent the suffering and death of hundreds of thousands of people. I'd say that is a good place to start."

"It's an excellent place to start," Terrek said.

He patted Celarus on the shoulder. "You're beginning to become a very honorable man, Celarus, and a very moral soldier. I'm glad you decided to switch sides."

"So am I, Commander," he said seriously.

Both men moved down the small hill on which they'd been standing to rejoin the others. Selate and her winglings were all huddled together and the few soldiers he had with him were in a large group conversing with each other. Diana, Zyron and the other aides walked to Terrek and Celarus.

Suddenly Selate's children became excited. A strange illuminating presence moved through the forest nearby. A strong wind accompanied and proceeded it. Terrek drew his weapon, as did the others.

Slowly the light form walked from the trees. It was a being sent by the Maker. It resembled a man but was enveloped in a bright light. It was more beautiful than anything they had seen in their lives and it's face invited confidence from all present.

"I have come from the Maker to give you a message," the being said.

It paused and raised it's arm and a warm beam of light struck Terrek in the temple. Although his aides were frightened they somehow realized that the beam was not harming him. Terrek knew what he had to do.

"I understand," he addressed the light being.

It nodded respectfully and moved off into the forest and disappeared from sight. Terrek faced the others.

"It's time to get the crystals back," he said passionately.

Selate and her children hid in the bushes, Zyron remained with them as Terrek and the others moved across the courtyard, weapons drawn. The palace temple guards had just disappeared into the forest. Terrek and his soldiers quietly crept inside the Vicar's temple. Inside, the dank smell of incense hovered around every corner. They moved through a massive chamber.

From the look of most of the objects in the room this must have been where the Vicar's men conducted their orgies and other 'wholesome' recreational activities, Terrek thought sarcastically in disgust. Undoubtedly many had been tortured and raped here simply to entertain the Vicar and his men. Terrek was deeply sickened.

Descending a few steps, they went through a large doorway into another vast area. This place had a wide walkway that was suspended above a huge bubbling swamp below. There were many joint walkways branching off toward other doors, but they followed straight ahead toward another gigantic doorway. The swamp below smelt rancid as though it was made up of dead remains.

As they entered the next door they surveyed the cathedral. Farther away they saw the adjoining room, and above, the spiraled platform. A luminous glow of great intensity throbbed from it's upper surface.

"I think we've found what we're looking for," Terrek smiled.

Terrek and his group looked forward as a person walked out from beneath the platform. Terrek raised his sword.

"Indeed, you have," Murack eyed them darkly. .

Terrek went to move forward but Murack raised his voice, "guards!"

Doors on either side of the cathedral exploded with rows of soldiers. They also moved in through the door Terrek had entered not far behind. Murack's face was dark and lethal.

"It's time to die, Terrek."

140

CHAPTER 17: FINAL VENGEANCE

$\mathfrak{R}$icsis and the others lingered in the underbrush, not far away was Victory City. Camped between them and the city was a huge army of the Vicar's hordes. They seemed to be waiting now. Their first attempt to overcome the enormous city walls had failed. Ricsis just wished he knew what they were waiting for.

Ricsis had ordered all women and extra family members, with exception of the remaining aides to set up camp on a small stream a quarter day travel behind them. With the other aides gone, they were down to six: Ricsis, John, Jason, Adam, Jessica and Juliana. Juliana had reluctantly left Timothy with one of the other mothers at the stream.

Ricsis conversed with the others. "We've got to figure out how we are going to attack them. They are still outside the city walls. This means that we'll have to wait until their next attempt to seize the city before we try. We can't hope to get inside the city, but perhaps if we attack from behind, the army in Victory City will follow suit."

"The element of surprise is very helpful in this situation. We are extremely fortunate that the men we rescued from the Tower of Descite decided to join us. But there are a few thousand within the hordes, they outnumber us almost ten to one. We can't afford a wrong move," he explained.

The remaining aides nodded in agreement.

"We should also have large quantities of John's new crossbow reproduced and spread among the soldiers. I just wish I knew what the Vicar's army were waiting for," Ricsis finished with an uncertain disposition.

Terrek scanned his few soldiers and Murack's men. He looked at Diana. He leaned toward Hemoth.

"Keep her from harm," he said.

Spinning around, he raced toward Murack yelling like a madman. Instantly Murack's men rushed him and Terrek's men counter-attacked. Diana moved on top of a small, elevated floor nearby, dagger drawn. Hemoth blocked everyone's path to her. He swung his club and stuck Murack's men with his dagger as they approached.

Terrek's path to Murack was littered with warriors. Suddenly he was plowed over by many of them. Terrek, with lightning reflexes, began quickly dispatching them. All of Terrek's warriors were also being occupied. Maybe he'd been wrong, maybe they were hopelessly outnumbered. Murack moved toward a vacant wall. A large iron chain hung to the floor suspended from the ceiling.

Unexpectantly a large number of soldiers jumped upon Hemoth pulling him to the floor. At the same time Murack clasped to the chain and swung.

"Help – Help me!" Diana began screaming as Murack swung by her, pulling her from the floor. The dagger was knocked from her hand by the impact.
Hemoth broke the soldier's hold on him and began decimating them, but he was already too late. Murack swung across the cathedral, landing on the first step of the spiral staircase to the crystal platform. Terrek moved from the fighting crowds, free from the soldiers he advanced

toward Murack. Terrek's mind sped in all directions.

"Leave her alone it's me you want. You want a fight? I'll give you one!" he said hoping to intimidate him.

"Maybe it is her I want," Murack smiled moving his face close to hers. She lurched at the foul smell of his breath.

"Such a tasty harlot, she'll give me many a thrill when I've killed you. But I'm sure she'll be nothing compared to Beverly," Murack emphasized the name laughing.

Rage collected in Terrek's body and mind. He moved forward.

"Stay where you are," Murack said calmly bringing a knife to Diana's throat.

Terrek held back.

"Throw me your sword," he yelled.

Terrek had no choice. Murack caught his blade and threw it behind him.

He squeezed Diana's cheeks and kissed her. Instantly she turned in his grip and kneed him in the groin, hard.

Murack roared in agony, his manhood tasted the bitterness of nausea.

He grabbed her by the hair, pulled her head down and smashed her in the neck with his fist. She hit the floor, out cold. Terrek rushed Murack impulsively and was also struck by his iron fist as he fell to the floor.

"Time for a little entertainment," Murack said as he unsheathed a spectacular dark sword.

Terrek had heard many stories about Murack's magical sword. Legend said the sword had never been beaten.

Terrek, almost to his feet, was struck by Murack's iron boot. He fell back, colliding with a large door on the cathedral wall. His body busted right through and he careened down the stone steps into one of the Vicar's dungeons. Murack entered at the top and galloped down toward him. Terrek quickly moved down the remaining stairs. Bruised and disoriented, he backed into the dungeon's central area and searched for a weapon.

Murack came toward him, a man impassioned with never-ending evil. Smiling, he circled Terrek. Terrek found a small rusted blade upon the floor and brought it to bear.

"You'll never know how satisfying your wife was Terrek," Murack said blatantly jeering at him, "even my men had their turns on her."

Terrek erupted and swung violently at Murack. The warlock leader swung back. Terrek was brought to his knees, barely able to hold Murack's blade from cutting his cheek with the rusted relic he held.

"Now I kill the husband as well, what a shame," he said sarcastically.

Terrek's strength gathered and he struck Murack back to the ground. He quickly recovered as Terrek got to his feet.

"Perhaps you will be more of a challenge," he said, "Beverly was never much of a fighter was she? No she screamed and begged more than anything. But that one," he said, referring to Diana, "she's got a bit more life to her doesn't she."

Murack moved forward and they both commenced swinging. The battle raged with Terrek continually being forced back. But somehow he struggled on.

Finally Murack caught his side with the edge of his sword; blood streaked his abdomen as he hit the floor.

"You are nothing!" Murack raged bringing his sword across Terrek's blade.

To Terrek's astonishment his own blade shattered, the handle hit the floor. He rolled sideways to escape Murack, pain rippling through his side.

He stared up at Murack and tore a skeleton's ribcage from the floor. He held it as a shield just in time for the sword to impact upon it. It was also smashed. Murack's fist struck Terrek in the side of the head, sending him disoriented across the floor. Terrek, exhausted and injured, brought himself to his knees but Murack was already upon him, sword held high to plunge into his heart.

In that moment Terrek noticed someone behind Murack. It was Perrin. Terrek, determined not to let Perrin see the fear within him, remained hard faced. But Perrin's face no longer held anger. That's when he tossed him the knife.

Immediately Terrek slashed it across Murack's chest. Murack rolled away coughing. It had been a surprising blow, but not a fatal one. Murack had lost his sword in the fall. Terrek moved toward him tightening his teeth. Blood stained both men and fell from their faces.

Terrek, with a slight advantage, tightened his grip on Murack's collar and began pummeling him repeatedly. Each strike shattered more and more of Murack's features. The bones in his face became exposed through his skin, which was violently marred. Blood collected in his eye sockets, yet he struck back with the fury of hell.

Terrek and Murack traded blow after blow, Terrek gaining much of the leeway. He released all his rage, anger and bitterness upon Murack. Until eventually Murack hardly had the will to stand or raise his arms.

Gathering his strength, with one tremendous blow, Murack managed to knock Terrek to the floor once again. He removed a small dagger from his belt and jumped toward Terrek.

A painful cry filled the dungeon. Murack had been impaled by his own sword. Terrek had brought the sword to bay just in time to save his life. His hands on the handle he stood and pulled it from Murack's stomach. Incredibly Murack stood.

Terrek moved toward him. Murack, barely able to breathe, backed toward a shallow trench of muddy water behind him, he was obviously dying.

Suddenly, Murack began yelling, and savagely lunged at Terrek one last time, arms outstretched. Terrek slashed with the sword completely decapitating Murack's head from his body. Blood splattered everywhere. Terrek's eyes stung from the foreign blood. Murack's head rolled into the darkness, and his body took a few steps back and morbidly landed in the disease-ridden water.

Terrek stared down at the headless corpse; blood flowed forcefully from his inner neck. The blood merged with the muddy water. Terrek thought of the morbid irony of Murack ending up dead where he'd been born in the filth and waste.

Terrek relaxed, and collapsed to the floor.

"My blood oath has been fulfilled, now maybe you will both have peace," he said, silently addressing Beverly and Jonathan.

"They will," Perrin said solemnly.

Terrek turned, once again angered. He raised the sword.

"Wait," Perrin said calmly.

Terrek paused.

"I know you don't want to ever see my face again after all I've done to you, to everyone, but I want another chance. I thought I wanted something that the Vicar was offering, but I had no idea what serving under the Vicar entailed. Even if you take me back to Victory City to be executed as a traitor, I would rather go with you than stay here," Perrin confessed, eyes lowered.

Terrek looked at him and lowered his sword.

"I never realized until the past few years how much jealousy had eaten me up inside. But that's what it was. I suppose I could never accept the fact that you accomplished everything so much better than I did. But I didn't realize how much harder you worked to attain what you wanted."

Terrek sighed.

"I don't expect you to trust me ever again but I hope in time you might think of me in the same way as you once did," he finished sorrowfully.

"After all you've done I should kill you. But I won't. You saved my life Perrin, but I don't know if I can ever forgive you for what you've done. You will rejoin us, because I believe your feelings are genuine, otherwise you wouldn't have aided me in Murack's death," Terrek said

His tone now held the hurt. "If I'm ever to forgive you or trust you in the same way again you will have to earn it. I'm sure the others will feel the same. It's not going to be easy."

"I know," he said sadly.

"Come with me," Terrek said ascending the stairs.

The battle still raged above.

At the top of the stairs Terrek surveyed the fighting. His men had done much better than he'd thought possible and most of Murack's men were fleeing. Terrek, still wielding Murack's sword rushed to help, as did Perrin.

Soon all of Murack's men had been killed, or had fled. All Terrek's aides eyed Perrin. Terrek nodded his approval of him to the others, and they silenced their rage against him for his betrayal.

Terrek approached Diana who was now awake.

"I'm sorry," Terrek said, "I should never have let you come with us, you could have been killed."

Diana's face comforted him.

"Don't blame yourself for anything. I'm alright. I wanted to come. And it's over now, don't worry, all right?" she said caressing his cheek with her hand.

Terrek took her hand and kissed it. He walked away toward the crystal platform. His aides and the remainder of his soldiers gathered and gazed upward toward him.

Terrek reached the platform and stared into the central crystal. As soon as he removed it from the stone table the beam shooting skyward was discontinued. He removed the others as well and placed them once again in a sack. He descended the spiral and exited the cathedral followed by his group. As they left the temple Terrek dropped the dark

148

sword into the swamp below the branching walkways.

Ricsis and the others were ready to fight. They now
knew why the Vicar's men had stopped. Dozens of massive
battering rams, siege towers and even catapults had been
brought into their camp and they were probably planning
on their use soon.

Like right now, Ricsis thought, as he saw them moving
the gigantic contraptions toward the walls. Instantly the
guards upon the walls began shooting arrows down upon
the Vicar's armies, while arming their own catapults and
other mounted weaponry upon the walls. But there seemed
to be some kind of magical power protecting the Vicar's
army. Most of the arrows missed their targets.

Ricsis faced all the soldiers.

"Our main objective if they conquer the walls is to
move in and try to get in front of them and prevent them
from advancing too far into the city. With the help of John's
crossbows it will be much easier to try and defeat their
forces. We will attack them from behind and then proceed
into the city and join the Victory City army in their
defensive efforts -"

Ricsis was interrupted as the sound of a catapult
boulder impacted with one of the guard towers on the city
wall reducing it to splinters and collapsing part of the wall.
More boulders were hurled as the siege towers were moved
into position, and the battering rams were released upon the
gates.

"Make Commander Terrek proud," bellowed Ricsis,
"Charge!"

Every soldier, girded for battle, sailed toward the city
walls, anxious for the first enemy that crossed their path.
They moved through the Vicar's men hacking and slashing,
wrestling to move past them and enter the cracks in the

wall, gaining access to the city. The crests upon the army led by Ricsis prevented the men in the city from attacking them. They scurried within the city ahead of them, like mice down a hole.

CHAPTER 18: REBIRTH

"Where are we going?" exclaimed Diana.

They clung once again to Selate's back in the sky; her winglings were close behind carrying the other soldiers. Selate was slightly discomforted with more weight on her back: Perrin was the extra.

"We must find the ancient ruins in the Central grasslands," Terrek said.

Everyone on Selate's back looked at him puzzled.

"What?" asked Celarus and Zachary in unison.

Terrek continued to survey the land below.

"When the being of light visited us outside the Vicar's temple I was given a message. The Maker told me that I am to take the crystals to an ancient ruin in the central grasslands. There we are to fulfill prophecy."

Everyone still seemed a bit perplexed. Zyron's eyes glowed with anticipation.

"I have the direction in my mind, I will guide us there. The Maker told me I would know what to do when I arrived," he explained.

"You will," Zyron beamed.

Terrek looked in the sack and held out the triangular dark crystal.

"But I'm unsure where this crystal came from?" he said to Zyron.

Zyron took one look at it and removed it from his hand. "We must rid ourselves of this, it has the taint of evil."

Zyron tossed the gem from them. It plummeted toward the ground far below.

"We have no need of it," Zyron said, Terrek didn't question him.

Far below, a sinister hand clasped the fallen gem.

The place was a large room in one of the stone homes on the inner part of Victory City. Flimsy articles of furniture surrounded a large table. Around the table and on nearby chairs, rested Ricsis, John, Jason, Adam, Jessica, Juliana, several Council members, as well as the few remaining military officials.

Juliana sat against the wall; her arm had been badly damaged in their attack on the Vicar's men as they infiltrated the city walls. Jessica was tending to her.

One of the council members spoke to Ricsis. "Your Commander failed. And now we are about to lose Zyconia."

Ricsis stared at the pompous, elite, inexperienced man. He'd no idea what anything was like in Zyconia. He'd always been sheltered and well pampered in his rich and easy environment. Ricsis felt contempt for him.

"Commander Terrek has fought for Zyconia for his entire life, and has nearly given his life for you people on many occasions. What have you ever fought for? You who sit behind your numerous armies and enjoy life, while others in Zyconia have nothing."

The Council member's jaw dropped open.

"You would not be speaking to me in such a manner if we were not in such a dire situation and required your help," he said madly.

"Perhaps not, but it's time you heard the truth from

someone," Ricsis said.

The man looked red in the face.

"Would you like to be removed from this meeting? There are still some loyal soldiers around who obey us."

"Shut up, Belan!" another Council member yelled at the man.

He turned toward Ricsis. This Council member's name was Tommeron.

"You must forgive Belan, even some of us are feeling the evil power that has been spreading. We all must do our best to control our tempers."

As Tommeron finished, Belan grunted and looked away from them.

"We have the utmost respect for Commander Terrek, and I know we are not perfect, but some of your statements about us are too harsh. We have always done our best to help everyone in Zyconia. But Zyconia is a dangerous land. We can't be everywhere," Tommeron explained.

Ricsis lowered his head slightly.

"Yes I know, I'm sorry," he said.

Tommeron nodded, then faced everyone at the table.

"May I have your attention please?" Everyone in the room focused on him.

"We have managed to dig up almost two-thousand soldiers for our final attempt to push the Vicar's men out of Victory City. If we fail, Victory City will fall. At this moment the rest of our forces are spread incredibly thin in an attempt to keep the Vicar's men from advancing, but we are being heavily eradicated," Tommeron paused, his face grave.

"The Vicar's men have complete control of the walls, the outer edges of the city, as well as control of most of the inner streets. The city being circular, they are slowly squeezing us in from the outer edges. They can't be far away and since the Council's castle is at the center of the city, if they break through the city streets and capture the

153

Council's castle, Victory City will be theirs."

"Many of the other Council members have been assassinated by the Vicar's spies, or have been killed attempting to lead men into battle themselves. Most of the people who've lived here for generations have fled in sheer terror instead of fighting for their homes. But may the Maker grant that we come out of this victorious, if not, the dead will be the most fortunate. There's no telling what sort of atrocities the Vicar will perform on us. Let's be on our way," Tommeron finished.

Everyone in the room began donning armor. Ricsis moved to Jessica.

"Stay with Juliana, if the Vicar's men get close to this area get to the Council's castle or if possible flee the city. If they make it this far chances are we'll already be dead," he said grimly.

Ricsis moved to Tommeron. "We can still hope that Terrek retrieved the crystals from the Vicar's palace temple."

"Maybe, but when the presence of evil like this begins, it's hard to stop," he replied sadly. Tommeron pulled on shoulderplates.

Ricsis thought about something else. "Was Walker killed in the attack?" He remembered the influential member of the Council well. He was one of the few who didn't seem spineless to him.

Tommeron seemed to think this over. "N - No, he's away on a secret mission."

"I suppose he probably won't return if we aren't victorious then, will he?" Ricsis asked.

"I doubt it," said Tommeron.

"There it is!" yelled Terrek.

Below them, a massive stretch of ruins could be seen.

The ancient city that once stood here must have been grand indeed. The stretch of ruins was much larger than Victory City. Selate sailed down into a centralized area of the ruins. Her children followed. Everyone stood on the ground. Terrek looked at his men and aides and then turned to Selate.

"I may need my men here, you never know where evil lurks. But I want you and your children to fly to Victory City and try to help Ricsis. If you are worried your children are not mature enough yet to fight, you don't have to go."

Selate smiled, "I've never told you this I didn't know if it would matter but, while avians are in their growth stage they are protected by an extremely tough skin. I doubt any blade could penetrate them."

Terrek smiled as well.

"Then destroy the Vicar's men and return for us."

"I'll do my best," she said. As she flew into the sky once more, her children followed.

Terrek looked across the stone surface. This was the center of the ruins. It was fairly barren. A stoned circular plain.

Suddenly an earthquake shook the ancient ruins. The flat surface cracked and a huge rock formation erupted from the ground not far away from them. Terrek gazed up in amazement.

It was a gigantic, steeply constructed pyramidal shape. Ingrained into the rock walls were small steps all the way to the pinnacle. Upon the pinnacle's small surface rested a circular stone table. Terrek vaguely recalled a legend once told to him by Zyron. Terrek turned to him.

"That's the altar of the Maker, my son," Zyron said. Terrek's eyes went wide.

"Legend predicted that one day the Maker's power would return in full force to purge the land of Zyconia and restore it to it's once great splendor," Terrek said remembering.

"That is the gate and you have the key, complete the prophecy, my son," Zyron smiled.

Terrek stood for a moment then took slow strides toward the nearest steps.

Suddenly, dark, menacing soldiers rushed from behind the ruins and blocked his path. Behind them stood Keldar the Soothsayer, apprentice to the Vicar and Colar the leader of the Sorcerers. Out of thin air the tall presence of the Vicar appeared on the steps of the altar.

His dark robes seemed out of place here, but his very presence seemed more prominent, more powerful than when Terrek last saw him. The Vicar had reached a new level of evil. The sky grew dark and the wind blew up a small swirling tornado of dirt and grime. Rain sprinkled and splattered upon everyone emptying the contents of the dark clouds filling the sky overhead.

"COMMANDER TERREK, WE ACQUAINT ONCE MORE. YOU MAY HAVE VANQUISHED MURACK, BUT YOUR TRAIL ENDS HERE, I COMMIT YOUR DEATHS TO THE LORD OF DARKNESS. DESTROY THEM, AND SCATTER THEIR REMAINS, THAT THE FLIES AND MAGGOTS MAY CONSUME THEM," the Vicar boomed.

Once again the Vicar's men rushed toward them as Terrek's small army drew their weapons. Keldar also waded into the fray against Terrek's men. Again battle commenced. This time Terrek moved Diana away from the battle. She and Zyron watched from behind a fallen pillar as Terrek rejoined the fight.

Celarus somehow managed to rush through the soldiers and started toward the Vicar. Instantly Colar appeared.

"Celarus, you traitor!" he roared.

A beam of dark energy shot from his arms directly toward Celarus. Celarus dodged the shot and reached the edge of the stone plain. He speedily scrambled down the small slope that presented itself and stole into the ruins,

Colar close behind.

Meanwhile the bloodshed continued.

Hemoth moved through the Vicar's men with little trouble. But he suddenly realized he had a very powerful adversary ahead. Not far away, he saw one of Terrek's men lifted from the ground and mutilated. The man fell to the stone plain bludgeoned, after his arms had been torn off. A huge portion of his middle section had been devoured. Keldar had torn the man's vital organs from his body with his grotesque, deformed mouth and massive teeth. Hemoth would have to stand against the powerful hunchback.

Quickly he ran forward and slammed his club into Keldar's large hump. Keldar howled and spun, swinging his clawed hand at Hemoth. Leading Keldar away from the other soldiers Hemoth lured him into a small ruined temple nearby. Large stone pillars barely held the wreck of a ceiling in the structure.

Keldar looked upon his prey. "You are the strongest warrior in Terrek's army, and perhaps the strongest that serves the Council. I must make an example of you."

Ricsis lifted his heavy brow. Blood covered his face, a mosaic of hurt and pain. A large laceration streaked from his ear almost to the corner of his mouth. He could see other warriors nearby dying and suffering from the endless charge of the Vicar's warlocks and sorcerers. An unseen force drove the Vicar's hordes. The savagery with which they fought was unsustainable for normal men. Ricsis was injured but he got to his feet. John, nearby, also rose and prepared to once again engage the enemy.

Velerion concentrated. She'd slept, and now felt more power than ever. Slowly she felt the entire domed city in her mind. It vibrated and slowly lifted from the bottom. She felt tremendous triumph. She tightened her telekinetic gift on the outer edges of Kaldoria and caressed the sea slowly. Ever so slightly the city moved toward the surface.

It would take time to reach it, but she knew it could be accomplished. Then she would take her revenge on the Vicar and seize control of Zyconia for herself. She was enthralled by the concept.

Celarus hid himself.

"You traitor," Colar said scanning the ruins, "come out and fight!"

Suddenly he was attacked from behind. Celarus struck him in the face with a tree branch. Colar was sent sprawling as he spun round. Celarus had evaded his vision once more.

"Enough of your parlor tricks, Celarus," Colar sneered.

Instantly Celarus moved toward Colar again. This time the Sorcerer wasn't fooled. Colar stretched his arm to him as he dove behind a nearby pillar.

A burning knife of energy shot from Colar's hands scorching Celarus's skin as it grazed his side. He landed behind a fallen pillar in pain. Colar grinned and moved toward the pillar. Suddenly a rock struck him in the head. He flashed his gaze toward Zachary nearby.

Zachary had angered him. Colar ran toward him allowing pulse after pulse to escape his hands. Zachary jumped and weaved bravely as Celarus regained feeling and rose.

Perrin dropped from a pillar above directly in Colar's path. With a glimmer Perrin pulled his arm up and slashed

Colar across the face. In his hand he held a bronze claw. The triple blade had scarred Colar's eyes. He was blind.

"Argh!" Colar's vocal upsurge grew.

In overwhelming rage and revenge, he allowed his power to flow. A fierce energy beam slammed Perrin's body to the ground. He lay immobile. Colar went mad, flailing his arms everywhere determined to kill Celarus and Zachary without his sight. He began moving toward a small cliff that had been created by the earthquake.

At once Celarus and Zachary moved from their positions and each locked onto one of Colar's arms. They tossed him, flailing over the cliff.

Colar spiraled downward and struck the flat surface with a deafening echo. Dead.

Celarus and Zachary ran to Perrin. He was severely injured.

Keldar didn't make many wrong moves in combat but Hemoth had managed to exploit a few thus far. Both men were weary and covered in blood, but neither would back down. Both men were driven by purposes greater than themselves.

"You are strong but you lack something," said Keldar. Hemoth looked at him.

"What do I lack?" he taunted, "deformation?" This angered Keldar and he charged. With a violent smash Keldar toppled into one of the pillars and the roof began to shake. Hemoth attacked him from behind. He clubbed him swiftly in the legs laying him to the floor and drove his dagger into Keldar's back. He buried it repeatedly. Cries of anger came from Keldar who struggled to his feet. At once Hemoth swung his club into Keldar's head. The resounding impact served to extenuate the beast man's injury. His body sailed into another pillar. A large section of ceiling landed on his legs. The entire structure began collapsing all around them.

Hemoth almost thought of helping him, but when Keldar threw his sword at him, he knew he couldn't and ran for the door.

"Darklord, I append my spirit to thee!" Keldar roared.

Keldar's prayer frightened and disturbed Hemoth. He felt horrendous pity for Keldar and what his existence had become.

Hemoth reached the doorway in time to jump as the entire ceiling and much of the walls collapsed behind him.

Terrek had scraped his way through the soldiers by this time and approached the Vicar.

"TERREK, AT LAST YOUR LIFE IS MINE," he rasped.

Terrek felt anger.

"My life is the Maker's," he stated.

The Vicar's eyes glowed.

"NOT FOR LONG," the Vicar said holding the pyramidal crystal of darkness high over his head. It glimmered. Terrek, surprised, brought his sword to ready.

"No!" Zyron screamed as he ran from a nearby hiding place and jumped in the way just in time to catch the energy bolt offspring of the translucent dark crystal parent directly to the chest. The energy blast from the dark crystal knocked Zyron to the ground.

Terrek, enraged, threw his dagger into the Vicar. The Vicar roared, his wound drew no blood but he dropped the crystal. As it hit the stone at the Vicar's feet it shattered. An enormous explosion threw Terrek to the ground as a dark cloud of smoke filled the air.

He stood. Still feeling the heat, he surveyed the area. There was no sign of the Vicar, but numerous fragments of his robe were strewn about. The explosion must have ended his life, Terrek thought.

He jumped to Zyron's side. Surprisingly, the seer got to his feet.

"Are you alright, Zyron? I'm sorry, I should have moved faster," he said fearfully.

Zyron's face was taut and pale.

"You are still blaming yourself for things outside your control, don't," he said weakly.

Diana appeared at Terrek's side. "I'm sorry, I saw what happened and I had to come."

"Are you all right, Zyron?" Terrek asked.

"We have no time for this. Come," Zyron said leading Terrek up the altar steps.

Terrek and Diana followed.

Below, as they walked, Terrek saw Hemoth return to the battle. He dove in, his size and skill giving a new advantage to the fight. Although slightly outnumbered, his men were doing amazingly well despite the evil passion the Vicar's men harbored. Even Lynx, who Terrek at one time suspected of being the traitor, was doing well as a warrior.

When they reached the top Terrek was overwhelmed by the feeling that he had seen the surface of the altar before. The stone table displayed before them was much like the one in the Vicar's palace temple except it had no central opening for a pyramidal crystal. Terrek looked to Zyron for counsel. Zyron still held his sceptre. He nodded and Terrek placed the crystals in the outer openings.

Amazing white beams of light flowed from each crystal shooting skyward from the top of the table. Overhead the dark clouds began to part. Suddenly Terrek felt something change.

The tide had turned.

Within the Caverns of Death, a plague infected the deathworms. They writhed in agony until every one of them lost their lives.

Spontaneously the ghouls returned to their swamp and were suctioned below. Their swamp suddenly transformed, taking on solid form. Shocked, the ghouls suffocated encased in stone.

The sandstorms in the Northern Desert ceased: permanently. The acidic mists of Fog Valley were lost to the Western Sea.

Suddenly the maze around the Tower of Descite collapsed and the Minotaurs within fled. All Minotaurs across Zyconia, struck with xenophobia, ran with extreme haste far up to their homeland; the Minotaur mountains.

To Celarus and Zachary's disbelief Perrin's deadly wounds were suddenly and miraculously healed. As Jessica looked on, Juliana's badly injured arm was also healed before her eyes.

Terrek's small army, below the altar, beamed with power as they slaughtered the Vicar's men and sent many fleeing.

162

Far away, an extreme mental pain hit Velerion. The strain hit her like nothing she'd ever faced.

"Help!" Velerion screamed losing her mental grip on the massive domed city. Her soldiers entered the room as she hit the floor. They suddenly felt weightless. Their city plummeted toward the bottom of the sea.

She ran past them through the door and out onto the street. Through the dome she could see they were falling fast. She concentrated, totally frantic. She had to at least slow their descent.

"No!" she yelled out loud, she no longer had the power even to slow them. She felt the impact before she heard or experienced it.

The city crashed to the sea floor. The last thing Velerion knew, as she fought internal injuries from the impact, was the collective scream of thousands within the city as the buildings began collapsing, and finally the huge fractured dome was reduced to enormous shards of broken glass.

Ricsis, who was racing forward, suddenly felt his wounds leave him. The scar disappeared from his face and he was filled with energy. He swung and maneuvered himself with new life. Ricsis gazed around. All the wounded were healed and each one retrieved their weapons. They nearly matched the Vicar's horde in number now, and were fighting so fiercely that they were starting to drive them back.

Immediately Ricsis noticed a massive armed crowd moving from behind the Vicar's men. For a moment his heart sank, were they reinforcements? But no, it was the people who inhabited Victory City. Something had encouraged them to return and fight for their homes. A huge wave of them slaughtered the Vicar's men from behind. Fear began to invade their enemies.

Suddenly, from the skies, Ricsis spied twenty-six Avians and smiled. Selate swooped down and picked one of the Vicar's men up with her claws, throwing him from high above into a few of his companions. All at once the Avian winglings swooped into the Vicar's men pecking and clawing. This incited terror in their forces. Many began to flee rising into a massive exodus.

This time the earthquake that rocked the ruins was stupendous and lasting. Terrek held fast to the stone table with Zyron and Diana. Below, Terrek's men moved to the altar's base. Everywhere, as far as they could see, stone structures erupted from beneath the ground. Some were grand; others were small but still well constructed. A city was forming from beneath.

Suddenly, on the outskirts of the ruins, huge walls erupted. They paralleled the ones of Victory City yet they were wider, higher and much more splendid. Then at once, not far from the altar, a huge palace spewed forth. It was more beautiful then any structure Terrek had ever seen. Adorned in strange markings the walls glowed with life, the high turrets molded from some unworldly blue rock. All the ruined wreckage that had covered the area for centuries seemed to disintegrate and disappear from sight.

"It's a city sent from the Maker. It has been foretold that one day Zyconia will be united under a king. And his subjects will be happy and Zyconia will prosper," Zyron coughed.

Zyron stumbled to the surface beside the stone table.

"Yet I fear I will not see that day."

"What's wrong, Zyron?" he said, panicking.

Diana knelt as well, looking on worriedly. For the first time Terrek noticed the blood on Zyron's chest seeping through his robes. He had been more injured by the Vicar's blast than he had let on. Diana looked as though she would cry. Terrek's face went white as he stared into the seer's eyes. Zyron was dying.

"Don't grieve my son. I have lived a full life and am ready to rejoin the Maker in paradise. Wence I have come, so shall I return," Zyron clasped Terrek's hand.

Terrek fought back tears, "I should have listened to you in the beginning, I - I shouldn't have made you feel obligated to join me."

"You did what was right, you performed the Maker's will as you should have. As you will continue to do, not just for me, but for yourself," he said calmly.

Terrek could no longer hold the tears as they streamed down his face. He knew a part of him was dying with the old man.

"Promise me you'll never forget what I've given you," Zyron said.

Terrek shook his head, "I will never forget as long as I live; I promise."

Diana hid her face in her hands and trembled.

"Take this," Zyron choked, handing Terrek the sceptre, "and follow your destiny."

"Goodbye my son," with those last words Zyron closed his eyes, and his breathing slowed.

Terrek pulled Zyron close and laid the seer's head against his shoulder. He lifted his head toward the heavens. The clouds were beginning to part.

"Please take good care of him," Terrek said, shaking.

The clouds parted and a beautiful multi-colored rainbow shone across the skies. A feeling of unexplained relief filled Terrek.

Terrek smiled through tears. "Thank you."

And with that Zyron became silent.

EPILOGUE: CORONATION

Terrek and Diana stepped from the altar unto the flat, stony ground. They rejoined the others. Terrek looked one last time at the altar. Atop, Zyron had been laid to rest. Silently the altar disappeared from sight, vaporizing as the ruins had. This left a barren plain directly in front of the palace. Terrek stared at Zyron's sceptre. He knew that the old seer was gone to a place where he would no longer feel pain. But he'd always miss him. A piece of Terrek's soul was vacant now and would never be filled again.

He released his emotions. He still felt guilt but he knew the seer was at peace and that he'd lived a full life. He knew Zyron would want him to remember their times together but also look to the bright future ahead.

"Terrek," Lynx said, approaching.

His voice was much louder than he'd ever heard it before. It sounded very familiar. Terrek looked at him. Suddenly he removed his hood and took off the false hair that was on his head and beard. Terrek's eyes went wide. Lynx didn't exist. The man who'd been using that alias was Walker. The influential member of the Council smiled and stepped to Terrek.

"Surprised to see me?" he asked.

The answer was obvious.

"Walker why have you been pretending that you're

someone you're not?" Terrek asked, totally perplexed.

"The Council wanted a representative to go with you. But we figured it would be best not to allow anyone, even you, to know I was here. We had to be cognizant of many things. Come, we all have duties to perform," Walker said.

Many days later in the new city, things were dramatically changed. All of the Vicar's men had been driven from the Council's cities and ultimately from Zyconia itself. The Forest of Darkness had been burned to the ground, the Vicar's palace temple destroyed by the Council's soldiers.

The surviving Council members had announced throughout Zyconia that those who had lost their homes to the Vicar's attack could now take up residence in the new city. Thousands had answered their invitation, both young and old, until the city became well populated. Meanwhile, the other cities were slowly being rebuilt.

Terrek's aides were all reunited in the new city and Juliana was reunited with her Timothy. The barren plain in front of the new palace was to be transformed into a grand garden: a main courtyard. Later that day, Terrek was to go to a Great Hall in the southern part of the new city. He was to be honored for his actions by the Council before the massive crowds that now populated the city. But at the moment, he had other matters to address.

In the new city, Terrek and Diana stood before a small altar in one of the newborn temples to the Maker. One of Zyron's closest followers had come all the way from Victory City to perform the joining of Terrek and Diana. He stood between them and the altar. Behind them stood Terrek's former aides, the Council members, as well as crowds of well-wishers who'd heard of his acts to preserve Zyconia against the Vicar. His legend was already spreading throughout Zyconia. In fact, the crowds were so large that people packed the streets outside the temple.

Terrek gazed into Diana's eyes and knew that he loved her with every fiber of his being. He would spend the rest of his life with her. He took her by the hand, and she smiled. The quest had matured her somewhat. She was no longer so nervous and withdrawn. In his eyes, she was perfect. Both of their gazes seemed connected, in essence they were already one form.

Terrek looked at her, and smiled.

"We have come to this place to witness the joining of Terrek and Diana," the man indicated.

"Terrek, you wanted to declare your love to the bride," stated the seer. Diana was surprised and looked at him lovingly, questioning.

Terrek faced Diana.

"There was once a time when I never thought I'd feel love again. When I thought that I'd lost my only chance for happiness. For so very long, it was the truth. But then I met you," he said.

Tears came slightly to her eyes, she was so happy.

"When I first met you. I merely thought of you as another pretty face, perhaps a friend. I never imagined then that we would be here, this way, together. Now I know how much I really do love you. I'd die for you. I want to spend the rest of my life with you," Terrek declared.

Diana delved deep into his eyes with her soft gaze.

"I love you," she said as she embraced him. They began to kiss.

"Hurrah!" a cry erupted from the crowds all around.

"What was two is now one. May the Maker grant you all the happiness you deserve. You are now husband and wife," the seer announced happily.

They both turned and walked toward their former comrades, now their friends.

The small wooden boat slowly drifted across the dark murky sea. A hooded boatman gently maneuvered the craft toward the nearby island. The vinework of vegetation covered the shoreline; the sky above was dark and foreboding. Large spikes of rock littered the landscape and not far away the dim lights of a settlement could be seen. The place was called the Island of Evil. His passenger sat at the other end of the vessel.

The passenger contemplated the future, his dark tattered robes, fluttered in the sea breeze. A time would come again when he would return. This time evil was vanquished but it would never be destroyed. The Vicar would return: in strength.

The Great hall where Terrek was supposed to attend the victory ceremony was much too hot in this season. So the Council held the ceremony in a central area of the city within a large open garden. From here, down a long street through the city everyone got an incredible view of the new palace.

A small platform had been placed on the ground at the center of the garden. Nearby, Selate and her children perched on the strangely sculpted rock formations that filled the garden. On the platform stood Terrek, Diana, all of his former aides and the few remaining Council members. The two Council members well known by Terrek and his former comrades were Walker and Tommeron.

Completely surrounding the platform stood vast crowds of people who had all come to see the honoring of

170

Zyconia's greatest hero. The crowds stretched so far in every direction that they filled the enormous garden. In fact some people were so far down the street that they probably had great trouble seeing the heroes. Walker went forward to address the crowd.

"This is a great day in Zyconia my friends! We have vanquished the Vicar and all his evil forces," Walker's voice instilled patriotism in all present.

"The Maker has granted us victory and given us this great city. The other Council members and I have decided on its name. From this day forward this city will be Zyconia's capital. It is thus christened New Victory City so that we will always remember how within this very city the Maker launched his power allowing us to destroy our enemies."

"Hurrah!" an explosive roar volcanoed throughout the crowds, as they expressed their joy.

Walker turned and beckoned Terrek to his side.

"No one understands this better than Commander Terrek, whom you've undoubtedly heard about. He fought an exhausting battle with the Vicar, and emerged victorious, saving all that dwell in this land. The other Council members and I were attempting to decide how we could possibly reward such an extremely selfless act. We couldn't decide, until last night when we all agreed."

Walker looked away from the crowd but still spoke to them. He directed his gaze at Terrek.

"We've decided to make him the first king of Zyconia," the murmuring in the crowd subsided. Everyone was shocked, including Terrek, who stared vacantly at Walker.

"The legends spoke of a great leader who would one day clear the path, making Zyconia a great kingdom. Terrek is that man. He even possesses the sceptre with the Amit yus on it," Walker exclaimed. Diana walked to Terrek's side as he withdrew the sceptre from his belt in plain view.

"The Council has always used this symbol because it was patterned after the ancient symbol of the power of good. That is why it appears on this sceptre."

"Terrek won't be alone in the responsibility of ruling, this is Diana," Walker said pointing her out, "she is Terrek's wife and will be your new queen."

Walker paused a moment. "But this decision must be their own. What say you, Commander Terrek? Will you accept the chance to rule Zyconia and lead all of us in the ways of the Maker."

Diana moved his hair from his face. Still in shock he looked down at the Sceptre in his hand, and thought about one of the last things Zyron told him on the altar of the Maker, 'take the sceptre and follow your destiny' he'd said: now he understood.

He raised his head proudly.

"Yes, I do accept," he said triumphantly.

A high-pitched ecstatic roar once again erupted from the crowd as they showed their approval.

Two rows of servants moved onto the platform. They fastened large elaborate gold threaded robes upon both Terrek and Diana, and placed jewel encrusted golden crowns upon their heads. Terrek held the sceptre out for all to see. Out of the corner of his eye he saw an elaborate carriage approaching the platform from the street. Behind it, many beautifully crested horses strode.

Walker looked at Terrek and Diana.

"From this day forward the Council relinquishes it's rule over Zyconia. I crown you King Terrek the first of Zyconia and you Queen Diana the first of Zyconia," Walker proclaimed.

He sensed their happiness.

"May your children rule as well as I know you will," he finished.

"Hurrah!" the roar of the crowd reached a nearly unattainable height.

172

Walker lead the newly weds off the platform. The soldiers that once served the Council pushed back the crowds to give them a path to the carriage. Terrek's former aides mounted the horses behind them as did the Council members, and they paraded through the streets toward the palace.

The crowds moved with them.

"Long live King Terrek! Long live Queen Diana!" the crowds cried.

Terrek moved his head close to Diana and looked at the sceptre.

"Who knows what tomorrow holds," he smiled.

She smiled as well, and put her arms around him. They closed their eyes and kissed.

Their future together would be very interesting indeed. But for now they had gained their just rewards and a rest from all their adventures. They were happy as the first true Rulers of Zyconia.

THE END

LEGENDS OF ZYCONIA
INVASION

Written and illustrated by

Hugh Stephens

FOREWORD/ACKNOWLEDGEMENTS:

In the last couple years my life has been filled with many trials and tribulations. Although I have changed in this time there is still a lot of myself within these two books. So if you really want to know me just read between the lines.

I still want to thank those I thanked at the beginning of Odyssey, particularly Melonie Gilchrist, Gina Kloetstra, Amanda Graham and Robert Allan. Other than these four there are a great number to which I'm still grateful, you all know who you are.

I'd like to thank Dylan Richards; you really are a true friend. A lot of the time you were on the same level of understanding as I was and I'm glad. We had a similar sense of humor and we looked at the world in the same way. I'm glad I know you.

I want to thank Catherine Secord for her support over the last little while. We've had quite a few conversations and I have discovered how much we have in common. Thank you for helping me through everything, it means a lot to know you're out there.

Last but certainly not least I would like to thank Jenn Windle. Without your help I don't know if my work would have ever reached the public in the form it has now. You are a very selfless person and I am very grateful.

Thank you all for your support and I'll see you at the release party!

TABLE OF CONTENTS:

PART 1

PROLOGUE: BOUNTIFUL KINGDOM

Terrek was king. He stood on the balcony of his new palace surveying the vast reaches of New Victory City. It had been nearly a year since his coronation and Zyconia had made incredible progress in that time.

It had taken some getting used to for he and Diana to fulfill their new roles both as King and queen and as husband and wife. But they were beginning to feel normal, even comfortable with their new royal positions. It just seemed that their work was never done, and they found it hard to make the difficult decisions.

In times past Terrek had often turned to Zyron for help but the seer was gone and Terrek had to move on with his life. He knew that Zyron was in a better existence now and no harm would ever come to him again.

With the threat of the Vicar gone, the people lived happily, free from persecution. Zyconia was no longer the volatile land it had once been. The Forest of Darkness had been burnt down, and all of the Vicar's raiders had been driven from Zyconia.

Zyconia had been divided into five distinct provinces; one controlled centrally by New Victory City known as Wercim, the others controlled by loyal subjects.

Celarus was now Duke of Letrinia, northwestern province of Zyconia, seemingly the most prosperous of

Zyconia's territories. His capital, recently built, was named Utona. Celarus had numerous mines set up, and so far the amount of gold retrieved was enormous.

Zachary, after his marriage to Juliana, became Duke of Separa, the southeastern province, and the most abundant agricultural territory in Zyconia. Terrek knew it would take some time for Timothy to accept Zachary as his new father. Terrek had attended Zachary and Juliana's recent marriage and it didn't seem as though Timothy was happy with the idea.

Ricsis became Duke of Astrana, northeastern province of Zyconia. Now that Terrek was King of Zyconia the Utopian people had decided to live in their above ground city, and bow before his rule. This is where Ricsis made his capital.

The southwestern province, now called Dernaca, possessed three cities required two administrators. Adam and Jason had become the Dukes of this territory. The destruction of the Forest of Darkness had created a large pass that was now opened through the Minotaur Mountains into southern uncharted territory. Adam and Jason had reported some contact with the inhabitants from the south and knew that another kingdom existed south of the mountains called Xanica. Terrek looked forward to peaceful relations with Xanica, and to meeting it's monarch.

Zyconia had already made contact with traders and merchants from other lands now unafraid to stop at Zyconian shores. The majority of these were from a large group of islands far away in the Northern Sea called the Radrialion Islands. The King of this ship-faring people was rumored to be Manakar, but Terrek had not yet come in contact with any ship sent from Manakar seeking relations with their kingdom.

Walker, formerly the most prominent Council member, had been appointed by Terrek as one of his two chief advisors. He was an intelligent individual and had guided Terrek with great wisdom. Terrek needed strong advisors, being very new to such enormous responsibility. Perrin was his second advisor, and although less experienced than Walker, Terrek trusted his judgment. He had forgiven Perrin for his once traitorous acts and trusted him wholeheartedly. He was confident this time that he knew where Perrin's loyalties lay.

John became military architectural advisor to Terrek and was in charge of weapon design. His ideas had revolutionized Terrek's armies, and given them great strength. Hemoth worked very closely with John to keep up to speed on his latest innovations.

Selate's children were now full grown and had become an elite part of Zyconia's vast new army. If there was a battle Selate and her children could be armored and carry crossbow men on their backs. They would also attack soldiers with their claws and beaks.

The new leader of all Zyconia's armies was Supreme Military Commander Hemoth. Zyconia was more organized than it had ever been, with outposts even in remote regions of the land. The largest section of the army, stationed at New Victory City had swelled to almost ten thousand in the last year, a fact in which Hemoth took great pride. He was also held leadership of the small fleet of ten warships that Terrek had constructed.

With the new organization of resources in Zyconia Jessica, now leader of all healers in Zyconia, she had a lot more knowledge and muscle at her disposal. Her knowledge of herbs and healing techniques had multiplied tenfold. She was now capable of much more than she thought possible.

Terrek's former aides now filled the roles of governing society, and they were leading Zyconia as no one else could.

Terrek smiled, the grand walls of New Victory City

catching his eye in the distance. Zyconia was a fully functional, bountiful kingdom.

CHAPTER 1: RETURN

$\mathbb{K}$ing Terrek sat at the head of a large table in the High chambers of his palace. Others around this table included his wife Queen Diana, Supreme Commander Hemoth, both Terrek's advisors: Perrin and Walker, Chief Military Architect John, and High healer Jessica. Also present were the administrators of Zyconia's few provinces: Duke Celarus, Duke Ricsis, Duke Adam, Duke Jason, Duke Zachary and his new wife Duchess Juliana. All were here to give reports to their king.

The administrators of Zyconia's provinces had made the journey to New Victory City and would soon be returning to their respective homes.

Terrek was pleased with how they had adapted to their new positions as he and Diana had. He turned to Hemoth and John first. Terrek enjoyed hearing about the growth and strength of the armies of Zyconia and of how the new weapons, created by John, could be used to give them an advantage over other armies that might attack Zyconia.

"Since Selate's children are now fully grown, and almost as intelligent as their mother, they are a valuable asset to our military forces. This allows us to initiate attacks from the air as well as from sea and land," pronounced Hemoth.

"Each avian can fly half a dozen soldiers into battle on his or her back. When armed with John's new multiple shot crossbows, they become an incredible danger to soldiers on the ground, peppering them with arrows," explains John.

"The avians are also able to attack soldiers themselves with their claws and strong beaks. We have an edge no army does," finished Hemoth.

"Very good," Terrek replied, "at least I know we aren't vulnerable to attacks from our surrounding neighbors."

Celarus was the next to speak.

"Letrinia continues to prosper Terrek. We have discovered vast amounts of gold throughout the northern part of the province. Most of this bounty is on route to New Victory City and the palace treasury."

"Thank you Celarus, that is very reassuring, but you know I have allowed you to take as much of Letrinia's wealth as you see fit in order to protect her from sea raids," Terrek said.

"So far there have been no attempts, and Letrinia is a fortress," assured Celarus.

"Well done," Terrek responded as he turned to Ricsis, "How is Astrana, Ricsis?"

The centaur smiled, "we are also prospering, although not as wealthy as Letrinia, everyone lives happily and the people of Utopia city have forever pledged their allegiance to you and the kingdom of Zyconia."

Terrek was pleased. He had been reluctant to force Utopia under his rule but they had not objected and seemed to welcome it.

"Separa is also benefiting our kingdom. The land is fertile and we have just retrieved an incredible harvest. No one in Zyconia will go hungry for many seasons," chimed in Zachary.

"This is excellent, everyone has done well," Terrek replied happily.

"Adam, Jason, is Dernaca under such organization?"

asked Terrek.

"Yes, much of Dernaca is peaceful, but we feel there is unrest in the most southern parts and are unsure of it's nature. We think that the people are fearful of the unknown Xanicans and there kingdom," said Adam.

"These people should be welcomed as allies," Terrek said.

"We understand that, but the few Xanicans that have come in contact with our people have been fairly hostile. We don't know if they welcome us as allies. It's as though they hate us, and we don't know why."

Grelkon scowled as he moved through the sky on another battle drill. He'd been told over and over that being an avian was an advantage. He hated the drills, and he hated the army, but his mother constantly rebuked him and scowled upon his misgivings. She told him that he should be grateful to king Terrek for their high position, and then she rambled off on stories of King Terrek's heroism and her rescue from the Caverns of Death.

So Grelkon continued, reluctantly, hating it.

"Grelkon, come on! Why are you moving so slowly?" asked Hecron, one of his brothers, who flew ahead of him in the air.

Grelkon sped to his brother's side, he disliked Hecron. Grelkon despised the way he obeyed every command their mother gave him. Never questioning, warming up to her like a good child, it made him sick. He looked at his brother as a weakling.

Both avians swooped down onto a large stone surface outside New Victory. Nearby a forest loomed and screeching could be heard from within.

"There's our sisters that were supposed to have been captured in this drill. We must move quietly if we are to fool our other siblings and get them free," Hecron whispered.

Not far away five of their avian brothers and sisters guarded three more of their avian sisters in a mock kidnapping. Grelkon was so tired of the drills.

"If they want us to join the army they should have us fighting battles not playing games," Grelkon sneered.

"Keep your voice down, they'll hear us! Anyway, Zyconia is at peace now. There are no more battles," Hecron frowned.

"That's why our king has us all running around like rats, even when there is no enemy. He's afraid of attack," Grelkon rasped.

"King Terrek is not cowardly in any way!" Hecron said loudly losing his temper.

"If you ask me, everyone in Zyconia has gotten so weak they wouldn't know what a true battle was anymore!" Grelkon looked at Hecron, "it's the same weakness I see in you."

Hecron exploded, lashing out at Grelkon with outstretched claws. Grelkon lifted from the ground on spread wings and ferociously struck his brother to the ground.

"I've had enough for one day," Grelkon said as he flew off into the skies.

Hecron got to his feet.

"Wait! The drill, we have to finish the drill..." his voice was lost on the winds.

Jessica, now the most influential healer in all Zyconia had enormous responsibilities, but she seemed to be seeing her queen a lot lately. Diana had been feeling fairly sick the past couple of days. Although Jessica had cures to many things, this she did not have a cure for. But, she had an idea as to the cause of the ailment.

"Terrek seems to fit the mold of King now doesn't he?" asked Jessica.

"That he does. It seems strange sometimes that he can be so gentle yet in extreme situations be so strong and authoritative," Diana smiled.

"Have you been eating regularly," Jessica asked offhand.

"Yes, I'm always eating well in the palace."

Jessica began smiling slightly as Diana watched her.

"You say the sickness usually manifests itself in the morning?" asked Jessica, removing a small flask from one of her pouches.

Diana looked at her.

"Yes, you've heard this all before I..." she stopped in mid-sentence, realization dawning on her.

"This should ease some of the nausea," Jessica said, as she handed Diana the flask that contained a greenish fluid, "but I'm afraid there's no cure for pregnancy."

Emperor Koiban sat in his throne room in Dystara city the capital of Xanica. He was happy. Once again Xanica was a strong land and it's people were united. The clans were satisfied with his rule and praised his judgment.

Finally, after nearly a century of clan wars, torn Xanica was reunited. Koiban couldn't have accomplished this without his new chancellor. It was his power that had cleansed the land and helped place him on the thrown.

Nearly a century before, Xanica's king had died leaving no heir. This set off the clan wars, all clan leaders vying for the thrown, and when they died, their children carried the torch. Koiban's clan had always been the strongest and had been one of the few that survived since the beginning of the wars. At last, a few years ago Koiban had gained the respect and allegiance of two other clans and had created safety for their families. But his chancellor had brought on the real move to the throne.

Koiban never knew from what land he hailed but he had appeared before him nearly a year ago and had offered to help him take the throne without resistance. Koiban had agreed.

For months, this mysterious man used his powers to heal the sick and injured, to raise crops to incredible growth, all in Koiban's name. This helped recruit more soldiers for Koiban's army. The clans that were not allied with Koiban saw what he was doing and slowly gave in, seeing their families happy and in good health. They decided on peace and succumbed to his leadership because of what he could do for them.

Koiban became emperor as his new chancellor built his armies and performed vast miracles across the land. Xanica had become strong. His Chancellor had even given Xanica it's first religion, and had anointed a powerful high priest named Yirdak. Koiban questioned this new religion at first, but concluded that someone who could accomplish so much good couldn't be wrong. Indeed, Xanica had been driven to the pinnacle of strength. He was eternally grateful to the Vicar.

CHAPTER 2: UNDERGROUND

Selate watched Grelkon swoop unto the balcony of their castle home. Not far away was an incredible view of King Terrek's palace.

He looked at his mother apprehensively.

"Your brother told me what happened," she said angrily.

"What of it? He attacked me," replied Grelkon rudely.

"But you provoked it! You were doing it intentionally. You know how to anger him. You've got to know where to draw the line. Your arrogance and instability are going to destroy you if you don't," she reasoned.

Grelkon moved into the open tower and sat in his living area.

He looked at her.

"Very well, I will carry on like everyone else," he folded.

She looked at him again and turned toward a nearby door to exit.

"Goodnight Grelkon, rest well," she murmured as she exited.

"Goodnight mother," angrily he watched her go.

The throne room of Xanica was empty except for it's monarch Emperor Koiban. He sat contemplating the changes he would make in the new dynasty now that it had attained such strength. There was now a large army of necromancers. The Vicar as Chancellor had appointed Yirdak as their High Priest. The Vicar had also taken the liberty of forming a vast army of select warriors as an elite force for Koiban's protection. This was in addition to his allied clan army, which was also an incredible asset.

Koiban's thoughts were interrupted as an armor-clad soldier with a royal shield and a fiery beard entered the chambers with a violent shove on the main doors.

"Koiban I am tired of this," the man yelled.

The man's name was Bratain. He was General of the allied clan armies and had always supported Koiban's leadership, until now.

"The Vicar is going to corrupt what little order we've managed to bring to Xanica before he arrived. The other clan leaders may be blind to that, but you've got to see it," Bratain pleaded.

Koiban looked at him, "Bratain, Xanica was always falling apart, we needed help to restore it. What the Vicar is doing for our land is a miracle."

Bratain, angered, moved forward slamming his gauntlet into a nearby ceremonial brazier. The red coals crumbled across the stone floor.

"I've seen the Vicar's necromancers do things that are far beyond decency. I won't stand by any longer. Don't you see what necromancy represents? Even you have one of these tiny altars now," he said pointing at the fallen brazier.

"It can't be as terrible as all that. Look at the good they've done," Koiban said.

"If you don't rid this kingdom of the Vicar I will no longer support you. I will leave Xanica," Bratain stared piercingly at Koiban.

Koiban's face went stone cold white.

"Bratain, be sensible about this -" he was cut of in mid-sentence.

"I'm serious," Bratain asserted.

Koiban lowered his gaze.

"All right," Bratain said, "but remember how loyal the clan armies are to me. If I leave, the majority of them will follow!" he finished as he stormed out of the room.

"Bratain, wait!" Koiban yelled, but he was gone.

The Vicar entered a door nearby.

"LET HIM GO. I WILL BRING YOU MORE ARMIES. I HAVE ALREADY SENT WORD TO MY HOMELAND. NUMEROUS WARSHIPS WILL BE SENT WITH NEW SOLDIERS TO SUPPORT YOU," the Vicar rasped.

"Yes, but who will replace Bratain, he was an incredible General and a close friend," Koiban said sadly.

"HE DOESN'T REALIZE THE POTENTIAL OF YOUR EMPIRE, IT'S TIME TO MOVE ON TO MORE IMPORTANT MATTERS," he replied.

"It's not that easy to discard someone who's been so loyal, " Koiban said back.

"PERHAPS, BUT IT'S FOR THE GOOD OF THE EMPIRE THAT YOU CONTINUE," he finished.

"HAVE YOU THOUGHT ABOUT WHAT WE DISCUSSED?" the Vicar walked a little closer.

Koiban shifted in his chair. "Do you really think that Xanica has a chance of conquering another kingdom just after we've come out of civil war?"

"YES. ONCE I HAVE ASSEMBLED THE FORCES MYSELF I WILL HELP YOU TO CAPTURE THE LAND," he stated.

Koiban thought for a moment.

"I feel a bit uneasy about this. I have no wish to persecute any nation of people," Koiban explained.

The Vicar scoffed, "YOU'RE NOT. THE RACE OF THIS NORTHERN LAND IS TYRANICALLY

IMMORAL AND EVIL. SOMEONE MUST STEP IN AND DO SOMETHING ABOUT THEM. I HAVE ALREADY WARNED THE PEOPLE NOT TO TRUST ANY THEY ENCOUNTER IN THE NORTHERN PARTS OF XANICA. ONLY YOU CAN BRING ORDER TO THEIR CHAOS AND HELP THEM BY MAKING THEM PART OF XANICA."

Koiban hesitated for a few moments, taking this in.

"If you believe I should help these people, I suppose I should," Koiban said finally.

"AS YOU WISH, SOON THE KINGDOM OF ZYCONIA WILL BE APPENDED TO YOUR REALM."

A father.

Terrek could hardly believe Diana, but it was true. He was to have a child. He and Diana had only been together for a year, and already a birth!

He smiled. Diana would make an excellent mother. She knew what a sad childhood was like, and she wouldn't let her child go through that. But he wondered if he would father the child well. He wasn't sure.

Diana had once said that he was good with children because of his good-natured attitude toward Juliana's little boy, Timothy. But he wondered if he would ever be as good a father as he'd once been. He knew that things would be different now than they had been once. Diana and his child wouldn't suffer the same tragedy as Beverly and Jonathan. Zyconia was different now and he was in command.

Terrek sat for a moment gazing at his sceptre.

Whenever he saw it he thought about Zyron. He missed his guardian. Zyron had been an old man and his health had been failing, but deep down Terrek had felt that Zyron was indestructible. But everyone dies. Life is a terminal illness.

14

He took comfort in the knowledge that Zyron was probably watching him and protecting him now that he was with the Maker. This was the knowledge that kept Terrek's demeanor as king in check.

He was young and unskilled as a king, but he was gaining experience. Soon he would learn not only to rule his kingdom well, but he would learn to be a parent again.

And as he became familiar with his role as king in the years ahead, he would also have the task of training his child for the position. He would have an heir. His child, male or female would someday rule in their father's place, how well they ruled would depend on both he and Diana's teaching. He knew his child would rule well.

He sat in silence and wondered what they would name the child.

His mother angered him. She continuously took sides with his siblings, in everything. And she wondered why he disliked spending time with them.

A strong wind blew inconsistently through the trees and shrubs below. Grelkon had never flown this far from New Victory City before, but he felt calmed by flight. His wings had grown stronger than those of his brothers and sisters. While they pranced around at home or slept, he flew. They did nothing of any physical nature other than their pathetic battle drills. Grelkon scowled as he thought of them.

Hecron had attacked him, yet his mother had treated him as the attacker. True he had shamed Hecron, but it was the truth, as Grelkon saw it. He felt like he craved something that was just out of his reach. But what was it?

Grelkon peered down through the tropical vegetation below. A few ruined stone structures could be seen below. Out of curiosity, he moved in closer. May as well take a rest before heading home, he thought. His body a pinwheel,

15

he careened downward from the sky.

The structure had been built in the distant past, long before Terrek's kingdom, or the Council ruled Zyconia. Overgrowth covered most of it. A large pavilion stretched out in front of it. The doorway was a dark oval against the smooth stone wall of the building. It was easily large enough for his frame.

Slipping through, he entered the darkness. Upon his entrance several oil lamps ignited, and a cloaked figure moved slowly from the darkness.

"Welcome," the man said.

"What is this place?" Grelkon asked.

"You would probably never guess that this was once an avian sanctuary," replied the man, shocking Grelkon.

"Long ago many of your kind lived here but they were eventually destroyed by other beings both monster and men," the stranger said.

Grelkon looked at him.

"You mean by your kind," he sneered.

"I'm not from this land," the man said to him.

"Then how do you know what happened here?" Grelkon said looking around at ancient artifacts cluttering the room.

"I know many things, Grelkon," he said looking toward the door.

"How do you know my name? Are you a seer, old man?" Grelkon stared at him.

"I have very deep powers," the man replied.

Grelkon rested himself on the stone floor observing the figure closely as he continued.

"I'm very familiar with your kind. In my homeland your kind once thrived. They were feared for their strength and power. They were much stronger than the weak ones

16

that once inhabited this dwelling. I see that power in you Grelkon, if only you'd release it."

The avian looked across the room at the stranger, hesitating. For the first time he was a bit confused but somehow grasped what the stranger meant.

"I - I don't know what you mean," Grelkon said quietly.

"You are different from your brothers and sisters aren't you? You want something more, something that eludes you. I think what you want is the power that has been stifled inside you since birth. You know it's dark but you still want to embrace it," he voiced.

Grelkon lowered his head, "I - I'm not sure."

"There is a land to the south, a place where I can teach you to understand. A place where you will be free to be what you want, without restriction. All you have to do is come with me," he stared at Grelkon, making him think about what he was saying.

He felt uneasy but inside he yearned for something new. That is what he was being offered, but he had little idea where the stranger was going.

He lifted his gaze to the cloaked stranger, "I'm unsure. I don't think I can leave."

"If you ever change your mind, I will be here occasionally. Simply return to this place and we will make the journey together. I sincerely hope to see you again. Don't be a slave like your siblings. You've got to allow yourself to live," he beckoned.

Grelkon turned and moved toward the door. Realizing he didn't know the man's name, he turned back.

"What's your - name?"

Nothing could be seen but a thin layer of mist where the stranger had stood.

CHAPTER 3: FIRST DEATH

Koiban stood gazing out into Dystara's harbor. Xanica's capital was alive with excitement at the arrival of allies from Wicketai. He could see that the Vicar's homeland was indeed powerful. Large, weapon-clad warships slowly slid into the bay, the wicketus fluttering above their masts. Koiban had counted Nearly two dozen vessels filled to the brim with soldiers. Besides Koiban's soldiers, crowds of people had gathered to greet the ships. Next to him, the Vicar looked on.

"YOU SEE, YOUR MAJESTY, I HAVE GIVEN YOU WHAT YOU NEED," he said.

"Indeed," Koiban said.

The lead ship moved toward the deepened waterfront and a large bridge was extended. The soldiers on the ship were lined up at attention. But instead of a military captain, the first to greet Koiban and the Vicar was a dark haired woman accompanied by a small boy.

"Greetings. I am Kridelia," she said softly, extending her hand.

"Greetings," moving forward Koiban kissed her hand.

She was cold. Her hand. Her body. Her gaze. She was cold. Her hair was dark, as were her eyes. Her body was slender and for some reason it reminded him of a cobra.

Upon seeing her you wouldn't have thought she belonged in the position as leader of these soldiers, but if anyone could instill fear in an enemy, it was her.

"GREETINGS KRIDELIA, YOU WERE ABLE TO BRING THE FORCES NEEDED," the Vicar stated.

"Yes," the woman smiled.

"Xanica thanks you for your extremely generous contribution to it's forces. It must have been difficult to gather so many soldiers in such a short time," Koiban said.

She faced him again with her deep eyes. "Yes, but when the Vicar told me of the need, I came as quickly as I could," she replied.

The small boy stood beside her, a cold statue. Koiban had never seen such control from such a small child. It was erie. The boy's face and body were thin and pale; he had the dark eyes of his mother.

"And what is your name, child?" Koiban knelt in front of the child.

The boy's eyes affixed on him and he moved to raise his arm, which was grasped quickly by his mother.

"My son's name is Koran, he can't speak Emperor."

"That is unfortunate," Koiban frowned looking at the boy whose eye's had once again taken on a vacant stare.

"I'll have my military commanders guide your soldiers to their new homes in the city, for now you will accompany the Vicar and I to my palace," Koiban explained.

Koiban beckoned the Vicar and Kridelia to follow. The Vicar walked close to Kridelia as the boy followed behind.

"These forces aren't enough, we will have to receive help from elsewhere," Kridelia whispered.

The Vicar turned

"WE WILL."

The walls of the cave were dark and menacing. These

19

caverns had once covered a vast reach of subterranean territory beneath both Zyconia and Xanica. But surface men who feared the underground beings had collapsed most of the caverns.

They were no different than surface men except for their pale white skin and greater physical strength. Once, their people had numbered in the hundreds of thousands. Now a lot of that kin had been lost and the beings had been driven to deeper caverns beneath the Minotaur Mountains where few men roamed.

When they realized how they were hated because they were different, they were forced to protect themselves. Their female leader, Delara, led her people to embrace the dark arts. It was this power that halted their extinction by men. In the past they were referred to as the Whitesouls.

Few from the surface had seen them in more than twenty years, until now.

The Vicar had been one of the few. Delara's search for a power to protect her people had taken her only so far. During the time when the Vicar lived in the Forest of Darkness he discovered her people and he lead her much farther into the dark arts. Now she was more powerful than the followers of the former Dark Circle had been. Now the Vicar saw a use for her people.

Slowly they entered the subterranean throne room. Panning the room, the Vicar and Kridelia took in their surroundings. The walls were carved out of solid rock and torches lined them. Dark shadows flickered about the room dimming everything. The floor was dry, but in the corridor behind them much of the caverns was covered with patches of dark mud. Beside them stood several pale guards. Before them perched upon her thrown was Delara.

"DELARA, IT'S GOOD TO SEE YOU, AND GOOD TO FEEL THAT THE POWER I'VE GIVEN YOU HASN'T GROWN DULL," the Vicar rasped.

"Yes, I have used my new found power to raise my

20

army to the pinnacle of fighting strength. They are incredible warriors now. I owe you a great debt for that," Delara's eyes were even.

The Vicar realized his advantage.

"I'M GLAD TO HEAR YOU SAY THAT, I KNOW HOW HONOUR BOUND YOU AND YOUR PEOPLE ARE TO SUCH THINGS, I HAVE COME TO COLLECT ON YOUR DEBT."

"Wha - what do you mean?" Delara said uneasily.

He walked forward Kridelia watching him, "I'VE HELPED YOU AQUIRE THE POWER TO PROTECT YOUR DOMAIN AND NOW YOU MUST HELP ME."

"How?" she asked.

"I'M GOING TO ATTACK ZYCONIA. I NEED YOU TO HELP ME WITH THE INVASION."

Delara's face lost all composure as her mind flowed against forgotten memories. She thought about this.

"I don't think it's in my people's best interest to be included in a war," she said.

"I DON'T THINK YOUR FATHER WOULD SEE MUCH HONOUR IN REFUSING SOMEONE TO WHOM YOU OWE SO MUCH," he rasped.

"Don't speak of the dead with your scheming tongue," she yelled. Delara stood, angered, and brought her arm up glowing blue.

The Vicar lifted his palm in her general direction. Delara fell back into her chair pinned by an unseen restraint. Her arm returned to normal as she struggled against the invisible force. Her guards also seemed to be trapped in position.

The Vicar came closer.

"YOU'RE VERY STRONG IN THE DARK ARTS MY DEAR, BUT NEVER THINK THAT THE STUDENT CAN OUTWIT THE TEACHER!"

She stopped struggling and the Vicar released her and her guards. She raised her hands to signal the guards to remain where they were.

"DON'T DESPAIR, YOUR PEOPLE WILL ALSO BENEFIT. WHEN CONTROL OF ZYCONIA IS MINE YOUR PEOPLE WILL BE GIVEN MUCH LAND FOR NEW SUBTERRANEAN DWELLINGS OR YOU MAY LIVE ABOVE GROUND, I WILL SEE THAT NO HARM COMES TO ANY OF YOUR PEOPLE. YOU WILL HAVE YOUR OWN AUTONOMY."

Delara pondered this information.

"If you give me your word that my people will benefit from this, than I will pledge my assistance," Delara conceded.

"ON MY HONOUR, YOUR PEOPLE WILL BENEFIT GREATLY QUEEN DELARA," he said.

"Very well. My army will await your command. May we be successful," she finished.

The Vicar and Kridelia exited the throne room escorted by two guards.

Delara sat alone. What was she doing rushing into position for more bloodshed, she had experienced too much death in her life. She didn't want this, but was honor bound. Delara hoped that she could trust his word.

In Koiban's throne room three individuals sat discussing a ruthless and traitorous plan. Koiban was absent. Nearby sat Kridelia's son Koran. The three were sitting crosslegged on the floor: The Vicar, Kridelia and Yirdak.

Yirdak wore a dark tunic and a blood red cape. His hair was black with twinges of white. He had derived his powers from a small group of witches that had raised him in southern Xanica. They were killed when he was a small boy, but they had left him a gift.

The Vicar had discovered Yirdak. As an incredibly powerful necromancer he had brought him into royal company. He hated Koiban but was loyal to the Vicar who had built him up as a necromancer spiritual leader throughout Xanica. Now he had a large army of necromancers.

"WE ARE ALMOST READY. I HAVE INCREDIBLE FORCES NOW. YIRDAK'S ARMY, THE ARMY YOU COMMAND FROM WICKETAI KRIDELIA, DELARA'S ARMY A SMALL ARMY OF KILLERS AND THEIVES I'VE COLLECTED IN THE PAST YEAR THROUGHOUT XANICA AND WHAT'S LEFT OF THE CLAN ARMIES," he finished.

"Which isn't much," continued Yirdak, "Bratain left with a great deal of clan forces taking many of Koiban's warships. Maybe you shouldn't have let him live."

"HE WASN'T A MAN TO BE DECEIVED EASILY," the Vicar said.

"But Koiban is. When are we going to execute him?" she said quietly.

"WE MUST ENTER BATTLE FIRST. ANY SOLDIER WHO IS STILL LOYAL WILL BE IN THE FRONT LINE OF OFFENSE AND WON'T BE HERE TO KNOW WHAT HAS HAPPENED TO THEIR PRESCIOUS KING. THEN I WILL FIND HIS MAJESTY AND TELL HIM THAT HE'S BEING DETHRONED TO MAKE WAY FOR A NEW KING, MYSELF. BOTH XANICA AND ZYCONIA UNDER ONE RULE," rasped the Vicar.

Nearby, they heard a creak and saw a door move ever so slightly. The Vicar looked at Yirdak and Kridelia his eyes glowing.

Frecan rushed down the hall and into his chambers. He knew what they were planning and he had to tell his friend Koiban, but first he had to send a message away.

23

Hemoth stood before King Terrek.

"We've been receiving reports that large warships have been seen traveling from Wicketai to Xanica. I'm worried Terrek. If they form a military alliance with Wicketai that may pose a great threat to Zyconia," he said.

"Then maybe it's time we made contact with Xanica ourselves. We must know what kind of people they are. If they're mislead or whether they're just like those from Wicketai," Terrek said.

"What do you wish me to do?" asked Hemoth.

"I suppose a military contact is out of the question. If they feel threatened you never know what might happen. Send a messenger with a message of goodwill and ask to meet with them. If they prefer I will talk face to face with their king," Terrek decided.

"You're a young king but a very wise one King Terrck," he said emphasizing the King.

"Why thank you, Supreme Commander Hemoth," he said smiling.

Carefully Frecan wrote out the message. He knew he had no time waste if he truly wished to stop their plan. He wrote the words very thickly to make sure they could not be blurred or washed off, then he handed it to a servant standing nearby.

"You know where to go, waste no time or Emperor Koiban will have your head," he said strongly.

The servant left the room.

Frecan moved to his bed placing the pen and paper beneath. Then he turned and picked up his walking stick. He'd been in the king's service for many years. When his father died he'd been a very close friend.

He stopped for a moment to decide where Koiban would be right then. Wasting little time he realized that he was in the courtyard. This was the time he always reserved for walking in the courtyard. He turned toward the door.

Suddenly the door swept open and there stood the Vicar, Necromancer Yirdak and Kridelia. The Vicar's eyes glowed yellow with malice.

"Guards!" Frecan bellowed, his voice merely echoed in the hallway beyond.

The Vicar moved forward, a dark towering figure shadowing the frailty that was Frecan. The old man stood in front of him in defiance of growing fear.

"You won't get away with this," he said.

The Vicar said nothing. In a sudden attempt to run past the Vicar Frecan felt the taste of his own blood from within. Carefully, calculatingly the Vicar brought a large sword up through Frecan's torso and lifted it from the floor.

A scream hung in the old man's throat. Pain and the realization that he was going to die destroyed Frecan's composure as the Vicar, with great strength held the sword out in front of him. Frecan's body clung suspended upon the blade.

"Your time will come," he gasped through dying breath.

"Ptuu," the amalgamation of saliva and blood splattered in the Vicar's face. In anger, the Vicar threw Frecan against the wall and took back his blade. The Vicar and his minions withdrew from the room as Frecan's vision blurred. And then he was gone.

CHAPTER 4: DECLARATION

$\mathfrak{G}$relkon was tired. Tired of the army stupidity. Tired of his siblings and mother. Tired of his life. He had to have something else. Perhaps what he had been offered was worth leaving Zyconia for. As he reached his home he shook the rain from his feathers. It was storming, and the weather had made him miserable. He'd abandoned the drills, which had been worse. Quickly he went inside to his dwelling.

"How can you constantly shirk your responsibilities, I don't understand you," it was Selate, she was very angry, but Grelkon didn't care.

"I have no wish to be a soldier, not in this pathetic kingdom," he roared.

Selate looked at him dumbfounded.

"We all owe our lives to King Terrek! He rescued me from a spell which could have held me forever."

"You owe him, not me!" he said as his hate began to break through at the sound of their king's name.

"I want another life, I won't return to anymore drills," Grelkon asserted.

"Yes, you will," Selate commanded, placing her wing on his shoulder firmly.

Grelkon looked into her eyes as his blood reached it's

boiling point, "No I won't!"

Incredibly, he pushed her into a nearby table as it collapsed. She looked at him, crying from the floor. Hecron entered the room as Grelkon fled back the way he'd come, into the storm.

"Mother are you all right?" asked Hecron, helping Selate to her feet. Behind him another brother, Fernok, had also heard the commotion and come.

"What's going on?" asked Fernok.

"Did - did Grelkon hurt you?" Hecron asked perplexed.

"Something is wrong with your brother. Please Hecron go find him. Bring him back if you can," Selate quickly replied.

"Of course mother," he said as he flew away into the storm.

Fernok helped Selate back to her room.

He hated her. She deserved it. His life here was over. He would accept the old man's offer. Rage burned inside him as he spiraled through the wind and rain, unafraid of the thunder and lightning.

Soon he felt his brother behind him. Didn't his mother give up? Why couldn't they just leave him alone?

"Wait, Grelkon you must come home," Hecron bellowed.

"Go away," Grelkon yelled back to him as he began flying faster.

Hecron tried to keep pace but seemed at a loss.

"If something is wrong, mother will fix it. If you're sick let her help you."

"That's what you think isn't it! That I'm sick! You're an idiot Hecron, go home!" Grelkon's loathing grew.

"I'm not going home without you!" Hecron yelled angrily.

Grelkon suddenly turned and beat his wing across his brother.

"Go away!" he screamed.

He went to turn but Hecron wrapped his wings around him. They fell from the skies wrapped in combat. As they struck the ground they began hitting one another. Then all at once Grelkon's rage exploded.

"I told you to leave me alone!" he screamed as he descended upon his brother biting and clawing with an untamable ferocity.

Screeches escaped Hecron's throat as Grelkon tore and pecked deep into his flesh, beating relentlessly upon his bruised body. All the rage he felt was released as he attacked again and again succumbing to his darkest instincts.

"Go away!" he yelled as he pulverized his brother's body. His throat was horse and his beak and claws stung from the assault. Soon he tired and drew back, his energy drained.

He looked down at the body of his brother, unmoving. Both Grelkon and Hecron were peppered with blood, but the blood belonged to Hecron.

"I told you to leave me alone, why didn't you listen?" he roared hoarsely looking toward the sky.

"Why doesn't anyone ever listen to me?" he said in a low tone resting his gaze on the broken form of his brother.

The rain beat down upon Grelkon washing blood from his face. He let everything overwhelm him.

Hecron's eyes were vacant. Grelkon moved away slowly, his face cold. He stood looking down. Then all at once he flew away. Grelkon had torn too deep.

Hecron was dead.

All the armies were in position and the signal to begin

invasion had just been received. Once a foothold in Zyconia was established the Vicar was supposed to visit the army encampments. Delara and her soldiers were already moving inland to raid and conquer some of the outlying castles of southern Zyconia. They had the element of surprise on their side.

The Castle Alexium had only be taken once and that was by the Vicar when he dwelled in the Forest of Darkness. But now it was a very peaceful spot. Until this untimely moment.

Suddenly guards atop Alexium's walls were stricken with streams of arrows. Soldiers were instantly called to arms climbing the walls to protect them. When they reached the top they saw what faced them, and knew the castle was lost. The conquest of Zyconia had begun.

Koran sat in a dark room with his mother Kridelia.

Kridelia was a powerful witch and had joined forces with the Vicar for more than the conquest of Zyconia. She had come to exact revenge on Terrek. Her husband Murack had been part of the Dark circle and had been killed by Terrek. A dark irony clouded this revenge because Murack had been responsible for the death of Terrek's former wife, Beverly. Kridelia wanted to finish what her husband had started, only she would destroy Terrek. First they would take his kingdom, then his new queen and finally she would torture him to death.

Koran looked at his mother. He was merely a puppet. She had conjured evil spirits into his body. She felt no love for him and hated him because he questioned Wicketai's society and his parent's dark powers. If he were not her child she would have slit his throat.

Terrek sat in his thrown room at a small banquet table enjoying the mellow flowing music of a lute. John had acquired a new talent and a delightful one it was. Around the table sat Queen Diana, Supreme Commander Hemoth, Chief Advisors Perrin and Walker, John, Jessica and visiting from his province, Celarus.

"You play beautifully John," said Hemoth.

"Thank you," he said continuing.

Terrek smiled but suddenly felt a cold feeling come over himself. He looked around. No one seemed to notice. He recognized something, he thought, something too intangible to be real, but it was.

Suddenly the doors of his throne room erupted with numerous guards.

"Forgive the intrusion," the leader said but your messenger has returned he said agitatedly.

The messenger with help of the guards staggered into the room. Terrek rose from his chair in shock, as did the others. The man had been beaten severely and blood marred his brow. Terrek helped the man to a chair.

"I'm sorry your majesty, I tried to relay a message of peace but they wouldn't listen," he cried.

Terrek felt he had made his first real mistake as king by sending this man to be maimed by what was obviously a very dangerous race.

"Jessica, take him to your healers," he said quietly.

"Wait!" the messenger cried as he took a letter bearing a seal from his pouch, "they left me alive to give you this."

Two healers carried the messenger away. Terrek opened the seal and stared at it's surface. Everyone saw his eyes change.

"What is it Terrek," asked Diana.

31

Terrek looked up.

"A letter from Emperor Koiban, of Xanica," he said evenly, "a declaration of war."

CHAPTER 5: REAWAKENING

Hecron should have stayed away. It was his fault.
Grelkon would wipe away the memory of his past to
prepare for his future. Now that he had traveled with the
old man to Xanica's capital he saw what strength was.

The old man was the Vicar. The same Vicar that had
once nearly conquered Zyconia, had once nearly killed
King Terrek and his mother. He knew this, but it made little
difference. He hated them, now seemingly more than ever.
The Vicar promised to help him erase his past and give him
something more. He would be transformed, and then the
Vicar would use his powers to create duplicates from his
body. He would be the grand leader of an entire army of
Avians, and then he would lead them into battle against
Zyconia. He would fight for the Vicar.

He would destroy with the hate that had given him
strength to kill Hecron. He would help the Vicar conquer
Zyconia and he would look down on those that looked
down on him. He would help ravage Zyconia. He would
destroy his family. And he would have no remorse.

Terrek stood, head lowered. How could this have
happened? First a declaration of war, and then a murder of

one so close to him he felt that part of his family had died. He had known Hecron. He was a very moral and honorable soldier.

Nearby, the funeral procession was taking place. Many people from the cit y had come. Some from the army, some out of respect for the avians. Hemoth was there. He had trained the Avians and had known Hecron personally. He was shocked to learn what had happened. All of Hecron's family in a long line placed a hand on Hecron as his body was slowly carried toward his grave to be laid to rest. All of Hecron's family had attended. All but Selate.

Terrek would never forget the look on her face when she saw his broken body brought back by two of his brothers. She simply couldn't handle it. She knew he had been killed by her other son Grelkon. She had gone into some emotional fit that had totally overwhelmed her. She'd locked herself in her private chambers, where she remained. She'd been in there for more than a day and would not come out to eat nor would she let anyone inside.

When one of her children tried to tell her through the door that Hecron would be placed to rest in a crypt, she began screaming that he must have a grave, that he must go back to the earth. Terrek obliged. A large stake-like iron marker had been fashioned with Hecron's name bronzed upon it. He hoped following her wishes would help her to attend the funeral. He hoped she was all right.

Koiban had sworn to behead the person guilty of Frecan's murder. As of yet, the Vicar couldn't find the assassin, but he said he would find him. Frecan had been a close and Koiban was shocked to learn that one of his most noble subjects could be killed right in his palace. Dealing with pain wasn't alien to him; Xanica had just resurfaced from civil war not long before. Losing family and friends was common throughout his life. It had made him much less sensitive than he'd been once, but there were always chinks in his emotional armor; one of them had been Frecan.

Koiban had discovered that an Avian had been brought to Dystara by the Vicar and, since the Vicar didn't feel it was necessary to keep him informed, came to see what was going on. Upon entering the throne room Koiban became uneasy. The Avian stood in front of the Vicar conversing with him.

"May I speak wit h you, Vicar," called Koiban.

The Vicar turned and moved toward him.

"WHAT IS IT?" he said insubordinately.

"Can you tell me why you've brought one of them here?" Koiban said, pointing to Grelkon, "and why you aren't looking for Frecan's killer?"

"I HAVE SOLDIERS SEARCHING FOR THE MURDERER, AND GRELKON IS HERE TO HELP GAIN OUR VICTORY," the Vicar said, showing contempt.

Koiban looked at the Vicar. Something had changed; he wasn't the pleasing servant he had been when he came to Xanica.

"When you have the time, I think we'd better discuss some issues. I think that maybe we should listen to the Zyconians. Maybe recall our forces. We must talk soon," he said leaving the room.

"AS YOU WISH," the Vicar sneered.

The Vicar spun back and approached Grelkon.

Koiban didn't realize his powerlessness before the Vicar. All loyal guards in the palace had been taken to the front and replaced with men who served the Vicar. But the Vicar knew that Koiban could still stir unrest among the people, his death would be soon.

"Is that the Emperor of Xanica," asked Grelkon.

"YES, BUT SOON I WILL REPLACE HIM AND

RULE XANICA MYSELF," he said.

Grelkon knew what he had in mind but had no qualms about it. He had chosen the Vicar and wouldn't question his actions.

"I'VE INSTILLED AS MUCH COMBAT STRENGTH IN YOU AS I CAN, ARE YOU PREPARED FOR ME TO USE MY POWERS TO MAKE DUPLICATES OF YOU," asked the Vicar.

"Yes," said Grelkon without emotion.

The strength he now possessed had come at a cost. It had warped his form slightly. He was darker, his feathers deep black. His claws were longer, sharper, and much stronger. He had been given small, razor sharp teeth within his beak. Grelkon had been the least attractive of his family anyway, his appearance little to him.

The Vicar raised his arms high over his head and began chanting with vitriolic passion. His words, unlike any Grelkon had ever heard, appeared to rock the very throne room itself. Swiftly his arms and hands began rippling with a supernatural glow as drafts from nowhere moved about the room rattling braziers and other inanimate objects.

The sound of far away rumbling reached his ears. Slowly the commotion around him grew as an undeniable mixture of uneasiness and excitement coursed through his veins.

Grelkon suddenly felt incredible physical and mental stress. A burning sensation flooded his brain. And he felt like his body was being torn apart from the inside out. His vision was clouded with both tears and foreimages of something he was not sure existed. He now was nearly completely detached from everything around him as a high pitched buzzing sound filled his entire hearing perception. He slowly looked down at himself and became aware that his wings seemed to be doubling, that his entire body was being duplicated, the new form was being extracted from

36

his.

He could taste success. The Vicar knew that all he had to do was hold the power a few moments longer and they would accomplish the first of many creations. He stared at Grelkon's body, suddenly his head seemed to fade as it moved into two distinct heads. The Vicar concentrated as the unseperated siamese twin mass of Grelkon and his counterpart struggled and vibrated in pain. Striking the floor they writhed in agony. Then with a burst of intense light they were no longer one entity.

Terrek and Diana stood on the grand balcony of Terrek's palace watching the march through the streets of New Victory City. A large force was being sent to fight the invaders from Xanica, Terrek prayed they'd move quickly.

"I received a message from Adam and Jason, the Xanicans are driving hard into Dernaca," he said gravely.

Diana squeezed his arm in comfort and love.

"But Celarus, Ricsis and Zachary have sent reinforcements as you've commanded, surely this will halt them," she reasoned.

"They believe they can hold them away from their cities with the reinforcements, perhaps they will be able to drive them back as well," he said optimistically.

Celarus came onto the balcony and moved toward them.

"Letrinia has sent a large force directly to Dernaca, I sent a message telling them to stop for nothing. Don't worry, these foreigners will be pushed out of your kingdom," he said loyally.

"Thank you," he smiled at Celarus, "I hope your right."

"I understand Ricsis is coming to New Victory City tomorrow," Celarus gazed out toward the gates.

"Yes, he wants to have first hand knowledge of the

battles, so that he can help in any way he can," Terrek replied.

"You can't say we aren't loyal," Celarus smirked.

"No, and with so much loyalt y who can really be defeated," Terrek said smiling.

Hemoth walked swiftly behind him and took his attention.

"I'm sorry to be the bearer of bad news but we've just received word that Separa has also been attacked," he said darkly.

Terrek lowered his head.

"The soldiers of outlying castles are being attacked by a brutally savage race of pale white skinned beings," he continued.

"White skinned beings," Celarus blurted in a shocked tone.

"Yes. The army commanders think they live underground in caves in the Minotaur mountains. Some say there were once a few colonies of this subterranean race in Zyconia."

Celarus became agitated, "I - I think I'll send a message to Letrinia to send the majority of our army. If you'll excuse me, Terrek," he said and hurried away.

They watched him go.

"I wonder what that was all about," Diana frowned.

Terrek pondered this as well but he had to move quickly.

"See that we send another force to Separa, and send a message to Astrania and tell Ricsis to send a larger force as well," he ordered Hemoth.

"At once," he answered leaving them.

Terrek looked at Diana.

"This may be more serious than we thought".

They met in an old bear cave.

He was fourteen and while exploring the forest he hurt his leg and took shelter in the cave to escape the rain. Although when he first saw her he was frightened, he overcame the fear. Her skin was pale white, very different from his pink. She was gentle and innocent, and very beautiful.

She helped him clean his wound.

Even when the rain stopped he stayed for a long time talking with her. She lived beneath the ground and had never seen the surface world. So he told her everything about it. The animals, the plants, the trees, everything beautiful that she'd missed by staying below. And in turn she told him about the world below. She told him how strict and pigheaded her father was, and how he always told her never to go to the surface because it was dangerous.

They laughed together and enjoyed eachothers company. Before they parted they agreed to meet again at the same cave.

They continued to return to the cave day after day. Each time he would bring her something from the surface. She was still too scared to come with him to the mouth of the cave to see for herself. He brought her a few colored leaves, a piece of bark, some grass and strange shiny pebbles from a brook. She treasured them as though they were priceless jewels. And she gave him a small amulet that had belonged to her mother. They were so close that they could speak about anything without worrying what the other would say.

But then came the fateful day.

He knew that she would love a flower, but he wanted to give her the greatest he could find. He knew that it was a rose. The only place he had ever seen these flowers was in a small garden that belonged to a rich nobleman. And he knew this man was a tyrant, but he would not let this stop him. Before he went to the caves he crept into the garden and stole many. Two guards saw him and chased him, threatening his life.

After he escaped he found that all but one of the flowers had been destroyed in the chase. It was the most beautiful white rose he'd ever seen. He knew she'd love it.

He reached the cave just as he always did and went inside. He didn't know he'd been followed.

She smiled widely upon seeing him and embraced him. He still held the rose behind his back. They both sat on a nearby rock and talked a bit. Then he surprised her with the rose. Upon revealing the rose, her face lit up as he had never seen before. She was so happy she placed her arms around his neck and kissed him with more passion than either of them had expected. Then they merely sat staring into eachothers eyes. They were in love.

Unexpectedly, her father came up behind her and began yelling at her as he grabbed her hand and began pulling her back down the cavern. The boy tried to explain to her father but he simply got an evil stare. That's when he heard the footsteps behind him. Her father tried to draw his sword but it was too late, the dagger was thrust deep into his heart.

She began screaming as the boy turned toward some mercenary soldiers that had followed him seeing him enter the cave. He picked up a rock and stood between her, her fallen father and the mercenaries who saw these strange white-skinned people as monsters of some kind. He'd seen these men before. They had raided many homes, killed and raped many people.

Her screams had summoned more of her race that came running from deep within the caverns. The mercenaries pushed the boy aside as the pale-skinned swordsmen attacked them. More men came from both ends of the cave, and soon dozens were fighting in close quarters.

The boy knelt across from her in a quiet corner, the girl's father lying on his back between them. She simply stared down at her father crying uncontrollably. He looked

40

down at the man, his body still.

The boy's eyes rested on the white rose clutched tightly in her small hand. One of the petals had touched her father's blood and was now forever tainted. He'd done the same to her. Her tears fell upon the petals streaming down onto her father, every drop a wish for his life. Slowly she looked around at the men, and looked into his eyes. He felt so ashamed that he was part of their race. What was there left for them now?

She began stroking her father's hair back as she began moaning and crying as well as rocking back and forth. This pushed the boy over the edge and he broke down looking at her. He tried to calm her, and reached over to brush away the tears, but this only seemed to make her cry louder. He couldn't take it anymore, so he ran.

He ran from the cave, he ran and didn't stop. If running meant his death he would not stop. But it didn't.

He collapsed face down in a small field, his lungs feeling as though they'd explode. He released all of his emotions. He coughed and choked in the dirt. He stood and smashed his fists, kicking nearby trees and bushes until he finally lay down bloody, bruised, and completely exhausted. His hand brushed the amulet around his neck as he continued crying. He gripped it tightly in his hand and knew what he'd lost.

Anger swelled within him, and he returned to the mouth of the cave. It had collapsed, but a large trail of hoof-prints led away from the cave. He followed them for more than a day, and finally came upon the mercenary encampment. That night he gathered herbs and poisoned their water. The next day everyone fell ill. Most died. The others were so weak they didn't have the strength to lift a blade as they watched him kill them in their own beds.

Now he was like them. They had taken every bit of innocence he had in less than two days. Did that mean he was a man now? Was this what manhood was?

Celarus came out of his thoughts sitting on his bed. Not long after, he heard about numerous massacres of the white-skinned race throughout southern Zyconia. After he killed those men he became an assassin and later leader of the Vicar's Assassin Army. It had taken Terrek and a near death experience to remove him from that life. It had been nearly twenty years since he'd killed those mercenaries. Celarus looked down at the amulet in his hand.

Was his past coming full circle?

CHAPTER 6: REALIZATIONS

The clouds were dotted with black specks. The Vicar felt totally drained as he stood in the courtyard gazing skyward. He had multiplied them as much as his powers allowed him. There were as many of his dark avians as there were avians in Terrek's army. Grelkon was leading them away now to battle his own family. He could only imagine their surprise.

They would realize it was him when they were close enough. Although his counterparts had come from him, none of them were identical. But one thing flowed through all of them, and that was evil.

Terrek's army of avians had never been in a battle and neither had his dark avians. But the dark avians fed on Grelkon's hatred. They would be totally ruthless and would kill without hesitation.

Could Terrek's avians do the same?

Selate had not resolved her emotional state but she knew there was a war going on and Terrek needed her. She had just left New Victory City with her children heading southward to the front. They had to reach Dernaca by nightfall.

She did not look forward to fighting but she was a powerful avian, as were her children, and they had the advantage of flight. The soldiers on the battlefields would be very surprised.

She forced herself not to think about the events of the last few days. If she did she would never be able to function in the battle.

Terrek sat in his throne room.

He told Selate she didn't have to go, but she had. He was relieved that they would help in the battle. But he felt guilty for sending them so soon after Hecron's death. He ran his hands through his long curly dark hair. He needed to know what to do. He needed guidance. Terrek lowered his head to his hands.

"Maker, please give me the wisdom to overcome the enemy," he said softly.

When he lifted his gaze he was aware of a presence in the room.

"I think you've got to overcome the enemy within first, my son."

Terrek knew the voice before he'd fully lifted his head.

"Zyron!" Terrek said incredulously.

Not far away stood the figure of Zyron. His face was bright and his form a light with a heavenly glow. Terrek stood and moved toward him, but he held up his hands.

"You can not touch me as I am only here in spirit and am no longer part of this world," Zyron said.

"How - Here, I mean, you were gone," he sputtered.

"The Maker heard your prayer, he sent me, but my time here is little," he said sadly.

"I need to know how to handle this war. I don't know if I'm the king everyone wants me to be," he said explaining.

Zyron walked to the throne and looked down at the

Amityus crested sceptre.

"This sceptre was given to you because of a prophecy that you were to fulfill. The Maker put you on the throne. You've must have faith, in the Maker and in yourself," he replied.

Terrek lowered his head.

"The Maker can only help you if you let him," Zyron's eyes twinkled as he'd seen them do so many times throughout his life.

"I've missed you so much. You've been there for me my entire life and then you were gone. I wish you could stay here now," Terrek said softly.

"I know, but part of me will always be with you," he replied easily.

Zyron's form began to ripple.

"Zyron wait, I still need answers," he said quickly trying to keep him there.

"I'm not here to provide all the answers, but I will return very soon," he smiled. Then he vanished.

Terrek slowly returned to his throne.

Perhaps things were not as bleak, he thought. He had accomplished so many feats and overcome so many obstacles in the past. This was another of those obstacles, and now he had much more strength under his command.

The Vicar had turned up nothing when searching Frecan's room or so he had said, but Koiban wouldn't leave it at that. He had entered Frecan's room in search of anything that might point to the killer. So far he'd turned up nothing. The only thing he knew was that he'd been murdered with a small sword.

Frecan was an elderly man and had accumulated many objects within his lifetime. His chambers were divided into three rooms. The larger outer room that adjoined to the palace hallway was the one in which he'd been murdered. It held little that took up his time. But Koiban didn't think it was likely there would be anything else in the other rooms.

He entered another room and sat on Frecan's bed looking in his vanity mirror.

"What happened, Frecan?" he said under his breath, looking into his reflection.

He sighed and shifted his weight.

"Maybe I'll never know," he said, depressed.

He stood, and as he did, a small bundle of paper fell to the floor from beneath Frecan's bed. Turning around Koiban retrieved the bundle from the floor.

The paper on the front of the bundle had been underneath a letter and had received a good deal of imprints from the heavy writing. This unnerved Emperor Koiban as he swiftly brought the paper to a candle.

Koiban began reading and his face took on an expression of outrage. Some of the letter was unreadable. Koiban couldn't tell whom it had been sent to, but what he could read accused the Vicar of conspiring to steal his throne. Could the Vicar be trying to take his throne? Did he kill Frecan?

Koiban exited Frecan's chambers and rushed down the great hall making his way to the Vicar's personal chambers. He knocked, and hearing no reply entered and began rummaging through everything, pushing over furniture in a growing rage.

Then he saw the glint from the corner of his eye. He thrust his hand behind a large oak chair against the wall and removed it.

It was a small broad sword.

He looked at it closely. It had been cleaned, but not well enough. Surrounding the base of the blade just above the hilt were small fragments of dried blood. Koiban's eyes welled up with tears, and his rage exploded as his hand tightened around the blade staining it with his blood. In

46

outrage he threw the blade against the wall and stormed out of the Vicar's chambers.

As he moved down the hall toward his throne room, he realized no guards would be there at the moment. They were on the lower levels having their meals. He decided to make sure the Vicar was there before he ordered the guards to take him to the dungeon. He would have the Vicar tortured and killed.

As he reached the door he heard others inside. Perhaps coconspirators, he thought, listening outside the door.

Inside sat the Vicar, Kridelia and Yirdak.

"We're gaining more territory as we speak, Kridelia and I are ready to proceed with the abduction," he said looking at Kridelia.

"VERY GOOD, YOU WILL HAVE THE PRIZE YOU CAME FOR KRIDELIA AS I HAVE PROMISED," he replied.

"Thank you," she smiled, "I understand you will kill Koiban tonight," she said sadistically.

"YES, WE WILL MEET TO DISCUSS MAKING PEACE WITH ZYCONIA, THEN I WILL SLIT HIS THROAT," he rasped.

Koiban's temper flared.

"IT NO LONGER MATTERS NOW, ALL GUARDS IN DYSTARA HAVE BEEN MOVED TO THE FRONT AND REPLACED WITH MEN LOYAL TO ME. I HAVE THE POWER NOW, EVEN THE PEOPLE KNOW WHO REUNITED XANICA AND HELPED IT PROSPER," the Vicar said.

Koiban's heart sank as he drew away from the door and leaned against the wall. The Vicar was right. How could he have been so blind? He had allowed his good judgment to be clouded by the gifts the Vicar had given Xanica. Using his powers to please his people, the Vicar had wormed his way onto his throne. He had allowed himself to be ruled by him, he was nothing more than a puppet.

Maybe he would be able to halt the invasion and try to reclaim his throne but he had to get away from Dystara, now!

When the Vicar had finished Yirdak and Kridelia left the throne room. Silently the Vicar focused his powers and slipped from normal reality into his small dark realm. There stood Delara.

Surrounding them were cloudy blue mists. They stood firmly but no solid footing could be seen beneath them. In all directions objects seemed to partially form and then dissipate, as though this place were clinging to reality but just too far removed.

"My soldiers have attacked Separa as you've requested," she said sullenly.

"HOW STRONG ARE THEIR DEFENSES," the Vicar began.

"They aren't weak, but the border is wide and they are spread thin, it has been easy to overcome them," she reported quietly.

"VERY GOOD, KEEP ME INFORMED," he ordered.

"Wait, my army believes reinforcements are arriving as we speak. We can't take Zyconia without the loss of many lives. I have no wish to see my men killed, many have families and I -" her passionate speech was cut off by a metallic chain cuff that suddenly appeared around her neck. Using his powers the Vicar magically pulled the collar to the firmament beneath them making her bow.

"YOU WILL CONTINUE TO BATTLE," he rumbled.

Delara placed her hands on the collar and it disintegrated as she stood defiantly. She'd used her powers to remove the collar, the Vicar was angered.

His eyes glowed yellow.

Suddenly a huge stone appeared behind Delara. She felt

herself knocked back against it's surface painfully as chains and cuffs wrapped her spread eagle against it's surface. She screamed and attempted to use her powers but to no avail, the Vicar's rage overwhelmed them. Instantly, a wall of fire rushed in front of her, so close that it singed stray hairs from her head, the heat was intense, but it stopped.

The Vicar moved his hood so close to her face she could almost make out the shadowy form of his face. She clenched her eyes shut. He had once told her that to look upon his face was to look upon death. She didn't want to know if it was a lie.

"YOU WILL CONTINUE TO FIGHT," he spat, "IF YOU DON'T I WILL HUNT DOWN EVERY MEMBER OF YOUR RACE AND ERADICATE THEM MYSELF."

With that he turned and disappeared.

Pushing her powers to the limits she freed herself from the chains. Instantly the rock vanished. She stood, her body sore. She lowered her head, she had no choice.
She waved her hand and returned to her caverns.

Selate and her children, shocked, had come to a halt at Victory City. It seemed the situation was more drastic than first thought. Some of their reinforcements had arrived, but the bulk of the forces were still on their way. That morning the Xanican armies had broken through the Zyconian lines and now were marching on Victory City. A large force had been raised to defend the city, and soldiers scattered throughout Dernaca turned from fighting the Xanicans, and rushed to defend the city.

Most of the Xanican force was headed to Victory City. The rest was spread throughout southern Dernaca plundering small castles and solidifying their hold on them. Some soldiers had also joined the assault on Separa, which had been spearheaded thus far by a race of pale subterranean beings.

From the reports they were a very ruthless and brutal enemy. Zachary's armies had thus far managed to keep them from the inner parts of Separa but he would need reinforcements soon or they would break through.

Zachary stood in his chambers with Juliana in Vatiria the capital of Separa.

"If the reinforcements arrive soon we can continue to fight," he said.

She looked understandingly at him.

"Even if they do, it may be prudent to leave Vatiria and go to New Victory city to Terrek's palace, I don't want to take any risks that you and Timothy will be harmed no matter how small they are," he continued.

Juliana embraced him, "I don't think we are in that much danger. Remember all we've been through in the past."

He did. He remembered how many things all their friends had gone through. If not for Terrek's excellent leadership they would all have surely perished. He hoped he would not dishonor Terrek as Duke of Separa, and wished he could be such a great leader.

As the armies of Xanica closed on Victory City the Zyconian forces rushed to meet them. Selate and her children leapt from the city walls and flew toward them. They had no time to allow crossbow men to mount their backs. If they could, they would stop them before they reached the walls. That's when they saw something that jarred everyone. Dark specks moved through the air toward them.

"Charge!" ordered one of the leaders from below.

Selate faced her children in the air.

"I don't know what they are but we've got to attack them before they attack our men, do you understand," she said strongly.

They nodded.

She spun and led them swiftly to the oncoming dark specks. As they loomed closer she could vaguely make out their forms. They appeared to be avian. But their bodies were so dark, so evil looking. Where had they come from?

Selate plowed into the leader as her children attacked the others. He spiraled downward as she followed. Suddenly their eyes met. His were deadly and cold.

"Goodbye, mother," he said vehemently as he lunged toward her.

It was Grelkon.

CHAPTER 7: DARK ALTERNATIVE

𝕿errek sat in his library, in near total darkness. His body felt numb and disabled: racked by the situation. He had been there since Selate returned. Victory City had been captured.

Selate had informed him that Xanica had their own force of winged soldiers, dark avians, and that her son Grelkon had become their leader. She had grappled with him herself. He had been changed. Selate and many of her children had been wounded, many of them severely. They were lucky none of them had been killed. As Selate fought with Grelkon, he told her who was behind the attacks and the sadistic dark avian army: the Vicar.

Terrek plunged deeper into the darkness of his soul as he considered what possibilities the future could have. He thought that the Vicar had been killed a year ago when the magical power of the dark crystal erupted in explosion, but he was alive. He knew the Vicar would stop at nothing to reclaim Zyconia. The last time Terrek had won, now a lot more had entered the equation. Terrek was responsible for all of Zyconia; he had Diana, and soon would have a child. So much more was at stake.

Since his childhood he had always been a leader. Now he wished he'd been different. There was so much weight now he could barely breath, let alone think.

In a sudden flash of light Zyron appeared, and looked down at him as hc lay on a large number of cushions upon the floor. Terrek stood and paced the room. He had a feeling that Zyron was there to tell him not to despair and to have faith.

"You've gathered many of Zyconia's lost parchments and scrolls," he declared surveying the abundance of the library.

Terrek leaned on a nearby windowsill staring outside.

"Yes, when I became king I wanted to preserve what records of Zyconia's past had not been destroyed. I managed to recover many chronicles and legends," he muttered.

"You are losing what I taught you," Zyron said softly.

"How can I think straight with this happening?" Terrek roared emotionally, moving from the window to a nearby table. He dropped into a chair and brought his hands to his face.

"You must believe," Zyron asserted quietly.

"I wish someone else were in this position! I don't want to be king!" he didn't fully mean it, but he was very upset.

"Sometimes I think Zyconia would be better off without me," Terrek said sadly.

"So be it," Zyron nodded as he vanished.

"So be what?" Terrek asked the empty room.

Terrek rubbed his eyes. He was very tired. He stood and dragged himself over to the mound of pillows. Diana would understand if he didn't come to bed that night. She knew the pressures on him and that he needed to think. He lay down and closed his eyes.

After what seemed like moments Terrek became aware of a slight draft and the loud commotion of people all around him. He quickly opened his eyes, perplexed. He was outside his palace lying under a tree and it was the middle of the day. Only moments before it had been night. He sat up looking around and what caught his sight jarred him deep within.

Not far away crowds of men dressed in rags filled the palace courtyard. They were being forced to erect a large statue of some kind near the center of the courtyard. Armored men waded among them hitting and whipping them. Terrek was angered but shock prevented him from reacting. He slowly waded into the crowd. He knew some of these people. They were prosperous citizens, but they were so scarred and dirty. What was going on?

Terrek walked a few steps more and saw a man being beaten profusely by one of the armored men. Angrily he grabbed the man's wrist and head smashing his face into a nearby pillar. Then he reached out to help the man who had been beaten. Two of his companions had come from nearby. Terrek jumped back, terror filling his face.

The man he'd helped up was Zachary, and the other two were Adam and Jason. They appeared as shocked as he was.

"Adam, Jason, Zachary what's going on?" Terrek asked in amazement.

They stood before him in rags. Their faces bruised and dirty. Zachary looked at Terrek helplessly with tears in his eyes.

"Terrek," he sobbed his eyes were those of a broken man.

Terrek stood staring. Something terrible was going on here.

"Where have you been?" Adam questioned sadly trying to understand.

"What do you mean?" he replied choking on his words, fear growing inside him.

"Take him!" the voice echoed behind him as two

armored guards pinned Terrek's arms and began dragging him away.

"Wait," cried Jason as he and the others ran forward. More guards pushed them back and began attacking them.

"Stop it!" Terrek roared, writhing in their grips.

They moved him slowly to the palace. Suddenly he became aware of the blood red banners streaming from his balcony. On the banners was the Wicketus. He also caught view of the enormous statue; it was the Vicar's likeness. Terrek erupted with emotion as he looked to the balcony. Atop stood Selate's son Grelkon, and a small group of dark people fronted by the Vicar.

"No!" Terrek screamed escaping the guards.

Desperately he grasped one of their blades and ran to a banner climbing up to the balcony. As he reached the top, he leapt with all his strength swinging at the Vicar, who carefully sidestepped his desperation. Grelkon, another man, and a dark haired woman moved back. Instantly guards were upon him pinning him to the balcony's small wall. The Vicar stared for a long time, standing perfectly still before he spoke.

"TERREK," he rasped.

The dark haired woman nearby looked at him with hatred. The Vicar moved forward and looked him up and down.

"WHERE HAVE YOU BEEN? DO YOU LIKE WHAT I'VE DONE WITH YOUR KINGDOM," he sneered.

"DO YOU THINK WE SHOULD GIVE HIM THE CELL WITH A VIEW, KRIDELIA?" asked the Vicar.

"Yes!" she said staring at Terrek through eyes of hatred that could have burned a hole through lead, not unlike the stare Terrek gave them all. One of the guards withdrew a club and slammed it into the back of his head.

Terrek groaned as his vision and memory returned. He sat up in the dark dungeon cell sensing four faces staring at him.

"Walker, John, Perrin, Celarus," he cried.

They looked at him, their faces bright, but they appeared as though joy was an alien emotion to them.

"What's going on?" he said incredibly frustrated.

"You don't know?" said Walker amazed.

"No, I don't!" cried Terrek.

Walker looked at the others, then sat across from him on the floor.

"You've been missing for weeks Terrek. After you disappeared, we tried to lead the armies and protect the kingdom, but we didn't have your leadership. The Vicar won in the end and he has been deforming New Victory city and all of Zyconia ever since," Walker said sadly.

Terrek sat there staring blankly. Walker looked away as he continued.

"Some have been executed," it was a cold sentence that made Terrek turned his head sharply.

"Selate was burned to death not long ago, with all of her children. Grelkon merely stood by as though he didn't care. I think he might have been the one who ordered their deaths," Walker said.

Tears rolled slowly from Terrek's face.

"Ricsis was one of the first killed. The Vicar thought his death was a great irony because he tied a horse to each limb of his centaur body and had them rush in separate directions," Walker paused, "he thought it was humorous that half of what he was tore him in half."

Terrek was horrified.

"And just two days ago Jessica, Juliana and Timothy poisoned themselves in their cell. They were to be tortured and killed the next day. The tortures would have been unspeakable. Jessica made the poison and they took it.

Juliana had to give it to Timothy, who cried and cried, but he swallowed it. What else could they have done," Walker finished, beginning to lose control of his emotions.

Terrek remembered Zachary's face outside. It had been so dead, so destroyed. Now he knew why. Terrek thought he would be sick. How could this have happened?

"But Diana is safe, at least for now," Perrin put in.

Terrek experienced slight relief. Diana and his child were alive.

"She's been imprisoned in one of the palace towers," Celarus confirmed.

Everyone present was tearful.

"Where have you been, Terrek?" asked John.

"I don't know. All I can remember is falling asleep in my library a few hours after Selate had returned. Victory City had just been taken. I woke up here!" he said slowly thinking.

"Nothing happened that night that can account for -" Terrek stopped in cold realization.

He had said that Zyconia would be better off without him. The Maker must have taken his upset ravings to heart. So he'd been removed. This is what Zyconia had become without him. This can't be happening, he thought.

Terrek slowly stood and for the first time noticed a huge mass sitting on the floor in a dark corner.

"Hemoth," he said, softly moving forward.

John blocked his path. "Please, don't," he pleaded.

Terrek peered into his eyes, slowly he moved past him.

He slowly approached, looking down it was too dark to see his face in the shadows. He knelt down in front of him. Immediately he knew that Hemoth was naked and that a nauseating odor wafted from his body. Despite this he was compelled to look upon his friend's face one last time. Behind him the others watched, tears streaming from each face, they lowered their gazes as Terrek laid his hand on Hemoth's shoulder to pull his face to the light.

Hemoth's face fell forward directly into a stream of light flowing through a barred window. What Terrek saw was the single most horrifying and grotesque sight he had seen in all his life. Most of Hemoth's face had been torn off leaving little flesh and dangling facial bones. He drew back in horror and sank against the wall. He felt like the wind had been knocked out of him. He was so overcome that he couldn't even scream.

"Hemoth was killed this morning. His face was torn off with a trident!" screamed Perrin in the throws of emotion. Everyone lowered their heads gravely.

Footsteps passed by them and Terrek lifted himself to the barred window and peered outside.

Outside, not more than fifteen strides away, was an elevated single noose gallows. Standing at the steps was the dark haired female he'd seen on the balcony when attacking the Vicar. She stared at him; totally aware he was watching her. Two guards came from behind a nearby door herding someone up to the noose. As they reached the platform Terrek realized who it was. Diana.

"No!" he screamed pulling on the bars and thrashing around crazily. The others behind him looked outside with shocked expressions.

"Diana!" Terrek yelled realizing what was about to happen.

The noose was fastened as she realized he was there.

He stretched out his hand futily crying to the dark haired female to release her.

"Terrek!" she screamed looking directly at him.

Her words were cut off as the trapdoor beneath her feet dropped. She died instantly, her neck broken. Her eyes rolled back in her skull as her face became pallid, her entire body limp as a ragdoll. Small trickles of blood fell from her torn neck streaking her once pregnant stomach. A life never to be realized.

"No!" Terrek roared falling away from the window

barely able to stand. The others came close.

"Don't touch me! No, No, No, No, no..." he began screaming convulsively, and collapsed on the floor. Overwhelmed he brought his hands to his face.

"Terrek," a voice echoed.

"I said leave me alone!" he screamed.

"Terrek," it came again but he realized whose voice it was.

He lowered his hands; he was sitting in his library. And there before him was Diana.

"Diana," he said crying as he embraced her. It was such joy to feel her in his arms. Streams covered his face.

"What's wrong?" she said, startled and concerned. He smiled through tears.

"Nothing, nothing's wrong. And I'm going to make sure it stays that way!" Terrek said.

Not far behind them, Zyron nodded to Terrek and disappeared.

CHAPTER 8: ABDUCTION

Zyron had come to see Terrek after his experience. He knew that it had been an incredible strain. It had been a hard lesson, but Terrek had gotten the point. Zyron told him that this was what Zyconia would have been if he had disappeared the night before. If he were not there Zyconia would have been captured, but he was there, and he had to do everything possible to defeat the Vicar. To do that he had to believe, to believe in the Maker, to believe in himself.

Zyron told him that what he had seen would never happen exactly as he'd seen it, but he had to overcome the Vicar to prevent similar events from occurring. Just the thought of what could happen was enough to refuel him. He wouldn't let it happen.

King Terrek sat at the head of a large table in his throne room. Around him sat Queen Diana, Supreme Commander Hemoth, Royal Advisor Perrin, Military Architect John, Royal Advisor Walker, Dukes: Adam, Jason, Zachary, Ricsis, Celarus, High Healer Jessica, Duchess Juliana, and Selate. He had just finished telling them what the Maker had made him experience. He'd told them that it had been hard, but it taught him and given him insight.

He also told them of their deaths, but in all instances he

tried to be kind. He wouldn't give them full details. Terrek left out Juliana's administering the poison to her own son, and he couldn't tell Zachary that he became a shadow of the man he was because of it. He said little about Hemoth's dead form in the dungeon. He thought it best not to tell Selate that Grelkon had sentenced her and her children to death, but he had to tell everyone that Grelkon was with the Vicar. But he couldn't bring himself to say anything about Diana other than that she died as well. It was too painful.

Everyone descended into docile forms of themselves completely absorbed in their thoughts.

"I know this comes as a shock," Terrek said quietly.

Diana's eyes clouded with tears as she looked around the table at everyone, heads lowered. Then she looked at Terrek beside her with loving sympathy. He had told her a few hours earlier about his experience, but it still brought tears to her eyes when he explained it to everyone else. She placed her hand on his in compassion.

"So," Walker began slowly, "what does this all mean? Where do we go from here?" he asked.

"What this means, is that we have one chance here and now to stop the conquest of Zyconia. It may take all we have, but we must succeed, no matter what the cost," Terrek said powerfully.

"I think we all understand," Hemoth said.

And they all did.

"He is nowhere to be found," Yirdak told the Vicar, "Koiban has escaped the palace, and perhaps the city."

"HE MUST HAVE DISCOVERED THAT I MURDERED FRECAN. NO MATTER, HE CAN DO LITTLE DAMAGE NOW. HAVE A DOZEN SOLDIERS SEARCH FOR HIM, AND HAVE OUR LOYAL MEN ON THE FRONT WATCH FOR HIM. HE MUST BE

KILLED ON SIGHT," the Vicar rasped.

"As you wish, my lord," Yirdak said.

"YOU AND KRIDELIA MUST LEAVE AT ONCE FOR ZYCONIA, IF SHE WISHES HER REVENGE," the Vicar said.

"We will leave within the hour, my lord," he finished.

"VERY GOOD," he hissed diabolically.

Terrek sat with Diana, Hemoth, Perrin and Juliana. The others had sprung into action, the Dukes sending word to their respective provinces to bring to bear their collective forces. Only small groups of guards would be left behind to keep civil order. John had set to work on building new weapons, and Jessica was with Selate seeing to her children's battle injuries.

"I saw some things that may give us some answers. A dark haired woman and a scarlet caped man stood with the Vicar. I can only guess that they are powerful individuals that are supporting him. They may possess dark powers as the Vicar's past servants have," he said, thinking back to the battle that had occurred on the very spot where his palace now sat.

"We also know what Selate's son, Grelkon, has become," Hemoth said gravely.

"I fear that Selate may not be able to kill her son in battle," Perrin said.

"I know. I hope one of her children can accomplish it. I understand Selate's feelings. But Grelkon must be killed. He is too evil, and he leads the dark avians. Without the leader they will begin to flounder. I hope one of Selate's children can bring themselves to do it. Hopefully they will also be physically strong enough," Terrek explained.

Grelkon was perched upon a huge fallen oak stretching his gigantic wingspan. Scattered around him were the dark avians. Although not used to it, Grelkon ate the raw dead animals they killed and brought to him. Nearby, many of them ravaged dozens of antelope corpses. He was not accustomed to hunting or eating raw meat. He was not accustomed to the taste of blood. He abstained from the hunt.

They were supposed to be like him, but he found them to be very different. They were darker, and not just physically.

Nearby, a large camp of the Vicar's soldiers prepared for the drive further into Zyconia. Soon the twin cities of Geritus and Batera would be attacked. It wouldn't be long before they moved toward New Victory City.

The cloaked figure of Emperor Koiban rode his stallion deep into the Xanican wilderness. He knew the Vicar would try to follow, but he was far from Dystara. So far that he didn't recognize most of the country.

Koiban thought about how weak willed he had been with the Vicar and grimaced. All the time being manipulated and used. The Vicar had slowly wormed his way into all parts of Xanica. He should have never accepted the Vicar's proposition. Perhaps eventually he could have ascended to the throne himself. Bratain had been right, he knew he should have listened. He thought there might be a chance, if he could contact enough soldiers on the front loyal to him, that perhaps he could retake Xanica, but to do that he needed King Terrek's help. He hoped he was a reasonable man, and could forgive Koiban's errors.

Slowly he reined his horse back and surveyed the

country. Ahead of him stretched a lengthy mountain range. Where was he?

Although the Vicar's realm powers had been strained Yirdak, Kridelia and three soldiers had transversed the distance from Xanica to Zyconia in seconds. They knew they could not return the way they had come. The Vicar had drained his power once again to send them. Only the Vicar could pass to and from his realm anywhere he wished, and only so far. Just outside New Victory City in the underbrush they hid, waiting.

"We will wait until nightfall," whispered Yirdak.

Kridelia's eyes glazed, her face glowing. Soon.

Night had fallen and Terrek had been called to his courtyard by Hemoth, who was joined by two dozen guards.

"Some of our soldiers reported spotting people outside the city walls. We fear a few rogue soldiers from Xanica's armies may have broken through our lines. We must capture them before they manage to infiltrate the city. They may be spies," Hemoth breathed.

"Wait a few moments, I'm coming wit h you," Terrek said.

Hemoth looked at him worriedly.

"I know one of your duties is to protect the king, but it's only a few spies," he said smiling.

Hemoth nodded slowly as Terrek moved away. Hemoth knew their king missed the joy of roaming the countryside and even engaging in battle.

Soon Terrek returned wearing some armor, his sword sheathed. He rode upon Streak. They exited the city's front gates and moved toward the nearest forest.

Diana entered the couple's personal chambers she lay in her bed and thought about their child to be. They had not yet decided on a name for their child. Terrek had a vast knowledge of names because he had traveled throughout Zyconia. The names she knew were few, but Terrek said they should make this decision together.

Diana felt strange being alone in their chambers. She felt like she was being watched. She stood and walked out of their chambers. Perhaps doing some reading would make her feel a little better.

She entered the library and sat on a chair overlooking a table covered with ancient maps. Terrek had collected so many artifacts from ancient Zyconia. She stared at the large pile of cushions on the floor and smiled. Terrek had a bad habit of lounging on the cushions on the floor a lot, looking at the artifacts, or thinking. Sometimes she thought they should move their bed into his library so he could get some sleep.

Suddenly the window nearby blew open, sending a gust of cold wind through the room. Diana spun quickly, looking out into the dark night. She ran to the window and closed it pushing down the latch. The erie feeling became elevated and persistent.

Diana left the library and made her way to the throne room. It was disturbing being without Terrek in the castle.

Upon entering the throne room she realized the guards were gone too. Most of the New Victory City army had left the city early that morning for Dernaca and Separa. The soldiers remaining in the cit y were at that moment patrolling the streets or were with Hemoth and Terrek looking for the spies. The possibility that spies might enter their city made her feel insecure.

Their friends were all attending to their duties still and had not returned to the palace.

She shut the doors that led to the balcony and moved to the throne next to Terrek's and sat. She didn't understand this unexplained fear. Instantly Diana stood. She could hear something very close. She walked about the room.

Suddenly she looked toward the balcony doors as they burst open. Splinters landed everywhere. It was too late.

Terrek plunged deeper into the thick forest. He'd told Hemoth it would be better to split up and find the men. Hemoth felt very uneasy but had capitulated to his king's demands. Terrek entered a dark clearing.

Suddenly a twig snapped.

Terrek spun as a soldier jumped from the trees pulling him from his horse. Two more men ran into the clearing. The soldier swung his dagger at Terrek's head but Terrek caught his wrist bringing his sword down hard on the man's bicep. The soldier screamed in horror his arm chopped cleanly off. He struck Terrek with his other arm but Terrek thrust his sword swiftly through his chest. The man fell as Terrek pulled away with his sword to face the other two.

Terrek tired of the night, threw his sword into the abdomen of one of the men and struck the other. The man he struck was large and used his weight to his advantage. He quickly pinned Terrek to a tree withdrawing a dagger. But Terrek reached up grabbing a small branch. With total control he pushed it into the big man's face, the little branches poking his eyes. With tremendous force Terrek pushed him back against a jagged, broken tree limb jutting from a trunk.

Shock crossed his face as his back collided with the sharp spear of wood. One moment the soldiers torso was fine, the next it housed the shattered limb and the globular outpourings of his insides. The man trembled for a few moments then his head fell slightly forward, his legs relaxed and he hung limply from the tree. Terrek had great respect for human life. He felt sorry that these men had wasted theirs.

"Terrek!" Hemoth yelled, terribly concerned, as he ran into the clearing.

Looking around he saw the man Terrek had thrown his sword into choke on his blood and die. Hemoth looked shocked.

"We were nearby, why didn't you cry out?" he panicked.

"I suppose I should have," Terrek said seriously looking at him.

"Zyconia can't lose it's king, remember," exclaimed Hemoth.

Terrek withdrew his sword tiredly.

"Zyconia hasn't lost me yet," he finished, "let's return to the palace. We've accomplished what we had to do."

Tired, Terrek entered the throne room. Hemoth and a few of the guards were close behind. The other guards were patrolling the palace. He felt the cold wind from the balcony. Instantly Terrek saw the shattered doors that led to his balcony.

"Diana?" he said as he saw a smashed chair nearby.

"Diana!" he moved toward the balcony.

"Check their personal chambers," Hemoth ordered the guards.

Hemoth searched the room looking at the few smashed chairs and splinters of glass and wood from the balcony doors. Nearby he spied a few drops of blood.

Rushing out unto the balcony Terrek saw a piece of paper hanging from the inside of the railing. A seal on

which the Wicketus was featured held it. Terrek tore the
paper off and read:

> Surrender Zyconia and we will release your
> wife. If you don't we will return both her and
> your unborn child in pieces.

Terrek swallowed, looking out at the dark sky above.
The cold wind caressed his white features taking his tears
away from his face. It was a night of great darkness and it
would be a dark day tomorrow. Diana had been abducted.

END OF PART ONE

CHAPTER 9: INFILTRATION

"We must get her back," Terrek said trembling.

Terrek stood looking out the high chamber windows. His face was grave, his complexion ashen. His back was turned to everyone present.

His Dukes and Advisors had assembled and sat around the huge table of the royal high chambers. They looked upon their monarch wishing they had the power to make things right, but they didn't.

"I don't understand how they managed to travel this deep into Zyconia without being spotted," Hemoth said quietly.

"But they must be captured before they reach Xanica," Perrin voiced in a concerned tone.

"Someone has to go after them," Jessica said.

Silence sat for a moment.

"I'm going," Terrek said.

"But Terrek, Zyconia must have you here to make sure the troops are properly guided. We can't afford to lose you," Hemoth cried pleadingly.

"I'm the king of Zyconia and you will obey me!" Terrek asserted.

"I'll take a small band of soldiers and all of you except Perrin, Selate, John and Walker will accompany me. Perrin and Walker, you will remain to hold the armies of defense together, John will help as a military aide. Selate, you and your children must attempt to keep the dark avians away from New Victory City. I only pray that they don't continue their drive in my absence," he said darkly.

Blackness.

Slight haze. There was a fabric to her eyes. It was a blindfold. Suddenly it was torn away roughly. A raven-haired individual rode her horse alongside the horse Diana had been bound to and slung over. The dark-haired woman looked at Diana with contempt.

"You'll be the first of my revenge upon your husband," she said gutturally.

Kridelia's metal boot collided violently with Diana's head sending her world reeling. Kridelia rode ahead. Senses dulling, Diana clasped her bound hands together slipping her royal ring from her finger. It fell away to the ground as she lost consciousness.

The Vicar surveyed his armies. At a distance Grelkon and his dark avians once again fed on antelope remains. Waves of soldiers prepared for the attack on the twin cities of Batera and Geritus. Not far away he could see forces gathering outside Batera's city walls. Across the river on the opposite side of Batera he knew more soldiers were gathering to defend Geritus. This would be a difficult battle, but it would be a triumph, he thought.

After they captured Batera and Geritus, their hold on the Dernacan province would be nearly impenetrable and they would concentrate their forces on Separa and it's capital, Vatiria.

Grelkon had grown accustomed to the dark avians. One in particular that he identified with was Cramin. He was the only one Grelkon had named. The others remained nameless.

Cramin incited all of what he had left Zyconia for. He and Grelkon had attacked various soldiers on the drive to the twin cities and seemed to share the same passion for battle. Cramin understood Grelkon more than the others.

Grelkon finally knew what it was to have a friend. The other dark avians appeared jealous of their master's favoritism of Cramin.

Terrek rode upon Streak fully gilded for battle against whatever the Vicar had in his power. He would not rest until Diana was in his arms again.

Soldiers near Separa's border had spotted Diana's captors heading south deep into central Separa. The soldiers had no idea who the individuals were when they saw them or they would have been captured. Terrek could only guess that they were going to return to Xanica through some unknown pass in the Minotaur Mountains. All they had to do was find the horse tracks, and they would have somewhere to begin, but it was going to be very difficult to track them.

Quieting his horse, Koiban moved through the underbrush. He had transversed the difficult mountain range and now rode into southern Separa. When he heard hoof beats, he hid. He knew it might be as dangerous for him here in Zyconia as it had been in Xanica.

Peering out from the bushes he was shocked. It was Kridelia and Yirdak. They also led a horse on which an unknown woman was bound. Trying to hold in his malice toward them, he watched as they galloped back the way he'd come from the Minotaur Mountains, into a small valley from which small streams of smoke wafted.

If not for an uneven saddle Terrek might never have seen it. The small word upon it's surface read: Forever. It was gold, with a large inset array of diamond and sapphire clusters, centralized by one large emerald. He'd given it to Diana. It was her wedding ring. Terrek squeezed it in his palm, flooded with dread, then anger. His company sat on their horses silently. A small group of select warriors from Zyconia's army lingered not far behind.

Terrek looked up and saw the small imprint of horse hooves. They were on the right track. Diana's captors couldn't be that far ahead. He remounted his horse and rode off in the direction of the tracks.

Perrin and Walker had just received word that the twin cities were being attacked. It was up to them now. All they could hope for was Terrek's return. They weren't used to the responsibility, but they would do their best.

John was corresponding with messengers being sent to the military leaders on the war front. And at that moment Selate and her children were probably in the heat of battle. Perrin looked across the vacant meeting table at Walker.

"I - I think we'd better go over our battle plan to protect this province and perhaps New Victory city as well," he swallowed.

Walker lifted his head and instead of a shocked expression he gave one of realization, "I think you're right."

Koiban had stopped to eat and had erected a fire. Unfortunately, he'd dozed off. After receiving no sleep in the last two days he was exhausted. Soon the approach of hoof beats woke him. As he clambered to his feet the lead horse entered the clearing. The armor and insignia upon both horse and rider were extravagant. They had to be royalty. He froze to his spot as Terrek and the other riders halted mere footsteps from him.

"Who are you, what are you doing here?" Terrek asked seeing fear in the man's eyes.

CHAPTER 10: LIVING DEAD

Koiban floundered as Terrek spied the royal insignia of Xanica beneath his dirty cloak. Terrek's eyes reddened with rage as he leapt from his horse.

"Wait! Yes, I am Emperor Koiban, but I'm not responsible for the assault on your people, the Vicar is!" he yelled.

Terrek grabbed him by the front of his uniform with both hands.

"You allowed him into your kingdom, you gave him your armies, do you expect me to believe that," Terrek growled through clenched teeth.

Koiban understood his rage.

"It's true that I accepted the Vicar as my chancellor, but only because my people were torn apart. He helped everything. When he convinced me that we should attack your kingdom, he led me to believe that your race was savagely evil and immoral."

"So slaughtering a savage race would have been alright?" Terrek said.

"No, my intent was never to slaughter, but I realized to late that the Vicar had ideas of his own," he finished quietly.

Terrek still held him, staring angrily into his eyes.

Celarus, the nearest to Terrek put a hand on his shoulder.

"We all know how the Vicar can cloud a person's judgment and worm his way into their life," he said slowly.

Terrek pushed Koiban back as he released his grip. He turned around bringing a hand to his lowered brow.

"Do you understand what he's doing here now?" Terrek said quietly.

Koiban realized now that everything the Vicar had said about the Zyconians was false. Their monarch obviously cared about them. What had he done?

"The only thing I can do is help you stop him. Many in the army are still loyal to me; they are just in battle and don't realize I've been dethroned. I will help you if that's what you want," Koiban offered.

"Fine, you help us get my kingdom back, you help us get my wife back and just go wherever you want..."

"Wait, did you say get your wife back?" Koiban asked remembering the woman Kridelia and Yirdak had on the horse.

"Yes, some of his minions have captured her," he voiced.

"I saw them not long ago pass by!" Koiban said.

"Lead us!" Terrek yelled as everyone mounted their horses.

"I didn't agree to this! Why have you brought her here?" Delara said loudly to Kridelia.

Delara stood in one of the main corridors of her underworld. Half a dozen guards flanked her. Standing before her were Kridelia, Yirdak and a bound disheveled young woman. The woman struggled in Kridelia's iron grip. Delara knew who it was.

"I want you to take us to the subterranean Oblivion pits," Kridelia replied.

"The entrance has been sealed for years. It's to dangerous," Delara said stubbornly.

"You'll take us there or the Vicar will destroy you and your people," Kridelia's eyes darkened.

Delara's blood boiled. Kridelia didn't have the power of the Vicar. Delara was more than a match for her, but Kridelia had Yirdak as well. Delara's temper was hot but she didn't know what long-term consequences acting on impulse would bring. She couldn't afford to do that.

Angrily, Delara turned and headed down the corridor. Satisfied, Kridelia and Yirdak followed dragging Diana. Delara's guards stared bitterly at them.

Soon they reached a large oak door set into solid rock. Delara used a skeleton key to open it and all entered. Descending a narrow tunnel downward the faint odor of brimstone reached them. Soon, Kridelia thought.

Walker and Perrin had heard the reports. The twin cities were floundering. They weren't expected to hold out much longer, and scout reports indicated that they were already marching toward Victory City and Vatiria. Selate and her children had been forced to retreat to Victory City, where some of her children lay severely injured. The dark avians gave no mercy, they were lucky none of them had been killed. The armies moving toward Vatiria were comprised mainly of the white beings.

John spread a large sketch over the table before Perrin and Walker.

"I have devised the battle plan for the city. It uses every defensive and offensive capability we have," he asserted.

They scanned the scroll markings.

"Our fleet of warships will catapult fire balls and rocks upon them from Wercim Lake right outside the city. Hopefully they'll be deterred before they reach our forces.

The main battle will be fought outside the castle walls. Most of our force will meet the incoming Xanican army head on. All soldiers will be utilized. Our main objective is to keep them from the walls. If they reach them, soldiers atop and inside will have to halt them. Boiled oil will be mounted on the walls, piles of boulders, anything we can use as a mass weapon," John halted.

"If they get past the soldiers inside the walls, it will be up to the people to protect their homes," John sighed gravely.

"If it comes to that, there won't be much of Zyconia left to protect," Perrin continued.

"The fate of every man, woman and child in Zyconia rests upon the outcome of this war. We must defeat them, at all cost," Walker finished grimly.

As Kridelia, Yirdak and Delara made their way down the stone steps with Diana in tow, the guards following Yirdak whispered to Kridelia.

"Perhaps I should go and slow them down. It will give you more time to prepare for their arrival," Yirdak offered.

"If you want, just don't kill them," she sneered.

Yirdak turned, slowly facing away from Kridelia, and smiled a cold chilling grin that would have been enough to frighten a minotaur. He moved back the way that they'd come, Delara stared after him. Turning, they continued downward.

Bratain stood staring out to the south, into the sea. He hated leaving Xanica. He had first helped Koiban to build confidence among the people, to convince them that he was worthy of leadership. But he knew what the Vicar was, and it was wrong.

He and most of the clan armies had taken the Xanican warships to the Radrailian Islands far to the north of Xanica and Zyconia. Looking along the shoreline he saw the several dozen ships spread along the vast wharf. The city on shore was the Radrailian capital of Haken. It's people offered Bratain food and anything they needed, in return for protection from pirates and sea raiders. Besides that Bratain and the army had skills to hunt game.

He looked to the south again and saw another ship moving toward the wharf. It wasn't a pirate, it carried no markings. It was just a merchant vessel. Once ashore the few on board dispersed and went their own ways. All but one man, who approached his vessel.

"I'm looking for a man by the name of Bratain," the man bellowed to him from the wharf.

"That's me, come aboard," Bratain looked up amazed. He pushed a small bridge down to the wharf and the man walked up onto the deck. The man ruffled through his pouches and pulled a scroll with a Xanican royal seal from within.

"This is for you," he said finally.

Worriedly, Bratain tore open the seal and opened the scroll. He read quickly, his face turning pale. He looked quickly out to the south, the sea.

King Terrek and his small band had thus far avoided enemy soldiers but they were deep into occupied Zyconia now. They could barely see the peaks of the Minotaur Mountains on the horizon. Emperor Koiban had told them that the Vicar had enlisted the white skinned race and that they did indeed live in caverns in the mountains. He assumed that Kridelia and Yirdak had taken her there. Soon they would reach the mountains but what lay before them at the moment made them down hearted.

The small valley that surrounded them was scorched, the earth black and red. One of the first battles had taken place here. All around were the remains of destroyed chariots and wagons. Weapons and armor and men lay strewn across the plain. The carnage was everywhere.

The dead was mostly Zyconian and the White Souls but some Xanican lay dead as well. Terrek dismounted and walked to the nearest casualty, looking down into the face not of a soldier but a young boy. Many had lived in Southern Zyconia; some felt the need to defend their homes. They had paid for it with their lives.

Dismounting from his horse Koiban, with lowered head, walked out among the dead. Terrek had no fear that he would run from them. Where would he go? Both Xanica and Zyconia were his enemies at the moment. He was safer in their company than anywhere else.

Those behind held their heads solemnly, they knew the gravity of emotion their new king felt, and they shared it. Terrek looked at the young boy and thought about all his life could have been. If the war had never occurred Zyconia would have remained an unvolatile region, a safe kingdom to raise children, where they could grow up and prosper. Terrek would have seen to it as a totally well intentioned king. He swallowed.

Blood marred the boy's face and his eyes stared at him as if to say, why? Terrek lowered his face as he knelt down and took the young boy by the hand.

"I'm sorry…may the Maker guide you home," he whispered.

Unable to withstand the piercing eyes any longer, he placed a nearby cloak over the boy's body and covered his face.

Swooping down out of the sky Cramin and Grelkon had sighted the prey. The lone antelope stricken with desperation was racing into the nearby forest. Grelkon felt strange hunting and killing live prey and eating the raw, blood-ridden meat, but he had succumbed to the taste. There was just something about it that excited him. Now he had begun to thrive on that, whether in the hunt or battle.

The hunt had slowly evolved into a game, they would follow the prey and come close enough to scare it and then fall away. They almost enjoyed seeing the fear in their eyes. Eventually they would capture and kill, but for now they would only follow close. Two black shadows of death, coming ever closer.

Both were grinning.

"So what will happen once Zyconia is taken and the war is over?" asked Cramin.

Cramin and the other dark avians didn't speak very well and sometimes Grelkon had a hard time understanding them. But Cramin was more intellectual than the others as well as stronger. There was always an intelligence to his fighting style, more than just pure instinct in battle.

"I haven't really thought about it," Grelkon said, "the Vicar will have more for us."

Perhaps when it was over the Vicar would attack another land, there was much more out there, there had to be more.

"Grelkon, what was your family like?" asked Cramin.

Grelkon scowled slightly but held it in.

"They were self righteous and didn't understand me, maybe they didn't want too. They had no idea who I was. Besides you and the others are my family now," he replied.

Cramin eyed the prey again as Grelkon and he swooped and spiraled around it in the air.

"Do you miss them?" he asked.

Grelkon looked sideways as anger flooded his eyes.

"Enough of this! Don't ask me about them again! No I

do not miss them, they rejected me long before I rejected them, I hate them!" Grelkon yelled.

Powerfully Grelkon dived out of the sky his eyes seeing nothing but red, his brain on fire, the brown mass coming closer. The eyes full of fear, the eyes of the antelope: the eyes of Selate. He felt such an overwhelming feeling of power. Opening his beak and barring his claws Grelkon slammed into the antelope ripping, tearing and shredding into it's flesh. Screams erupted from the beast as Cramin swooped in and helped to mutilate the prey.

Emperor Koiban stumbled back toward the group, he had touched the dead, and his arms were reddened with blood. His face was pale and his eyes clouded with grief.

Koiban had been through many years of civil war and seem many atrocities but he'd never been responsible for the death of innocents. There were young men and woman, even children that had fought for their homes, and he knew the soldiers would still be alive had he not been so weak. He recognized a few of the men from his army and he had known them personally. It was as the Vicar had said; the loyal men had been placed in the front lines to die.

Emperor Koiban looked up at King Terrek full of regret.

"I – I didn't realize…" he said quietly.

His eyes had seen enough of what the Vicar represented and he knew it was evil.

"We'll stop him I swear, for both our kingdoms," Koiban promised.

"No, you won't," The voice belonged to a cloaked figure nearby.

"Yirdak," Koiban said in disgust.

Terrek withdrew his sword and stepped forward, in mid-stride he stopped. Yirdak's eyes glowed red. Looking around the field of death, Terrek and the others gasped. The dead was rising.

CHAPTER 11: DEATH BATTLE

Everywhere the bodies from the former battle rose from the ground, picked up their weapons and slowly descended upon the group. Many had missing arms, eyes, and even heads, but they were aware of their direction none the less. There was little doubt that Yirdak was controlling them. Terrek knew now that Yirdak had deep evil powers.

"To arms, protect yourselves!" Terrek ordered his small army, everyone withdrew their weapons and awaited the onslaught. There were hundreds of them all slowly marching toward them.

"Stop this Yirdak, don't you have any respect for the dead!" Koiban yelled angrily throwing a knife at the man. For a moment the dead fell limp as Yirdak retreated slightly behind them and concentrated again. The dead resumed their march.

Terrek and the others charged into the crowd swinging their weapons, hacking and silencing the dead in all directions. Even the small child Terrek had seen jumped upon his comrades swinging a small dagger he had picked up. Too many were closing in, Terrek and his men were going to be slaughtered!

"We're going to have to retreat!" Hemoth yelled to Terrek. He had just finished throwing half a dozen dead, who clung to his body, back into the crowds.

"No! I won't retreat, not when we're this close to finding Diana! Keep fighting!" he yelled. Koiban looked at Hemoth worriedly. There were hundreds. This small army was no match for them.

"We – we can't win Terrek!" Koiban said as he held back several of the dead with a spear. Their force was like a tidal wave crashing down on Terrek's small army.

Terrek looked around. They were all struggling. Very few of the dead had weapons, the field had been picked clean by the living after the battle. None-the-less they were overcoming them with shear numbers. Terrek squeezed his fist in defiance against Yirdak and in his desperation to save Diana.

"Terrek, we're going to die! We must retreat!" Celarus yelled to him.

His armor was already marred by the onslaught of these lifeless creatures attacking with rocks, tree branches and bare hands.

"Then go, you are freed from any obligations to me, Go! But I won't stop!" Terrek roared as he ran forward and dove headfirst into the nearest crowd of dead and savagely swung his sword in all directions.

He gritted his teeth and strained his muscles, killing and killing. Or at least attempting too, if they weren't completely severed or deterred, they would rise again. Terrek's every stroke was a plea to the Maker for Diana's life. He just couldn't retreat now.

They all stared at Terrek, then groaning they plunged forward as well, even more fiercely than before. Terrek looked at his comrades and continued fighting, but he wondered if they were right. The dead were very powerful.

"You won't get away with this! Why have you brought me here!" Diana yelled.

84

She was standing inside a small narrow cage that hung suspended from the ceiling of the surrounding cave. Directly below her was a steaming pit of liquid. It bubbled ominously, as if to show it's deadly presence to her. Nearby at the cave entrance stood Delara and her guards, at the edge of the chasm of lava, Kridelia and her son Koran.

"Once upon a time your husband had a family. They were killed by my husband, as they should have been! I have now lost my husband and my son is nothing to me. I'm here to claim vengeance! As your husband did to me, I will do to him!" Kridelia said vehemently.

Diana stared down at her from her cage and realized, for the first time just who Kridelia was. "You are Murack's widow!" she said.

"Yes, I am!" she said.

"Terrek's family were innocents there was no reason for Murack to have murdered them! You are crazy to be here on behalf of that man!" Diana reasoned.

"Silence wench, or I'll release that cage!" she rasped grabbing the nearby chain attached to the wall.

Diana was silent but looked upon her captor with disgust. Kridelia paced back toward the entrance to the cave that led up toward Delara's underground kingdom.

"What are you going to do to her?" Delara asked.

"That isn't your concern!" Kridelia said angrily.

Delara stared up at Diana wondering if she should step in now. That's when she heard the whistle beginning from the other caverns leading into the cave.

"The creatures are coming Kridelia, I'm leaving now! If you don't they'll kill you, for sure!" Delara spoke fearfully.

"I have no fear of the Crabnids. As a small child I found one when it was very young, before it's predatory instincts set in. I've learned to communicate with them and, with special powers, to control them," Kridelia smiled evilly.

Delara stared at her in disbelief.

"They will be Terrek's death. I will watch them tear the flesh from his bones and feast upon him while he's still alive. I want him to die slowly!" she said.

"I feel sorry for you," Delara scowled in disgust as she exited the cave entrance and closed the strong iron door on the outside sealing it.

"Don't feel sorry for me! Feel sorry for him and the others I will burn in my wake!" she screamed after her as she descended the steps beyond the door, her guards following. Kridelia turned with a sadistic expression and stared up at Diana.

The nearby caverns echoed with the high-pitched whistle now as large creatures reached the openings and showed themselves.

Diana's face went white as they appeared.

"What are they!" she screamed.

Kridelia smiled.

The throne room of the palace in New Victory City was full of officials. At the head of a large table were Perrin, Walker and John. Selate stood nearby with her children about the room, most were injured in some way. Victory City and Vatiria had been taken earlier that day and they were preparing for the battle of New Victory City.

Timothy sat against the wall nearby, a healer looking after him as his parents, Zachary and Juliana had accompanied Terrek. Juliana for her healing abilities that both she and Jessica possessed.

"Grelkon and the dark avians are just too strong for us," Selate explained to the three at the table.

"Don't blame yourself Selate, it hasn't been easy for any of us," Perrin said.

"We'd like to call this meeting to order!" Walker announced to the crowd of military officials. Everyone silenced and sat down.

"We must prepare for the battle. At this very moment the combined forces of the Whitesouls and the Xanican army under the Vicar are marching toward New Victory City. It is true that mercenaries and forces of our armies are slowing them but this is where the final stand will be. We must protect New Victory at all costs!" Walker paused.

"All soldiers across Zyconia have gathered just outside the city walls. If we lose this battle Zyconia belongs to the Vicar!" Perrin finished Gravely.

"So fight for your lives."

"So what has the master asked you to do today, Cramin?" scowled one of the dark avians.

All of them were on a hunt searching for antelope that they could bring back for their meal before the army attacked New Victory City.

"What do you mean?" Cramin asked angrily.

"We all know that you're the master's favorite. Will you be cleaning his claws today or making him a good nest?" mocked another.

Cramin looked at the half dozen with him and jumped upon the first biting and clawing.

"I do for myself, we simply relate!" yelled Cramin attacking the dark avian.

The others grew suddenly angry and all attacked Cramin with extreme ferocity. Grelkon, seeing them, swooped down from the skies. Confused, he pushed the group over into the grass.

"Stop it! Now!" he rasped as they ceased their feud.

"What's going on here?" Grelkon asked the claw-marked group.

They were silent.

"You know I would never start a fray with my brethren Grelkon," Cramin began.

Again one of the others angered, attacked Cramin.

"You liar, you struck first" he yelled.

"Only after you said that I was the masters little slave," Cramin roared, fighting back.

"Stop that I said!" Grelkon opened his wingspan. Both stopped again. Grelkon looked at them and thought for a moment. He knew they were all becoming very jealous of the time he was spending with Cramin.

"We don't have time for this! Find an antelope and return to the camp," he ordered staring at the one who had attacked Cramin he finished, "and do it quickly!"

"Whatever," said Cramin's attacker.

All of them turned and flew into the sky. Grelkon stared after them. That last word had been the first small act of defiance he had heard from any of the dark avians. This situation seemed so familiar to him, only before he had been on the opposite side of the argument.

Terrek and his group had been pushed back to a large steep rock hill that jutted up from the death field. The steep hill was completely surrounded by the dead now, the entire band of soldiers squeezed together desperately striking at the foe in attempts to keep them off their moor. The dead rasped and yelled at them in anger, their words only nonsense to the soldiers they attacked. Yirdak had moved closer too. They could just make out his twisted expression from the position he held behind the soldiers.

"Yirdak, stop this, as ruler of Xanica I command you!" Koiban yelled angrily.

Yirdak smiled, "you are very far from your throne room, emperor, and even farther from the power that you once held. Better you die now than later."

Terrek looked sideways at Koiban and shook his head, "your title means nothing to him Koiban, just keep fighting it's our only chance."

Koiban looked away embarrassed, as he began pushing and hacking away at the dead attempting to clamor up onto the rock face.

The dead gained strength slowly. As Yirdak became totally entranced, his eyes glowed stronger and brighter. The dead were empowered as one managed to pull himself up upon their moor followed by another and another. The group was pushed together as the dead began attempting to pull them from the moor into their waiting clutches.

"Fight, or we all die!" Terrek roared, but it was too late. Several of his men were pulled from the huge rock hill into the massive crowds of the dead.

That's when they pulled Hemoth from the moor. A wave of dead washed over the moor pulling all of them apart. Terrek looked back and realized almost everyone had been pulled from the moor or were being overcome by the massive numbers of the dead. They were all below screaming and fighting for their lives with every last breath. That's when he felt his sword being pulled from his grip as half a dozen dead pinned him with his chest against the stone surface.

A dead man sat on his back and lifted his dagger over his head ready to plunge it into Terrek and end his life.

"No!" Terrek screamed, barely able to breathe. He grabbed a rock nearby, and with one last, defiant effort, threw it at Yirdak.

Surprisingly the rock rebounded off Yirdak's head with a loud crack. Everything seemed frozen in place for just a moment. Terrek shut his eyes tightly, waiting for the dagger to descend into his back. He felt the knife fall onto his back, but suddenly realized there was no force behind it. Yirdak stumbled from the blow and keeled over onto the ground. Opening his eyes he saw the dead falling away from the moor and collapsing on the ground below. Terrek pushed his way free of the immobile dead and jumped from the hill.

All around him his men wrenched free, helping Jessica and Juliana who had accompanied them as healers. Zachary ran to Juliana and kissed her hugging her. Yirdak slowly rose to his feet. Terrek picked up a nearby spear and ran toward Yirdak. Disoriented, Yirdak opened his eyes and summoned the dead once more as he rose.

"Kill Yirdak! If we get to him, the dead will cease to attack us!" Terrek yelled.

The dead jumped upon Terrek once more and began attacking everyone around him. Terrek pushed forward dragging half a dozen dead with him. Everyone was armed again and fighting to reach Yirdak. They knew if they killed the man, the power in the dead would leave them. Once again several dozen dead bodies pulled Terrek to the ground mobbing him. Looking through the bodies he could see Yirdak standing several strides away, totally entranced. Before the dead could kill Terrek, Hemoth came plowing into them, pushing them away from him. Collapsing nearby, they attacked Hemoth.

Terrek, roaring, grabbed his spear, jumped to his feet, and took two running strides toward Yirdak. The dead reached for him as he leapt with all his might over the remaining enemies. Terrek plunged down with tremendous force, his spear tearing right through Yirdak's heart. It erupted from his back spraying the ground in blood. Yirdak opened his eyes, separated from his trance, as Terrek fell over on the ground and looked up at him.

A yell of agony escaped his throat as he looked angrily at Terrek. The dead fell everywhere, ceasing their attack on the group. Yirdak reached down and grasped Terrek around the throat, lifting him to his feet. Anger slated Yirdak's face as he attempted to strangle Terrek. Terrek hit him once and his grip to kill became a grip to hold himself up as he began choking on his own blood. He dropped one of his hands to his hip as the others came closer.

"Terrek look out!" cried Zachary.

Terrek looked down and caught Yirdak by the arm as he brought a dagger up toward his belly in his last attempt to kill. Terrek pushed it into Yirdak as he gave up his life and sank to the ground. Blood flowed forcefully from his throat. He sat silent propped up by the spear protruding from his back, as his eyes became dark.

CHAPTER 12: DISCOVERY

The Vicar stumbled sideways as he felt Yirdak die. Soldiers around the Vicar began surrounding him, very concerned.

"Sir, sir, are you all right!" a soldier asked trying to help him to his feet.

"DON'T TOUCH ME!" rasped the Vicar recovering himself. In anger he roared to the skies and moved into his tent entering a trance. He knew that Terrek had been responsible for Yirdak's death. He would now talk to the next person who had an opportunity to kill the king of Zyconia, in order to coerce the proper cooperation.

The Vicar closed his eyes and concentrated. Slowly his surroundings changed to his unreal realm, sliding into the non-corporeal. He stood and yelled thunderously, "DELARA!"

Hearing the roar in her mind Delara halted in place grumbling. She had become very wary of this evil game and wanted out of it, but she had not found her way yet. She closed her eyes and concentrated allowing herself to slip into the Vicar's realm.

Opening her eyes she faced the Vicar.

"WHAT HAS HAPPENED? WHERE ARE YIRDAK AND KRIDELIA?" he roared.

Delara stared at him, he was obviously very angry about something. "Kridelia is in the lower pits far below my kingdom awaiting Terrek who should be here soon. She has a plan to cause him to die painfully. As for Yirdak, I don't know. He arrived with Kridelia but returned to the surface to stall Terrek while Kridelia prepared."

The Vicar roared causing his realm to vibrate, Delara looked around realizing that something was very wrong.

"YIRDAK HAS BEEN KILLED BY TERREK," the Vicar rasped.

Delara looked at him, surprised. She found it amazing that one without possession of any special powers had vanquished Yirdak. Her mind slowed a little as she went over many thoughts.

"I AM HEADING BACK TO DYSTARA. I DON'T CARE ANYMORE IF KRIDELIA WANTS HER REVENGE! AS SOON AS TERREK ARRIVES IN YOUR CAVERNS I WANT YOU TO KILL HIM! DO YOU UNDERSTAND!" he yelled.

Delara gazed upward, "But if he can kill someone as powerful as Yirdak what makes you think I can stop him?" she said angrily, just a little too angrily.

The Vicar increased in size taking on the form of an incredibly grotesque monster. He reached down and scooped Delara up in his grasp crushing her severely. She had little control over the situation. The Vicar was so filled with rage that his powers were too much for her to fight.

The new monster pulled her close to it's massive mouth which featured two massive almost wild pig-like tusks. But they were sharp like fangs. Delara stared in horror at the face. Horns covered most of the scalp, and red slime flowed from pores upon the surface. The skin was scaled and the eyes piercing red and green. It brought forth nothing but fear from her. She used her powers to prevent herself from being crushed but that was all she could accomplish.

"YOU WILL KILL HIM, DELARA!" the beast roared.

Delara struggled as the monster's claws dug into her arms.

"Yes," she said, compliantly.

Suddenly the realm rushed away as Delara hit the floor of her cavern kingdom. Her guards helped her up very concerned as she held her arms painfully. Large scratches covered them.

The man peered over the side of his ship into the water staring down at the rising waves caused by his vessel. After receiving the message from Xanica he had set sail right away, he had to return, out of honor. Raising his gaze he saw the horizon and knew that just beyond lay home. On both sides of his vessel traveled dozens of other warships filled with soldiers. Soon they would fight a great battle.

Walking across the ship he went below and removed the sea charts from his chest unscrolling them on the floor. He knew they would be choosing a different route than just directly home. They would have to fight to go home.

"I can see land!" someone cried from outside.

Leaving his charts he ran out onto the deck within the crowd of soldiers. Squinting he surveyed the horizon. Then it caught his eye, it was land! Smiling he stepped back into the lower reaches of the vessel. Picking up his sea chart he placed his knife on their destination: New Victory City.

Leaving the field of death behind Terrek and the others had reached the edge of the Minotaur Mountains. No one had been severely injured by the onslaught of the dead bodies, which had surprised Terrek, but he knew his men were very resourceful in battle, especially when fighting to survive. The peaks were deceivingly majestic, but their name came from the fact that minotaurs lived throughout the mountains. This was an incredibly dangerous area to be in, let alone live. Very few men had ever traveled among the mountains and survived.

But this was not their destination. They traveled beneath the mountains in a massive collection of caves and caverns, where Kridelia had taken Diana. Emperor Koiban had confided in Terrek already that the Vicar had enlisted the help of the Whitesouls. They lived beneath the mountains and Koiban expected that this was where she had been taken.

"Terrek! I've found a small cave!" Adam said.

Terrek and his group rushed around a small bend in the rock formation and spied the cave. Both Adam and Jason were peeling away large portions of moss and vines that had obviously been used to conceal the entrance.

"Draw your weapons and follow me inside," Terrek ordered.

Everyone did as they were told. Terrek moved past Jason and Adam pushing his way into the moss-laden cave.

Celarus stood at the mouth of the cave thinking about the past. Flashbacks went through his brain as his stomach churned. Would he find answers inside these caverns? Would he like what he found?

"Celarus? Are you coming?" asked Zachary.

"Yes – yes, ah, just tired that's all," he replied.

"You look a little pale. Are you sick?" Zachary asked.

Celarus shook his head moving past him into the cave.

"No, just tired. Well let's not keep Terrek waiting he's going to need our help."

"Right," said Zachary following, a little puzzled.

Perrin, Walker and John stood upon the walls of New Victory City viewing the vast armies that Terrek had recruited within the past year. Their number was massive but they knew that clashing with the forces of both Xanica and the Whitesouls that it would be an extreme battle. They honestly didn't know if their soldiers could repel the enemy.

All soldiers sat about the outside of the city completely surrounding more than half of the wall. For now they ate and prepared, soon it would be a matter of survival. Not far away the lake outside the city was filled with their small fleet of warships ready to attack the enemy with the use of flaming projectiles. John had carefully mapped out the battle plan for all military officials below.

"Do they know what we're facing?" John asked Perrin and Walker.

Both looked down at the soldiers.

"Yes," they replied in unison.

John clapped his breastplate against his chest and prepared his armor to join the men below.

"I know that we're supposed to remain in the palace to give orders to the lines if the city is compromised, but if that happens I don't think we will be able to do much. I think we should join you on the battlefield," Perrin said.

"Yes, but –," John started.

"I think maybe he's right," Walker cut him off.

John thought for a moment and realized there was no arguing now. He also knew they were probably right.

After entering the cave Terrek and the others had walked a great distance through an endless number of caverns. They were unsure that the path they'd chosen was the correct one until they reached the double bronze doors before them.

The doors were aged and dirty but after Terrek examined the crack between both, he realized they had been opened recently. Then he looked to the cave floor and realized he could make out a thin sliver of light coming from beneath the door. Carefully he pushed on the doors, they didn't move. Terrek looked between the doors. There had to be a locking mechanism between the doors.

Turning to the silent group he surveyed the cave. With Hemoth's help they could probably break down the door with the use of several huge boulders within the cave but he decided that approaching with stealth was the best. Receiving a small dagger from Adam he wedged it between the doors. Then, with all his might, he brought both his clasped gauntlets into the dagger. The old door groaned as the lock on the opposite side shattered. Hemoth and Terrek braced themselves each on a door and pushed. The doors flew open as everyone raised their weapons.

The hall beyond was silent, but obviously part of an inhabited area. Along the walls were torches for lighting, several doors lined the walls on both sides.

They moved carefully down the large hall. After passing several more halls they came to a vast throne room. Entering, they began to look about in curiosity. Celarus wandered about the room and into a tunnel nearby, at the end of the tunnel was a vast bedchamber. Undoubtedly fit for royalt y.

Moving next to the bed he sat down and surveyed a wide array of gems and artifacts in a glass cabinet beside the bed. There were emeralds, rubies even diamonds. Then something else caught his eye. It seemed to be a vase containing some type of embalming fluid and within the fluid a flower. Celarus stood quickly and pried open the cabinet. Grabbing the flask with the flower inside he stared in disbelief. Floating inside the fluid was an aged white rose. Expressed on one of the rose petals was a single red stain. A drop of blood.

Celarus spun and ran down the tunnel into the throne room where the others still looked about. He held out the flask and started to address Terrek.

"Terrek, I found something important, something you should -," he stopped, hearing a roar.

Suddenly a battle cry arose as a white-skinned soldier entered the throne room. Suddenly white-skinned beings flooded the room followed by a decorated queen, Delara.

CHAPTER 13: REMEMBERING

The battle exploded as everyone, white-skinned and otherwise withdrew their weapons. Quickly Terrek's army defended themselves. Celarus stood, motionless. Then he backed against the cave wall and looked at the flask in his hand. He looked across the room at the white-skinned queen a tear reaching his eye. He let his breath out heavily, realizing he had to stop this.

Moving forward sword in hand he was stalled by several white-skinned guards swinging their blades.

Terrek and the others fought brutally with the white-skinned men. Finally Delara moved past everyone and reached Terrek.

"I'm sorry, you must die," she said as she flung him against the cave wall with her unseen powers. Terrek rebounded off of the wall barely conscious. Delara grabbed a blade and started forward. Suddenly Celarus barred her way.

"Stand aside or die!" she commanded. Looking down she realized that he was holding something that belonged to her.

"How dare you!" she cried, pushing him against the rock face pulling the flask from his hands and bringing her blade to his throat, "what gives you the right to touch my possessions. I'm going to kill you!"

"Delara," Celarus said softly.

Delara loosened her grip on the blade, her features became confused. He knew her name; the voice and face were familiar. She gazed into the face of Celarus, then down to the flask. She looked upon the white rose with the red stain and looked again at Celarus. Her face lost it's evil nature and became that of an innocent adolescent once again.

"Celarus!" she cried with tears in her eyes.

"Only a few more hours and we attack New Victory City, are you ready Cramin?" asked Grelkon.

"Of course master, very ready!" he said.

Nearby the other dark avians listened to both in disgust.

"The master doesn't give the rest of us any sort of talks or attention like Cramin receives. It's as though he is more important than the rest of us," one growled.

"The master has become weak and stupid. I don't even think we need him anymore," erupted a comment from the dark avian who had attacked Grelkon previously.

They grumbled among themselves but one of them was much more vehement. He picked up a small stone from the ground and threw it at Cramin. The pebble bounced off Cramin's head as he spun around. Grelkon had also seen the pebble rebound and turned angrily toward the nearest group.

"Which one of you threw that stone?" asked Grelkon.

No one said a word. Approaching the group Grelkon looked upon the culprit.

"Was it you?" Grelkon asked.

The dark avian was the same who had attacked Cramin previously, Grelkon had come to call him Darcet. He looked up at Grelkon with defiance on his face.

"Yes, I did!" he roared.

"One of you hold him," Grelkon yelled to the group. They merely moved off as Grelkon turned to Cramin, "hold him."

Cramin nodded and flung his wings around Darcet whom struggled in his grip.

"What are you doing, let go!" he roared.

Carefully retrieving a branch from the ground Grelkon hit Darcet upon his back a few times. Not enough to really hurt him, just enough to embarrass him in front of the others. The others looked surprised at Grelkon. Finally Cramin released Darcet who fell over into a small stream of mud on the ground.

"I want all of you to remember this," Grelkon said to the dark avians, "if you are out of line you will be punished. I will not tolerate disobedience!" he affirmed.

"You'll regret that!" Darcet roared as he got to his feet and spun off into the sky. Grelkon watched him go very worried.

"Stop!" Delara yelled to her men, "stop fighting! I command you!" Delara's men drew back from their fray with Terrek's small army.
Terrek, now back on his feet, looked puzzled. He stared at the white-skinned queen, and confirmed the order.
"Halt men! Don't attack!" he ordered his army.
Delara moved closer, both she and Celarus held the flask now, fingers interlaced. She caressed his cheek with her hand, her eyes wandering over his face.
"Celarus," she whispered softly.

Their eyes met for the first time in nearly twenty years, and for the first time in nearly twenty years Queen Delara smiled.

"I –," they both started but stopped, not wanting to interrupt the other. Celarus squeezed her hand gently. Then Delara remembered the horrid consequences of her encounter, and she recovered. Staring around at her soldiers and the gathering Zyconian men she regained her royal composure.

"All right! Everyone outside except Celarus and King Terrek!" Delara ordered.

Everyone stared at Terrek for his approval; he nodded slowly, puzzled. The mixed crowd shuffled outside the throne room and closed the large doors, remaining outside.

Delara turned away from both men for a moment, a tear rolled down her face as she held herself stable basing her arm against her throne.

"You should know that I avenged your father, and I made them pay for what they did," he said to her, referring to the soldiers that he had poisoned and murdered so long ago.

"I'm very confused," Terrek interrupted.

"Is it all right if I try to explain to him Delara?" asked Celarus.

She nodded turning and sitting on her throne, her mind very deep in thought.

"A long time ago Delara and I met in a cave, we became very close," he began.

"One day I returned to the cave to see her and brought her that white rose," he pointed to the flask of embalming fluid containing the flower, "I didn't realize that I had been followed. Several mercenaries killed Delara's father and there was a small battle within the cave. I – I ran from the cave," he said in a low tone.

"I followed the mercenaries, I poisoned their water and killed the ones who weren't poisoned to death. After that, I slowly became an assassin and eventually became the leader of the Vicar's assassin army," he finished.

Delara's head snapped back.

"Wait! You were dealing with the Vicar?"

"Yes. For a long time I was so bitter toward everything. Not long ago King Terrek helped me to escape that; I let go of my past. I'm a Zyconian Duke now," he replied.

"I'm only surprised because it was the Vicar who taught me in the ways of the dark arts. He, in essence, gave me my powers," she said.

"It seems both of you were dealing with the Vicar around the same time. Just not aware of eachother," Terrek injected.

"I believe I remember the Vicar leaving the Forest of Darkness upon occasion and traveling among the mountains. I guess now I know why," Celarus remembered.

Delara got up from her throne and approached Celarus.

"Thank you for avenging my father Celarus," she began softly.

"But I need to ask you, why did you run?"

"I realized you knew my people would protect me, that I would be taken from the battle and you weren't afraid of the men. You tried to protect me when they first entered the cave. So why did you bolt from the cave?" she asked softly.

Terrek took a few steps away to allow them a few moments of privacy.

"I – I was so overwhelmed with what had happened. I was just so ashamed with what my race had done to your father. I knew you had to blame me for what happened," he trembled sadly.

"No!" she began a caring expression on her face. She took him by the hand and moved closer.

"I could never blame you for what happened. What happened that day was an accident on our part. We didn't know the danger was coming and we couldn't have known.

I know that you would do anything to erase what happened, right?" she said.

Celarus nodded without hesitation.

She wrapped her arms around him as they embraced.

"I've missed you."

They drew close slightly faces almost touching.

"I've missed you too, Delara, so much," Celarus said. Slowly they moved forward and kissed. It almost seemed as though this moment had continued where their first kiss left off.

"Ahem," Terrek cleared his throat.

Both withdrew and faced him.

"Delara, you must help us," he said quickly.

Delara, still focused on Celarus, wrenched her mind back to reality.

"Yes, I believe it's time for me to stop giving in to the Vicar and stand up for what's right. I will send an order for my forces to withdraw from Zyconia and return home."

"Thank you Delara," Terrek replied, "do you know where Kridelia has taken my wife?"

"Yes, I can take you to her," Delara thought for a moment.

"I will accompany you, she is in the lower caverns. But I must warn you, she has a group of monsters under her control and it may be best for us to descend only with a small group. Your wife is in a cage hanging over a lava pit, we don't want to agitate Kridelia."

"Very well, but let's move quickly," Terrek said. Both Delara and Celarus nodded.

Terrek had chosen Hemoth, Zachary, Celarus, and Ricsis to accompany him, all others remained above. Delara stopped at the door and pushed it open, entering. Far across the expanse of the cave floor stood Kridelia and her son, Koran. The monsters of these caverns were no where to be seen. Terrek and the others stood inside the darkness of the doorway.

"I must talk with you!" Delara said walking out toward her. Kridelia stared at her with suspicion. Delara had almost reached Kridelia when she moved toward the chain suspending Diana above the lava pit.

"I know you're out there Terrek, come in and see your wife die!" she yelled. Kridelia brought her hand up to release the chain but before she could Delara plowed into her. Both women went rolling across the cave surface as Terrek and the others entered the cave and rushed in their direction. Suddenly several monsters crawled up from inside the lava pit barring their way. Terrek and the others drew their swords in horror.

CHAPTER 14: SIEGE

The sun rose from the darkness shining it's all too familiar light upon New Victory City. Thousands of warriors stood ready for the onslaught of the Xanican forces. Among them their leaders: Walker, Perrin and John. Everyone was prepared for death.

Not a man showed fear but deep inside everyone was aware of the odds and wishing that they were not part of them. Not far behind lay the city walls, rows and rows of soldiers upon them. Most of the battle would be fought from the outside of the city. If their stand outside failed and they allowed anyone to get through into the city, it would be all over.

Suddenly a lone soldier rode up the hill toward the army and approached the leading three. He wore the marks of battle but also the garments of the Zyconian army. Out of breath he collapsed before them.

"They're – they're coming, sir, all other resistance has failed. We are just too few and scattered to push them away from the cit y!" he gasped.

Perrin merely glanced down at him and to the others.

"Go further north, find somewhere to tend to your wounds, you've done all you can," he said quietly. The man looked back the way he came then nodded, mounted his horse and moved past the army riding away.

All three leaders drew their swords, thousands behind them followed suit. The thunder of hoof-beats came to them now as a dark line of endless horsemen crested the horizon. They loomed closer and closer. Between both armies lay the large lake in which all Zyconia's warships were gathered. Already they began catapulting fireballs and rocks from their decks attempting to deter the oncoming forces. They kept coming. Both Xanican and Whitesoul. Above, the dark avians soared as well.

Perrin roared as he moved his horse forward into a gallop, everyone rushed forward into battle. Overhead Selate and her children engaged the dark avians.

Terrek was mortified. The creatures before him were the most grotesque he had ever seen. They were a cross between a crab and a tarantula. They had several hairy legs but also claws like a crab, several hundred eyes covered what appeared to be their heads. Opening their mouths they screamed with a piercing shrillness. Green venom hung from their fang-toothed mouths. They were larger then men, and they were fearless. Rushing forward they advanced on Terrek and the others.

Terrek swung at one of the beasts burying his blade deep. The others attacked the monsters as well.

Kridelia screamed hitting Delara in the stomach as they grappled.

"What are you doing?" Kridelia roared, "the Vicar will kill you for this!" Kridelia wrapped her hands around Delara's neck.

"I'm through with the Vicar," Delara yelled as she planted her fist into the black haired witch's face. Both fell over onto the cave floor again. They were fighting power to power as well, Kridelia had a stronger will than Delara had anticipated. Her anger over her husband's death drove her. Finally, Delara conquered Kridelia's power forcing her up against the cave wall with an invisible barrier.

Kridelia mumbled strange words as she closed her eyes. "You are beaten, give up!" Delara said with confidence. "Not yet!" she cried.

"Ow!" suddenly Delara spun, Koran had stabbed her in the leg. Kridelia must have mumbled a spell to make him fight for her. Delara swung her arm striking the child unconscious as she stumbled to the cave floor losing her hold on Kridelia. Recovering, she raised her face in time only to receive a blow to the forehead as Kridelia brought a large stone down upon her. She stumbled backwards, disoriented.

Not far away Terrek, Hemoth, Zachary, Celarus and Ricsis backed up into a small, enclosed area of the cave. There were dozens of Crabnids cornering them, too many. Terrek surveyed the immediate area and crawled up the walls of the caverns, as did the others. The creatures covered the floor below as all the men began pushing the spiked rocks on the ceiling, gravity did the rest. With several cracking sounds, it began raining rocks on the creatures below, piercing one after another.

Everyone jumped off the walls attacking once again. Hemoth brought his club down heavily on one of the creatures heads crushing it's skull as the others moved quickly, pushing the wounded beasts over the edge into the acidic pit below. They waded into the remaining ones slicing and hacking at their multi-legged bodies.

Kridelia hit Delara across the face with an armored glove sending her sprawling to the edge of the chasm. Quickly Kridelia jumped toward the wall and began to loosen the steel chain that held Diana's cage.

Diana saw her and screamed, "Terrek!" but he was still to far away dispatching the Crabnids.

Diana's high-pitched scream filled the cave as Kridelia let the chain go and the cage plummeted down directly for the acidic liquid.

Kridelia turned and moved to the edge of the pit. She was surprised to see the cage rising above the surface of the liquid. She looked sideways at a disoriented Delara, barely conscious, holding her arm out. Her power kept Diana from her burning death.

"Let it go!" Kridelia roared as she raced forward striking her in the ribs. Delara collapsed again as Kridelia pulled her to her feet by her neck. Delara's eyes floated in their sockets as blood flowed across her face from the gash in her forehead she'd received previously. She hung limply, but still managed to point her arm toward the pit in defiance.

"Let go of the cage or I'll kill you," she screamed unsheathing her dagger.

Delara looked at her, totally unmoved by her statement.

"I'm going to kill -," suddenly Kridelia felt a grip around her wrist as she dropped the dagger and Delara to the cavern floor. Picking Kridelia up Celarus hurled her into the pit below as she screamed in terror. Fear invaded her features as she forgot her powers and fell down into the yawning pit.

Terrek, Hemoth, Zachary and Ricsis stood covered in cuts. Celarus held Delara up into a sitting position. Behind them lay the carnage of several dozen Crabnid bodies. Delara stretched her arm far above her head as the cage containing Diana rose from the depths and found a resting place on solid ground. Inside, Diana smiled through tears. Terrek broke the lock from the cage with his sword and Diana ran forward into his arms, he embraced her happily.

"I knew you'd come," she cried happily, tears of joy mixed with those of relief from the evil she'd endured. Terrek kissed her forehead and held her close. After a moment they heard screaming from below. Moving to the

edge of the chasm everyone peered down through the rising acidic mist.

Kridelia sat below on a collection of jagged rocks crying. Her head was down and her hands covered it. She looked up and Terrek realized what had happened.

"Look, look what you have done to me!" she rasped.

She had landed on the rocks below and was covered in blood, severely injured from the fall, but this wasn't the most horrifying result. She had tasted the sting of the acid below as well. Her hair was burned and frayed, here and there sections were completely missing. Her face had been disfigured, burned, leaving her with a disturbing appearance. No longer was her skin the smooth white color it had been; now it displayed blood vessels and burned bubbly skin. She felt her face as she continued to scream and scream.

"Look what you've done! Look what you've done!" Kridelia covered her face with her arms. Slowly using her power she rose from the pit, hovering.

"You will die!" she cried futilely as she flew across the landing where they stood and into one of the cavern passages that the creatures had used to enter the cave not long before.

Delara raised herself in Celarus's arms.

"It will be no use following her, that tunnel leads back to the surface eventually," she said groggily. Delara fell back into Celarus, she looked at him and smiled.

"Thank you for the save," she said referring to his action of stopping Kridelia from killing her.

"Thank you too Delara," Terrek said, still holding Diana's hands. Delara smiled again, she knew that after the entire ugly episode, she was finally doing what was right. She felt good, and knew that she was on the right side of the battle.

Perrin waded into crowds of soldiers fighting for his life as they struck at him from all directions. He'd lost sight of Walker and John and was afraid that soon he would lose his sight altogether. Here and there his soldiers filled his view, but the number of enemies was just so overwhelming. The Whitesouls possessed a fighting ability unmatched by the Zyconian force or the remainder of the Xanican forces. Deep down, Perrin didn't think they had a chance.

The more he killed the more came forward. Sooner or later he knew he would tire or they would simply exploit a weakness and he would be gone. Nonetheless he continued to fight, keeping in his mind what he was fighting for.

Suddenly, one of their Whitesoul enemies slashed Perrin across the arm. Then, from behind several soldiers pushed him to the ground. He rolled over in the dirt gripping his bleeding arm. A heavy boot stepped upon his chest as he looked up at one of the Whitesouls with sword in hand.

"You must die," he roared over the noise of battle lifting his sword to strike.

Suddenly a shrill blast filled the battlefield the Whitesoul paused for a moment. Not far behind their armies a lone Whitesoul messenger blew a huge horn. Almost everyone stopped for a moment. The crowd wondered what was going on.

The Whitesoul removed his boot from Perrin's chest who used this opportunity to scramble through the crowds to several of his men. He used a rag as a makeshift bandage for his arm. Perrin looked awestruck as the crowd thinned out, every Whitesoul had retreated to the position where their messenger stood. The remaining Xanican forces appeared angered as they returned their attention to the Zyconian force. Perrin didn't know if the Whitesouls were just discussing a battle plan or whether they'd decided to back out, but either way he knew now was the time to attack.

"Charge!" he ordered the Zyconian army, not far from him he heard Walker and John echo his words. The Xanican army was still a massive force but the Whitesouls had comprised nearly half of their forces. Perrin knew they had more than a chance of winning the battle if they merely had to clash with this force.

Plowing forward they kept their eyes on the Whitesoul forces, suddenly they began to leave the battlefield completely.

"What's going on!" Perrin yelled to Walker who was now in his view.

"I don't know but we can win now!" Walker yelled back.

The battle was slowly pushed down next to the nearby lake. Soldiers on the Zyconian warships came ashore to battle now. Instantly something caught everyone's eye, it was a warship flying a Xanican flag. Perrin's heart sank. Were they reinforcements? The ship was followed by another and another as they flooded the entire lake. Atop the deck of the lead ship stood a decorated warrior with a red beard.

Surprisingly the Xanican warships had not attacked the Zyconian vessels. As they reached the docks Perrin noticed that despite the Xanican markings on the vessels their tunics were colored differently than those of the men they fought presently. Suddenly drawbridges were dropped from all of the ships as soldiers waded to the shores, and the most bizarre thing was whom they chose to attack. Perrin was breathless as this new force lead by the red-bearded man joined the Zyconian army in their defense of New Victory City. They attacked the same force that threatened them.

Not about to lose his head Perrin returned to the battle, as he noticed that their foe was already retreating, the enemy was severely outnumbered now. Their men below began firing spears and objects skyward as well as attempting to slay the dark avians. It was amazing but they were having luck.

Above, Selate tried to keep her flock from Grelkon as best she could. She knew what he was capable of now, but she still loved him, he was her child. She fought him herself in every battle. Before, he had been ruthless, but now something was different, he was holding back now for some reason.

"You don't have to be like this, Grelkon, you can come back to us!" Selate tried to tell him as she flew forward hitting him and scratching with her claws.

Grelkon said nothing for awhile merely fighting her and pushing her back.

"No," he managed, "I can't!" he yelled at her as he renewed his attack with strength. Finally Fernok came to his mothers rescue. As they fought Grelkon noticed the crossbow man on his back attempting to hit him. He pushed Fernok as the man held on for dear life.

"Did king Terrek think equipping you with those men would help you?!" he roared.

Several spears flew past Grelkon causing him to look down, he saw the Vicar's Xanican forces retreating. Projectiles of all kinds were flying in their direction as the other dark avians began to peel off.

"We – we're losing!" Grelkon realized.

"No, keep fighting! Where are you going?" he stared back at his dark avians.

Suddenly a small hammer struck him in the head as he struggled to remain conscious. Fernok flew in close as the soldier on his back fired a huge spear into Grelkon's back.

Grelkon screamed turning, his wing fell limp as he spiraled toward the ground. His wing was severely injured. The ground approached faster as he prepared for his death, blood fell from the side of his head and wing. Out of

nowhere Cramin swooped in low and caught the barely conscious leader of the dark avians.

"Cramin," Grelkon forced drowsily.

He held Grelkon in his claws flying higher away from the battle.

"We must keep fighting! We must!" Grelkon yelled weakly.

"We can't, we'll die, the battle is theirs," Cramin whispered as he immersed them both in the cloud cover.

Terrek and Diana sat on the cave floor their foreheads resting against one another as they stared into eachothers face. He smiled, so happy, as he lost himself in the blue of her eyes. Nearby Zachary, Ricsis and Hemoth surveyed the cave for any more enemies while Celarus sat with Delara tending to her wounds.

"Do you feel faint?" Celarus asked her worriedly.

"Not now that you are here," Delara smiled.

Crying reached their ears as Terrek stood, looking to Delara curiously. The crying echoed from a small ditch in the cave floor nearby. Everyone approached looking down into the small chasm. Within sat Koran.

Delara turned to Terrek, "Koran is Kridelia's son, I think that he has been controlled by spells she has cast upon him. I think her power has lifted, he seems to have his own free will now."

Terrek moved forward and stepped into the ditch sitting beside the child trying to wipe away his tears. The child stared at him.

"My mother – she makes me do things, things that aren't right – things that are bad," he said sadly.

Terrek lowered his head for a moment as he realized what this small boy must have experienced throughout his childhood.

"Her power is gone now Koran, would you like to come with us? I promise we will find you someone that will never do that to you," he assured Koran.

Displaying an expression of relief, the boy nodded through his tears.

CHAPTER 15: DEVOURING THE DEAD

Terrek and the others had ascended to Delara's throne room. Delara told them that the only way the Vicar could be defeated was if his realm was destroyed. That had been how he escaped the explosion of the dark crystal during their last battle at the ruins that once lay where New Victory City now stood. The Vicar merely passed through his realm to escape the explosion. Delara told Terrek that since she was not in good physical condition after her combat with Kridelia she couldn't enter the realm and do battle. However, she could feed her power to him, although she was not a match for the power of the Vicar. But Terrek agreed to enter the realm and battle the Vicar. He knew he had to do it.

Diana sat beside Terrek holding his hand. She was distressed once again, as she knew that he was about to take another risk. She disliked him being in danger but she knew his mind was made up.

Both Whitesouls and Zyconian men filled the throne room. Approaching the center of the room Delara and Terrek faced eachother as they closed their eyes. Delara placed her palm against his forehead as she entered a trance. Her hand glowed, and when Terrek's eyes opened again, they glowed blue. Delara remained motionless as she summoned the Vicar into his realm with her mind.

Suddenly, Terrek disappeared from their sight as he reappeared on a non-corporeal plain.

He lifted his gaze as he saw the Vicar before him. Before he could react, the phantom reached out and struck him down to the firmament below them. Then the Vicar's form dispersed into a million rays of light as he disappeared. The floating blue existence surrounded Terrek and changed as it formed into a large pit. The swamp beneath his feet moved with life. Over head, the opening to the pit revealed black clouds racing across an evil sky. Guttural sounds filled the air.

"SO DELARA HAS CHOSEN TO SIDE WITH YOU! THAT IS UNFORTUNATE FOR HER, IT MEANS HER RACE WILL HAVE NO PLACE IN THE NEW ORDER WHEN I AM RULER OF BOTH XANICA AND ZYCONIA. THEY MUST DIE!" the Vicar's voice boomed, echoing from all points of this newly created illusion. Or at least what Terrek perceived to be an illusion.

"You will never hurt anyone again!" Terrek cried vehemently as the fierce winds of this newly formed world played havoc with his breath, "I'm here to make sure of that!"

"HOW DARE YOU! The Vicar boomed. All around Terrek green snakes rose and eyed him as their new prey. Terrek focused, and a sword appeared in his hand. The snakes moved forward, biting at him, as he sliced and slashed them to keep them down. As each snake's head was cut off it grew back to continue the attack. Focusing, Terrek caused his sword to be engulfed in flames. Now as he severed their heads, the flesh remained burnt and their heads didn't grow back, but there were still too many of them. He had to escape the pit. He rushed to the walls and began climbing for his life. Pulling himself up on the walls he raced to reach the top.

Looking below, for an instant he was horrified, as the ground beneath the swamp lifted revealing a huge monster.

The entire surface beneath the swamp had been the head of this monster. Now lifting itself Terrek saw the thousands of eyes and fang-toothed mouths that covered the surface. Hundreds of small snakes rose from the face stretching to grip him. Several spiraled around his legs and torso trying to pull him down to be devoured.

"YOU CAN'T ESCAPE," bellowed the Vicar's voice from within the horrible monster. As fear flooded him Terrek saw the Vicar's piercing stare of satisfaction in every eye below. He closed his eyes, tightened his grip and concentrated Delara's power.

Instantly, the sides of the pit erupted as shards of rock began shooting from the walls into the snakeheads, severing them. Loosening their grip on his legs he cut them with his sword and sprang upward with the gift of flight from the pit. Reaching the top he ran from the pit and focused on his next defense as the Vicar roared behind him.

"There is no game, the only thing left to eat is our dead," Darcet said menacingly.

The dark avians were slowly starving to death, after losing the battle and being pushed back, they had no luck finding food. The entire army nearby was also starving. Only small rations had been circulated. After being pushed back several times, rations had been seized and unfortunately it had become difficult to find animals to feed on. The dark avians were about to cross the line of all things decent.

"Grelkon will be very angry!" Cramin yelled at Darcet and the others who surveyed the three bodies of their dead comrades nearby.

"We have no choice!" Darcet roared back, "would you have us starve to death," he finished vehemently.

"I – I won't be part of this!" Cramin said weakly.

Quickly the scavengers rushed at the dead bodies picking and tearing at flesh much like their own. Stripping away feathers and meat, gnawing on cartilage and bone.

Although intrigued by the depth of their depravity, Cramin looked at them feeling sickened, angry and sad. During the process that created him he knew he had been different than the others somehow. It was true that he harbored Grelkon's passion and strength, but he had been created from the one last shred of compassion and respect Grelkon had left for the world, his past life, his mother, and his family.

Suddenly Grelkon ran from his tent still injured but moving quickly.

"What is going on Cramin? Where did they find food?" Grelkon yelled over the gluttonous sounds of the black birds.

"I tried to tell them not to do this," Cramin choked, backing away from him.

Confused Grelkon stared at the ravaging group. Instantly Darcet withdrew his head from the center mass. Covering his sharp toothed beak was blood and hanging from inside his mouth was black feathers. Darcet saw him and grinned, it was a grin that burned through him. Grelkon, shaken by overwhelming shock, ran toward the group realizing that they were devouring their dead from the previous battle.

"Stop, stop it, I command you!" he roared, but none of them heard him, they were too hungry. Attempting to push them away from the bodies Grelkon was thrown back to the ground landing on his wing. Wincing at the pain shooting through his appendage he gazed up to see the ruthless face of Darcet peering down at him from the group of ravaging birds. They shrieked as they tore more and more flesh in a cannibalistic manner. Cramin came from nearby and helped Grelkon away from the gruesome scene.

The pit boiled out of the earth exploding a supernova on the celestial plain skies. The scene began to dissolve as the Vicar's essence flowed through the sky like a space-born river. His roars shattered everything as a jungle surrounded Terrek. Mentally he created his sword again causing it to grow and allow him the ability to clear the underbrush. Hacking away at the encompassing vines, he peered skyward to see the Vicar's newest form.

Piercing the clouds with strong bony, outstretched wings was a dragon. The bat-like wings glistened black, it's tail was forked, and it spiraled through the sky with little effort. Smoke rose from the Vicar's throat as his dark pupils rolled to face Terrek, staring at him like a snake does a mouse. The black shape dove out of the sky much in the same manner Terrek had seen the avians do, only this time he knew it meant danger. Opening his sparking mouth, the Vicar swooped low over the jungle hurtling straight at Terrek as his mouth sprayed flames, blasting the trees to charred splinters.

At that moment, Terrek had erected an invisible shield against the blast. Squinting hard, he held his protection in place. The fire was so hot, so powerful, maybe he couldn't do this, he thought. Terrek opened his eyes and for a moment it felt as though time had stopped. Looking forward into the scorched burning trunks of the jungle Terrek saw Zyron. He lifted his arm high over his head and tightened his hand into a fist, his face became strong. Terrek nodded as he closed his eyes and focused, straining Delara's powers.

In disgust the Vicar passed over Terrek. Ceasing his fiery attack, he landed on a nearby hill. Terrek spun just in time to see the dragon rushing directly for him. Terrek held his large shield in front of his body as a turbulent storm of fire bore down on him. Kneeling behind his shield he grabbed at the dirt to keep from being blown away.

Instantly the Vicar-dragon swung it's massive tail, sending Terrek flying through the air into some nearby tree trunks. Terrek gasped as he sat up. Blood poured from his nose, and the wind had been knocked out of him. Staring up he saw the Vicar dragon staring down at his fallen form.

The Vicar smiled with the massive teeth of the dragon.

"GOODBYE TERREK!" the dragon roared as spikes appeared on it's tail. The dragon lifted the tail high ready to strike. Terrek saw a flash as Zyron appeared to him again, this time at his side. Zyron placed his arm on Terrek's shoulder. Terrek felt something flow through him.

As the tail descended it found only trees as the Vicar-dragon winced in pain. Terrek leapt high into the air as his sword reappeared glowing with an unworldly light, he descended blade first into the dragon's tail severing it completely.

The Dragon roared as Terrek fell to the ground rolling over. The Vicar dragon faced Terrek and opened it's mouth gathering wind to breathe fire once again. Terrek, straining his muscles pulled his sword back and threw it with all his might. The sword sailed skyward and sunk into the Vicar's right eye. In agony, the dragon screamed releasing flames in all directions as he toppled back, crashing down into the dense underbrush. For a moment the world was silent as the dragon was lost beneath the massive jungle vegetation.

"I SENSE THAT YOU ARE IN COMMAND OF MORE THAN DELARA'S POWER!" the vicar roared, "SHE COULD NOT HAVE INJURED ME AS YOU HAVE JUST DONE! WHERE DOES THIS POWER COME FROM?"

"The Maker has sent someone to protect me!" Terrek yelled back, "you are finished!"

Once again the world around him changed. The ground and surrounding area became flat stone with jutting jagged

124

knives of rock here and there. He was standing on a mountain plateau. The clouds overhead became dark, and the wind blew ferociously. Menacing thunder and lightning rocked the world, as hail beat down on Terrek. Terrek held up invisible defenses as he approached the nearest cliff.

Terrek suddenly backed away from the cliff as he saw the Vicar's new form. He had appeared only to Delara in this form. The Vicar lifted himself to his massive height as he rose above the cliff several times taller than Terrek.

The monstrous form opened it's mouth wide as both massive fangs vibrated with a roar so fierce Terrek had to resist the instinct to run. Besides the fangs, several horns covered his head as red flowing slime trickled across his scaly face. The Vicar beast raised his clawed hands skyward as he focused on Terrek with his burning red and green eyes.

"FARE THEE WELL!" the Vicar beast rasped.

Terrek was afraid, but he noticed that one of the beast's eyes was cut open. Then he realized that this monster still had the wound received in his previous form.

"You're injured!" Terrek mocked the Vicar monster.

The monster swung it's clawed hand down, attempting to swat Terrek like a fly. Terrek brought his sword to bear and slashed a deep wound into the beast's palm as it cried in pain. Tearing bedrock loose with his other hand the Vicar monster threw the debris at him in rage. Terrek ran from the falling rock, collapsing face first to the ground. Turning over, he looked up just in time to see the Vicar-monster scoop him up in one hand. The monster's grip tightened around his body as he struggled in pain.

The Vicar viewed him menacingly through the monster's eyes.

"I AM NOT FINISHED, YOU ARE!" he spat upon Terrek.

Terrek breathed harder as the Vicar roared with sadistic laughter, gripping his hands ever tighter as Terrek began losing control of Delara's power.

"Maker, help me," he whispered. Suddenly Terrek felt two familiar hands on his shoulders, turning his head in the monster's grip he saw the face of Zyron. Terrek closed his eyes as he felt himself change. Zyron's translucent form flowed into Terrek's body as he breathed in deeply. Terrek's eyes glowed with blue light as unimaginable power flowed through his body.

The Vicar monster paused, staring at Terrek.

Suddenly the Vicar monster's hand exploded as he fell back from the cliff gripping his handless arm in anguish. Terrek hovered, arms outstretched, floating above the cliff. Powerful energy rippled across his body as he changed form. A suit of armor appeared, covering him. His skin and armor glowed deep blue. Instantly, the blue soldier grew in size until he matched the Vicar's monstrous form. Terrek felt unbelievable energy as he lifted his arms instinctively. Lightning rippled through his grip and supplied him with a glowing blue staff.

Howling, the Vicar leapt up on the cliff and gripped Terrek by the torso attempting to squeeze the life out of him. Terrek slammed his massive blue gauntlet into the monster's neck and was released. Terrek smashed his staff into the beast's head knocking it to it's knees. Then, pulling it high above, he brought it down onto the Vicar's back sprawling him to the dirt.

Terrek dropped his staff and lifted the dazed Vicar monster from the stone surface. Holding it by the throat with one hand he brought his fist into it's grotesque face again and again. Finally, blood appeared, or what seemed to be blood. Terrek released it's neck and grabbed both massive fangs protruding from the monster's mouth. With a great cry of horror from the beast, Terrek tore both fangs from it's mouth. The Vicar-monster sank to it's knees

126

screaming, one severed arm folded beneath the other arm holding it's injured mouth. Blood flowed upon the stone surface, puddling, as the beast continued to scream. The Vicar looked up at Terrek through the eyes of the beast. No longer did they cause fear; they were filled with fear.

"HOW DID YOU GAIN SUCH POWER?" the Vicar cried.

"The Maker!" Terrek said triumphant ly.

The Vicar took one last swing at Terrek with his uninjured claw. Terrek moved quickly, rotating his staff heavily into the Vicar's temple. The monster collapsed unconscious.

"You have lost, and now your realm must be destroyed," Terrek finished.

Instinctively Terrek's armor enveloped with ripples of powerful energy as he lifted his staff over his head once more and brought it down directly into the stone surface beneath them. A great chasm erupted as Terrek hovered above the surface. All around them the ground quaked as the skies exploded with scorching fire. The Vicar lifted his head as his realm began to crumble.

"WE WILL MEET AGAIN SOON!" the Vicar monster roared as his form disappeared. Terrek felt the realm fading as he watched the remainder of the ground disintegrate and the clouds disappear. He felt himself change back into his familiar self having shed the blue armor.

Suddenly he appeared back in reality as he fell to the cave floor adjacent Delara. Delara's eyes opened and widened as all in the cave surrounded Terrek's exhausted form.

CHAPTER 16: THE END IS NEAR

The Vicar's forces had been pushed far from New Victory City. Most had fled, as the overpowering combination of the Zyconian army and this new force was unmatched. Now Walker, Perrin and John approached the leader of their new allies to converse.

"Hello," Perrin began curiously.

"Hello," he said heartily, "I suppose you have many questions, don't you?"

"Yes, we do," Walker smiled.

"Well, I may as well tell you that we are Xanican, I am Bratain. The army I command was once a large portion of the Xanican clan armies. When Emperor Koiban decided that the Vicar would be his advisor, and when he began believing in his lies, I personally knew I couldn't stand by and watch, so I left Xanica. The clan armies had always been loyal to me and so they followed," he finished.

"Why did you return, and how did you know we were under attack?" John asked.

"There is a servant in Koiban's service named Frecan, he sent a messenger North in search of me. In the message he begged me to return because he'd overheard the Vicar plotting to take control of Xanica and assassinate Koiban. Frecan is a close friend to Koiban as am I, so I took the message seriously. Koiban may have been foolish, but I don't believe he truly wanted the destruction of your nation," he reasoned.

Pausing for a moment Bratain scratched his beard, "I chose to come to Zyconia to enlist your help in saving Xanica from the Vicar's clutches. You can imagine my surprise as our warships entered the lake and saw the forces the Vicar had gathered. It seems we are fighting the same battle, doesn't it?"

"Yes. We're very lucky you arrived when you did. Much later and you may not have had any help to enlist. The Vicar might have gained control of both Xanica and Zyconia. We will order our armies to push the Vicar's forces into Xanican and drive to your capital to help you regain control," Perrin smiled.

"Very well. I will add my forces to yours and keep only skeleton crews for my warships. If you will have your war vessels accompany us I would be privileged if you would come aboard and travel with us to Dystara directly. The Vicar has warships as well that must be destroyed in order for us to free Xanica," Bratain explained.

"We understand, we will accompany you," Walker answered.

The Vicar sat in the throne room in Dystara; he was solemn. The room was dark and shadowy, a small brazier burned in the center of the room. A small puddle of blood had collected beside him on the floor. His arm lay wrapped in a dirty tourniquet; a horrifying collection of spoiled blood and clumping veins covered a grimy stump where his hand used to be. His robe, just below his hooded face, was also stained in dried blood; two large streaks flowed from each corner of his mouth. For the first time in his existence the Vicar had been wounded.

He meditated to keep his powers from fading. With the loss of his realm he had been considerably weakened.

Quietly the door to the throne room opened as Kridelia walked inside. She stood before the Vicar in a drained state. He looked upon her face, it had changed. She now wore the ugliness of a thousand hags. She walked with a limp, holding her side in pain. He knew she had fallen into the pits below Delara's caverns.

"Delara has gone over to their side," Kridelia said hoarsely.

The Vicar remained silent.

"We're both injured," she commented.

"WHERE IS YOUR SON, KORAN?" the Vicar asked.

Kridelia looked at him for a moment.

"I left him to their clutches. I had neither the time nor strength to retrieve the puppet. I believe when I was injured my hold over his mind was broken."

The Vicar stared straight ahead, "YOU SHOULD NOT BE SO CARELESS, IF YOU BURN A TREE AND DON'T CONTAIN THE BLAZE, THE WHOLE FOREST WILL BURN, TAKING YOU WITH IT."

Kridelia stood, puzzled, running her palm over her deformed face in disgust.

"He's a helpless child, in the grand scheme of things his life or death means nothing. He made his choice at a young age when he renounced our ways. If Terrek doesn't execute him, then let him rot in Zyconia," she said, vehemently cursing her son.

The Vicar was silent for a moment as he collected his thoughts, "I'VE ORGANIZED THE REMAINDER OF OUR FORCES TO DEFEND DYSTARA. OUR WARSHIPS ARE ARMED AND READY IN THE HARBOR, SO WE ARE PROTECTED FROM SEA INVASION. OUR VESSELS OUTNUMBER THE ZYCONIAN FLEET FOUR TO ONE."

"We could still flee this place, but I want to destroy Terrek. If it means my life, I will have his death," she rasped.

"WE BOTH STILL POSSESS GREAT POWERS. TERREK WILL COME TO DESTROY US BEFORE HIS ARMIES REACH DYSTARA, AND WHEN HE DOES WE WILL BE WAITING FOR HIM," the Vicar roared.

Terrek stood surrounded by his aides: Hemoth, Ricsis, Perrin, Zachary, Adam, Jason, Jessica, Juliana, Delara, Diana, Koiban, the Whitesouls and his army. All cheered as they congratulated him for his Victory in the Vicar's realm. Then they began talking amongst themselves as Delara, Koiban and Terrek's aides moved in to speak with him.

"How – how did you defeat him?" asked Delara, "my power alone couldn't have accomplished what you did!"

"The Maker was smiling on me today, he saved me," Terrek replied staring off into space for a moment.

Those surrounding him looked around at eachother puzzled. Diana took Terrek by the hand.

"I'm glad you're alright, I was so worried!" she scolded him. Terrek pulled her close and kissed her forehead.

"I wouldn't leave you after having just found you again," Terrek promised.

"I know," she smiled, brushing his dark locks from his face, "I really do."

Suddenly Terrek remembered the others, "I – I suppose we should decide our next move. The Vicar's realm is gone and he is injured, but he is still alive. With the loss of your force on the front Delara, I believe my armies can push the Vicar's men out of my kingdom. I think we should infiltrate Xanica and head to the Dystara palace."

"Will you lead us there?" Celarus spoke to Koiban.

"We have the same enemy, I will," Koiban answered.

"What about the boy?" Delara asked, speaking of Koran, Kridelia's son.

Terrek watched Koran curled up in a sitting position in a nearby corner. He felt a pang of sadness for the child.

Koran rested his back against the cave wall and pulled himself close, his knees up against his chest. He kept his eyes low, not looking at those around him. Never staring. He shivered slightly, aware of the draft in the caverns. He was hungry. He thought about his past, and about his future, and was unsure.

Terrek approached the boy and sat against the wall beside him. Koran's gaze remained fixed straight ahead. Terrek draped an animalskin around the boy and removed a small flask and a dried piece of meat from a pouch and gave it to him. He looked at the boy somberly.

"We'd like you to come with us to Xanica Koran," he began, "your mother may choose to stand against us when we attack the Vicar. We want you to help us talk to her, perhaps convince her that she should simply leave Xanica."

"She won't leave," Koran released his small voice quickly. "She will stop at nothing to destroy you. She will stop at nothing to avenge my father Murack."

Terrek lowered his gaze and whispered.

"What of you? Do you hate me for his death?"

Koran turned his head finally and looked at Terrek.

"No, I understand your reason, but now in a way it has become hers too. I realize that she has no right to seek vengeance when both she and my father have caused so much pain and suffering to others."

Terrek turned his face to the child once again as if seeing him through different eyes. He was very mature and intelligent for a small boy. He was older inside.

132

"I loved my father and I love my mother, but I know the path they've chosen has no room for compassion. When I was younger the Maker sent an angelic servant to me. He told me that I would come to fulfill a great purpose and that I must reject the ways of those around me. I chose to follow the Maker and he has walked with me since. But my mother cast spells and conjured evil into my body to use me as a puppet for death and destruction," he paused.

Terrek met the boy's eyes and he knew what he said about the Maker was true.

"I still believe the Maker wants to use me, I have a purpose. I will come with you to Xanica, I will help you to overcome my mother so that no more death will be caused by her or the Vicar," he finished as he returned his gaze to the wall. The movement had such finality that Terrek knew the conversation was over.

He stood and walked away from the boy. The child held no resentment toward Terrek for his father's death, and he was willing to help them even though he understood it could mean his mother's death. Terrek also knew that the Maker was with the boy. Despite the fact that Kridelia's power was gone he felt so much energy of the power of good in him that he knew that he had a great destiny to fulfill.

"He will accompany us," Terrek said, speaking of Koran.

Delara returned to the group from another cavern.

"Some of my soldiers have returned from the front, their report is surprising. It seems that as they left the battlefield another large army, decorated with altered Xanican uniforms, entered the lake beside New Victory City in warships. The new soldiers are fighting for your side," she remarked to Terrek.

The surrounding group stared at Emperor Koiban whose face lit up, "Bratain! When the Vicar first came I was blinded, but my commander of the clan armies, Bratain, wasn't. He chose to leave and to my dismay, so did the majority of the clan armies. It seems he has returned."

"My scouts say that the Vicar's forces are being driven south and that the armies will drive them right into Dystara," Delara declared.

"Thank the Maker!" Terrek sighed in relief; Perrin, Walker and John had managed to push the Vicar's soldiers away from New Victory City.

He turned to Koiban, "I believe that you were blinded by the Vicar, Emperor Koiban, and I have decided that it's in my nation's best interests to help you reclaim your throne. If you give me your word that nothing like this will ever happen again, when Dystara is taken, we will help you rid Xanica of any opposing forces."

"I never wanted this King Terrek, I give you my word. I allowed my judgment to disappear once, but I never will again. I welcome your help. When this is all over Xanica and Zyconia will live together in peace," he said honorably.

Terrek and Koiban shook hands smiling.

"I will help you as well," Delara said, "I will leave word that when all of my army has returned, they are to drive into Xanica to Dystara."

"Very well, I will have one of my soldiers sent to my forces to let them know your people are on our side now. I believe we should head for Dystara now. The Vicar will be waiting," Terrek finished.

CHAPTER 17: BURNING THE CANDLE AT BOTH ENDS

Cramin flew high through the clouds, he was so hungry. The others, following, were as well. Floating down out of the clouds the flock came to rest. They had captured little prey in the past few days. Fate was not on their side.

"We've been hunting all day and have found nothing!" Darcet cried to Cramin, "Grelkon has condemned us to starve to death!"

Cramin scowled at him and looked at the others who showed their support for his ravings with strong expressions.

"It isn't Grelkon's fault! We've just had a bad few days, it has been difficult to find prey!" Cramin spoke up.

"But he certainly isn't helping us is he? Where is he now!" Darcet screamed.

"You know he is recovering from wounds sustained in the battle at New Victory City!" Cramin looked at him in disgust.

"If he had any skill at all he could have evaded the spears. What sort of a weak leader are we following into battle," Darcet spat.

"Darcet is right," cried another.

Cramin was surprised; it had been the first real outburst from one of the others. Cramin stared off away from the group into the forest as though if he squinted hard enough he would see a field of antelope for them to devour.

"And you want to know something else?" Darcet said, coming close to Cramin's ear, "you're as weak as he is!"

Cramin had enough. He spun, lashing out as he knocked Darcet back. Stumbling, Darcet recovered but Cramin was upon him again. With a flourish of his wing he knocked Darcet violently to the ground. Angrily, he started toward the fallen Darcet only to be pushed sideways by several of the other Avians. Cramin slipped in the mud and landed heavily on his wing.

Cramin cried as a muffled crack resounded from his wing. He looked up as Darcet got to his feet, and the others looked on, moving in around him. None of them were with him. He jumped from the mud and attempted to run, half flying away from them. The group sensed his weakness and, with Darcet in the lead pursued him.

Cramin looked behind just in time to see Darcet swooping down on him.

"You didn't help us find prey, now you are the prey!" he yelled, a sadistic look in his eyes. He fell heavily into Cramin his claws scratching deep, pecking and clawing. Cramin hit the ground as the other avians attacked as well biting, tearing, killing.

The Vicar raised himself from the throne as he stretched out his arm. The tourniquet fell away as, magically, his blood vessels and skin molded into a hand. He flexed his new hand testing it's ability. He had sustained a blow that might never be recovered with the loss of his realm, but he had managed to harness the power that remained. Now he would use it to destroy Terrek and his friends once and for all.

Kridelia smiled as she saw his new hand. She had been meditating as well attempting to heal herself. Her face was still grotesquely marred, she didn't have the abilities of the Vicar, and the Vicar couldn't waste what power he still had. She would have to continue with her scarred appearance.

"WE MUST PREPARE FOR TERREK'S ARRIVAL, COME!" the Vicar commanded, as Kridelia followed him.

Bratain's ship, the Guarnadine, rose up and down on the open sea. The water was rough and the winds increased in strength. Beside Bratain stood Walker, Perrin and John. His crew moved about the deck preparing the vessel for battle and speeding it to their destination. It was night, but they had to push forward. They had nearly reached the channel between the edge of Xanica and Wicketai the homeland of their enemies.

"Just ahead, to the west, you might see the tip of Wicketai," Bratain roared over the crashing waves.

"I wonder what life is like there?" Perrin said.

"Judging from the Vicar, not very good," Bratain replied. "I would suspect it is an evil place filled with so much misery and strife, not to mention dark magic, that the weak would have a very short lifespan."

"That sounds like a correct assessment," Walker finished.

"Merchant vessel captains that have gone through the Wicketai waters and survived say that the population is vast for an island it's size. Perhaps one of the reason's the Vicar chose to attack our lands is to give his homeland colonies," Bratain reasoned.

"Perhaps," John said, "but I hope we never have to find out."

Darcet and the others flew out of the sky next to Grelkon who was awaiting their return. All of the avians swooped down behind him as Grelkon looked among them.

"Were you successful in finding game? Where is Cramin?" he voiced concern.

Grelkon looked at Darcet. Blood covered his beak and a single black feather clung to the dried blood. Grelkon peered into his eyes and saw the evil that had transpired not long ago.

"Cramin attacked us, we had to kill him!" Darcet yelled.

"No! What have you done!" Grelkon roared running forward he hit Darcet hard with his good wing. Darcet stumbled back but swung back striking Grelkon in his injured wing. It was healing but it was painful, Grelkon stumbled back having received the first real blow ever from another dark avian. The shock held him in check as he held his wing in pain staring at Darcet.

"How could you kill him, he was practically your -," Grelkon paused as he lingered on his final word, "brother."

"You – you must be punished," Grelkon said weakly.

"No," another dark avian said fiercely, "there will be no more punishing."

Suddenly Grelkon examined the entire group. He saw the hate in their eyes, he also saw Cramin's blood on all of their beaks. None of the dark avians were on his side any longer. He was alone.

"You – you will regret this," Grelkon finished, frustrated. Darcet and the others turned their backs on him talking amongst themselves. Grelkon moved away from them wandering into the nearby forest. Reaching a small brook he looked down into the crystal water at his reflection.

138

He thought about his past, about his mother Selate, about Hecron and Cramin. The dark avians had fed on his hate. They had become what he was. Grelkon finally understood, finally saw things clearly. They had murdered Cramin just as he had murdered Hecron. How could he have let things come down to this? What had he done?

For the first time in his life Grelkon brought his wings to his face and cried.

Emperor Koiban knew the terrain of Xanica well. He'd led them past several groups of soldiers, undetected, as they made their way to Dystara. It had been night so it wasn't overly difficult, but now the sun was rising. Exiting the underbrush of a dense forest, cresting a hill, they caught sight of the great city. Koiban halted for a moment as did Terrek and the others. Small stone homes and peasant dwellings surrounded the outer edges of the city. Strong massive structures filled the inside confines of the great walls. The large towers of the palace could be seen far in the distance. From this distance, Terrek was surprised at how much Dystara looked like New Victory City.

"The city is beautiful Koiban," Terrek said.

Koiban breathed in the fresh air as he replied, "I'm home, and will not rest until Xanica is back in my hands."

Terrek was afraid of taking Diana to Dystara to face again the evil she had just been rescued from. He would make sure she was safe when they entered the palace. This venture was already becoming a couple's outing but the danger was real. Delara and Celarus, Diana and himself and Zachary and Juliana. Delara had powers, her strength was evident. And Juliana and Jessica were present because they were healers. Diana could defend herself, but he was very protective where she was concerned.

Terrek took a moment to survey their small force. Terrek's army was following in stealth, as were several Whitesouls that had accompanied their queen. Terrek's aides followed close, as he and Koiban led the way.

"I alone know a small subterranean passage that leads under the city walls and into the palace dungeon. We will enter that way. Best we get this over with," Koiban whispered to Terrek. Both men marched onward to the city.

CHAPTER 18: DEATH AND DESTRUCTION

𝕿he sun shone desperately in the seaside sunrise, bars of light filtering through black clouds. Bratain stood at the bow of his vessel as it led several dozen warships into the Dystaran bay. Several dark vessels raised their anchors and sailed out to do battle with them. Behind Bratain's ship, the Guarnadine, the combined clan vessels and the Zyconian fleet spread out and caught up to their pace.

"All men to arms!" cried Bratain as Walker, John and Perrin rushed from below halting beside Bratain. Nearly a hundred soldiers stood above deck ready and willing to do battle. The Dystaran bay hung heavy with fog clouding their vision of the approaching darkened vessels. Squinting through the mist, Bratain saw their flagship and his face went white.

"The vessel in the lead is called the Helios. I have seen it raid and destroy many ships traveling through the large channel between Xanica and Wicketai. It is a very powerful warship," he voiced his agitation to the three Zyconian leaders.

The evil warship was very well constructed of reinforced solid broad wood with several iron markings and armaments. Atop it's deck, several catapults could be seen. The most prominent feature was a huge section of the bow that had been fitted with a massive section of iron shaped into several large spikes. The sails were as black as death, and it rode higher on the sea than the Guarnadine. It's massive oars protruded from the lower decks. The huge ship seemed to hold back as the other ships of this vicious pack encompassed and surged ahead of it.

More fog rolled into the bay as soft glows began to appear on the decks of each evil vessel. The sound of voices and crackling fire reached them, as they loomed closer.

The entire crew of the Guarnadine prepared their catapults, as well as the special gelatinous tar and oil projectiles. Men stood by with torches to light them ablaze. Other weapons, single boulder and large crossbow type arms, were also being prepared. Every free soldier held a crossbow or longbow with flaming arrows. Alongside the Guarnadine the other Zyconian and Xanican vessels also prepared themselves. There were several dozen on each side; both sides prepared to fight to the death. The ships moved ever forward through the increasing mist.

"When I give the word we must give them everything we have!" Bratain yelled to the men aboard his own ship as well as the to the soldiers listening aboard the other ships on each side of the Guarnadine.

Bratain raised his hands as he prepared to give his order. Suddenly a distant thump and whistling of wind pricked his ears. His eyes opened wide.

A huge boulder sailed out of the skies and directly into the Guarnadine's sail cracking a small section of railing at the back of the ship completely off, before it sank into the sea.

"Fire!" Bratain bellowed, realizing the other side had already begun their attack. Men lit and released volley after volley of flaming ooze and solid boulders across the seas great expanse and onto the enemy, as they did the same. Every soldier on each side began dodging and weaving as they got close enough to fire their bows. Arrows, flaming and otherwise, peppered the Guarnadine as Bratain and the others scrambled for cover. Suddenly, a pile of flaming fluid collided with the Guarnadine's mast, running down the base and splashing the deck with puddles of flame. Fire rose up the mast igniting the sail.

"Put it out!" Bratain roared to his men as several grabbed buckets and in panic ran across the deck, climbed the mast and doused the fire in streams of water. The sails lay a blackened, tattered wreck but Bratain pushed the men below to increase the pace to the oars. The ships of both forces came alongside each other as they savagely attacked one another. A few collided and men began boarding each other's vessels, the soldiers fighting hand to hand.

A huge boulder smashed into the deck of the Guarnadine crashing through more than one deck. Walker took cover as showers of splinters sprayed nearby. Peering for a moment through the hole he saw the boulder resting on the lowest deck. They had been lucky that the amount of force behind the weapon was no greater or it would have gone completely through the hull, causing the ship to sink. The Guarnadine traveled beyond the battle area and swung around to coast back into the fighting.

As the ship got close again, several clouds of fog blanketed them. Bratain noticed that since the beginning of the battle he had not seen the Helios anywhere. The fog was so thick now that Bratain could barely see the ships in battle just ahead and to the sides of them. He squinted, trying to see through the thick fog. The attack on the Guarnadine had died down as several vessels were engaged in individual combat and the amount of projectiles available had been exhausted.

"Can you see the Helios!" he cried to Walker, Perrin and John.

"No, it seems to have disappeared -," Perrin stopped short as he turned and glanced off the starboard of the

143

Guarnadine. His head snapped back focusing on a huge bulky shadow in the fog, "Bratain!" he roared.

A moment later, the massive Helios rushed out of the fog into view it's oars churning the sea aggressively, heading directly for them. The metallic spikes mounted on it's front hurtled toward them; a predator about to strike with fury. It made everyone aboard the Guarnadine gasp in horror.

"They're trying to ram us! Pull those oars!" Bratain screamed to the oarsmen below deck.

But it was already too late. The spikes at the bow of the Helios crashed into the starboard side of the Guarnadine. Cracks tore into the side and deck of Bratain's ship as splinters of wood exploded in every direction. All of the crew was thrown to the deck as the soldiers on the Helios began firing arrows upon them. Bratain looked about as the sound of rushing water reached his ears. The Guarnadine was taking on water!

Scrambling above deck the former oarsmen of the Guarnadine took up arms, as did the entire crew. Bratain leapt, hiding behind several planks of broken wood, as the rest of the crew took similar cover across the Guarnadine's deck. He fired his crossbow, as did the three Zyconians beside him, but the crew of the Helios had the upper hand and higher ground. The enemy's arrows rained down on them from the elevated deck. Soon they began bombarding them with flame and debris. The Guarnadine caught fire as the crew fought for their lives.

"The ship is sinking, and it's on fire. We must abandon ship!" John yelled to Bratain.

"Even if we tried we'd be picked off when we left our cover, if only there was some way we could get aboard their ship!" Bratain said.

Just then, two Xanican vessels came through the mist converging on the Helios scattering and distracting it's crew as they were blanketed with a veritable fountain of flaming arrows.

"Come on!" Bratain roared, taking advantage of their momentary distraction. Running to the spiked bow of the Helios, he drew his sword and climbed up unto the deck. The entire crew followed suit as they scaled the spikes, and launched themselves into the Helios' soldiers. A moment later, the other two Xanican ships ceased their bombardment. Several grappling hooks were swung unto the Helios' deck as the soldiers aboard pulled their ships next to the massive vessel. Wasting no time, they scaled the side of the ship, running above deck, aiding Bratain and their comrades in attacking the Helios' crew. The fog began to clear revealing the other vessels, still in very heated battle, strewn about the bay.

Opening a large grate Emperor Koiban climbed up through the floor of the Dystaran palace dungeons. Behind him Terrek surfaced, extending his hand to Diana. One by one the others rose single file from the grate filling the lower dungeon with several dozen soldiers. Terrek looked to Koiban for guidance now.

"Do you think the Vicar could have detected us?" Terrek asked.

"Not yet, but he will soon. I have several secret tunnels throughout these walls that can lead us to the throne room, but from there we will have to travel in the open hallways where soldiers may bar our way. We must move quickly. Follow me!" Koiban said.

Approaching the wall, Koiban pushed a stray brick that opened a passage. Quickly everyone entered single file then the door closed. After navigating several twists, turns and ladders Koiban paused in a hollowed cavern behind a brick wall. He silently directed Terrek to peer through a small hole. Terrek looked through to see Koiban's throne room; several guards patrolled just inside.

"Ready?" Koiban whispered.

Terrek withdrew his sword, as did the others. Koiban removed a small latch as he heaved on the wall. It spun on a central axis as it swung open. In surprise the soldiers inside reached for their weapons, but they were already being attacked. Delara used her power to throw the enemy against the walls. Diana and the others threw daggers at the soldiers. The only one immobile was Koran. Soon enough all but one of the men were dead. Koiban gripped the survivor.

For a moment Koiban peered cautiously out the window. In the distance, just beyond Dystara's walls, a dark smoke was rising. Looking below he saw soldiers rushing through the streets.

"The armies are attacking!" Koiban faced Terrek. "It has begun!"

"Where is the Vicar?" the Emperor roared at the young man who had survived their assault.

"He – he went to the main towers," he replied, cowering beneath Koiban's gaze. The direction he pointed was far down the great hall where the palace split into two separate staircases and towers. Hemoth grabbed the soldier and held him. Emperor Koiban dropped the man and, with Terrek following, rushed down the great hall. The group followed as well, but as they approached the door to the great hall a huge iron door fell from the ceiling. Koran and Diana managed to jump clear before it completely fell separating Terrek, Koiban, Koran and Diana from the rest of their small army. Terrek and Koiban spun around and approached the iron door, it was incredibly solid.

"Delara, can you use your powers to move it?" Terrek yelled through the door.

After a moment they felt the door vibrate slightly.

"I'm sorry, I'm still somewhat weakened from battling Kridelia. It's too heavy," a muffled voice said.

"We can't move it either!" rose the voice of Hemoth, Zachary and Celarus.

Terrek and Koiban paused, then Terrek replied.

"Very well, if any soldiers enter the palace, keep them away from this part of the castle. We will ascend and face the Vicar."

"As you wish," several voices replied.

Terrek and Koiban looked at Diana and Koran as they walked away from the door down the hall together.

"When we reach the next room I want you to stay with the boy. Keep him from harm while Emperor Koiban and I ascend the towers. Will you do that?" Terrek asked.

"As long as you promise to be cautious," she warned him.

"I promise I will Diana," he replied.

"All right, I will remain with the boy," she finished.

After coming down the lengthy hall they entered a massive den. Two staircases spiraled up in different directions. Suddenly a small band of soldiers ran into the room from another hallway, roaring with battle cries. Diana moved and pulled Koran back into the hallway away from the room slightly as Terrek and Koiban loosed their swords. The soldiers swarmed them.

Terrek swung his sword piercing man after man. Finally, two of the soldiers managed to grab him by the arms as another rushed him with a spear. Koiban was busy dealing with several men as well and couldn't help him. Loosing her dagger Diana ran from the darkened hall and buried her weapon in the back of one of the soldiers. One arm freed, Terrek pulled the other man in front of him as the spear entered the soldier's stomach. He leapt around the speared soldier retrieved Diana's dagger and slit the spearman's throat. Pausing for a moment, Terrek looked at

Diana raising his eyebrows in surprised approval at her assistance.

"You were in danger, remember your promise," she scolded, "I can't be there to save you all the time," she chided with gentle sarcasm.

Terrek smiled at her as he ran to aid Koiban with the remainder of the fray. Soon enough all the soldiers had been silenced. Terrek and Koiban glanced from staircase to staircase.

"We're going to have to split up," Koiban said nervously.

"I know," Terrek replied.

"I'll take this one," Koiban pointed to the far left.

"Very well," Terrek said.

Koiban wished him the guidance of the Maker and ascended the stairway. Terrek faced Diana.

"Do be very careful, and come back to me safely. Remember that you have a child to father," she said touching her belly.

"I can't do it without you," she whispered in a low tone.

Terrek looked at Diana; she was truly scared for him. He embraced her, brushing her hair away he kissed her.

"I will return, I've been through this sort of thing many times in my life, and I'm still here, right?" Terrek forced a smile trying to make her feel better.

Diana nodded wiping her eyes, near to tears.

"I – I know you have," she said trying to be stronger.

"I will be back, wait here and keep Koran safe," he said glancing down at the boy.

Terrek squeezed her hand and backed away ascending the staircase to the far right.

Darcet and the others had become incredibly evil. The dark avians were stubborn and still attempted to defend

Dystara, pushed on by the Vicar. Grelkon's wing was still slightly sore, but he had to help them. Entering battle again, Grelkon flew with faked ferocity among his former siblings, biting and clawing. He was still overcome with grief for Cramin. He didn't want this anymore, he felt so sick inside.

Grelkon held back for a moment watching the battle. Far below, the soldiers on both sides fought and killed. Smoke rose causing him to choke. Suddenly, several spears projected from soldiers towards his sibling's backs flew right by him. Flying away quickly, he stared at the avians around him. Death was on every face and in every eye. Looking around he saw Hecron and Cramin's faces on both flocks. Each way he turned they were there staring at him. They were lashing out, attacking him, and hurting him.

Grelkon's face became distorted as he broke down, tears erupting from his eyes.

"Why?" he whispered.

In his upset state Grelkon turned away from the attack and flew. With all his wing power he blazed a path away from the pain, away from the dark avians, and away from his own guilt. Selate watched him go through the clouds. Surveying the battle, she saw that her children were winning. She felt worried about leaving them but Grelkon was still her son. She followed him, but so did Darcet.

The Helios glided across the waters as it approached the docking system of Dystara's harbor. Standing upon the spiked bow of the massive warship was Bratain. Behind him stood Walker, Perrin and John, surrounded by a mixture of Xanican and Zyconian warriors. The Vicar's men had been vanquished. Several dozen ships followed them into the harbor; some were of Xanican and Zyconian origin. The others came from Wicketai. The difference was that now either Xanican or Zyconian soldiers commanded them.

Farther behind them slicks of burning gelatin and pieces of wreckage floated about the sea. Crackling erupted from the floundering ships as they sank slowly beneath the choppy waves. They had won the battle; who would win the war.

The Helios came to a stop alongside the wharf as Bratain and the others dropped planks from the side of the ship to the dock. The other ships did the same. Hundreds of the Vicar's soldiers ran from within the city to meet them as they stormed upon the shore, weapons drawn. In the distance, they could already hear the cries of battle. The Zyconian armies had driven the Vicar's forces back into Dystara and the city was being attacked from the other side.

Racing up the spiraled staircase, Koiban entered the western tower. The vast room was cluttered with unfamiliar artifacts and strange idols, all of which reminded Koiban of the Vicar. Here and there blood red curtains hung from ill-constructed rods. Wandering through the darkness of the room he looked to the nearby window shutters. They had been fitted with pieces of iron to keep them permanently closed. It seemed the Vicar had been busy in this part of the castle. Koiban knew these artifacts belonged to the Vicar and had probably been brought here from aboard the Wicketai vessels after he'd escaped Dystara.

Nearby, there was a large altar with steps that led to the surface Koiban stared as he saw a movement on it.

"Vicar!" Koiban yelled. Suddenly a blinding magical light flickered on the ceiling. The brightness was so strong Koiban was forced to shield his eyes in an attempt to view the altar. Sure enough, atop the metallic altar was the Vicar.

"SO YOU HAVE RETURNED TO RECLAIM YOUR THRONE," the Vicar rasped mockingly.

"Yes, I have," he said. As he moved forward to the altar, suddenly someone barred his way. The bright light died down. Koiban looked up. All around him dozens of identical men wearing the same face stared at him, their faces evil, covered in blood. Each had a small sword pierced through his heart. Koiban was horrified. He saw the face and knew the man. It was Frecan, they all were.

Terrek walked up the steps into the eastern tower. The room was very dark; almost no light could be seen. As he pushed his way into the room it became pitch black. He could hardly see anything. Suddenly, not far away from him, a woman appeared, her face shadowed; it was Kridelia.

"This must end!" Terrek yelled, "I've spoken to your son. If you leave now I won't kill you. I have no wish to kill both Koran's parents."

"You had no problem with one," Kridelia rasped, "and look what you've done to me!" Kridelia displayed her distorted face; the skin had been eaten away by the acid from within the subterranean pit.

"I didn't murder Murack in cold blood. He was responsible for the deaths of many innocents, including my once wife and child. You know that! We wouldn't have harmed you either except to protect ourselves. Don't attempt to paint us as the evil ones. Just go! Go far away, and don't return," Terrek offered.

"No, the never ending circle of vengeance between us will end here, but not with my departure, only yours from the realm of the living!" Kridelia screamed.

Terrek, angered, ran forward, "I gave you a chance!" he yelled as he brought his sword down into Kridelia. A violent smash of glass exploded on him as he realized he'd swung his sword into a mirror. Shards of glass clattered to the floor as Terrek spun in the dark room. Kridelia appeared again not far away, taunting him.

"I'm over here," she roared vehemently.

Terrek took a few steps forward as she disappeared and reappeared in another position.

"No, I'm here," she yelled.

"No more games," Terrek yelled.

"No? Very well. Here I am!" Kridelia appeared beside him knocking his blade away into the dark. Terrek leapt away from her as she slashed at him with her dagger catching his arm. Crying out in pain, Terrek fell backwards crashing into several mirrors that splintered, sending glass shards across the floor as Kridelia moved forward. Terrek lifted himself from the pile of glass as he faced her. Again she disappeared in the darkness.

He stood perfectly still holding his bleeding arm trying to hear her movements.

"I have no wish to kill you, just leave now!" Terrek said.

She appeared next to him again, but this time he pushed her before she could strike. She hit the floor as her dagger rolled away into the dark. She screamed, cursing him, as she disappeared again. Not wanting to be a sitting duck, Terrek walked through the dark trying to move about as he fumbled around for anything to use as a weapon.

Not far away Terrek heard a low grinding noise as the floor vibrated. It sounded as though a stone door was opening.

Suddenly, Terrek looked up to see Kridelia running right at him as though to tackle him. He held his ground as she collided with his body. Terrek felt a hard impact as a massive mirror crashed into him, sending him backwards, once again covered in glass. He rolled over, and instantly found himself falling. Reaching out, he grasped the ledge as he realized there was an open pit in the floor. He saw Kridelia standing above him as he hung on the edge of the chasm. She waved her hand and illuminated the pit. Terrek fought back fear as he saw the bottom, far below, covered in metallic spikes. Kridelia smiled.

"Goodbye Terrek!" she said in satisfaction. She brought her foot down on one of his hands as he yelled in pain. Pulling his hand from beneath her foot he grabbed at it as she fell to the ground. She backed away quickly. Terrek tried to place his hand back on the ledge, but couldn't regain his grip. He was slipping.

Angrily she approached again, "I hope you die slowly," she grinned menacingly as she lifted her boot to kick his face.

Suddenly her head snapped back as someone pushed her violently from behind. Kridelia screamed as she fell head first down into the pit. Terrek heard her land with a sudden violent thud as he placed his hand back on the ledge, finding his grip. With all his strength he heaved himself back onto the solid floor as he spun to see the pit. Far below, Kridelia lay face down, several spikes jutting from her back and torso, as blood flowed in pools across her body. She was dead.

Terrek turned to see her killer, and was gripped with surprise. There, standing before him, was Koran. The boy lowered his head and collapsed to the floor in a sitting position, bringing his hands to his face, he began crying. Terrek stood immobile, unsure of what to do. He moved close and sat beside him.

The child paused and spoke through tears.

"Sometimes I'd ask my mother to stop causing me to do evil. I knew it was wrong and I knew she could hear me in her mind crying out as she controlled me, making me a puppet. Why couldn't she stop hurting me? Why did she have to be so evil? Why couldn't she stop? Why?" Koran broke down as he began crying again. Terrek was moved

154

by the child's words and, even though he was unsure if it was his place, he reached out and hugged Koran. The boy wrapped his arms around Terrek's as he buried his face in his tunic.

Suddenly Terrek turned as footsteps came from behind them. Diana stepped softly into the dimly lit area.

"I only glanced away for one moment and he was gone!" she whispered.

"What happened?"

"It's okay, we're both safe," he said.

Diana was overcome with the emotion Koran displayed as well, so she knelt down and hugged him, squeezing his arm in support.

Emperor Koiban raised his arms to protect himself as the Frecan duplicates moved slowly toward him. They moaned in pain and anguish, asking him why they were in such torment, asking him what had happened, and how he could have let it happen in his kingdom. Koiban fell back against the stone wall. The dead approached him, their eyes dark and eroded.

"Stop this!" Koiban cried.

The Vicar laughed evilly, "WHAT'S WRONG KOIBAN? DON'T YOU WANT ONE LAST CHANCE TO SAY GOODBYE?"

The Frecans came close as Koiban flattened himself against the wall. He withdrew his sword realizing what he had to do. Closing his eyes, he lashed out at the zombies slicing into the nearest one's chest. As he hit the ground, Koiban felt himself dying inside. The Vicar looked on as he attacked the dead illusions. They began to fall, calling out for him to stop, questioning him as to why he would do this. Koiban fought down sadness as he struck again and again.

The Vicar lifted his robe slightly and withdrew an enormous sword. It was the sword of darkness that had been used in the past by one of the Vicar's evil warlocks; Murack. The sword pulsed with a flowing darkness across the blade. Descending the steps, the Vicar approached Koiban as the zombies parted to allow him entry.

Koiban lifted his sword just in time to ward off a heavy blow from the Vicar as the sword of darkness rebounded with crackling energy on his own blade. Koiban ducked away from the wall backing into the center of the room. The Vicar spun as well, both men swinging, the Vicar the aggressor. Koiban could barely believe he possessed so much strength as blow after blow of the sword of darkness staggered him and pained his grip. The emperor was still distressed by the presence of several dead Frecans, which followed the battle about the room. Koiban was breathing hard as he backed into the stairs of the altar slowly ascending.

The Vicar smiled as Koiban stumbled up the steps moving higher toward the upper surface. Finally they reached the landing. With a mighty blow the Vicar roared as Koiban, on his knees before the altar, held his sword and closed his eyes. The sword of darkness smashed completely through Koiban's blade. Broken fragments of Koiban's iron sword fell to the floor below as Koiban jumped to his feet, grabbing at the Vicar trying to stop the next blow. Now he was defenseless.

The Vicar sneered at his feeble attempt, as he struck him in the forehead with the sword's hilt. Koiban fell in a dazed state, blood flowing across his face, his back against the altar. The Vicar threw the sword of darkness to the floor on the lower landing as he leaned into Koiban on the altar, withdrawing a dagger. The Vicar gripped Koiban by the jaw pushing his head up and bringing the knife forward. In his weary state, Koiban placed both his hands on the Vicar's arm, holding the knife back from slitting his throat.

"I HAVE SPOKEN WITH THE DARK LORD. I CAN REGAIN MY FORMER POWER AND A NEW REALM. ALL I NEED IS A SACRIFICE, THE LEADER OF A NATION, YOU EMPEROR KOIBAN!" the Vicar roared.

Koiban's heart raced as he looked up into the Vicar's glowing eyes so full of sadistic power. Behind him the duplicates of Frecan looked on, smiling, as though they enjoyed the thought of him dying. Koiban began to lose his grip on the Vicar's arm, his strength failing. The dagger came forward slightly; Koiban's expression becoming desperate, as the edge of the blade caressed his neck sliding across the surface skin. Blood flowed from the shallow cut. At any moment his strength would give way and the knife would kill him.

"No," he whispered, "Maker, god of Terrek and his people, please help me," he spoke.

The Vicar screamed suddenly, as Koiban looked up at him. The sword of darkness was now housed in the phantom's front. The Vicar released the dagger in horror and grabbed the blade that had been thrust through his back and exited his chest. The sword bearer pushed the hilt sideways as the Vicar fell from the altar, careening down the steps, landing on the floor below. Koiban stared at the one who'd saved his life: Terrek. Behind him stood Diana and Koran. Koiban, coughing, joined the other three at the edge of the altar platform to view the screaming Vicar below.

"NO!" the Vicar knelt on the floor as he roared, holding the blade. His form combusted with a wide array of flashing colors as his robes and body caught fire. Roaring, he writhed on the floor in agony, cursing Terrek with his last breaths. Then he became silent and unmoving. The crackling fire was engulfing not only him but the sword of darkness as well. Finally nothing remained but dust. At long last the Vicar was dead.

Emperor Koiban faced Terrek.

"Thank you," he said.

He stared back at the smoldering dust that was once the Vicar. The ghost duplicates of Frecan faded from the room.

"Perhaps now you will rest in peace old friend," Koiban whispered.

Grelkon raced across the skies, his mind rebounding from guilt and grief. There was nothing left for him. No one to see, no where to go. His only companions now were pain and guilt. The unstable emotions exploded through his brain as he cried compulsively, unable to contain the flow of tears. Below him, huge rivers of lava flowed across this area of the Minotaur Mountains. Steam and smoke rose, reaching his nostrils.

Out of the corner of his eye, through translucent tears, Grelkon caught sight of another avian. Spinning, he saw Selate following him. This compounded his grief, he knew she thought she could save him somehow. As if she could take away his pain! He could no longer bear to face her.

"Grelkon please! Stop! You can come back, we can sort through this together," she cried to him tears in her eyes as well.

"N – no! How can I go back? No one will ever accept me again. Why should they?" he screamed, "I – I can't."

"They will accept you if you show your willingness to change, please," she sobbed afraid he would escape.

Grelkon broke down, every word stuttering, "please go away mother, I – I can't think, please," he bawled.

Suddenly he saw another shadow. It was Darcet.

"Yes, mother," Darcet roared, "go away!"

He descended heavily on Selate and attacked. With a stroke of luck he knocked her cold. Selate fell out of the sky as Grelkon spun around. He flew into Darcet fiercely pushing him back, another avian joined the battle attacking

Darcet, it was Fernok. Darcet and Fernok were locked in combat as Grelkon stared below. His mother hurtled directly toward the rivers of lava.

"No!" he screamed as he dove out of the sky. Grelkon pushed himself harder than he'd ever done before, channeling all his emotions into physical effort, as he plunged downward faster and faster. The lava became dangerously close as he reached Selate. With one final movement of bravery he flew beneath his mother as both splashed into the lava.

Selate was not harmed, but for an instant Grelkon shut his eyes as the front of his body was immersed in the burning liquid. For a moment he felt the scorching sensation of being burned alive. Frantically, he pushed against the liquid clumsily lifting himself and his dead mother from the ooze. Splotches of molten magma clung to his wings and body, still burning him. Screaming inside, Grelkon flew to the nearest section of dry solid land as he collapsed, rolling away from his mother. Grelkon shook frantically as the magma on his body began to solidify. His breath became erratic.

Selate lifted herself from the ground and looked upon Grelkon's burned body. His feathers were almost all scorched away as burns revealed flesh and muscle. Sections of molten rock still burned him. He was dying.

"No! Grelkon!" she screamed, moving to him. Cradling his head, she frantically attempted to knock the molten lava from his body as he cried out in pain. There was no way to remove it.

"Mother," Grelkon cried, "I'm so sorry, so sorry..." he forced the words, his lungs tightening.

Fernok, having killed Darcet, landed behind her. Selate cradled Grelkon's head in her wings. She lost control of herself breaking down, trembling. She knew Grelkon had caused her pain, but he was still her son. She knew he was dying.

"I – I didn't realize, I just didn't understand," he cried, "I love you mother, please forgive me."

"I forgive you my son," Selate wept.

Grelkon began to cry as he felt his body slipping away, his vision faded as he lost sight of Selate.

"I didn't mean it, I, mother, where are you mother? I'm sorry! I…please don't leave me," Grelkon choked on his words as his body shook, then became still. There was silence for a moment as Fernok lowered his head. Selate buried her face in Grelkon's shoulder and cried.

EPILOGUE: WELCOMES AND FAREWELLS

𝒳anica and Zyconia had been liberated. The Vicar and his servants were dead, and now both nations looked to the future. The necromancy adopted by the Xanicans had been outlawed and destroyed by Koiban. All across the nations the people picked up the pieces of their lives. Cities were repaired. Everyone helped eachother.

The vessels lost in the battle of Dystara Bay had been easily replaced with the captured Wicketai warships. After they'd been modified, they joined both nation's fleets. King Terrek and Emperor Koiban had announced the news of a great feast at New Victory City throughout both kingdoms. But first, there were some things left undone, which needed to be dealt with.

Terrek stood, head bowed, slightly outside the mouth of the cave. Several soldiers stood guard. Inside, Delara and Celarus spoke. Not far away, inside the cave, Delara's guards stood as well. She smiled at Celarus staring deep into his eyes. Finally, they had a moment alone, but it was not to be the grand reunion.

"You could come and be with me in the surface world," Celarus said weakly.

"And you could come and live with me in the underworld," she smiled, "but we both have important rolls now. I am the Queen of an entire nation, and you are a duke, responsible for a province of many people."

He knew it was goodbye. His heart sank as she drew close to him.

"I know now that there are many in the surface world like you who are full of good but there are still many like the Vicar that are so evil. For this reason, I fear my people and I will once more retreat deep into the caverns," she reasoned.

His eyes were low as she looked at him sadly. Celarus pulled his hand from behind his back, revealing a single white rose.

"I – I wanted to give you this so that this time you could receive the rose without painful memories to accompany it. Please don't forget me Delara," he spoke softly.

She smiled, eyes watered slightly. Placing her arms around his neck she leaned forward, pressing her lips against his. He ran his hand across her back, her long hair flowing over his arm one last time, as he held her close in the embrace.

She withdrew slightly.

"I care a great deal for you. We will meet again Celarus, I promise you. Maybe then we can…" her words trailed off as she leaned forward and kissed him again, then withdrew, retreating into the cavern.

"Maybe then," she spoke again. Reluctantly, Delara turned around and walked slowly down into the cave. Turning around, her guards followed. Celarus stared as her form disappeared into the darkness, then he lowered his head.

After a moment, Terrek entered, and placed his hand on Celarus's shoulder.

"You will meet again Celarus," he asserted.

"Yes we will," he smiled slightly.

"Come on, let's get back to New Victory City," Terrek said easily. Celarus nodded slowly as he exited the cave. Celarus looked back one last time in the direction Delara had gone, and thought about the future.

Emperor Koiban stood upon the balcony of his palace as the wind from the sea flowed through his hair. He breathed in deeply, overjoyed to be home. Bratain came out and stood beside him. He faced his old friend, an uneasy expression on his face.

"I am grateful that you returned Bratain. Without your help, we may not have been able to vanquish the Vicar's armies," he said.

"It was the honorable thing to do," Bratain said softly.

"I will miss Freecan, he was almost like a father to me. Even in death he managed to save me with one valiant letter," Koiban said quietly.

"Yes, I know, he was a very noble subject. I will miss him too," Bratain spoke up, sharing his connection with the old man.

Koiban lowered his gaze. "I should have listened to you. You were right to mistrust the Vicar. I just couldn't see it, I'm sorry. But now I have a second chance to raise Xanica to the pinnacle of strength, as we began together. Will you stand with me?"

Bratain faced him and lost his somber expression for a smile.

"I know you see that you made a mistake. I won't hold it against you. We have been friends a long time. I always knew you were meant to be the ruler of Xanica, and so did Freecan that is why he did what he did."

Koiban smiled, "thank you."

The wind blew across the hill ruffling the feathers of two avians. Selate and Fernok stood before two metallic stakes, one with the bronzed name of Hecron, the other with the bronzed name of Grelkon. Selate stared at the two stakes, her eyes raw. In her wing, she held two small bouquets of flowers woven together with vines. Placing the first on the stake featuring Hecron's name she stood back.

"Do you think Grelkon could have been helped mother?" Fernok asked sadly.

Selate looked to the stake. "I honestly don't know. Good and evil were battling inside him. In the end good prevailed, but only at the expense of his life. If he had lived, I don't know if the demons inside him would have eventually taken control again or not."

Selate moved to the stake and placed the flowers upon his stake. She touched the stake with her wing.

"Thank you for my life Grelkon. Despite all you have done, I will miss you. I will love you always Grelkon. Let the maker take care of you now."

Tears fell from Selate's eyes as she descended the hill. Fernok stood for a moment looking to the stake that featured Grelkon's name.

"Be at rest my brother," he whispered. "Both of you," he finished, acknowledging Hecron as well.

Koran smiled and laughed as he and Timothy played together, running about the Zyconian palace courtyard. Terrek and the child's new guardians, Zachary and Juliana, looked on. Now the couple had two children.

"He's actually laughing and having fun," Terrek remarked slowly, as the two boys chased one another through the hedges.

"Children are resilient," Juliana smiled, "even after such a sad life."

Terrek had not revealed to them that Koran had been responsible for his mother's death. He knew Koran's mind had suffered greatly from all that had happened, and it would be a long time before it would be completely healed, if ever.

"You're right," Terrek replied, "he is still young. Be gentle with him. He's been through a lot."

The roar of the crowd was intense as thousands of men, women and children from all across Zyconia and Xanica filled the palace courtyard and the streets of New Victory City. On a small hill in the courtyard sat Emperor Koiban, King Terrek and Queen Diana. They were surrounded by those close to them and by their armies. Throughout the crowd cookfires had been erected as mountain upon mountain of food was fed to the people. Everyone cheered the three monarchs as they feasted.

Finally, all three stood as Emperor Koiban addressed the crowd.

"Good people of Zyconia and of course Xanica!" Koiban began as the multitude quieted.

"The Vicar's armies have been driven from both our nations and now it is time to look to the future. The armies of both our kingdoms are scouring the countryside, helping all to find food, to rebuild their homes, and to rebuild their lives. King Terrek and I have both signed a treaty that represents a new beginning for both our kingdoms!" Koiban said. Then Terrek began.

"To ensure that nothing like this ever happens again, from this day forward there shall be an alliance between Xanica and Zyconia. If one nation is threatened, the other will take up arms to defend it," Terrek said.

Finally Diana completed the circle. "May the peace of our two nations last forever. Now everyone make merry, sing and dance, and feast upon what has been prepared," she finished smiling. She turned to Terrek and kissed him.

The crowd roared with cheerfulness. The Dukes and the duchess, together with Bratain, raised their goblets in a toast to their nation's leaders, and to their health. All was joyous and wonderful.

Terrek paced the stone floor outside Diana's chambers. Surrounding him were his friends, the Dukes and the duchess. Inside the next room Jessica was with Diana, who was in labor. Terrek stopped as Jessica rushed to the door. She smiled as she addressed him.

"I have good news for you, you're a father! It's a boy!" she paused for a moment, "and a girl!"

Terrek looked at her for a moment, as he absorbed her words.

"You have twins! Your wife wishes to see you now," she smiled.

Getting to his feet he walked through the door, as his friends patted him on the back and congratulated him. Walking through the door and into the next threshold. Quietly entering their chambers, he saw Diana lying on the bed holding two small crying bundles. She saw him and smiled.

"Say hello to your new children Terrek," she said.

Terrek drew close staring down at them with joy. Terrek leaned forward gently and kissed Diana on the forehead.

"Thank you for bringing me so much happiness," he whispered.

Diana beamed as she lifted them to Terrek who cradled one child in each arm. Terrek stared down at them. They

166

both had chosen a name, Terrek a boy's and Diana a girl's, but now that it was both they would use both names.

"Prince Daniel and Princess Ilona," Terrek remembered, vocalizing their choices. Diana glowed as she took him by the hand.

Suddenly with a flash Terrek saw Zyron standing near the wall of their chambers. He smiled as he looked upon their children. Terrek realized that Diana couldn't see Zyron.

"Teach them well," he whispered.

"I will," Terrek whispered back.

With another flash he was gone.

Terrek stared into the faces of his newborn children. The future would be grand indeed for these two heirs.

THE END

On the heels of *Legends of Zyconia: Odyssey Invasion,* comes a new science fiction action/adventure of the futuristic societal struggle which pits man against machine in:

FLESH AND CIRCUITS

Turn the page for a special advance preview of *Flesh and Circuits* the new novel by Hugh Stephens.

PROLOGUE: ESCAPE

The sky burned a dim red. Darkened, sulfuric clouds flowed across the horizon: a thick smog. It was a desolate blue grey plain littered with thorny unforgiving vegetation and haunted by wild animals: a realm full of hate, misery and strife. The planet was Corona gamma, an occupied world.

Xertron peered from the shadows. Dark, shaded tritanium structures stretched in all directions. Not far above through the mist small Scorpions patrolled the atmosphere, their red lights blinking ominously.

All around them large edifices of steel and circuits rose. And high above clasped to each edifice an android, their internal circuitry torn open and several thousand optic cables bleeding them dry of knowledge and energy. Occasionally they struggled, their eyes full of pain. At one time these edifices had been inside buildings but there were so many brought to the death camps now. The level of extermination was horrible. Xertron looked at them sadly and wished they had time to save them as well as themselves, but knew they couldn't.

The death camp was huge, and incredibly well guarded. From behind him Berillna squeezed his hand. Moments ago they had escaped their cell, killing two guards. She was trying to show her support. Xertron and Berillna had both been imprisoned in the death camp for over a year and were desperate for freedom.

Their captors were a ruthless race, one so bent on anothers destruction it was hard to believe they had never destroyed one another. They knew that their only chance lay in the compound on the opposite side of the camp. There they would find several prison ships, the same ones that had brought them to this awful place. Xertron peered one last time into the darkness with his cybernetic eyes and gripped Berillna's metallic hand in his. Rushing from the side of the building the two androids moved from one building to another.

"We're going to make it Berillna," he said.

She looked at him, worried, but still nodding.

Suddenly they stopped dead in their tracks. A human guard came around the corner of the nearest building. His eyes widened and filled with the all too familiar bloodlust they had seen in the eyes of his entire race. Xertron and Berillna moved quickly behind the next building as the human male withdrew his laser rifle and began firing. They heard the scorching of laser fire on tritanium as they broke into a run.

"Come on Berillna!" Xertron yelled.

"Stop, android trash!" the human screamed from behind them.

Xertron and Berillna were now the hunted. Reaching the middle of the camp, they entered a large area with several metallic pyramids. Some were low to the ground; others were massive, reaching toward the sky. The loud echoing of security alarms screeched overhead, and far away human voices could be heard, hungry for death.

Out of nowhere, laser fire began erupting all around them. Rolling over into the dirt and mud on the ground, Xertron and Berillna came up with their lasers ready. The laser fire came from several small robotic laser towers nearby. Firing wildly, they began systematically destroying

2

reaching the compound. They had to travel the rest of the way through an alternate route.

Xertron knelt to the ground and pried away a sewer grate. He and Berillna dropped down into the rushing water of the sewer below. As they struck the water they were carried away becoming very aware of the odor and the low temperature.

The voices of the approaching guards died as the toxic water soaked into their circuits. Xertron tightened his grip on Berillna's hand. Occasionally their heads floated above water and they could see the terror in the other's eyes. Perhaps they wouldn't make it, the toxic water could be enough to kill them, he thought. He went through the events of the last year in his head; he couldn't let this be the end. Finally Xertron managed to pull Berillna close in his arms, he wouldn't let her die, not here in this place.

Reaching out of the water he grasped a nearby ledge, and with all his might he pulled himself and Berillna from the waste. Staring back they saw not far ahead the toxic sewage falling as a waterfall into a machine known as the Disintegrator. Crackling pulses and stray bolts of energy rose from the machine as the sewage was burned from existence. If Xertron had missed the ledge that would have been them they realized.

Once upon the dry surface, they moved down a small corridor. Xertron's shoulder was sparking and hissing in pain from the exposure to the toxic waste. He couldn't feel it very well; the circuitry had been reduced to passive response. Upon reaching a dead end they ascended through another grate, coming out right beside the prison ship compound. Surprised the two guards at the entrance grabbed their rifles, but it was too late. Xertron and Berillna fired their weapons immobilizing both of them. The two soldiers fell to the ground as Xertron and Berillna used their new weapons to burn open the doors of the compound.

Inside the room, another firefight broke out. Xertron could hardly believe that they had made it this far. Firing back at the guards in the compound they jumped toward a bulky prison transfer ship, the only vessel within the vast compound bay. Xertron covered Berillna while she smashed the locking mechanism with her rifle and began crossing several fibre optic cables within. They would have their freedom Xertron knew, as Berillna released the lock on the ships pressure doors. Both took one last look at the hell they'd been forced to call home for more than a year, finally it was over.

Falling inside, the doors sealed behind them. Racing into the cockpit they activated the ship and, training the ship's pulsecanons skyward, created their own entrance in the compound's ceiling. From their console monitors they could see the guards firing upon the outer shell of the ship as it rose from the compound floor, through the hole in the ceiling. To their relief there was no sign of nearby Scorpion fighter patrols. Xertron activated the rocket boosters as the prison ship sped quickly out of the atmosphere.

CHAPTER 1: SURVIVAL INSTINCTS

Space exploded into view as their ship thrust itself from the red atmosphere and into the open depths. Their worries were diminished when they realized the orbiting battle station was on the other side of the planet at that moment. It would take several minutes for the massive station to reach their position, by then they would be long gone.

Xertron was seated in the pilot seat and Berillna was in the navigator's position of the small cockpit. The ship was small, but it had teeth and they were sharp.

"Hello, anyone out there?" a voice echoed behind them.

Spinning around, they realized that the small chamber behind a forcefield harbored a prisoner, undoubtedly being transported to their death camp. The chamber was dark and only a silhouette could be seen.

"Hello. Don't worry we've just escaped the camp. We'll release you. Berillna hit the lights," Xertron said as he lifted his metallic body from the cockpit and moved to deactivate the forcefield.

Berillna pushed the panel for light control illuminating the chamber behind her. For only a moment Xertron lifted his arm toward the switch but he stopped midway. He stood, and looked in disgust at the prisoner.

"You're one of them, a human!" he said bitterly.

"What did you do that your kind would imprison you on Corona Gamma?" asked Berillna from the cockpit.

The man within had long, tangled brown hair. He wore rough, dirty pilot clothing. His body revealed a few scars. His face was hard, like those of his kind. He sighed angrily. He knew they wouldn't let him out.

"It had to be androids, didn't it," he scoffed sarcastically.

Xertron looked at Berillna and returned to the pilot's chair.

"We can't trust his kind," he whispered coldly.

"My name is Tane. I'm a fighter pilot. The best there is Andy. You're going to need me if you want to get away from Corona alive!" he yelled.

Xertron looked back from his seat, angry at the derogatory term used, and at the pilot's arrogance.

"Tell me why we shouldn't just throw you out an airlock? Why would we need you?" Xertron yelled back.

Suddenly the ship was hit by laser fire. The violent jolt sent all three of them to the floor. Lighting began to flicker as they got their bearings.

"That's why!" Tane said strongly.

"We're being pursued by five scorpion fighters Xertron," Berillna stated with worried eyes.

"The death camp fighters! We're already at full speed, heading into the asteroid belt, we'll shake them there, ourselves!" Xertron affirmed.

Tane banged his fist on the forcefield in anger. The asteroid belt loomed closer, the density surprised Xertron.

"I – I don't know if we can maneuver in there. The asteroids are too close together, could be suicide," Xertron fumbled.

Again the prison ship rocked from an external explosion. This time sparks crackled from the control consoles as a large panel exploded overhead discharging showers of sparks, plasma flames, and frayed fibreoptics. Berillna screamed and shielded her eyes. The lighting flickered as Xertron activated the fire suppression system and sprayed the fire out.

"Are you all right?" Xertron asked her, the flames discontinued.

"Yes," she started, "but that was the shield generator they destroyed. I don't think we can survive another hit!" she said fearfully.

"Let me save us!" Tane bellowed from his cell.

Xertron looked at the man; his face was serious now, not evil.

"Do you really think you can get us out of here!" Xertron said strongly.

"Yes, I swear, I will!" he yelled.

Xertron jumped back out of the cockpit and hit the release on the forcefield. Instantly Tane was over the threshold and into the pilot seat. Xertron pulled an empty seat up between Tane and Berillna.

"All right I'm activating the weapon systems. Hard to starboard!" Tane explained. The ship veered severely from the other fighters and spun into the asteroid field. The five scorpion fighters increased speed and followed it in. Asteroids began appearing through the reinforced cockpit windows, careening in every direction. Suddenly one of the fighters smashed into an asteroid and exploded.

"Minus one Scorpion," Tane smiled.

He nervously began adjusting their direction to compensate. Beams of laserfire lanced across the cockpit window. Xertron expected them to be destroyed at any moment.

"They're still too close," Tane rasped, "I've got to increase speed!"

Xertron watched a huge asteroid spiral right overhead as they moved forward faster.

"I'm going to take them out," Tane yelled as he pushed the throttle to the limit. Moving forward Tane brought the ship upside down and blazed a path directly at the group of fighters. The prison ship's blue fluorescent laser cannons erupted in full fury, scattering the four remaining fighters. The nearest of the four was hit! Pulsing with crackling energy, the fighter exploded.

"Minus two Scorpions!" Tane yelled.

Moving in close, Tane maneuvered the ship into a pinwheel attack, spiraling toward the group of Scorpions. Catching one of them off guard he damaged it's wing. Suddenly one of the Scorpions turned and spun toward them, firing with vehemence!

Tane fired toward it, and then he realized what the pilot was doing.

"It's a suicide run!" he yelled to the others as he turned the ship left hard, but it was too late. The Scorpion tore into the hull of the prison ship tearing the pulsecanons right off. All three were thrown about the cockpit. Tane felt the wind knocked out of him as the atmosphere in the cockpit suddenly changed. A crack in the ship's ceiling was causing the cockpit to depressurize. The lights dimmed and their engines choked. The severely damaged Scorpion fighter flew out of control and crashed into an asteroid, exploding in a kaleidoscope of flame.

Hyperventilating, Tane hit the atmospheric controls. A mixture of nitrogen and oxygen began flooding the ship. Blood flowed across his face from a huge gash in his forehead. Xertron was trying to settle Berillna who had a damaged shoulder. The circuitry was discharging, causing her arm to go numb, but she was not severely hurt.

"We're going to have to seal the pressure leak or I'm as good as dead. It's hard to breathe now, and that crack may rupture. It may mean all our deaths!" Tane wheezed quickly to conserve oxygen.

Xertron turned to him. "Do you know if there is any welding equipment aboard?"

"I think that there are torches in the maintenance lockers at the back of the ship," he wheezed.

"I'll be back," he told them rushing from the cockpit.

"Hurry, I'm starting to feel a bit faint," Tane yelled in desperation, holding his hand to his forehead to keep the blood from his eyes. His other hand flew across the console trying to stabilize the ship. Not looking up, he was aware of the wind and cold temperature in the cockpit as the atmosphere was slowly being sucked into space. Berillna looked at him with pity as he struggled to remain conscious.

"If I go out, you will have to take control," Tane managed through labored breath, he looked down at her damaged arm, "one good arm is better than none."

Tane felt a merciless head rush as his vision was interrupted for a moment, but he didn't pass out. He'd managed to stabilize their speed, but the remaining two Scorpions were closing fast! And they were now severely damaged. Asteroids spun around them faster and faster.

"I got the torch!" Xertron yelled, as he rushed back into the cockpit and steadied himself on one of the ships inside structural beams. He quickly activated the plasma torch and got to work sealing the long crack in the ceiling.

Tane looked at him with relief, then turned his attention back out the window in front of the console.

"There are still two Scorpions left to deal with, only one of them is damaged. We no longer have weapons or shields, and there is very little life support. We can't fight or protect ourselves now, we can only run. Any ideas?" Tane asked Xertron.

Holding the torch steady on the ceiling Xertron answered.

"There is a small nebula on the edge of the asteroid belt can you see it?" he yelled.

Laser fire followed them from the two remaining Scorpions. They were very close. Tane squinted, his vision blurred.

"Yes, it's not far away," he realized.

"Head for the nebula we will hide there, maybe touchdown on one of the large asteroids inside!" he finished triumphantly.

Tane nodded, he could feel the atmospheric pressure rising as Xertron worked on sealing the fissure.

The prison ship reluctantly dodged and weaved through space, groaning under the stress of battle. The Scorpions raced after it, bent on its destruction. The bluish glow of the dense nebula loomed closer and closer. Then all at once the ship was enveloped by the cumulous mass. The two Scorpions paused at the outer edge, unsure, and then they too entered in pursuit of their prey.

The asteroid was large enough to be a small moon, the perfect place to hide. Scanning the surface the Scorpion pilots spied the damaged vessel on the dusty pockmarked landscape. All around lay strange spiked landmasses and small hills. They came to a halt landing adjacent the prison ship.

Donning spacesuits the pilots exited the Scorpions activating their locking mechanisms. The three men met in front of the prison ship, laser rifles in hand.

"They damaged our ship and Kerns is severely injured," one of the three stated pointing back toward his ship. A fourth pilot could be seen in the cockpit window of the Scorpion; his face was covered in blood. He lay limp, breathing hard.

"We don't have time for this," growled another. "I have the prison ship airlock encryption key, we go in, kill them and head back to Corona, come on!"

Moving quickly in their sleek spacesuits the three aggressors approached the side hatch of the vessel. The leader removed the bulky key and punched it into the locking mechanism. With a pop the hatch depressurized and they entered. Sealing the hatch they pressurized the chamber and removed their space suits and readied their rifles.

"Remember, the cockpit and seating area is just beyond this door, be prepared for a firefight," he said angrily.

Pushing the panel on the door it slipped sideways as they rushed into the room. Pointing their weapons into the cockpit they caught Xertron and Berillna seated in fear.

"I should have known, these Andys are nothing but pacifists!" the leader laughed evilly. Xertron and Berillna sat in humility staring at the floor. The human leader looked around at the room, smiling at the sloppy welding job on the ceiling. Then he looked at the empty cell nearby with it's forcefield deactivated.

"Wait, they said there was a human prisoner in that cell!" the leader shouted, "where is he?" he finished pointing his rifle at Xertron.

"There – there was no prisoner, I swear!" he started. The leader paused for a moment, no android would help a human, perhaps it was the truth. He moved his head very close, staring into Xertron's cybernetic eyes, then moved back.

"Bower, go search the rest of the ship!" he ordered one of the others. The man left the cockpit and moved into the rear of the ship. The leader and remaining man began making fun of their prey.

Bower headed down the small corridor and entered the large maintenance room. Small catwalks and ladders crisscrossed the vast double level maintenance room. It was poorly lit and smelled like crude oil. This ship was very misused and abused by the camps. Steam and exhaust rose from leaks around him, due to the heavy damage inflicted during the battle. Here and there panels and rubble lay strewn about. Sections of metallic structures hung low at the centre of the room, a slow hum emanating from them. These were the ship engines, they seemed very sluggish.

Moving down beneath the hanging structures he surveyed the area. If the human prisoner were here he would have to be on his guard. There was no telling how the encounter would play out.

Suddenly he saw a dark shape out of the corner of his eye. He spun around.

"Come out slave, and die!" he roared.

Instantly a fibre optic cable slipped around his neck from behind. Dropping his weapon he grabbed at the cable as it tightened.

Strengthening his grip on the cable Tane replied, "you first."

"You can't even imagine what we can do to you!" the leader laughed with his comrade at Xertron and Berillna.

"Even you circuit freaks can feel pain, especially if you know how to administer it," he replied removing a small black device.

"Do you know what this is?" he smiled.

Xertron knew perfectly well what it was, he had seen them used on many in the Corona Gamma death camps. It was called a MDM, which stood for Mind Destruction Module. On the forehead of every android was the direct interface to their brain. When the device was attached to an interface it would increase the intensity of the androids touch sensitivity circuits tenfold and induce the most painful sensation imaginable. Eventually the victims neural net would discharge, much like a human having a brain aneurysm.

"Yes I do," Xertron said quietly, Berillna placed her hand on his.

"Who said it was time for love?" the leader yelled hitting Berillna in her damaged arm, she winced in pain, "did I say you could move?"

"Leave her alone!" Xertron roared pushing the man onto the floor. Starting forward the other man leveled his rifle at Xertron's chest.

"Big mistake Andy, now you die," the leader stood and grabbed his weapon, pushing Xertron back into his seat. He leaned toward him with the MDM, his counterpart covering him with his rifle.

Suddenly the door opened at the rear of the cockpit. Both men turned.

"Bower! What took you so long?" the leader said.

"I'm not Bower," Tane yelled moving through the door firing his new laser rifle. The blast struck the leader's counterpart, killing him, as Tane pointed it at the leader.

"Drop it now!" Tane ordered. The man complied, placing both his rifle and the MDM on the cockpit floor.

Everyone stood outside the undamaged Scorpion fighter. Xertron helping Berillna along with her damaged arm. Tane had taken one of the pilot's space suits and now stood behind the Scorpion pilot leader. Tane had retrieved several weapons from the prison ship, and carried his armaments like a soldier. The laser rifle he held was based at the leaders back as he ordered from the communications device within the suit, "open it! Now!"

He referred to the locking mechanism he had placed on his Scorpion fighter.

"How do I know that when you get inside you won't just kill me?" the leader rasped.

"Well, I guess you'll just have to trust us, won't you!" Tane said knocking the man against the Scorpion hatch.

The leader recovered and entered the code at the keypanel on the side of the ship. With a small pop from within the hatch door slid sideways.

"Your trust was misplaced," Tane said coldly, as he grabbed the leader by the helmet tearing back on its release. The helmet of his space suit fell away as his oxygen supply escaped. Shock appeared on his face, but only for a moment, then he fell limp and settled slowly unto the ground drawn down by the gentle gravity of the asteroid. His face frozen, his mouth open, he settled into the alien dirt. Tane looked down for a second, unmoved by his action.

Starting back toward the prison ship he passed Xertron who was horrified at what he'd done.

"You didn't have to kill him. He was no longer a threat to us. We could have just left him here to be found!" he said.

Tane merely gave him a glance.

"Wait here, we have to destroy the other ships," he said removing two explosive devices from his suit.

Xertron helped Berillna to the hatch of the Scorpion.

"Head inside and find the living quarters, try to repair your arm, I'll be there in a moment," he said softly.

Tane placed a large explosive on the outer hull of the prison ship setting the timer. Then he walked toward the scorpion with the injured man inside.

"What are you doing?" asked Xertron as he reached Tane, "there is an injured man in there!"

"We don't have time for this!" yelled Tane as he brought his rifle to bear. Quickly he pointed it directly at

14

the Scorpion cockpit window, and increased the settings to full power.

"What are you doing?" Xertron yelled again as he jumped into Tane, tackling him to the asteroid surface, but not before he squeezed off the shot. The already cracked window shattered as the man inside was silenced.

Xertron spun to the ship then knocked the rifle from Tane's grip. Angrily Xertron grabbed him by the collar and shook him.

"What do you think your doing?" he roared, "that man was unarmed and injured. There was no threat involved!"

Tane showed no compassion. "This is a war. Wake up before you die."

Xertron pushed Tane back, releasing him. He stood and walked back toward the Scorpion shaking his head in rage. Tane recovered as well and retrieved his weapon. After placing the final explosive, he boarded the Scorpion they had chosen.

Blasting away from the asteroid, Tane looked back as the prison ship and damaged Scorpion exploded. As they exited one end of the nebula several more scorpions entered in search of their comrades. Clearing the nebula, Tane activated the hyperdrive as they sped away into deep space.

ABOUT THE AUTHOR

Twenty-one year old Hugh J. Stephens resides on Manitoulin Island, Ontario with his family. He is currently adding the finishing touches to his next novel: Flesh and Circuits as well as several side projects. In the near future he hopes to start a fiction magazine which features the stories of other young Ontario writers.

Correspondence to this author may be directed to:

Hugh Stephens,
Rural Route# 1, Little Current,
Ontario, Canada
P0P1K0

or

machineheart20@hotmail.com

ISBN 155212627-7